P9-BJX-034

Friends
—— OF ——
LAFAYETTE LIBRARY
AND LEARNING CENTER

generously provided
this book

WITHDRAWN

SHATTER ME

The Shatter Me Series by Tahereh Mafi

SHATTER ME

TAHEREH MAFI

HARPER

An Imprint of HarperCollinsPublishers

Library of Congress Cataloging-in-Publication Data

Mafi, Tahereh.

Shatter me / Tahereh Mafi. — 1st ed.

    p.   cm.

    Summary: Ostracized or incarcerated her whole life,
seventeen-year-old Juliette is freed on the condition that she
use her horrific abilities in support of The Reestablishment, a
postapocalyptic dictatorship, but Adam, the only person ever
to show her affection, offers hope of a better future.

    ISBN 978-0-06-274173-8 (trade bdg.)

    [1. Science fiction. 2. Ability—Fiction. 3. Love—
Fiction. 4. Soldiers—Fiction. 5. Dictatorship—Fiction.]
I. Title.

PZ7.M2695Sh 2011   2011019370

[Fic]—dc23   CIP

                                         AC

Typography by Ray Shappell

23 24 25 26 27 LBC 13 12 11 10 9

Revised edition, 2018

Dear Reader:

The strikethroughs in the Shatter Me books are intentional. The writing in this series is occasionally as erratic as its main character, and serves as a visual representation of the chaos in Juliette's mind. The repetition, the hyperbolic language, the obsession with numbers—these are not errors on the page. As our heroine grows and evolves, so too does the prose, and as she finds her voice, the strikethroughs disappear, the language softens, the repetition dissolves, and the numerals ease into written words. This is, ultimately, a story of change. Thank you so much for reading.

Two roads diverged in a wood, and I—
I took the one less traveled by,
and that has made all the difference.

—ROBERT FROST, "The Road Not Taken"

ONE

I've been locked up for 264 days.

I have nothing but a small notebook and a broken pen and the numbers in my head to keep me company. 1 window. 4 walls. 144 square feet of space. 26 letters in an alphabet I haven't spoken in 264 days of isolation.

6,336 hours since I've touched another human being.

"You're getting a ~~cellmate~~ roommate," they said to me.

"~~We hope you rot to death in this place~~ For good behavior," they said to me.

"~~Another psycho just like you~~ No more isolation," they said to me.

They are the minions of The Reestablishment. The initiative that was supposed to help our dying society. The same people who pulled me out of my parents' home and locked me in an asylum for something outside of my control. No one cares that I didn't know what I was capable of. That I didn't know what I was doing.

I have no idea where I am.

I only know that I was transported by someone in a white van who drove 6 hours and 37 minutes to get me here. I know I was handcuffed to my seat. I know I was strapped to my chair. ~~I know my parents never bothered to~~

1

~~say good-bye.~~ I know I didn't cry as I was taken away.

I know the sky falls down every day.

The sun drops into the ocean and splashes browns and reds and yellows and oranges into the world outside my window. A million leaves from a hundred different branches dip in the wind, fluttering with the false promise of flight. The gust catches their withered wings only to force them downward, forgotten, left to be trampled by the soldiers stationed just below.

There aren't as many trees as there were before, is what the scientists say. They say our world used to be green. Our clouds used to be white. Our sun was always the right kind of light. But I have very faint memories of that world. I don't remember much from before. The only existence I know now is the one I was given. An echo of what used to be.

I press my palm to the small pane of glass and feel the cold clasp my hand in a familiar embrace. We are both alone, both existing as the absence of something else.

I grab my nearly useless pen with the very little ink I've learned to ration each day and stare at it. Change my mind. Abandon the effort it takes to write things down. Having a cellmate might be okay. Talking to a real human being might make things easier. I practice using my voice, shaping my lips around the familiar words unfamiliar to my mouth. I practice all day.

I'm surprised I remember how to speak.

I sit up on the cloth-covered springs I'm forced to sleep on. I wait. I rock back and forth and wait.

I wait too long and fall asleep.

My eyes open to 2 eyes 2 lips 2 ears 2 eyebrows.

I stifle my scream my urgency to run the crippling horror gripping my limbs.

"You're a b-b-b-b—"

"And you're a girl." He cocks an eyebrow. He leans away from my face. He grins but he's not smiling and I want to cry, my eyes desperate, terrified, darting toward the door I'd tried to open so many times I'd lost count. They locked me up with a boy. A boy.

Dear God.

They're trying to kill me.

They've done it on purpose.

To torture me, to torment me, to keep me from sleeping through the night ever again. His arms are tatted up, half sleeves to his elbows. His eyebrow is missing a ring they must've confiscated. Dark blue eyes dark brown hair sharp jawline strong lean frame. ~~Gorgeous~~ Dangerous. Terrifying. Horrible.

He laughs and I fall off my bed and scuttle into the corner.

He sizes up the meager pillow on the spare bed they shoved into the empty space this morning, the skimpy mattress and threadbare blanket hardly big enough to support his upper half. He glances at my bed. Glances at his bed.

Shoves them both together with one hand. Uses his foot to push the two metal frames to his side of the room. Stretches out across the two mattresses, grabbing my pillow to fluff up under his neck. I've begun to shake.

I bite my lip and try to bury myself in the dark corner.

3

He's stolen my bed my blanket my pillow.

I have nothing but the floor.

I will have nothing but the floor.

I will never fight back because I'm too petrified too paralyzed too paranoid.

"So you're—what? Insane? Is that why you're here?"

~~I'm not insane.~~

He props himself up enough to see my face. He laughs again. "I'm not going to hurt you."

~~I want to believe him.~~ I don't believe him.

"What's your name?" he asks.

~~None of your business. What's your name?~~

I hear his irritated exhalation of breath. I hear him turn over on the bed that used to be half mine. I stay awake all night. My knees curled up to my chin, my arms wrapped tight around my small frame, my long brown hair the only curtain between us.

I will not sleep.

I cannot sleep.

I cannot hear those screams again.

TWO

It smells like rain in the morning.

The room is heavy with the scent of wet stone, upturned soil; the air is dank and earthy. I take a deep breath and tiptoe to the window only to press my nose against the cool surface. Feel my breath fog up the glass. Close my eyes to the sound of a soft pitter-patter rushing through the wind. Raindrops are my only reminder that clouds have a heartbeat. That I have one, too.

I always wonder about raindrops.

I wonder about how they're always falling down, forgetting their parachutes as they tumble out of the sky toward an uncertain end. It's like someone is emptying their pockets over the earth and doesn't seem to care where the contents fall, doesn't seem to care that the raindrops burst when they hit the ground, that they shatter when they fall to the floor, that people curse the days the drops dare to tap on their doors.

I am a raindrop.

~~My parents emptied their pockets of me and left me to evaporate on a concrete slab.~~

The window tells me we're not far from the mountains and definitely near the water, but everything is near the

5

water these days. I just don't know which side we're on. Which direction we're facing. I squint up at the early morning light. Someone picked up the sun and pinned it to the sky again, but every day it hangs a little lower than the day before. It's like a negligent parent who only knows one half of who you are. It never sees how its absence changes people. How different we are in the dark.

A sudden rustle means my cellmate is awake.

I spin around like I've been caught stealing food again. That only happened once and my parents didn't believe me when I said it wasn't for me. I said I was just trying to save the stray cats living around the corner but they didn't think I was human enough to care about a cat. Not me. Not ~~something~~ someone like me. But then, they never believed anything I said. That's exactly why I'm here.

Cellmate is studying me.

He fell asleep fully clothed. He's wearing a navy blue T-shirt and khaki cargo pants tucked into shin-high black boots.

I'm wearing dead cotton on my limbs and a blush of roses on my face.

His eyes scan my silhouette and the slow motion makes my heart race. I catch the rose petals as they fall from my cheeks, as they float around my body, as they cover me in something that feels like the absence of courage.

Stop looking at me, is what I want to say.

Stop touching me with your eyes and keep your hands to your sides and please and please and please—

"What's your name?" The tilt of his head cracks gravity in half.

I'm suspended in the moment. I blink and bottle my breaths.

~~He reminds me of someone I used to know.~~

"Why are you here?" I ask the cracks in the concrete wall. 14 cracks in 4 walls. The floor, the ceiling: all the same slab of stone. The pathetically constructed bed frames: built from old water pipes. The small square of a window: too thick to shatter. My hope is exhausted. My eyes are unfocused and aching. My finger is tracing a lazy path across the cold floor.

I'm sitting on the ground where it smells like ice and metal and dirt. Cellmate sits across from me, his legs folded underneath him, his boots just a little too shiny for this place.

"You're afraid of me." His voice has no shape.

"I'm afraid you're wrong."

I might be lying, but that's none of his business.

He snorts and the sound echoes in the dead air between us. I don't lift my head. My throat is tight with something familiar to me, something I've learned to swallow.

2 knocks at the door startle my emotions back into place.

He's upright in an instant.

"No one is there," I tell him. "It's just our breakfast." 264 breakfasts and I still don't know what it's made of. It smells like too many chemicals; an amorphous lump always delivered in extremes. Sometimes too sweet, sometimes too salty, always disgusting. Most of the time I'm too starved to notice the difference.

He hesitates for only an instant before edging toward the door. He slides open a small slot and peers through to a world that no longer exists.

"*Shit!*" He practically flings the tray through the opening, pausing only to slap his palm against his shirt. "Shit, *shit*." He curls his fingers into a tight fist and clenches his jaw. He's burned his hand. I would've warned him if he would've listened.

"You should wait at least three minutes before touching the tray," I tell the wall. I don't look at the scars gracing my small hands, at the burn marks no one could've taught me to avoid. "I think they do it on purpose," I add quietly.

"Oh, so you're talking to me today?" He's angry. His eyes flash before he looks away and I realize he's more embarrassed than anything else. He's a tough guy. Too tough to make stupid mistakes in front of a girl. Too tough to show pain.

I press my lips together and stare out the small square of glass they call a window. There aren't many animals left, but I've heard stories of birds that fly. Maybe one day I'll get to see one. The stories are so wildly woven these days there's very little to believe, but I've heard more than one person say they've actually seen a flying bird within the past few years. So I watch the window.

There will be a bird today. It will be white with streaks

of gold like a crown atop its head. It will fly. There will be a bird today. It will be white with streaks of gold like a crown atop its head. It will fly. There will be a—

His hand.

On me.

2 tips

of 2 fingers graze my cloth-covered shoulder for less than a second and every muscle every tendon in my body is fraught with tension that clenches my spine. I don't move. I don't breathe. Maybe if I don't move, this feeling will last forever.

~~No one has touched me in 264 days.~~

Sometimes I think the loneliness inside of me is going to explode through my skin and sometimes I'm not sure if crying or screaming or laughing through the hysteria will solve anything at all. Sometimes I'm so desperate to touch to be touched *to feel* that I'm almost certain I'm going to fall off a cliff in an alternate universe where no one will ever be able to find me.

It doesn't seem impossible.

I've been screaming for years and no one has ever heard me.

"Aren't you hungry?" His voice is lower now, a little worried now.

~~I've been starving for 264 days.~~ "No." I turn and I shouldn't but I do and he's staring at me. Studying me. His lips are only barely parted, his limbs limp at his side, his lashes blinking back confusion.

Something punches me in the stomach.

His eyes. Something about his eyes.

~~It's not him not him not him not him not him.~~

I close the world away. Lock it up. Turn the key so tight.

"Hey—"

My eyes break open. 2 shattered windows filling my mouth with glass.

"What is it?"

~~Nothing.~~

I focus on the window between me and my freedom. I want to smash this concrete world into oblivion. I want to be bigger, better, stronger.

~~I want to be *angry angry angry*.~~

I want to be the bird that flies away.

"What are you writing?" Cellmate speaks again.

~~These words are vomit.~~

~~This shaky pen is my esophagus.~~

~~This sheet of paper is my porcelain bowl.~~

"Why won't you answer me?" He's too close too close too close.

No one is ever close enough.

My eyes are focused on the window and the promise of what could be. The promise of something grander, something greater, some reason for the madness building in my bones, some explanation for my inability to do anything without ruining everything. There will be a bird. It will be white with streaks of gold like a crown atop its head. It will fly. There will be a bird. It will be—

"Hey—"

"You can't touch me," I whisper. I'm lying, is what I don't tell him. He can touch me, is what I'll never tell him. Please touch me, is what I want to tell him.

But things happen when people touch me. Strange things. Bad things.

Dead things.

I can't remember the warmth of any kind of embrace. My arms ache from the inescapable ice of isolation. My own mother couldn't hold me in her arms. My father couldn't warm my frozen hands. I live in a world of nothing.

Hello.

World.

You will forget me.

Knock knock.

Cellmate jumps to his feet.

It's time to shower.

THREE

The door opens to an abyss.

There's no color, no light, no promise of anything but horror on the other side. No words. No direction. Just an open door that means the same thing every time.

Cellmate has questions.

"What the hell?" He looks from me to the illusion of escape. "They're letting us out?"

~~They'll never let us out.~~ "It's time to shower."

"Shower?"

"We don't have much time," I tell him. "We have to hurry."

"Wait, what?" He reaches for my arm but I pull away. "But there's no light—we can't even see where we're going—"

"Quickly." I focus my eyes on the floor. "Take the hem of my shirt."

"What are you talking about—"

An alarm sounds in the distance. A buzzing hums closer by the second. Soon the entire cell is vibrating with the warning and the door is slipping back into place. I grab his shirt and pull him into the blackness beside me. "Don't. Say. Anything."

"Bu—"

"*Nothing*," I hiss. ~~It's a home, a center for troubled youth,~~ ~~for neglected children from broken families, a safe house~~ ~~for the psychologically disturbed~~. It's a prison. They feed us nothing and our eyes never see each other except in the rare bursts of light that steal their way through cracks of glass they pretend are windows. Nights are punctured by screams and heaving sobs, wails and tortured cries, the sounds of flesh and bone breaking by force or choice I'll never know. I spent the first 3 months in the company of my own stench. No one ever told me where the bathrooms and showers were located. No one ever told me how the system worked. No one speaks to you unless they're delivering bad news. No one touches you ever at all. Boys and girls never find each other.

Never but yesterday.

It can't be coincidence.

My eyes begin to readjust in the artificial night. My fingers feel their way down the rough corridors, and Cellmate doesn't say a word. I'm almost proud of him. He's nearly a foot taller than me, his body hard and solid with the muscle and strength of someone close to my age. The world has not yet broken him.

"Wha—"

I tug on his shirt to keep him from speaking. We've not yet cleared the corridors. I feel oddly protective of him, this person who could probably break me with 2 fingers. He doesn't realize how his ignorance makes him vulnerable. He doesn't realize that they might kill him for no reason at all.

I've decided not to be afraid of him. I've decided his actions are more immature than genuinely threatening. ~~He looks so familiar so familiar so familiar to me.~~ I once knew a boy with the same blue eyes and my memories won't let me hate him.

Perhaps I'd like a friend.

6 more feet until the wall goes from rough to smooth and then we make a right. 2 feet of empty space before we reach a wooden door with a broken handle and a handful of splinters. 3 heartbeats to make certain we're alone. 1 foot forward to edge the door inward. 1 soft creak and the crack widens to reveal nothing but what I imagine this space to look like. "This way," I whisper.

I push him toward the row of showers and scavenge the floor for any bits of soap lodged in the drain. I find 2 pieces, one twice as big as the other. "Open your hand," I tell the darkness. "It's slimy. But don't drop it. There isn't much soap and we got lucky today."

He says nothing for a few seconds and I begin to worry.

"Are you still there?" I wonder if this was the trap. If this was the plan. If perhaps he was sent to kill me under the cover of darkness in this small space. I never really knew what they were going to do to me in the asylum, I never knew if they thought locking me up would be good enough but I always thought they might kill me. It always

14

seemed like a viable option.

I can't say I wouldn't deserve it.

But I'm in here for something I never meant to do and no one seems to care that it was an accident.

~~My parents never tried to help me.~~

I hear no showers running and my heart stops. This particular room is rarely full, but there are usually others, if only 1 or 2. I've come to realize that the asylum's residents are either legitimately insane and can't find their way to the showers, or they simply don't care.

I swallow hard.

"What's your name?" he says. I can feel him breathing much closer than he was before. My heart is racing and I don't know why but I can't control it. "Why won't you tell me your name?"

"Is your hand open?"

He inches forward and I'm almost scared to breathe. His fingers graze the starchy fabric of the only outfit I'll ever own and I manage to exhale. As long as he's not touching my skin. As long as he's not touching my skin. As long as he's not touching my skin. This seems to be the secret.

My thin T-shirt has been washed in the harsh water of this building so many times it feels like a burlap sack against my skin. I drop the bigger piece of soap into his hand and tiptoe backward. "I'm going to turn the shower on for you," I explain, anxious not to raise my voice lest others should hear me.

"What do I do with my clothes?" His body is still too close to mine.

I blink in the blackness. "You have to take them off."

He laughs, amused. "No, I know. I meant what do I do with them while I shower?"

"Try not to get them wet."

He takes a deep breath. "How much time do we have?"

"Two minutes."

"Jesus, why didn't you say somethi—"

I turn on his shower at the same time I turn on my own and his complaints drown under the broken bullets of the barely functioning spigots.

My movements are mechanical. I've done this so many times I've already memorized the most efficient methods of scrubbing, rinsing, and rationing soap for my body as well as my hair. There are no towels, so the trick is trying not to soak any part of your body with too much water. If you do you'll never dry properly and you'll spend the next week nearly dying of pneumonia. I would know.

In exactly 90 seconds I've wrung my hair and I'm slipping back into my tattered outfit. My tennis shoes are the only things I own that are still in fairly good condition. We don't do much walking around here.

Cellmate follows suit almost immediately. I'm pleased he learns quickly.

"Take the hem of my shirt," I instruct him. "We have to hurry."

His fingers skim the small of my back and I have to bite

my lip to stifle the intensity. No one ever puts their hands anywhere near my body.

When we're finally trapped in the familiar 4 walls of claustrophobia, Cellmate won't stop staring at me.

I curl into myself in the corner. He still has my bed, my blanket, my pillow. I forgive him his ignorance, but perhaps it's too soon to be friends. Perhaps I was too hasty in helping him. Perhaps he really is only here to make me miserable. But if I don't stay warm I will get sick. My hair is too wet and the blanket I usually wrap it in is still on his side of the room. Maybe I'm still afraid of him.

I breathe in too sharply, look up too quickly in the dull light of the day. Cellmate has draped 2 blankets over my shoulders.

1 mine.

1 his.

"I'm sorry I'm such an asshole," he whispers to the wall. He doesn't touch me and I'm ~~disappointed~~ happy he doesn't. ~~I wish he would.~~ He shouldn't. No one should ever touch me.

"I'm Adam," he says slowly. He backs away from me until he's cleared the room. He uses one hand to push my bed frame back to my side of the space.

Adam.

Such a nice name. Cellmate has a nice name.

It's a name I've always liked but I can't remember why.

I waste no time climbing onto the barely concealed springs of my mattress and I'm so exhausted I can hardly feel the metal coils threatening to puncture my skin. I haven't slept in more than 24 hours. *Adam is a nice name* is the only thing I can think of before exhaustion cripples my body.

FOUR

I am not insane. I am not insane. I am not insane. I am not insane.
I am not insane. I am not insane. I am not insane. I am not insane.
I am not insane. I am not insane. I am not insane. I am not insane.
I am not insane. I am not insane. I am not insane. I am not insane.
I am not insane. I am not insane. I am not insane. I am not insane.
I am not insane. I am not insane. I am not insane. I am not insane.
I am not insane. I am not insane. I am not insane. I am not insane.
I am not insane. I am not insane. I am not insane. I am not insane.
I am not insane. I am not insane. I am not insane. I am not insane.
I am not insane. I am not insane. I am not insane. I am not insane.
I am not insane. I am not insane. I am not insane. I am not insane.
I am not insane. I am not insane. I am not insane. I am not insane.
I am not insane. I am not insane. I am not insane. I am not insane.
I am not insane. I am not insane. I am not insane. I am not insane.
I am not insane. I am not insane. I am not insane. I am not insane.
I am not insane. I am not insane. I am not insane. I am not insane.
I am not insane. I am not insane. I am not insane. I am not insane.
I am not insane. I am not insane. I am not insane. I am not insane.

Horror rips my eyelids open.

My body is drenched in a cold sweat, my brain swimming in unforgotten waves of pain. My eyes settle on circles of black that dissolve in the darkness. I have no idea how long I've slept. I have no idea if I've scared my cellmate with my dreams. Sometimes I scream out loud.

Adam is staring at me.

I'm breathing hard and I manage to heave myself upright. I pull the blankets closer to my body only to realize I've stolen his only means for warmth. It never even occurred to me that he might be freezing as much as I am. I'm shivering in place but his body is unflinching in the night, his silhouette a strong form against the backdrop of black. ~~I have no idea what to say.~~ There's nothing to say.

"The screams never stop in this place, do they?"

~~The screams are only the beginning.~~ "No," I whisper. A faint blush flushes my face and I'm happy it's too dark for him to notice. He must have heard my cries.

Sometimes I wish I never had to sleep. Sometimes I think that if I stay very, very still, if I never move at all, things will change. I think if I freeze myself I can freeze the pain. Sometimes I won't move for hours. I will not move an inch.

If time stands still nothing can go wrong.

"Are you okay?" His voice is concerned. I study the furrow buried in his brow, the tension in his jaw. This same person who stole my bed and my blanket is the same one who went without tonight. So cocky and careless so few hours ago; so careful and quiet right now. It scares me that this place could've broken him so quickly. I wonder what he heard while I was sleeping.

I wish I could save him from the horror.

Something shatters; a tortured cry sounds in the distance. These rooms are buried deep in concrete, walls thicker than the floors and ceilings combined to keep sounds from escaping too far. If I can hear the agony it must be insurmountable. Every night there are sounds I don't hear. Every night I wonder if I'm next.

"You're not insane."

My eyes snap up. His head is cocked, his eyes focused and clear despite the shroud that envelops us. He takes a deep breath. "I thought everyone in here was insane," he continues. "I thought they'd locked me up with a psycho."

I take a sharp hit of oxygen. "Funny. So did I."

1

2

3 seconds pass.

He cracks a grin so wide, so amused, so refreshingly sincere it's like a clap of thunder through my body. Something pricks at my eyes. I haven't seen a smile in 265 days.

Adam is on his feet.

I offer him his blanket.

He takes it only to wrap it more tightly around my body and something is suddenly constricting in my chest. My lungs are skewered and strung together and I've just decided not to move for an eternity when he speaks.

"What's wrong?"

~~My parents stopped touching me when I was old enough~~

21

to crawl. Teachers made me work alone so I wouldn't hurt the other children. I've never had a friend. I've never known the comfort of a mother's hug. I've never felt the tenderness of a father's kiss. I'm not insane. "Nothing."

5 more seconds. "Can I sit next to you?"

That would be wonderful. "No." I'm staring at the wall again.

He clenches and unclenches his jaw. He runs a hand through his hair and I realize for the first time that he's not wearing a shirt. It's so dark in this room I can only catch his curves and contours; the moon is allowed only a small window to light this space but I watch as the muscles in his arms tighten with every movement. Every inch of his body is raw with power, every surface somehow luminous in the darkness. In 17 years I've never seen anything like him. In 17 years I've never talked to a boy my own age. Because I'm a monster.

I close my eyes.

I hear the creak of his bed, the groan of the springs as he sits down. I unstitch my eyes and study the floor. "You must be freezing."

"No." A strong sigh. "I'm actually burning up."

I'm on my feet so quickly the blankets fall to the floor. "Are you sick?" My eyes scan his face for signs of a fever but I don't dare inch closer. "Do you feel dizzy? Do your joints hurt?" I try to remember my own symptoms. I was chained to my bed by my own body for 1 week. I could do nothing more than crawl to the door and fall face-first into my food.

I don't even know how I survived.

"What's your name?"

He's asked the same question 3 times already. "You might be sick," is all I can say.

"I'm not sick. I'm just hot. I don't usually sleep with my clothes on."

Butterflies catch fire in my stomach. I don't know where to look.

A deep breath. "I was a jerk yesterday. I treated you like crap and I'm sorry. I shouldn't have done that."

I meet his gaze.

His eyes are the perfect shade of cobalt, blue like a blossoming bruise, clear and deep and decided. He's been thinking about this all night.

"Okay."

"So why won't you tell me your name?" He leans forward and I freeze.

I thaw.

"Juliette," I whisper. "My name is Juliette."

His lips soften into a smile. He repeats my name like the word amuses him. Entertains him. Delights him.

~~In 17 years no one has said my name like that.~~

FIVE

I don't know when it started.

I don't know why it started.

I don't know anything about anything except for the screaming.

My mother screaming when she realized she could no longer touch me. My father screaming when he realized what I'd done to my mother. My parents screaming when they'd lock me in my room and tell me I should be grateful. For their food. For their humane treatment of this thing that could not possibly be their child. For the yardstick they used to measure the distance I needed to keep away.

I ruined their lives, is what they said to me.

I stole their happiness. Destroyed my mother's hope for ever having children again.

Couldn't I see what I'd done, is what they'd ask me. Couldn't I see that I'd ruined everything.

I tried so hard to fix what I'd ruined. I tried every single day to be what they wanted. I tried all the time to be better but I never really knew how.

I only know now that the scientists are wrong.

The world is flat.

I know because I was tossed right off the edge and I've been trying to hold on for 17 years. I've been trying to climb back up *for 17 years but it's nearly impossible to beat gravity when no one is willing to give you a hand.*

When no one wants to risk touching you.

It's snowing today.

The concrete is icy and stiffer than usual, but I prefer these freezing temperatures to the stifling humidity of summer days. Summer is like a slow-cooker bringing everything in the world to a boil 1 degree at a time. I hate the heat and the sticky, sweaty mess left behind. I hate the sun, too preoccupied with itself to notice the infinite hours we spend in its presence. The sun is an arrogant thing, always leaving the world behind when it tires of us.

The moon is a loyal companion.

It never leaves. It's always there, watching, steadfast, knowing us in our light and dark moments, changing forever just as we do. Every day it's a different version of itself. Sometimes weak and wan, sometimes strong and full of light. The moon understands what it means to be human.

Uncertain. Alone. Cratered by imperfections.

I stare out the window for so long I forget myself. I hold out my hand to catch a snowflake and my fist closes around the icy air. Empty.

I want to put this fist attached to my wrist right through the window.

Just to feel something.

Just to feel human.

"What time is it?"

His voice pulls me back down to a world I keep trying to forget. "I don't know," I tell him. I have no idea what time it is. I have no idea which day of the week it is, what month we're in, or even if there's a specific season we're supposed to be in.

We don't really have seasons anymore.

The animals are dying, birds don't fly, crops are hard to come by, flowers almost don't exist. The weather is unreliable. Sometimes our winter days hit 92 degrees. Sometimes it snows for no reason at all. We can't grow enough food anymore, we can't sustain enough vegetation for the animals anymore, and we can't feed the people what they need. Our population was dying off at an alarming rate before The Reestablishment took over and they promised us they had a solution. Animals were so desperate for food they were willing to eat anything and people were so desperate for food they were willing to eat poisoned animals. We were killing ourselves by trying to stay alive. The weather, the plants, the animals, and our human survival are all inextricably linked. The natural elements were at war with one another because we abused our ecosystem. Abused our atmosphere. Abused our animals. Abused our fellow man.

The Reestablishment promised they would fix things. But even though human health has found a modicum of relief under the new regime, more people have died at the end of a loaded gun than from an empty stomach. It's progressively getting worse.

"Juliette?"

My head snaps up.

His eyes are wary, worried, analyzing me.

I look away.

He clears his throat. "So, uh, they only feed us once a day?"

His question sends both our eyes toward the small slot in the door.

I curl my knees to my chest and balance my bones on the mattress. If I hold myself very, very still, I can almost ignore the metal digging into my skin. "There's no system to the food," I tell him. My finger traces a new pattern down the rough material of the blanket. "There's usually something in the morning, but there are no guarantees for anything else. Sometimes . . . we get lucky." I glance out the window. Pinks and reds filter into the room and I know it's the start of a new beginning. The start of the same end. Another day.

~~Maybe I will die today.~~

Maybe a bird will fly today.

"So that's it? They open the door once a day for people to do their business and maybe if we're *lucky* they feed us? That's it?"

The bird will be white with streaks of gold like a crown atop its head. It will fly. "That's it."

"There's no . . . group therapy?" He almost laughs.

"Until you arrived, I hadn't spoken a single word in two hundred sixty-four days."

His silence says so much. I can almost reach out and touch the guilt growing on his shoulders. "How long are you in for?" he finally asks.

~~Forever.~~ "I don't know." A mechanical sound creaks/groans/cranks in the distance. My life is 4 walls of missed opportunities poured into concrete molds.

"What about your family?" There's a serious sorrow in his voice, almost like he already knows the answer to that question.

~~Here is what I know about my parents: I have no idea where they are.~~ "Why are you here?" I talk to my fingers to avoid his gaze. I've studied my hands so thoroughly I know exactly where each bump cut and bruise has ravaged my skin. Small hands. Slim fingers. I curl them into a fist and release them to lose the tension. He still hasn't responded.

I look up.

"I'm not insane," is all he says.

"That's what we all say." I cock my head only to shake it a fraction of an inch. I bite my lip. My eyes can't help but steal glances out the window.

"Why do you keep looking outside?"

I don't mind his questions, I really don't. It's just strange to have someone to talk to. It's strange to have to move my lips to form words necessary to explain my actions. No one has cared for so long. No one's watched me closely enough to wonder why I stare out a window. No one has ever treated me like an equal. Then again, he doesn't know

~~I'm a monster~~ my secret. I wonder how long this will last before he's running for his life.

I've forgotten to answer and he's still studying me.

I tuck a piece of hair behind my ear only to change my mind. "Why do you stare so much?"

His eyes are careful, curious. "I figured the only reason they would lock me up with a girl was because you were crazy. I thought they were trying to torture me by putting me in the same space as a psychopath. I thought you were my punishment."

"That's why you stole my bed." To exert power. To stake a claim. To fight first.

He looks away. Clasps and unclasps his hands before rubbing the back of his neck. "Why'd you help me? How'd you know I wouldn't hurt you?"

I count my fingers to make sure they're still there. "I didn't."

"You didn't help me or you didn't know if I'd hurt you?"

"Adam." My lips curve around the shape of his name. I'm surprised to discover how much I love the easy, familiar way the sound rolls off my tongue.

He's sitting almost as still as I am. "Yeah?"

"What's it like?" I ask, each word quieter than the one before. "Outside?" ~~In the real world.~~ "Is it worse?"

It takes him a few heartbeats to answer. "Honestly? I'm not sure if it's better to be in here or out there."

I wait for his lips to part; I wait for him to explain. And then I try to pay attention as his words bounce around in the haze of my head, fogging my senses, clouding my concentration.

Did you know it was an international movement? Adam asks me.

No I did not, I tell him. I do not tell him I was dragged from my home 3 years ago. I do not tell him that I was dragged away exactly 7 years after The Reestablishment began to preach and 4 months after they took control of everything. I do not tell him how little I know of our new world.

Adam says The Reestablishment had its hands in every country, ready for the moment to bring its leaders into a position of control. He says the inhabitable land left in the world has been divided into 3,333 sectors and each space is now controlled by a different Person of Power.

Did you know they lied to us? Adam asks me.

Did you know that The Reestablishment said someone had to take control, that someone had to save society, that someone had to restore the peace? Did you know that they said killing all the voices of opposition was the only way to find peace?

Did you know this? is what Adam asks me.

And this is where I nod. This is where I say yes.

This is the part I remember: The anger. The riots. The rage.

My eyes close in an effort to block out the bad memories, but the effort backfires. Protests. Rallies. Screams for survival. I see women and children starving to death, homes destroyed and buried in rubble, the countryside a burnt landscape, its only fruit the rotting flesh of casualties.

I see dead dead dead red and burgundy and maroon and the richest shade of your mother's favorite lipstick all smeared into the earth.

So much everything all the things dead.

The Reestablishment is struggling to maintain its hold over the people, Adam says. He says The Reestablishment is struggling to fight a war against the rebels who will not acquiesce to this new regime. The Reestablishment is struggling to root itself as a new form of government across all international societies.

And then I wonder what has happened to the people I used to see every day. What's become of their homes, their parents, their children. I wonder how many of them have been buried in the ground.

How many of them were murdered.

"They're destroying everything," Adam says, and his voice is suddenly solemn. "All the books, every artifact, every remnant of human history. They're saying it's the only way to fix things. They say we need to start fresh. They say we can't make the same mistakes of previous generations."

2

knocks

at the door and we're both on our feet, abruptly startled back into this bleak world.

Adam raises an eyebrow at me. "Breakfast?"

"Wait three minutes," I remind him. We're so good at masking our hunger until the knocks at the door cripple our dignity.

They starve us on purpose.

"Yeah." His lips are set in a soft smile. "I wouldn't want to burn myself." The air shifts as he steps forward.

I am a statue.

"I still don't understand," he says, so quietly. "Why are you here?"

"Why do you ask so many questions?"

He leaves less than a foot of space between us and I'm 10 inches away from spontaneous combustion. "Your eyes are so deep." He tilts his head. "So calm. I want to know what you're thinking."

"You shouldn't." My voice falters. "You don't even know me."

He laughs and the action gives life to the light in his eyes. "I don't know you."

"No."

He shakes his head. Sits on his bed. "Right. Of course not."

"What?"

"You're right." His breath catches. "Maybe I am insane."

I take 2 steps backward. "Maybe you are."

He's smiling again and I'd like to take a picture. I'd like to stare at the curve of his lips for the rest of my life. "I'm not, you know."

"But you won't tell me why you're here," I challenge.

"And neither will you."

I fall to my knees and tug the tray through the slot. Something unidentifiable is steaming in 2 tin cups. Adam folds himself onto the floor across from me.

"Breakfast," I say as I push his portion forward.

SIX

1 word, 2 lips, 3 4 5 fingers form 1 fist.

1 corner, 2 parents, 3 4 5 reasons to hide.

1 child, 2 eyes, 3 4 17 years of fear.

A broken broomstick, a pair of wild faces, angry whispers, locks on my door.

Look at me, is what I wanted to say to you. Talk to me every once in a while. Find me a cure for these tears, I'd really like to exhale for the first time in my life.

It's been 2 weeks.

2 weeks of the same routine, 2 weeks of nothing but routine. 2 weeks with the cellmate ~~who has come too close to touching me~~ who does not touch me. Adam is adapting to the system. He never complains, he never volunteers too much information, he continues to ask too many questions.

He's nice to me.

I sit by the window and watch the rain and the leaves and the snow collide. They take turns dancing in the wind, performing choreographed routines for unsuspecting masses. The soldiers stomp stomp stomp through the rain, crushing leaves and fallen snow under their feet. Their hands are wrapped in gloves wrapped around guns that could put a bullet through a million possibilities. They don't bother to be bothered by the beauty that falls from the sky. They don't understand the freedom in feeling the universe on their skin. They don't care.

I wish I could stuff my mouth full of raindrops and fill my pockets full of snow. I wish I could trace the veins in a fallen leaf and feel the wind pinch my nose.

Instead, I ignore the desperation sticking my fingers together and watch for the bird I've only seen in my dreams. Birds used to fly, is what the stories say. Before the ozone layer deteriorated, before the pollutants mutated the creatures into something ~~horrible~~ different. They say the weather wasn't always so unpredictable. They say there were birds who used to soar through the skies like planes.

It seems strange that a small animal could achieve anything as complex as human engineering, but the possibility is too enticing to ignore. I've dreamt about the same bird flying through the same sky for exactly 10 years. White with streaks of gold like a crown atop its head.

It's the only dream I have that gives me peace.

"What are you writing?"

I squint up at his strong stature, the easy grin on his face. I don't know how he manages to smile in spite of everything. I wonder if he can hold on to that shape, that special curve of the mouth that changes lives. I wonder how he'll feel in 1 month and I shudder at the thought.

I don't want him to end up like me.

Empty.

"Hey—" He grabs the blanket off my bed and crouches next to me, wasting no time wrapping the thin cloth around my thinner shoulders. "You okay?"

I try to smile. "Thank you for the blanket."

He sits down next to me and leans against the wall. His shoulders are so close too close ~~never close enough.~~ His body heat does more for me than the blanket ever will. Something in my joints aches with an acute yearning, a desperate need I've never been able to fulfill. My bones are begging for something I cannot allow.

~~Touch me.~~

He glances at the little notebook tucked in my hand, at the broken pen clutched in my fist. I know he's staring at me.

"Are you writing a book?"

"No."

"Maybe you should."

I turn to meet his eyes and regret it immediately. There are less than 3 inches between us and I can't move because my body only knows how to freeze. Every muscle every movement tightens, every vertebra in my spinal column is a block of ice. I'm holding my breath and my eyes are wide, locked, caught in the intensity of his gaze. I can't look away. I don't know how to retreat.

Oh.

God.

His eyes.

I've been lying to myself, determined to deny the impossible.

I know him I know him I know him I know him

The boy ~~who does not remember me~~ I used to know.

"They're going to destroy the English language," he says, his voice careful, quiet.

I fight to catch my breath.

"They want to re-create everything," he continues. "They want to redesign everything. They want to destroy anything that could've been the reason for our problems. They think we need a new, universal language." He drops his voice. Drops his eyes. "They want to destroy everything. Every language in history."

"No." My breath hitches. Spots cloud my vision.

"I know."

"No." This I did not know.

He looks up. "It's good that you're writing things down. One day what you're doing will be illegal."

I've begun to shake. My body is suddenly fighting a maelstrom of emotions, my brain plagued by the world I'm losing and pained by this boy who does not remember me. The pen stumbles its way to the floor and I'm gripping the blanket so hard I'm afraid it's going to tear. I never thought it would get this bad. I never thought The Reestablishment would take things so far. They're incinerating culture, the beauty of diversity. The new citizens of our world will be reduced to nothing but numbers, easily interchangeable, easily removable, easily destroyed for disobedience.

We have lost our humanity.

I wrap the blanket around my shoulders but the tremors won't stop. I'm horrified by my lack of self-control. I can't make myself still.

His hand is suddenly on my back.

His touch is scorching my skin through the layers of fabric and I'm caught, so desperate ~~so desperate so desper-ate~~ to be close so desperate to be far away. I don't know how to move away from him. ~~I don't want to move away from him.~~

I don't want him to be afraid of me.

"Hey." His voice is soft so soft so soft. He pulls my swaddled figure close to his chest and his heat melts the icicles propping me up from the inside out and I thaw I thaw I thaw, my eyes fluttering fast until they fall closed, until silent tears are streaming down my face and I've decided the only thing I want to freeze is his frame holding mine. "It's okay," he whispers. "You'll be okay."

Truth is a jealous, vicious mistress that never ever sleeps, is what I don't tell him. I'll never be okay.

It takes every broken filament in my being to pull away from him. I do it because I have to. ~~Because it's for his own good.~~ The blanket catches my foot and I nearly fall before Adam reaches out to me again. "Juliette—"

"You can't t-touch me." My breathing is shallow and hard to swallow, my fingers shaking so fast I clench them into a fist. "You can't touch me. You can't." My eyes are trained on the door.

He's on his feet. "Why not?"

"You just can't," I whisper to the walls.

"I don't understand—why won't you talk to me? You sit in the corner all day and write in your book and look at everything but my face. You have so much to say to a piece of paper but I'm standing right here and you don't even acknowledge me. Juliette, *please*—" He reaches for my arm and I turn away. "Why won't you at least *look* at me? I'm not going to hurt you—"

~~You don't remember me. You don't remember that we went to the same school for 7 years.~~

You don't remember me.

"You don't know me." My voice is even, flat; my limbs numb, amputated. "We've shared one space for two weeks and you think you know me but you don't know anything about me. Maybe I *am* crazy."

"You're not," he says through clenched teeth. "You *know* you're not."

"Then maybe it's you," I say carefully, slowly. "Because one of us is."

"That's not true—"

"Tell me why you're here, Adam. What are you doing in an insane asylum if you don't belong here?"

"I've been asking you the same question since I got here."

"Maybe you ask too many questions."

I hear his hard exhalation of breath. He laughs a bitter laugh. "We're practically the only two people who are *alive* in this place and you want to shut me out, too?"

I close my eyes and focus on breathing. "You can talk to me. Just don't touch me."

"Maybe I want to touch you."

I'm tempted by recklessness, desperate for what I can never have. I turn my back on him but I can't keep the lies from spilling out of my lips. "Maybe I don't want you to."

He makes a harsh sound. "I disgust you that much?"

I spin around, so caught off guard by his words I forget myself. He's staring at me, his face hard, his jaw set, his fingers flexing by his sides. His eyes are 2 buckets of rainwater: deep, fresh, clear.

Hurt.

"You don't know what you're talking about."

"You can't just answer a simple question, can you?" he says. He shakes his head and turns to the wall.

My face is cast in a neutral mold, my arms and legs filled with plaster. I feel nothing. I am nothing. I am empty of everything I will never move. I'm staring at a small crack near my shoe. I will stare at it forever.

The blankets fall to the floor. The world fades out of focus, my ears outsource every sound to another dimension. My eyes close, my thoughts drift, my memories kick me in the heart.

I know him.

I've tried so hard to stop thinking about him.
I've tried so hard to forget his face.

I've tried so hard to get those blue blue blue eyes out of my head but I know him I know him I know him it's been 3 years since I last saw him.

I could never forget Adam.

But he's already forgotten me.

SEVEN

I remember televisions and fireplaces and porcelain sinks. I remember movie tickets and parking lots and SUVs. I remember hair salons and holidays and window shutters and dandelions and the smell of freshly paved driveways. I remember toothpaste commercials and ladies in high heels and old men in business suits. I remember mailmen and libraries and boy bands and balloons and Christmas trees.

I remember being 10 years old when we couldn't ignore the food shortages anymore and things got so expensive no one could afford to live.

Adam is not speaking to me.

Maybe it's for the best. Maybe there was no point hoping he and I could be friends, maybe it's better he thinks I don't like him than that I like him too much. He's hiding a lot of something that might be pain, but his secrets scare me. He won't tell me why he's here. Though I don't tell him much, either.

~~And yet and yet and yet~~.

Last night the memory of his arms around me was enough to scare away the screams. The warmth of a kind embrace, the strength of firm hands holding all of my pieces together, the relief and release of so many years' loneliness. This gift he's given me I can't repay.

Touching Juliette is nearly impossible.

I'll never forget the horror in my mother's eyes, the torture in my father's face, the fear etched in their expressions. Their child ~~was~~ is a monster. Possessed by the devil. Cursed by darkness. Unholy. An abomination. Drugs, tests, medical solutions failed. Psychological cross-examinations failed.

She is a walking weapon in society, is what the teachers said. *We've never seen anything like it,* is what the doctors said. *She should be removed from your home,* is what the police officers said.

~~No problem at all, is what my parents said.~~ I was 14 years old when they finally got rid of me. When they stood back and watched as I was dragged away for a murder I didn't know I could commit.

Maybe the world is safer with me locked in a cell. Maybe Adam is safer if he hates me. He's sitting in the corner with his fists in his face.

I never wanted to hurt him.

I never wanted to hurt the only person who never wanted to hurt me.

The door crashes open and 5 people swarm into the room, rifles pointed at our chests.

Adam is on his feet and I'm made of stone. I've forgotten to inhale. I haven't seen so many people in so long I'm momentarily stupefied. I should be screaming.

"HANDS UP, FEET APART, MOUTHS SHUT. DON'T MOVE AND WE WON'T SHOOT YOU."

I'm still frozen in place. I should move, I should lift my arms, I should spread my feet, I should remember to breathe.

The one barking orders slams the butt of his gun into my back and my knees crack as they hit the floor. I finally taste oxygen and a side of blood. I think Adam is yelling but there is an acute agony ripping through my body unlike anything I've experienced before. I'm immobilized.

"What don't you understand about keeping your mouth SHUT?" I squint sideways to see the barrel of the gun 2 inches away from Adam's face.

"GET UP." A steel-toed boot kicks me in the ribs, fast, hard, hollow. "I said GET UP." Harder, faster, stronger, another boot in my gut. I can't even cry out.

~~Get up, Juliette. Get up. If you don't, they'll shoot Adam.~~

I heave myself up to my knees and fall back on the wall behind me, stumbling forward to catch my balance. Lifting my hands is more torture than I knew I could endure. My skin is a sieve, punctured by pins and needles of pain. They've finally come to kill me.

That's why they put Adam in my cell.

Because I'm leaving. Adam is here because I'm leaving, because they forgot to kill me on time, because my moments are over, because my 17 years were too many for this world. They're going to kill me.

I always wondered how it would happen. ~~I wonder if this~~

~~will make my parents happy.~~

Someone is laughing. "Well aren't you a little shit?"

I don't even know if they're talking to me. I can hardly focus on keeping my arms upright.

"She's not even crying," someone adds.

The walls are beginning to bleed into the ceiling. I wonder how long I can hold my breath. I can't distinguish words I can't understand the sounds I'm hearing the blood is rushing through my head and my lips are 2 blocks of concrete I can't crack open. There's a gun in my back and I'm tripping forward. The floors are falling up. My feet are dragging in a direction I can't decipher.

I hope they kill me soon.

EIGHT

It takes me 2 days to open my eyes.

There's a tin of water and a tin of food set off to the side and I inhale the cold contents with trembling hands, a dull ache creaking through my bones. Nothing seems to be broken, but one glance under my shirt proves the pain was real. The bruises are discolored blossoms of blue and yellow, torture to touch and slow to heal.

Adam is nowhere.

I am alone in a block of solitude, 4 walls no more than 10 feet in every direction, the only air creeping in through a small slot in the door. I've just begun to terrorize myself with my imagination when the heavy metal door slams open. A guard with 2 rifles strung across his chest looks me up and down.

"Get up."

This time I don't hesitate.

I hope Adam, at least, is safe. I hope he doesn't come to the same end I do.

"Follow me." The guard's voice is thick and deep, his gray eyes unreadable. He looks about 25 years old, blond hair cropped close to the crown, shirtsleeves rolled up to his shoulders, military tattoos snaking up his forearms just like Adam's.

Oh.

God.

No.

Adam steps into the doorway beside the blond and gestures with his weapon toward a narrow hallway. "Move."

~~Adam is pointing a gun at my chest.~~

~~Adam is pointing a gun at my chest.~~

Adam is pointing a gun at my chest.

His eyes are foreign to me, glassy and distant, far, far away.

I am nothing but novocaine. I am numb, a world of nothing, all feeling and emotion gone forever.

I am a whisper that never was.

Adam is a soldier. ~~Adam wants me to die.~~

I stare at him openly now, every sensation amputated.

Death would be a welcome release from these earthly joys I've known.

I don't know how long I've been walking before another blow to my back cripples me. I blink against the brightness of light I haven't seen in so long. My eyes begin to tear and I'm squinting against the fluorescent bulbs illuminating the large space. I can hardly see anything.

"Juliette Ferrars." A voice detonates my name. There's a heavy boot pressed into my back and I can't lift my head to distinguish who's speaking to me. "Weston, dim the lights and release her. I want to see her face." The command is cool and strong like steel, dangerously calm, effortlessly powerful.

The brightness is reduced to a level I'm able to tolerate. The imprint of a boot is stamped into my back but no longer settled on my skin. I lift my head and look up.

I'm immediately struck by his youth. He can't be much older than me.

It's obvious he's in charge of something, though I have no idea what. His skin is flawless, unblemished, his jawline sharp and strong. His eyes are the palest shade of emerald I've ever seen.

He's beautiful.

His crooked smile is calculated evil.

He's sitting on what he imagines to be a throne but is nothing more than a folding chair at the front of an empty room. His suit is perfectly pressed, his blond hair expertly combed, his soldiers the ideal bodyguards.

I hate him.

"You're so stubborn." His green eyes are almost translucent. "You never want to cooperate. You wouldn't even play nice with your cellmate."

I flinch without intending to. The burn of betrayal blushes up my neck.

Green Eyes looks unexpectedly amused and I'm suddenly mortified. "Well isn't that interesting." He snaps his fingers. "Kent, would you step forward, please."

My heart stops beating when Adam comes into view. ~~Kent. His name is Adam Kent.~~

Adam flanks Green Eyes in an instant, but only offers a curt nod of his head as a salute. Perhaps the leader isn't nearly as important as he thinks.

"Sir," he says.

I should've known.

I'd heard rumors of soldiers living among the public in secret, reporting to the authorities if things seemed suspicious. Every day people disappeared. No one ever came back.

Though I still can't understand why Adam was sent to spy on me.

"It seems you made quite an impression on her."

I squint closer at the man in the chair only to realize his suit has been adorned with tiny colored patches. Military mementos. His last name is etched into the lapel: Warner.

Adam says nothing. He doesn't look in my direction. His body is erect, 6 feet of ~~gorgeous~~ lean muscle, his profile strong and steady. The same arms that held my body are now holsters for lethal weapons.

"You have nothing to say about that?" Warner glances at Adam only to tilt his head in my direction, his eyes dancing in the light, clearly entertained.

Adam clenches his jaw. "Sir."

"Of course." Warner is suddenly bored. "Why should I expect you to have something to say?"

"Are you going to kill me?" The words escape my lips before I have a chance to think them through and someone's gun slams into my spine all over again. I fall with a broken whimper, wheezing into the filthy floor.

"That wasn't necessary, Roland. I suppose I'd be

wondering the same thing if I were in her position." A pause. "Juliette?"

I manage to lift my head.

"I have a proposition for you."

NINE

I'm not sure I'm hearing him correctly.

"You have something I want." Warner is still staring at me.

"I don't understand," I tell him.

He takes a deep breath and stands up to pace the length of the room. Adam has not yet been dismissed. "You are kind of a pet project of mine. I've studied your records for a very long time."

"What?"

"We're in the middle of a *war*," he says a little impatiently. "Maybe you can put the pieces together."

"I don't—"

"I know your secret, Juliette. I know why you're in here. Your entire life is documented in hospital records, complaints to authorities, messy lawsuits, public demands to have you locked up." His pause gives me enough time to choke on the horror caught in my throat. "I'd been considering it for a long time, but I wanted to make sure you weren't *actually* psychotic. Isolation wasn't exactly a good indicator, though you did fend for yourself quite well." He offers me a smile that says I should be grateful for his praise. "I sent Kent to stay with you as a final precaution.

I wanted to make sure you weren't volatile, that you were capable of basic human interaction and communication. I must say I'm quite pleased with the results."

"Kent, it seems, played his part a little too excellently. He is a fine soldier. One of the best, in fact." Warner spares him a glance before smiling at me. "But don't worry, he doesn't know what you're capable of. Not yet, anyway."

I claw at the panic, I swallow the agony, I beg myself not to look in his direction but I fail ~~I fail I fail~~. Adam meets my eyes in the same split second I meet his but he looks away so quickly I'm not sure if I imagined it.

~~I am a monster.~~

"I'm not as cruel as you think," Warner continues, a musical lilt in his voice. "If you're so fond of his company I can make this"—he gestures between myself and Adam— "a permanent assignment."

"No," I breathe.

Warner curves his lips into a careless grin. "Oh yes. But be careful, pretty girl. If you do something . . . *bad* . . . he'll have to shoot you."

Adam doesn't react to anything Warner says.

He is doing a job.

I am a number, a mission, an easily replaceable object; I am not even a memory in his mind.

I didn't expect his betrayal to bury me so deep.

"If you accept my offer," Warner interrupts my thoughts, "you will live like I do. You will be one of *us*, and not one of *them*. Your life will change forever."

"And if I do not accept?" I ask.

Warner looks genuinely disappointed. His hands are clasped together in dismay. "You don't really have a choice. If you stand by my side you will be rewarded." He presses his lips together. "But if you choose to disobey? Well . . . I think you look rather lovely with all your body parts intact, don't you?"

I'm breathing so hard my frame is shaking. "You want me to torture people for you?"

His face breaks into a brilliant smile. "That would be wonderful."

I don't have time to form a response before he turns to Adam. "Show her what she's missing, would you?"

Adam answers a beat too late. "Sir?"

"That is an order, soldier." Warner's eyes are trained on me, his lips twitching with suppressed amusement. "I'd like to break this one. She's a little too feisty for her own good."

"You can't touch me," I spit through clenched teeth.

"Wrong," he singsongs. He tosses Adam a pair of black gloves. "You're going to need these," he says with a conspiratorial whisper.

"You're a monster." My voice is too even, my body filled with a sudden rage. "Why don't you just *kill* me?"

"That, my dear, would be a waste." He steps forward and I realize his hands are sheathed in white leather gloves. He tips my chin up with one finger. "Besides, it'd be a shame to lose such a pretty face."

I try to snap my neck away from him but the same steel-toed boot slams into my spine and Warner catches my face in his grip. I suppress a scream. "Don't struggle, love. You'll only make things more difficult for yourself."

"I hope you rot in hell."

Warner flexes his jaw. He holds up a hand to stop someone from shooting me, kicking me in the spleen, cracking my skull open, I have no idea. "You're a fighter for the wrong team." He stands up straight. "But we can change that. Kent," he calls. "Don't let her out of your sight. She's your charge now."

"Yes, sir."

TEN

Adam puts on the gloves but he doesn't touch me. "Let her up, Roland. I'll take it from here."

The boot disappears. I struggle to my feet and stare at nothing. I won't think about the horror that awaits me. Someone kicks in the backs of my knees and I nearly stumble to the ground. "Get *going*," a voice growls from behind. I look up and realize Adam is already walking away. I'm supposed to be following him.

Only once we're back in the familiar blindness of the asylum hallways does he stop walking.

"Juliette."

I don't answer him.

"Take my hand," he says.

"I will never. Not ever."

A heavy sigh. I feel him shift in the darkness and soon his body is too close to mine. His hand is on my lower back and he's guiding me through the corridors toward an unknown destination.

The distance we're walking is much longer than I expected. When Adam finally speaks I suspect we're close to the end. "We're going to go outside," he says near my ear and I'm almost too distracted by the feel of his voice to understand the significance of what he's saying. "I just thought you should know."

An audible intake of breath is my only response. I haven't been outside in almost a year. I'm painfully excited but I haven't felt natural light on my skin in so long I don't know if I'll be able to handle it. I have no choice.

The air hits me first.

Our atmosphere has little to boast of, but after so many months in a concrete corner even the wasted oxygen of our dying Earth tastes like heaven. I can't inhale fast enough. I fill my lungs with the feeling; I step into the slight breeze and clutch a fistful of wind as it weaves its way through my fingers.

Bliss unlike anything I've ever known.

The air is crisp and cool. A refreshing bath of tangible nothing that stings my eyes and snaps at my skin. The sun is high today, blinding as it reflects the small patches of snow keeping the earth frozen. My eyes are pressed down by the weight of the bright light and I can't see through more than two slits, but the warm rays wash over my body like a jacket fitted to my form, like the hug of something greater than a human. I could stand still in this moment forever. For one infinite second I feel free.

Adam's touch shocks me back to reality. I nearly jump out of my skin and he catches my waist. I have to beg my bones to stop shaking. "Are you okay?" His eyes surprise me. They're the same ones I remember, blue and bottomless like the deepest part of the ocean. His hands are ~~gentle so gentle~~ around me.

"I don't want you to touch me," I lie.

"You don't have a choice." He won't look at me.

"I always have a choice."

He runs a hand through his hair and swallows the nothing in his throat. "Follow me."

We're in a blank space, an empty acre filled with dead leaves and dying trees taking small sips from melted snow in the soil. The landscape has been ravaged by war and neglect and it's still the most beautiful thing I've seen in so long. The stomping soldiers stop to watch as Adam opens a car door for me.

It's not a car. It's a tank.

I stare at the massive metal body and attempt to climb my way up the side when Adam is suddenly behind me. He hoists me up by the waist and I gasp as he settles me into the seat.

Soon we're driving in silence and I have no idea where we're headed.

I'm staring out the window at everything.

I'm eating and drinking and absorbing every infinitesimal detail in the debris, in the skyline, in the abandoned homes and broken pieces of metal and glass sprinkled in the scenery. The world looks naked, stripped of vegetation and warmth. There are no street signs, no stop signs; there is no need for either. There is no public transportation. Everyone knows that cars are now manufactured by only one company and sold at a ridiculous rate.

Very few people are allowed a means of escape.

~~My parents~~ The general population has been distributed across what's left of the country. Industrial buildings form the spine of the landscape: tall, rectangular metal boxes stuffed full of machinery. Machinery intended to strengthen the army, to strengthen The Reestablishment, to destroy mass quantities of human civilization.

Carbon/Tar/Steel

Gray/Black/Silver

Smoky colors smudged into the skyline, dripping into the slush that used to be snow. Trash is heaped in haphazard piles everywhere, patches of yellowed grass peeking out from under the devastation.

Traditional homes of our old world have been abandoned, windows shattered, roofs collapsing, red and green and blue paint scrubbed into muted shades to better match our bright future. Now I see the compounds carelessly constructed on the ravaged land and I begin to remember. I remember how these were supposed to be temporary. I remember the few months before I was locked up when they'd begun building them. These small, cold quarters would suffice just until they figured out all the details of this new plan, is what The Reestablishment had said. Just until everyone was subdued. Just until people stopped protesting and realized that this change was *good* for them, *good* for their children, *good* for their future.

I remember there were rules.

No more dangerous imaginations, no more prescription medications. A new generation comprised of only healthy individuals would sustain us. The sick must be locked away. The old must be discarded. The troubled must be given up to the asylums. Only the strong should survive.

Yes.

Of course.

No more stupid languages and stupid stories and stupid paintings placed above stupid mantels. No more Christmas, no more Hanukkah, no more Ramadan and Diwali. No talk of religion, of belief, of personal convictions. Personal convictions were what nearly killed us all, is what they said.

Convictions priorities preferences prejudices and ideologies divided us. Deluded us. Destroyed us.

Selfish needs, wants, and desires needed to be obliterated. Greed, overindulgence, and gluttony had to be expunged from human behavior. The solution was in self-control, in minimalism, in sparse living conditions; one simple language and a brand-new dictionary filled with words everyone would understand.

These things would save us, save our children, save the human race, is what they said.

Reestablish Equality. Reestablish Humanity. Reestablish Hope, Healing, and Happiness.

SAVE US!

JOIN US!

REESTABLISH SOCIETY!

The posters are still plastered on the walls.

The wind whips their tattered remains, but the signs are determinedly fixed, flapping against the steel and concrete structures they're stuck to. Some are still pasted to poles sprung right out of the ground, loudspeakers now affixed at the very top. Loudspeakers that alert the people, no doubt, to the imminent dangers that surround them.

But the world is eerily quiet.

Pedestrians pass by, ambling along in the cold, frigid weather to do factory work and find food for their families. Hope in this world bleeds out of the barrel of a gun.

No one really cares for the concept anymore.

People used to want hope. They wanted to think things could get better. They wanted to believe they could go back to worrying about gossip and holiday vacations and going to parties on Saturday nights, so The Reestablishment promised a future too perfect to be possible and society was too desperate to disbelieve. They never realized they were signing away their souls to a group planning on taking advantage of their ignorance. Their fear.

Most civilians are too petrified to protest but there are others who are stronger. There are others who are waiting for the right moment. There are others who have already begun to fight back.

I hope it's not too late to fight back.

I study every quivering branch, every imposing soldier, every window I can count. My eyes are 2 professional pick-pockets, stealing everything to store away in my mind.

I lose track of the minutes we trample over.

We pull up to a structure 10 times larger than the asylum and suspiciously central to civilization. From the outside it looks like a bland building, inconspicuous in every way but its size, gray steel slabs comprising 4 flat walls, windows cracked and slammed into the 15 stories. It's bleak and bears no marking, no insignia, no proof of its true identity.

Political headquarters camouflaged among the masses.

The inside of the tank is a convoluted mess of buttons and levers I'm at a loss to operate, and Adam is opening my door before I have a chance to identify the pieces. His hands are in place around my waist and my feet are now firmly on the ground but my heart is pounding so fast I'm certain he can hear it. He hasn't let go of me.

I look up.

His eyes are tight, his forehead pinched, his lips ~~his lips his lips~~ are 2 pieces of frustration forged together.

I step back. He drops his gaze. Turns away. He inhales and 5 fingers on one hand form a fickle fist. "This way." He nods toward the building.

I follow him inside.

ELEVEN

I'm so prepared for unimaginable horror that the reality is almost worse.

Dirty money is dripping from the walls, a year's supply of food wasted on marble floors, hundreds of thousands of dollars in medical aid poured into fancy furniture and Persian rugs. I feel the artificial heat pouring in through air vents and think of children screaming for clean water. I squint through crystal chandeliers and hear mothers begging for mercy. I see a superficial world existing in the midst of a terrorizing reality and I can't move.

I can't breathe.

So many people must've died to sustain this luxury. So many people had to lose their homes and their children and their last 5 dollars in the bank for promises promises promises so many promises to save them from themselves. They *promised* us—The Reestablishment promised us hope for a better future. They said they would fix things, they said they would help us get back to the world we knew— the world with movie dates and spring weddings and baby showers. They said they would give us back our homes, our health, our sustainable future.

But they stole everything.

They took everything. ~~My life. My future. My sanity. My freedom.~~

They filled our world with weapons aimed at our foreheads and smiled as they shot 16 candles right through our future. They killed those strong enough to fight back and locked up the freaks who failed to live up to their utopian expectations. ~~People like me.~~

Here is proof of their corruption.

My skin is cold-sweat, my fingers trembling with disgust, my legs unable to withstand ~~the waste the waste the waste~~ the selfish waste in these 4 walls. I'm seeing red everywhere. The blood of bodies spattered against the windows, spilled across the carpets, dripping from the chandeliers.

"Juliette—"

I break.

I'm on my knees, my body cracking from the pain I've swallowed so many times, heaving with sobs I can no longer suppress, my dignity dissolving in my tears, the agony of this past week ripping my skin to shreds.

I can't ever breathe.

I can't catch the oxygen around me and I'm dry-heaving into my shirt and I hear voices and see faces I don't recognize, wisps of words wicked away by confusion, thoughts scrambled so many times I don't know if I'm even conscious anymore.

I don't know if I've officially lost my mind.

I'm in the air. I'm a bag of feathers in his arms and he's

breaking through soldiers crowding around for a glimpse of the commotion and for a moment I don't want to care that I shouldn't want this so much. I want to forget that I'm supposed to hate him, that he betrayed me, that he's working for the same people who are trying to destroy the very little that's left of humanity and my face is buried in the soft material of his shirt and my cheek is pressed against his chest and he smells like strength and courage and the world drowning in rain. I don't want him to ~~ever ever ever~~ ever let go of my body. I wish I could touch his skin, I wish there were no barriers between us.

Reality slaps me in the face.

Mortification muddles my brain, desperate humiliation clouds my judgment; red paints my face, bleeds through my skin. I clutch at his shirt.

"You can kill me," I tell him. "You have guns—" I'm wriggling out of his grip and he tightens his hold around my body. His face shows no emotion but a sudden strain in his jaw, an unmistakable tension in his arms. "You can just *kill me*—"

"Juliette," he says. *"Please."*

I'm numb again. Powerless all over again. Melting from within, life seeping out of my limbs.

We're standing in front of a door.

Adam takes a key card and swipes it against a black pane of glass fitted into the small space beside the handle, and the stainless steel door slides out of place. We step inside.

We're all alone in a new room.

"Please ~~don't let go of me~~ put me down," I tell him.

There's a queen-size bed in the middle of the space, lush carpet gracing the floors, an armoire flush against the wall, light fixtures glittering from the ceiling. The beauty is so tainted I can't stand the sight of it. Adam gentles me onto the soft mattress and takes a small step backward.

"You'll be staying here for a while, I think," is all he says.

I squeeze my eyes shut. I don't want to think about the inevitable torture awaiting me. "Please," I tell him. "I'd like to be left alone."

A deep sigh. "That's not exactly an option."

"What do you mean?" I spin around.

"I have to watch you, Juliette." He says my name like a whisper. "Warner wants you to understand what he's offering you, but you're still considered . . . a threat. He's made you my assignment. I can't leave."

"You have to live with me?"

"I live in the barracks on the opposite end of this building. With the other soldiers. But, yeah." He clears his throat. He's not looking at me. "I'll be moving in."

There's an ache in the pit of my stomach that's gnawing on my nerves. I want to hate him and judge him and scream forever but I'm failing because all I see is an 8-year-old boy who doesn't remember that he used to be the kindest person I ever knew.

I don't want to believe this is happening.

I close my eyes and curl my head into my knees.

"You have to get dressed," he says after a moment.

I pop my head up. I blink at him like I can't understand what he's saying. "I am dressed."

He clears his throat again but tries to be quiet about it. "There's a bathroom through here." He points. I see a door connected to the room and I'm suddenly curious. I've heard stories about people with bathrooms in their bedrooms. I guess they're not exactly *in* the bedroom, but they're close enough. I slip off the bed and follow his finger. As soon as I open the door he resumes speaking. "You can shower and change in here. The bathroom . . . it's the only place there are no cameras," he adds, his voice trailing off.

There are cameras in my room.

Of course.

"You can find clothes in there." He nods to the armoire. He suddenly looks uncomfortable.

"And you can't leave?" I ask.

He rubs his forehead and sits down on the bed. He sighs. "You have to get ready. Warner will be expecting you for dinner."

"*Dinner?*" My eyes are the size of the moon.

Adam looks grim. "Yeah."

"He's not going to hurt me?" I'm ashamed at the relief in my voice, at the unexpected tension I've released, at the fear I didn't know I was harboring. "He's going to give me *dinner?*" ~~I'm starving my stomach is a tortured pit of starvation I'm so hungry so hungry so hungry~~ I can't even imagine

65

what real food must taste like.

Adam's face is inscrutable again. "You should hurry. I can show you how everything works."

I don't have time to protest before he's in the bathroom and I've followed him inside. The door is still open and he's standing in the middle of the small space with his back to me and I can't understand why. "I already know how to use the bathroom," I tell him. ~~I used to live in a regular home. I used to have a family.~~

He turns around very, very slowly and I begin to panic. He finally lifts his head but his eyes are darting in every direction. When he looks at me his eyes narrow; his forehead is tight. His right hand curls into a fist and his left hand lifts one finger to his lips. He's telling me to be quiet.

I knew something was coming but I didn't know it'd be Adam. I didn't think he'd be the one to hurt me, to torture me. I don't even realize I'm crying until I hear the whimper and feel the silent tears stream down my face and I'm ~~ashamed so ashamed~~ so ashamed of my weakness but a part of me doesn't care. I'm tempted to beg, to ask for mercy, to steal his gun and shoot myself first.

He seems to register my sudden hysteria because his eyes snap open and his mouth falls to the floor. "No, God, Juliette—I'm not—" He swears under his breath. He pumps his fist against his forehead and turns away, sighing heavily, pacing the length of the small space. He swears again.

He walks out the door and doesn't look back.

TWELVE

5 full minutes under piping hot water, 2 bars of soap both smelling of lavender, a bottle of shampoo meant only for my hair, and the touch of soft, plush towels I dare to wrap around my body and I begin to understand.

They want me to forget.

They think they can wash away my memories, my loyalties, my priorities with a few hot meals and a room with a view. They think I am so easily purchased.

Warner doesn't seem to understand that I grew up with nothing and I didn't hate it. I didn't want the clothes or the perfect shoes or the expensive anything. I didn't want to be draped in silk. All I ever wanted was to reach out and touch another human being not just with my hands but with my heart. I saw the world and its lack of compassion, its harsh, grating judgment, and its cold, resentful eyes. I saw it all around me.

I had so much time to listen.

To look.

To study people and places and possibilities. All I had to do was open my eyes. All I had to do was open a book—to see the stories bleeding from page to page. To see the memories etched onto paper.

I spent my life folded between the pages of books.

In the absence of human relationships I formed bonds with paper characters. I lived love and loss through stories threaded in history; I experienced adolescence by association. My world is one interwoven web of words, stringing limb to limb, bone to sinew, thoughts and images all together. I am a being comprised of letters, a character created by sentences, a figment of imagination formed through fiction.

They want to delete every point of punctuation in my life from this earth and I don't think I can let that happen.

I slip back into my old clothes and tiptoe into the bedroom only to find it abandoned. Adam is gone even though he said he would stay. I don't understand him I don't understand his actions I don't understand my disappointment. I wish I didn't love the freshness of my skin, the feel of being perfectly clean after so long; I don't understand why I still haven't looked in the mirror, why I'm afraid of what I'll see, why I'm not sure if I'll recognize the face that might stare back at me.

I open the armoire.

It's bursting with dresses and shoes and shirts and pants and clothing of every kind, colors so vivid they hurt my eyes, material I've only ever heard of, the kind I'm almost afraid to touch. The sizes are perfect too perfect.

They've been waiting for me.

I've been neglected abandoned ostracized and dragged from my home. I've been poked prodded tested and thrown in a cell. I've been studied. I've been starved. I've been tempted with friendship only to be left betrayed and trapped into this nightmare I'm expected to be grateful for. My parents. My teachers. Adam. Warner. The Reestablishment. I am expendable to all of them.

They think I'm a doll they can dress up and twist into prostration.

But they're wrong.

"Warner is waiting for you."

I spin around and fall back against the armoire, slamming it closed in the craze of panic clutching my heart. I steady myself and fold away my fear when I see Adam standing at the door. His mouth moves for a moment but he says nothing. Eventually he steps forward so forward until he's close enough to touch.

He reaches past me to reopen the door hiding the things I'm embarrassed to know exist. "These are all for you," he says without looking at me, his fingers touching the hem of a purple dress, a rich plum color good enough to eat.

"I already have clothes." My hands smooth out the wrinkles in my dirty, ragged outfit.

He finally decides to look at me, but when he does his eyebrows trip, his eyes blink and freeze, his lips part in surprise. I wonder if I've washed off a new face for myself and I flush, hoping he's not disgusted by what he might see. I don't know why I care.

He drops his gaze. Takes a deep breath. "I'll be waiting outside."

~~I stare at the purple dress with Adam's fingerprints~~

I study the inside of the armoire for only a moment before I abandon it. I comb anxious fingers through my wet hair and steel myself.

I am no one's property.

And I don't care what Warner wants me to look like.

I step outside and Adam stares at me for a second. He rubs the back of his neck and says nothing. He shakes his head. He starts walking. He doesn't touch me and I shouldn't notice but I do. I have no idea what to expect I have no idea what my life will be like in this new place and I'm being nailed in the stomach by every exquisite embellishment, every lavish accessory, every superfluous painting, molding, lighting, coloring of this building. I hope the whole thing catches fire.

I follow Adam down a long carpeted corridor to an elevator made entirely of glass. He swipes the same key card he used to open my door and we step inside. I didn't even realize we'd taken an elevator to get up this many floors. I realize I must've made a horrible scene when I arrived and I'm almost happy.

I hope I disappoint Warner in every possible way.

The dining room is big enough to feed thousands of orphans. Instead, there are 7 banquet tables stretched across the room, blue silk spilling across the tabletops, crystal vases bursting with orchids and stargazer lilies, glass bowls filled with gardenias. ~~It's enchanting~~. I wonder where they got the flowers from. They must not be real. I don't know how they could be real. I haven't seen real flowers in years.

Warner is positioned at the table directly in the middle, seated at the head. As soon as he sees ~~me~~ Adam he stands up. The entire room stands in turn.

I realize almost immediately that there are empty seats on either side of him and I don't intend to stop moving but I do. I take quick inventory of the attendees and can't count any other women.

Adam brushes the small of my back with 3 fingertips and I'm startled out of my skin. I hurry forward and Warner beams at me. He pulls out the chair on his left and gestures for me to sit down. I do.

I try not to look at Adam as he sits across from me.

"You know . . . there are clothes in your armoire." Warner sits down beside me; the room reseats itself and resumes a steady stream of chatter. He's turned almost entirely in my direction but somehow the only presence I'm aware of is directly across from me. I focus on the empty plate 2 inches from my fingers. I drop my hands in my lap. "And you don't have to wear those dirty tennis shoes anymore," Warner continues, stealing another glance before pouring something into my cup. It looks like water.

~~I'm so thirsty I could inhale a waterfall.~~

I hate his smile.

Hate looks just like everybody else until it smiles. Until it spins around and lies with lips and teeth carved into the semblance of something too passive to punch.

"Juliette?"

71

I inhale too quickly. A stifled cough is ballooning in my throat.

His glassy green eyes glint in my direction.

"Are you not hungry?" Words dipped in sugar. His gloved hand touches my wrist and I nearly sprain it in my haste to distance myself from him.

~~I could eat every person in this room.~~ "No, thank you."

He licks his bottom lip into a smile. "Don't confuse stupidity for bravery, love. I know you haven't eaten anything in days."

Something in my patience snaps. "I'd really rather die than eat your food and listen to you call me *love*," I tell him.

Adam drops his fork.

Warner spares him a swift glance and when he looks my way again his eyes have hardened. He holds my gaze for a few infinitely long seconds before he pulls a gun out of his jacket pocket. He fires.

The entire room screams to a stop.

I turn my head very, very slowly to follow the direction of Warner's gun only to see he's shot some kind of meat right through the bone. The platter of food is slightly steaming across the room, the meal heaped less than a foot away from the guests. He shot it without even looking. He could've killed someone.

It takes all of my energy to remain very, very still.

Warner drops the gun on my plate. The silence gives it space to clatter around the universe and back. "Choose your words very wisely, Juliette. One word from me and your life here won't be so easy."

I blink.

Adam pushes a plate of food in front of me; the strength of his gaze is like a white-hot poker pressed against my skin. I look up and he cocks his head the tiniest millimeter. His eyes are saying *Please*.

I pick up my fork.

Warner doesn't miss a thing. He clears his throat a little too loudly. He laughs with no humor as he cuts into the meat on his plate. "Do I have to get Kent to do all my work for me?"

"Excuse me?"

"It seems he's the only one you'll listen to." His tone is breezy but his jaw is unmistakably set. He turns to Adam. "I'm surprised you didn't tell her to change her clothes like I asked you to."

Adam sits up straighter. "I did, sir."

"I like my clothes," I tell him. I'd like to punch you in the eye, is what I don't tell him.

Warner's smile slides back into place. "No one asked what *you* like, love. Now eat. I need you to look your best when you stand beside me."

THIRTEEN

Warner insists on accompanying me to my room.

After dinner Adam disappeared with a few of the other soldiers. He disappeared without a word or glance in my direction and I don't have any idea what to anticipate. At least I have nothing to lose but my life.

"I don't want you to hate me," Warner says as we make our way toward the elevator. "I'm only your enemy if you want me to be."

"We will always be enemies," I say. "I will never be what you want me to be."

Warner sighs as he presses the button for the elevator. "I really think you'll change your mind." He glances at me with a small smile. A shame, really, that such striking looks should be wasted on such a miserable human being. "You and I, Juliette—together? We could be unstoppable."

I will not look at him though I feel his gaze touching every inch of my body. "No, thank you."

We're in the elevator. The world is whooshing past us and the walls of glass make us a spectacle to every person on every floor. There are no secrets in this building.

He touches my elbow and I pull away. "You might reconsider," he says softly.

"How did you figure it out?" The elevator dings open

but I'm not moving. I finally turn to face him because I can't contain my curiosity. I study his hands, so carefully sheathed in leather, his sleeves thick and crisp and long. Even his collar is high and regal. He's dressed impeccably from head to toe and covered everywhere except his face. Even if I wanted to touch him I'm not sure I'd be able to. He's protecting himself.

From me.

"Perhaps a conversation for tomorrow night?" He cocks a brow and offers me his arm. I pretend not to notice it as we walk off the elevator and down the hall. "Maybe you could wear something nice."

"What's your first name?" I ask him.

We're standing in front of my door.

He stops. Surprised. Lifts his chin almost imperceptibly. Focuses his eyes on my face until I begin to regret my question. "You want to know my name."

I don't do it on purpose, but my eyes narrow just a bit. "Warner is your last name, isn't it?"

He almost smiles. "You want to know my name."

"I didn't realize it was a secret."

He steps forward. His lips twitch. His eyes fall, his lips draw in a tight breath. He drops a gloved finger down the apple of my cheek. "I'll tell you mine if you tell me yours," he whispers, too close to my neck.

I inch backward. Swallow hard. "You already know my name."

He's not looking at my eyes. "You're right. I should rephrase that. What I meant to say was I'll tell you mine if

75

you show me yours."

"What?" I'm breathing too fast too suddenly.

He begins to pull off his gloves and I begin to panic. "Show me what you can do."

My jaw is too tight and my teeth have begun to ache. "I won't touch you."

"That's all right." He tugs off the other glove. "I don't actually need your help."

"No—"

"Don't worry." He grins. "I'm sure it won't hurt *you* at all."

"No," I gasp. "No, I won't—I can't—"

"Fine," Warner snaps. "That's fine. You don't want to hurt me. I'm so utterly flattered." He almost rolls his eyes. Looks down the hall. Spots a soldier. Beckons him over. "Jenkins?"

Jenkins is swift for his size and he's at my side in a second.

"Sir." He bows his head an inch even though he's clearly Warner's senior. He can't be more than 27; stocky, sturdy, packed with bulk. He spares me a sidelong glance. His brown eyes are warmer than I'd expect them to be.

"I'm going to need you to accompany Ms. Ferrars back downstairs. But be warned: she's incredibly uncooperative and will try to break free from your grip." He smiles too slowly. "No matter what she says or does, soldier, you cannot let go of her. Are we clear?"

Jenkins' eyes widen; his nostrils flare, his fingers flex at his sides. He nods.

Jenkins is not an idiot.

I start running.

I'm bolting down the hallway and running past a series of stunned soldiers too scared to stop me. I don't know what I'm doing, why I think I can run, where I think I could possibly go. I'm straining to reach the elevator if only because I think it will buy me time. I don't know what else to do.

Warner's commands are bouncing off the walls and exploding in my eardrums. He doesn't need to chase me. He's getting others to do the work for him.

Soldiers are lining up before me.

Beside me.

Behind me.

I can't breathe.

I'm spinning in a circle of my own stupidity, panicked, petrified by the thought of what I'm going to do to Jenkins against my will. What he will do to me against his will. What will happen to both of us despite our best intentions.

"Seize her," Warner says softly. His voice is the only sound in the room.

Jenkins steps forward.

My eyes are flooding and I squeeze them shut. I pry them open. I blink back at the crowd and spot a familiar face. Adam is staring at me, horrified.

Jenkins offers me his hand.

My bones begin to buckle, snapping in synchronicity with the beats of my heart. I crumble to the floor, folding into myself like a flimsy crepe. My arms are so painfully bare in this ragged T-shirt.

"Don't—" I hold up a tentative hand, pleading with my eyes, staring into the face of this innocent man. "Please don't—" My voice breaks. "You don't want to touch me—"

"I never said I did." Jenkins's voice is deep and steady, full of regret. Jenkins who has no gloves, no protection, no preparation, no possible defense.

"That was a direct order, soldier," Warner barks, trains a gun at his back.

Jenkins grabs my arms.

NO NO NO

I gasp.

My blood is surging through my veins, rushing through my body like a raging river, waves of heat lapping against my bones. I can hear his anguish, I can feel the power pouring out of his body, I can hear his heart beating in my ear and my head is spinning with the rush of adrenaline fortifying my being.

I feel alive.

I wish it hurt me. I wish it maimed me. I wish it repulsed me. I wish I hated the potent force wrapping itself around my skeleton.

But I don't. My skin is pulsing with someone else's life and I don't hate it.

I hate myself for enjoying it.

I enjoy the way it feels to be brimming with more life and hope and human power than I knew I was capable of. His pain gives me a pleasure I never asked for.

And he's not letting go.

But he's not letting go because he can't. Because I have to be the one to break the connection. Because the agony incapacitates him. Because he's caught in my snares.

Because I am a Venus flytrap.

And I am lethal.

I fall on my back and kick at his chest, willing him away from me, willing his weight off of my small frame, his limp body collapsed against my own. I'm suddenly screaming and struggling to see past the sheet of tears obscuring my vision; I'm hiccupping, hysterical, horrified by the frozen look on this man's face, his paralyzed lips wheezing.

I break free and stumble backward. The sea of soldiers parts behind me. Every face is etched in astonishment and pure, unadulterated fear. Jenkins is lying on the floor and no one dares approach him.

"Somebody help him!" I scream. "Somebody *help* him! He needs a doctor—he needs to be taken—he needs—he—oh God—what have I done—"

"Juliette—"

"DON'T TOUCH ME—DON'T YOU DARE TOUCH ME—"

Warner's gloves are back in place and he's trying to hold me together, he's trying to smooth back my hair, he's trying to wipe away my tears and I want to murder him.

"Juliette, you need to calm down—"

"HELP HIM!" I cry, falling to my knees, my eyes glued to the figure lying on the floor. The other soldiers are finally creeping closer, cautious as though he might be contagious.

"Please—you have to help him! *Please*—"

"Kent, Curtis, Soledad—*take care of this*." Warner shouts to his men before scooping me up into his arms.

I'm still kicking when the world goes black.

FOURTEEN

The ceiling is fading in and out of focus.

My head is heavy, my vision is blurry, my heart is strained. There is a distinct flavor of panic lodged somewhere underneath my tongue and I'm fighting to remember where it came from. I try to sit up and can't understand why I was lying down.

Someone's hands are on my shoulders.

"How are you feeling?" Warner is peering down at me.

Suddenly Jenkins' face is swimming in my consciousness and I'm swinging my fists and screaming for Warner to get away from me and struggling to wriggle out of his grip but he just smiles. Laughs a little. Gentles my hands down beside my torso.

"Well, at least you're awake," he sighs. "You had me worried for a moment."

I try to control my trembling limbs. "Get your hands away from me."

He waves sheathed fingers in front of my face. "I'm all covered up. Don't worry."

"I *hate* you."

"So much passion." He laughs again. He looks so calm, so genuinely amused. He stares at me with eyes softer than

I expected them to be.

I turn away.

He stands up. Takes a short breath. "Here," he says, reaching for a tray on a small table. "I brought you food."

I take advantage of the moment to sit up and look around. I'm lying on a bed draped in damask golds and burgundies the darkest shade of blood. The floor is covered in thick, rich carpet. It's warm in this room. It's the same size as the one I occupy, its furniture standard enough: bed, armoire, side tables, chandelier glittering from the ceiling. The only difference is there's an extra door in this room and there's a candle burning quietly on a small table in the corner. I haven't seen fire in so many years I've lost count. I have to stifle an impulse to reach out and touch the flame.

I prop myself up against the pillows and try to pretend I'm not comfortable. "Where am I?"

Warner turns around holding a plate with bread and cheese on it. His other hand is gripping a glass of water. He looks around the room as if seeing it for the first time. "This is my bedroom."

If my head weren't splitting into pieces I'd be tempted to run. "Take me to my own room. I don't want to be here."

"And yet, here you are." He sits at the foot of the bed, a few feet away. Pushes the plate in front of me. "Are you thirsty?"

I don't know if it's because I can't think straight or if it's because I'm genuinely confused, but I'm struggling to reconcile Warner's polarizing personalities. Here he is, offering me a glass of water after he forced me to torture someone. I lift my hands and study my fingers as if I've never seen them before. "I don't understand."

He cocks his head, inspecting me as though I might've seriously injured myself. "I only asked if you were thirsty. That shouldn't be difficult to understand." A pause. "Drink this."

I take the glass. Stare at it. Stare at him. Stare at the walls.

I must be insane.

Warner sighs. "I'm not sure, but I think you fainted. And I think you should probably eat something, though I'm not entirely sure about that, either." He pauses. "You've probably had too much exertion your first day here. My mistake."

"Why are you being nice to me?"

The surprise on his face surprises me even more. "Because I care about you," he says simply.

"You *care* about me?" The numbness in my body is beginning to dissipate. My blood pressure is rising and anger is making its way to the forefront of my mind. "I almost killed Jenkins because of you!"

"You didn't kill—"

"Your soldiers beat me! You keep me here like a prisoner! You threaten me! You threaten to kill me! You give me no freedom and you say you *care* about me?" I nearly throw the glass of water at his face. "You are a *monster!*"

Warner turns away so I'm staring at his profile. He clasps his hands. Changes his mind. Touches his lips. "I am

83

only trying to help you."

"Liar."

He seems to consider that. Nods, just once. "Yes. Most of the time, yes."

"I don't want to be here. I don't want to be your experiment. Let me go."

"No." He stands up. "I'm afraid I can't do that."

"Why not?"

"Because I can't. I just—" He tugs at his fingers. Clears his throat. His eyes search the ceiling for a brief moment. "Because I need you."

"You need me to kill people!"

He doesn't answer right away. He walks to the candle. Pulls off a glove. Tickles the flame with his bare fingers. "You know, I am very capable of killing people on my own, Juliette. I'm actually very good at it."

"That's disgusting."

He shrugs. "How else do you think someone my age is able to control so many soldiers? Why else would my father allow me to take charge of an entire sector?"

"Your *father*?" I sit up, suddenly curious in spite of myself.

He ignores my question. "The mechanics of fear are simple enough. People are intimidated by me, so they listen when I speak." He waves a hand. "Empty threats are worth very little these days."

I squeeze my eyes shut. "So you kill people for power."

"As do you."

"How *dare* you—"

He laughs, loud. "You're free to lie to yourself, if it makes you feel better."

"I am not lying—"

"Why did it take you so long to break your connection with Jenkins?"

My mouth freezes in place.

"Why didn't you fight back right away? Why did you allow him to touch you for as long as he did?"

My hands have begun to shake and I grip them, hard. "You don't know anything about me."

"And yet you claim to know me so well."

I clench my jaw, not trusting myself to speak.

"At least I'm honest," he adds.

"You just agreed you're a liar!"

He raises his eyebrows. "At least I'm honest about being a liar."

I slam the glass of water on the side table. Drop my head in my hands. Take a steadying breath. "Well," I rasp, "why do you need me, then? If you're such an excellent murderer?"

A smile flickers and fades across his face. "One day I'll introduce you to the answer to that question."

I try to protest but he stops me with one hand. Picks up a piece of bread from the plate. Holds it under my nose. "You hardly ate anything at dinner. That can't possibly be healthy."

I don't move.

He drops the bread on the plate and drops the plate beside the water. Turns to me. Studies my eyes with such intensity I'm momentarily disarmed. There are so many things I want to say and scream but somehow I've forgotten all about the words waiting patiently in my mouth. I can't make myself look away.

"Eat something." His eyes abandon me. "Then go to sleep. I'll be back for you in the morning."

"Why can't I sleep in my own room?"

He gets to his feet. Dusts off his pants for no real reason. "Because I want you to stay here."

"But why?"

He barks out a laugh. "So many questions."

"Well if you'd give me a straight answer—"

"Good night, Juliette."

"Are you going to let me go?" I ask, this time quietly, this time timidly.

"No." He takes 6 steps into the corner with the candle. "And I won't promise to make things easier for you, either." There is no regret, no remorse, no sympathy in his voice. He could be talking about the weather.

"You could be lying."

"Yes, I could be." He nods, as if to himself. Blows out the candle.

And disappears.

I try to fight it
I try to stay awake
I try to find my head but I can't.

I collapse from sheer exhaustion.

FIFTEEN

Why don't you just kill yourself? someone at school asked me once.

I think it was the kind of question intended to be cruel, but it was the first time I'd ever contemplated the possibility. I didn't know what to say. Maybe I was crazy to consider it, but I'd always hoped that if I were a good enough girl, if I did everything right, if I said the right things or said nothing at all—I thought my parents would change their minds. I thought they would finally listen when I tried to talk. I thought they would give me a chance. I thought they might finally love me.

I always had that ~~stupid~~ hope.

"Good morning."

My eyes snap open with a start. I've never been a heavy sleeper.

Warner is staring at me, sitting at the foot of his own bed in a fresh suit and perfectly polished boots. Everything about him is meticulous. Pristine. His breath is cool and fresh in the crisp morning air. I can feel it on my face.

It takes me a moment to realize I'm tangled in the same sheets Warner himself has slept in. My face is suddenly on fire and I'm fumbling to free myself. I nearly fall off the bed.

I don't acknowledge him.

"Did you sleep well?" he asks.

I look up. His eyes are such a strange shade of green: bright, crystal clear, piercing in the most alarming way. His hair is thick, the richest slice of gold; his frame is lean and unassuming, but his grip is effortlessly strong. I notice for the first time that he wears a jade ring on his left pinkie finger.

He catches me staring and stands up. Slips his gloves on and clasps his hands behind his back.

"It's time for you to go back to your room."

I blink. Nod. Stand up and nearly fall down. I catch myself on the side of the bed and try to steady my dizzying head. I hear Warner sigh.

"You didn't eat the food I left for you last night."

I grab the water with trembling hands and force myself to eat some of the bread. My body has gotten so used to hunger I don't know how to recognize it anymore.

Warner leads me out the door once I find my footing. I'm still clutching a piece of cheese in my hand.

I nearly drop it when I step outside.

There are even more soldiers here than there are on my floor. Each is equipped with at least 4 different kinds of guns, some slung around their necks, some strapped to their belts. All of them betray a look of terror when they see my face. It flashes in and out of their features so quickly I might've missed it, but it's obvious enough: everyone grips their weapons a little tighter as I walk by.

Warner seems pleased.

"Their fear will work in your favor," he whispers in my ear.

"I never wanted them to be afraid of me."

"You should." He stops. His eyes are calling me an idiot. "If they don't fear you, they will hunt you."

"People hunt things they fear all the time."

"At least now they know what they're up against." He resumes walking down the hall, but my feet are stitched into the ground. Realization is ice-cold water and it's dripping down my back.

"You made me do that—what I did—to Jenkins? On *purpose?*"

Warner is already 3 steps ahead but I can see the smile on his face. "Everything I do is done on purpose."

"You wanted to make a spectacle out of me."

"I was trying to protect you."

"From your own soldiers?" I'm running to catch up to him now, burning with indignation. "At the expense of a man's *life*—"

"Get inside." Warner has reached the elevator. He's holding the doors open for me.

I follow him.

He presses the right buttons.

The doors close.

I turn to speak.

He corners me.

I'm backed into the far edge of this glass receptacle and I'm suddenly nervous. His hands are holding my arms and his lips are dangerously close to my face. His gaze is locked into mine, his eyes flashing; dangerous. He says one word: "Yes."

It takes me a moment to find my voice. "Yes, what?"

"Yes, from my own soldiers. Yes, at the expense of one man's life." He tenses his jaw. Speaks through his teeth. "There is very little you understand about my world, Juliette."

"I'm trying to understand—"

"No you're not," he snaps. His eyelashes are like individual threads of spun gold lit on fire. I almost want to touch them. "You don't understand that power and control can slip from your grasp at any moment and even when you think you're most prepared. These two things are not easy to earn. They are even harder to retain." I try to speak and he cuts me off. "You think I don't know how many of my own soldiers hate me? You think I don't know that they'd like to see me fall? You think there aren't others who would love to have the position I work so hard to have—"

"Don't *flatter* yourself—"

He closes the last few inches between us and my words fall to the floor. I can't breathe. The tension in his entire body is so intense it's nearly palpable and I think my muscles have begun to freeze. "You are naive," he says to me, his voice harsh, low, a grating whisper against my skin. "You don't realize that you're a threat to everyone in this building. They have every reason to harm you. You don't see that I am trying to help you—"

"By hurting me!" I explode. "By hurting others!"

His laugh is cold, mirthless. He backs away from me, disgusted. The elevator slides open but he doesn't step outside. I can see my door from here. "Go back to your room. Wash up. Change. There are dresses in your armoire."

"I don't like dresses."

"I don't think you like seeing *that,* either," he says with a tilt of his head. I follow his gaze to see a hulking shadow across from my door. I turn to him for an explanation but he says nothing. He's suddenly composed, his features wiped clean of emotion. He takes my hand, squeezes my fingers, says, "I'll be back for you in exactly one hour," and closes the elevator doors before I have a chance to protest. I begin to wonder if it's coincidence that the one person most unafraid to touch me is a monster himself.

I step forward and dare to peer closer at the soldier standing in the dark.

Adam.

Oh Adam.

Adam who now knows exactly what I'm capable of.

My heart is exploding in my chest. I feel as though every fist in the world has decided to punch me in the stomach. I shouldn't care so much, but I do.

He'll hate me forever now. He won't even look at me.

I wait for him to open my door but he doesn't move.

"Adam?" I venture, tentative. "I need your key card."

I watch him swallow hard and take a tiny breath and immediately I sense something is wrong. I move closer and a quick, stiff shake of his head tells me not to. ~~I do not touch people I do not get close to people I am a monster.~~ He doesn't want me near him. Of course he doesn't.

He opens my door with immense difficulty and I realize someone's hurt him where I can't see it. Warner's words come back to me and I recognize his airy good-bye as a warning. A warning that severs every nerve in my body.

Adam will be punished for my mistakes. For my disobedience.

I step through the door and glance back at Adam one last time, unable to feel any kind of triumph in his pain. Despite everything he's done I don't know if I'm capable of hating him. Not Adam. Not the boy I used to know.

"The purple dress," he says, his voice broken and a little breathy like it hurts to inhale. I have to wring my hands to keep from running to him. "Wear the purple dress." He coughs. "Juliette."

I will be the perfect mannequin.

SIXTEEN

As soon as I'm in the room I open the armoire and yank the purple dress off the hanger before I remember I'm being watched. *The cameras.* I wonder if Adam was punished for telling me about the cameras, too. I wonder if he's taken any other risks with me. I wonder why he would.

I touch the stiff, modern material of the plum dress and my fingers find their way to the hem, just as Adam's did yesterday. I can't help but wonder why he likes this dress so much. Why it has to be this one. Why I even have to wear a dress.

I am not a doll.

My hand comes to rest on the small wooden shelf beneath the hanging clothes and an unfamiliar texture brushes my skin. It's rough and foreign but familiar at the same time. I step closer to the armoire and hide between the doors. My fingers feel their way around the surface.

My notebook.

He saved my notebook. ~~Adam saved the only thing I own.~~

I grab the purple dress and tuck the notebook into its folds before stealing away to the bathroom.

~~The bathroom where there are no cameras.~~

~~The bathroom where there are no cameras.~~

The bathroom where there are no cameras.

He was trying to tell me, I realize. Before, in the bathroom. He was trying to tell me something and I was so scared I scared him away.

I scared him away.

I close the door behind me and my hands are shaking as I unfurl the familiar papers bound together by old glue. I flip through the pages to make sure they're all there and my eyes land on my most recent entry. At the very bottom there is a shift. A new sentence not written in my handwriting.

A new sentence that must've come from him.

It's not what you think.

I stand perfectly still.

Every inch of my skin is taut, fraught with feeling and the pressure is building in my chest, pounding louder and faster and harder, overcompensating for my stillness. I do not tremble when I'm frozen in time. I train my breaths to come slower, I count things that do not exist, I make up numbers I do not have, I pretend time is a broken hourglass bleeding seconds through sand. I dare to believe.

I dare to hope Adam is trying to reach out to me. I'm crazy enough to consider the possibility.

I rip the page out of the small notebook and clutch it close.

I hide the notebook in a pocket of the purple dress. The pocket Adam must've slipped it into. The pocket it must've

95

fallen out of. ~~The pocket of the purple dress. The pocket of the purple dress.~~

Hope is a pocket of possibility.

I'm holding it in my hand.

Warner is not late.

He doesn't knock, either.

I'm slipping on my shoes when he walks in without a single word, without even an effort to make his presence known. His eyes are falling all over me. My jaw tightens on its own.

"You hurt him," I find myself saying.

"You shouldn't care," he says with a tilt of his head, gesturing to my dress. "But it's obvious you do."

I zip my lips and pray my hands aren't shaking too much. I don't know where Adam is. I don't know how badly he's hurt. I don't know what Warner will do, how far he'll go in the pursuit of what he wants but the prospect of Adam in pain is like a cold hand clutching my esophagus. If Adam is trying to help me it could cost him his life.

I touch the piece of paper tucked into my pocket.

Breathe.

Warner's eyes are on my window.

Breathe.

"It's time to go," he says.

Breathe.

"Where are we going?"

He doesn't answer.

We step out the door. I look around. The hallway is abandoned; empty. "Where is ~~Adam~~ everyone . . . ?"

"I really like that dress," Warner says as he slips an arm around my waist. I jerk away but he pulls me along, guiding me toward the elevator. "The fit is spectacular. It helps distract me from all your questions."

"Your poor mother."

Warner almost trips over his own feet. His eyes are wide; alarmed. He stops a few feet short of our goal. Spins around. "What do you mean?"

The look on his face: the unguarded strain, the flinching terror, the sudden apprehension in his features.

I was trying to make a joke, is what I don't say to him. I feel sorry for your poor mother, is what I was going to say to him, that she has to deal with such a miserable, pathetic son. But I don't say any of it.

He grabs my hands, focuses my eyes. "What do you mean?" he insists.

"N-nothing," I stammer. "I didn't—it was just a joke—"

Warner drops my hands like they've burned him. He looks away. Charges toward the elevator and doesn't wait for me to catch up.

I wonder what he's not telling me.

Only once we've gone down several floors and are making our way down an unfamiliar hall toward an unfamiliar exit does he finally look at me. He offers me 4 words.

"Welcome to your future."

SEVENTEEN

I'm swimming in sunlight.

Warner is holding open a door that leads directly outside and I'm so unprepared for the experience I can hardly see straight. He grips my elbow to steady my path and I glance back at him.

"We're going outside." I say it because I have to say it out loud. Because the outside world is a treat I'm so seldom offered. Because I don't know if Warner is trying to be nice again. I look from him to what looks like a concrete courtyard and back to him again. "What are we doing outside?"

"We have some business to take care of." He tugs me toward the center of this new universe and I'm breaking away from him, reaching out to touch the sky like I'm hoping it will remember me. The clouds are gray like they've always been, but they're sparse and unassuming. The sun is high high high, lounging against a backdrop propping up its rays and redirecting its warmth in our general direction. I stand on tiptoe and try to touch it. The wind folds itself into my arms and smiles against my skin. Cool, silky-smooth air braids a soft breeze through my hair. This square courtyard could be my ballroom.

I want to dance with the elements.

Warner grabs my hand. I turn around.

He's smiling.

"This," he says, gesturing to the cold gray world under our feet, "this makes you happy?"

I look around. I realize the courtyard is not quite a roof, but somewhere between two buildings. I edge toward the ledge and can see dead land and naked trees and scattered compounds stretching on for miles. "Cold air smells so clean," I tell him. "Fresh. Brand-new. It's the most wonderful smell in the world."

His eyes look amused, troubled, interested, and confused all at once. He shakes his head. Pats down his jacket and reaches for an inside pocket. He pulls out a gun with a gold hilt that glints in the sunlight.

I pull in a sharp breath.

He inspects the gun in a way I wouldn't understand, presumably to check whether or not it's ready to fire. He slips it into his hand, his finger poised directly over the trigger. He turns and finally reads the expression on my face.

He almost laughs. "Don't worry. It's not for you."

"Why do you have a gun?" I swallow, hard, my arms tight across my chest. "What are we doing up here?"

Warner slips the gun back into his pocket and walks to the opposite end of the ledge. He motions for me to follow him. I creep closer. Follow his eyes. Peer over the barrier.

Every soldier in the building is standing not 15 feet below.

I distinguish almost 50 lines, each perfectly straight,

perfectly spaced, so many soldiers standing single file I lose count. ~~I wonder if Adam is in the crowd. I wonder if he can see me.~~

~~I wonder what he thinks of me now.~~

The soldiers are standing in a square space almost identical to the one Warner and I occupy, but they're one organized mass of black: black pants, black shirts, shin-high black boots; not a single gun in sight. Each is standing with his left fist pressed to his heart. Frozen in place.

Black and gray

and

black and gray

and

black and gray

and

bleak.

Suddenly I'm acutely aware of my impractical outfit. Suddenly the wind is too callous, too cold as it slices its way through the crowd. I shiver and it has nothing to do with the temperature. I look for Warner but he has already taken his place at the edge of the courtyard; it's obvious he's done this many times before. He pulls a small square of perforated metal out of his pocket and presses it to his lips; when he speaks, his voice carries over the crowd like it's been amplified.

"Sector 45."

One word. One number.

The entire group shifts: left fists released, dropped to

their sides; right fists planted in place on their chests. They are an oiled machine, working in perfect collaboration with one another. If I weren't so apprehensive I think I'd be impressed.

"We have two matters to deal with this morning." Warner's voice penetrates the atmosphere: crisp, clear, unbearably confident. "The first is standing by my side."

Thousands of eyes snap up in my direction. I feel myself flinch.

"Juliette, come here, please." 2 fingers bend in 2 places to beckon me forward.

I inch into view.

Warner slips his arm around me. I cringe. The crowd starts. My heart careens out of control. I'm afraid to back away from him. His gun is too close to my body.

The soldiers seem stunned that Warner is willing to touch me.

"Jenkins, would you step forward, please?"

My fingers are running a marathon down my thigh. I can't stand still. I can't calm the palpitations crashing my nervous system. Jenkins steps out of line; I spot him immediately.

He's okay.

Dear God.

He's okay.

"Jenkins had the pleasure of meeting Juliette just last night," he continues. The tension among the men is very nearly tangible. No one, it seems, knows where this speech is headed. And no one, it seems, hasn't already heard Jenkins' story. My story. "I hope you'll all greet her with the same sort of kindness," Warner adds. "She will be with us for some time, and will be a very valuable asset to our efforts. The Reestablishment welcomes her. I welcome her. You should welcome her."

The soldiers drop their fists all at once, all at exactly the same time.

They shift as one, 5 steps backward, 5 steps forward, 5 steps standing in place. They raise their left arms high and curl their fingers into a fist.

And fall on one knee.

I run to the edge, desperate to get a closer look at such a strangely choreographed routine. I've never seen anything like it.

Warner makes them stay like that, bent like that, fists raised in the air like that. He doesn't speak for at least 30 seconds. And then he does.

"Good."

The soldiers rise and rest their right fists on their chests again.

"The second matter at hand is even more pleasant than the first," Warner continues, though he seems to take no pleasure in saying it. "Delalieu has a report for us."

He spends an eternity simply staring at the soldiers, letting his few words marinate in their minds. Letting their own imaginations drive them insane. Letting the guilty among them tremble in anguish.

Warner says nothing for so long.

No one moves for so long.

I begin to fear for my life despite his earlier reassurances. I begin to wonder if perhaps I am the guilty one. If perhaps the gun in his pocket is meant for me. I finally dare to turn in his direction. He glances at me for the first time and I have no idea how to read him.

"Delalieu," he says, still looking at me. "You may step forward."

A thin, balding sort of man in a slightly more decorated outfit steps out from the very front of the fifth line. He doesn't look entirely stable. He ducks his head an inch. His voice warbles when he speaks. "Sir."

Warner finally unshackles my eyes and nods, almost imperceptibly, in the balding man's direction.

Delalieu recites: "We have a charge against Private 45B-76423. Fletcher, Seamus."

The soldiers are all frozen in line, frozen in relief, in fear, in anxiety. Nothing moves. Nothing breathes. Even the wind is afraid to make a sound.

"Fletcher." One word from Warner and several hundred necks snap in the same direction.

Fletcher steps out of line.

Ginger hair. Ginger freckles. Lips almost artificially red. His face is blank of every possible emotion.

I've never been more afraid for a stranger in my life.

Delalieu speaks again. "Private Fletcher was found on unregulated grounds, fraternizing with civilians believed to be rebel party members. He had stolen food and supplies from storage units dedicated to Sector 45 citizens. It is not known whether he betrayed sensitive information."

Warner levels his gaze at the gingerbread man. "Do you deny these accusations, soldier?"

Fletcher's nostrils flare. His jaw tenses. His voice cracks when he speaks. "No, sir."

Warner nods. Takes a breath.

And shoots him in the forehead.

EIGHTEEN

No one moves.

Fletcher's face is etched in permanent horror as he crumbles to the ground. I'm so struck by the impossibility of it all that I can't decide whether or not I'm dreaming.

Fletcher's limbs are bent at odd angles on the cold, concrete floor. Blood is pooling around him and still no one moves. No one says a single word. No one betrays a single look of fear.

I keep touching my lips to see if my screams have escaped.

Warner tucks his gun back into his jacket pocket. "Sector 45, you are dismissed."

Every soldier falls on one knee.

Warner slips the metal amplification device back into his suit and has to yank me free from the spot where I'm glued to the ground. I feel nauseous, delirious, incapable of holding myself upright. I keep trying to speak but the words are sticking to my tongue. I'm suddenly sweating and suddenly freezing and suddenly so sick I see spots clouding my vision.

Warner is trying to get me through the door. "You really must eat more," he says to me.

I am gaping with my eyes, gaping with my mouth, gaping wide open because I feel holes everywhere, punched into the terrain of my body.

"You killed him," I manage to whisper. "You just killed him—"

"You're very astute."

"Why did you *kill him* why would you *kill him* how could you *do* something like that—"

"Keep your eyes open, Juliette. Now's not the time to fall asleep."

I grab his shirt. I stop him before he gets inside. A gust of wind slaps me across the face and I'm suddenly in control of my senses. I push him hard, slamming his back up against the door. "You disgust me." I stare hard into his crystal-cold eyes. "You *disgust* me—"

He twists me around, pinning me against the door where I just held him. He cups my face in his gloved hands, holding my eyes in place. The same hands he just used to kill a man.

I'm trapped.

Transfixed.

Slightly terrified.

His thumb brushes my cheek.

"Life is a bleak place," he whispers. "Sometimes you have to learn how to shoot first."

Warner follows me into my room.

"You should probably sleep," he says to me. It's the first time he's spoken since we left the rooftop. "I'll have food sent up to your room, but other than that I'll make sure you're not disturbed."

"Where is Adam? ~~Is he safe? Is he healthy? Are you going to hurt him?~~"

Warner flinches before finding his composure. "Why do you care?"

~~I've cared about Adam Kent since I was in third grade~~. "Isn't he supposed to be watching me? Because he's not here. Does that mean you're going to kill him, too?" I'm feeling stupid. I'm feeling brave because I'm feeling stupid. My words wear no parachutes as they fall out of my mouth.

"I only kill people if I need to."

"Generous."

"More than most."

I laugh a sad laugh, sharing it with only myself.

"You can have the rest of the day to yourself. Our real work will begin tomorrow. Adam will bring you to me." He holds my eyes. Suppresses a smile. "In the meantime, try not to kill anyone."

"You and I," I tell him, anger coursing through my veins, "you and I are not the same—"

"You don't really believe that."

"You think you can compare my—my *disease*—with your insanity—"

"*Disease?*" He steps forward, abruptly impassioned. "You think you have a *disease*? You have a gift! You have an extraordinary ability that you don't care to understand! Your *potential*—"

"I have no potential!"

"You're wrong." He's glaring at me. There's no other way to describe it. I could almost say he hates me in this moment. Hates me for hating myself.

"Well you're the murderer," I tell him. "So you must be right."

His smile is laced with dynamite. "Go to sleep."

"Go to hell."

He works his jaw. Walks to the door. "I'm working on it."

NINETEEN

The darkness is choking me.

My dreams are bloody and bleeding and blood is bleeding all over my mind and I can't sleep anymore. The only dreams that ever used to give me peace are gone and I don't know how to get them back. I don't know how to find the white bird. I don't know if it will ever fly by. All I know is that now when I close my eyes I see nothing but devastation. Fletcher is being shot over and over and over again and Jenkins is dying in my arms and Warner is shooting Adam in the head and the wind is singing outside my window but it's high-pitched and off-key and I don't have the heart to tell it to stop.

I'm freezing through my clothes.

The bed under my back is too soft, too comfortable. It reminds me too much of sleeping in Warner's room and I can't stand it. I'm afraid to slip under these covers.

I can't help but wonder if Adam is okay, if he'll ever come back, if Warner is going to keep hurting him whenever I disobey. I really shouldn't care so much.

Adam's message in my notebook might just be a part of Warner's plan to drive me insane.

I crawl onto the hard floor and check my fist for the

crumpled piece of paper I've been clutching for 2 days. It's the only hope I have left and I don't even know if it's real.

I'm running out of options.

"What are you doing here?"

I bite down on a scream and stumble up, over, and sideways, nearly slamming into Adam where he's lying on the floor next to me. I didn't even see him.

"Juliette?" He doesn't move an inch. His gaze is fixed on me: calm, unflappable; 2 buckets of river water at midnight.

"I couldn't sleep up there."

He doesn't ask me why. He pulls himself up and coughs back a grunt and I remember how he's been hurt. I wonder what kind of pain he's in. I don't ask questions as he grabs a pillow and the blanket off my bed. He puts the pillow on the floor. "Lie down," is all he says to me.

They're just 2 words and I don't know why I'm blushing. I lie down despite the sirens spinning in my blood and rest my head on the pillow. He drapes the blanket over my body. I let him do it. I watch as his arms curve and flex in the shadow of night, the glint of the moon peeking in through the window, illuminating his figure in its glow. He lies down on the floor leaving only a few feet of space between us. He requires no blanket. He uses no pillow. He still sleeps without a shirt on and I've realized I'll probably never exhale in his presence.

"You don't need to scream anymore," he whispers.

I curl my fingers around the possibility of Adam in my hand and sleep more soundly than I have in my life.

My eyes are 2 windows cracked open by the chaos in this world.

A cool breeze startles my skin and I sit up, rub the sleep from my eyes, and realize Adam is no longer beside me. I blink and crawl back up to the bed, where I replace the pillow and the blanket.

I glance at the door and wonder what's waiting for me on the other side.

I glance at the window and wonder if I'll ever see a bird fly by.

I glance at the clock on the wall and wonder what it means to be living according to numbers again. I wonder what 6:30 in the morning means in this building.

I decide to wash my face. The idea exhilarates me and I'm a little ashamed.

I open the bathroom door and catch Adam's reflection in the mirror. His fast hands pull his shirt down before I have a chance to latch on to details but I saw enough to see what I couldn't see in the darkness.

He's covered in bruises.

My legs feel broken. I don't know how to help him. I wish I could help him.

"I'm sorry," he says quickly. "I didn't know you were awake." He tugs on the bottom of his shirt like it's not long enough to pretend I'm blind.

I nod at nothing at all. I look at the tile under my feet. I don't know what to say.

"Juliette." His face is a forest of emotion. He shakes his head. "I'm sorry," he says, so quietly I'm certain I imagined it. "It's not . . ." He clenches his jaw and runs a nervous hand through his hair. "All of this—it's not—"

I open my palm to him. The paper is a crumpled wad of possibility. "I know."

Relief washes over his face and suddenly his eyes are the only reassurance I need. Adam did not betray me. I don't know why or how or what or anything at all except that he is still my friend.

He is still standing right in front of me and he doesn't want me to die.

I step forward and close the door.

I open my mouth to speak.

"No!" His lips move but make no sound. I realize in the absence of cameras there might still be microphones in the bathroom. Adam looks around and back and forth and everywhere.

He stops looking.

The shower is made of marbled glass and he's pulling the door open before I have any idea what's happening. He flips the spray on at full power and the sound of water is rushing through, rumbling through the room, muffling everything as it thunders into the emptiness around us. The mirror is already fogging up on account of the steam and just as I think I'm beginning to understand his plan he pulls me into his arms and lifts me into the shower.

My screams are vapor, wisps of gasps I can't grasp.

Hot water is puddling in my clothes. It's pelting my hair and pouring down my neck but all I feel are his hands around my waist. I want to cry out for all the wrong reasons.

His eyes pin me in place. Rivulets of water snake their way down his face and his hands hold me up against the wall.

His lips his lips his lips his lips his lips

My eyes are fighting not to flutter

My legs have won the right to tremble

My skin is scorched everywhere he's not touching me.

His lips are so close to my ear I'm water and nothing and everything and melting into a wanting so desperate it burns as I swallow it down.

"I can touch you," he says, and I wonder why there are hummingbirds in my heart. "I didn't understand until the other night," he murmurs, and I'm too drunk to digest the weight of anything but his body hovering so close to mine.

"Juliette—" His body presses closer and I realize I'm paying attention to nothing but the dandelions blowing wishes in my lungs. My eyes snap open and he licks his bottom lip for the smallest second and something in my brain bursts to life.

I gasp. I gasp. I gasp. "What are you *doing*—"

"Juliette, *please*—" His voice is anxious and he glances behind him like he's not sure we're alone. "The other night—" He presses his lips together. He closes his eyes and I marvel at the drop drop drops of hot water caught in his eyelashes like pearls forged from pain. His fingers inch up the sides of my body like he's struggling to keep them in one place, like he's struggling not to touch me everywhere everywhere everywhere and his eyes are drinking in the 63 inches of my frame and I'm so I'm so I'm so

caught.

"I finally get it now," he says into my ear. "I know—I know why Warner wants you."

"Then why are you here?" I whisper. "Why . . ." 1, 2 attempts at inhalation. "Why are you touching me?"

"Because I *can*." He almost cracks a smile and I almost sprout a pair of wings. "I already have."

"What?" I blink, suddenly sobered. "What do you mean?"

"That first night in the cell," he sighs. He looks down. "You were screaming in your sleep."

I wait.

I wait.

I wait forever.

"I touched your face." He speaks into the shape of my ear. "Your hand. I brushed the length of your arm. . . ." He pulls back and his eyes rest at my shoulder, trail down to my elbow, land on my wrist. I'm suspended in disbelief. "I didn't know how to wake you up. You wouldn't wake up. So I sat back and watched you. I waited for you to stop screaming."

"That's. Not. Possible." 3 words are all I manage.

But his hands become arms around my waist his lips become a cheek pressed against my cheek and his body is flush against mine, his skin touching me touching me touching me and he's not screaming he's not dying he's not running away from me and I'm crying

I'm choking

I'm shaking shuddering splintering into teardrops

and he's holding me the way no one has ever held me before.

Like he wants me.

"I'm going to get you out of here," he says, and his mouth is moving against my hair and his hands are traveling to my arms and I'm leaning back and he's looking into my eyes and I must be dreaming.

"Why—why do you—I don't—" I'm shaking my head and shaking because this can't be happening and shaking off the tears glued to my face. This can't be real.

His eyes gentle, his smile unhinges my joints, and I wish I had the courage to touch him. "I have to go," he says. "You have to be dressed and downstairs by eight o'clock."

I'm drowning in his eyes and I don't know what to say.

He peels off his shirt and I don't know where to look.

I catch myself on the glass panel and press my eyes shut and blink when something flutters too close. His fingers are a moment from my face.

"You don't have to look away," he says. He says it with a smile the size of Jupiter.

I peek up at his features, at the crooked grin I want to savor, at the color in his eyes I'd use to paint a million pictures. I follow the line of his jaw down his neck to the peak of his collarbone; I memorize his arms, the perfection of his torso. The bird on his chest.

The bird on his chest.

A tattoo.

A white bird with streaks of gold like a crown atop its head. It's flying.

"Adam," I try to tell him. "Adam," I try to choke out. "Adam," I try to say so many times and fail.

I try to find his eyes only to realize he's been watching me study him. The pieces of his face are pressed into lines of emotion so deep I wonder what I must look like to him. He touches 2 fingers to my chin, tilts my face up just enough and I'm a live wire in water. "I'll find a way to talk to you," he says, and his hands are reeling me in and my face is pressed against his chest and the world is suddenly brighter, bigger, beautiful. The world suddenly means something to me, the possibility of humanity means something to me, the entire universe stops in place and spins in the other direction and I'm the bird.

I'm the bird and I'm flying away.

TWENTY

It's 8:00 in the morning and I'm wearing a dress the color of dead forests and old tin cans.

The fit is tighter than anything I've worn in my life, the cut modern and angular, almost haphazard; the material is stiff and thick but somehow breathable. I stare at my legs and wonder that I own a pair.

I feel more exposed than I ever have in my life.

For 17 years I've trained myself to cover every inch of exposed skin and Warner is forcing me to peel the layers away. I can only assume he's doing it on purpose. My body is a carnivorous flower, a poisonous houseplant, a loaded gun with a million triggers and he's more than ready to fire.

Touch me and suffer the consequences. There have never been exceptions to this rule.

Never but Adam.

He left me standing sopping wet in the shower, soaking up a torrential downpour of hot tears. I watched through the blurred glass as he dried himself off and slipped into his standard uniform.

I watched as he slipped away, wondering every moment why why why

Why can he touch me?

Why would he help me?

~~Does he remember me?~~

My skin is still steaming.

Hope is hugging me, holding me in its arms, wiping away my tears and telling me that today and tomorrow and two days from now I will be just fine and I'm so delirious I actually dare to believe it.

I am sitting in a blue room.

The walls are wallpapered in cloth the color of a perfect summer sky, the floor tucked into a carpet 2 inches thick, the entire room empty but for 2 velvet chairs punched out of a constellation. Every varying hue is like a bruise, like a beautiful mistake, like a reminder of what they did to Adam ~~because of me.~~

"You look lovely."

Warner whisks into the room like he treads air for a living. He's accompanied by no one.

My eyes involuntarily peek down at my tennis shoes and I wonder if I've broken any rules by avoiding the stilts in my closet I'm sure are not for feet. I look up and he's standing right in front of me.

"Green is a great color on you," he says with a stupid smile. "It really brings out the color of your eyes."

"What color are my eyes?" I ask the wall.

He laughs. "You're not serious."

"How old are you?"

He stops laughing. "You care to know?"

"I'm curious."

He takes the seat beside me. "I won't answer your questions if you won't look at me when I speak to you."

"You want me to torture people against my will. You want me to be a weapon in your war. You want me to become a monster for you." I pause. "Looking at you makes me sick."

"You're far more stubborn than I thought you'd be."

"I'm wearing your dress. I ate your food. I'm here." I lift my eyes to look at him and he's already staring straight at me.

"You did none of that for me," he says quietly.

I nearly laugh out loud. "Why would I?"

His eyes are fighting his lips for the right to speak. I look away.

"What are we doing in this room?"

"Ah." He takes a deep breath. "Breakfast. Then I give you your schedule."

He presses a button on the arm of his chair and almost instantly, carts and trays are wheeled into the room by men and women who are clearly not soldiers. Their faces are hard and cracked and too thin to be healthy.

It breaks my heart.

"I usually eat alone," Warner continues. "But I figured you and I should be more thoroughly acquainted. Especially since we'll be spending so much time together."

The ~~servants~~ ~~maids~~ people-who-are-not-soldiers leave and Warner offers me something on a dish.

"I'm not hungry."

"This is not an option."

I look up.

"You are not allowed to starve yourself to death," he says. "You don't eat enough and I need you to be healthy. You are not allowed to commit suicide. You are not allowed to harm yourself. You are too valuable to me."

"I am not your *toy*," I nearly spit.

He drops his plate onto the rolling cart and I'm surprised it doesn't shatter into pieces. He clears his throat and I might actually be scared. "This process would be so much easier if you would just cooperate.

"The world is disgusted by you," he says, his lips twitching with humor. "Everyone you've ever known has hated you. Run from you. Abandoned you. Your own parents gave up on you and *volunteered* your existence to be given up to the authorities. They were so desperate to get rid of you, to make you someone else's problem, to convince themselves the abomination they raised was not, in fact, their child."

My face has been slapped by a hundred hands.

"And yet—" He laughs openly now. "You insist on making *me* the bad guy." He meets my eyes. "I am trying to *help* you. I'm giving you an opportunity no one would ever offer you. I'm willing to treat you as an equal. I'm willing to give you everything you could ever want, and above all else, I can put power in your hands. I can make them suffer for what they did to you." He pauses. "You and I are not as different as you might hope."

"You and I are not as similar as you might hope," I snap.

He smiles so wide I'm not sure how to react. "I'm nineteen, by the way."

"Excuse me?"

"I'm nineteen years old," he clarifies. "I'm a fairly impressive specimen for my age, I know."

I pick up my spoon and poke at the edible matter on my plate. I don't know what food really is anymore. "I have no respect for you."

"You will change your mind," he says easily. "Now hurry up and eat. We have a lot of work to do."

TWENTY-ONE

Killing time isn't as difficult as it sounds.

I can shoot a hundred numbers through the chest and watch them bleed decimal points in the palm of my hand. I can rip the numbers off a clock and watch the hour hand tick tick tick its final tock just before I fall asleep. I can suffocate seconds just by holding my breath. I've been murdering minutes for hours and no one seems to mind.

It's been one week since I've spoken a word to Adam.

I turned to him once. Opened my mouth just once but never had a chance to say anything before Warner intercepted me. "You are not allowed to speak to the soldiers," he said. "If you have questions, you can find *me*. I am the only person you need to concern yourself with while you're here."

Possessive is not a strong enough word for Warner.

He escorts me everywhere. Talks to me too much. My schedule consists of meetings with Warner and eating with Warner and listening to Warner. If he is busy, I am sent to my room. If he is free, he finds me. He tells me about the books they've destroyed. The artifacts they're preparing to burn. The ideas he has for a new world and how I'll be a great help to him just as soon as I'm ready. Just as soon as I realize how much I want *this*, how much I want *him*, how much I want this new, glorious, powerful life. He is waiting for me to harness my *potential*. He tells me how grateful I should be for his patience. His kindness. His willingness to understand that this transition must be difficult.

I cannot look at Adam. I cannot speak to him. He sleeps in my room but I never see him. He breathes so close to my body but does not part his lips in my direction. He does not follow me into the bathroom. He does not leave secret messages in my notebook.

I'm beginning to wonder if I imagined everything he said to me.

I need to know if something has changed. I need to know if I'm crazy for holding on to this hope blossoming in my heart and I need to know what Adam's message meant but every day that he treats me like a stranger is another day I begin to doubt myself.

I need to talk to him but I can't.

Because now Warner is watching me.

The cameras are watching everything.

"I want you to take the cameras out of my room."

Warner stops chewing the food/garbage/breakfast/nonsense in his mouth. He swallows carefully before leaning back and looking me in the eye. "Absolutely not."

"If you treat me like a prisoner," I tell him, "I'm going to act like one. I don't like to be watched."

"You can't be trusted on your own." He picks up his spoon again.

"Every breath I take is monitored. There are guards stationed in five-foot intervals in all the hallways. I don't even have access to my own room," I protest. "Cameras aren't going to make a difference."

A strange kind of amusement dances on his lips. "You're not exactly stable, you know. You're liable to kill someone."

"No." I grip my fingers. "No—I wouldn't—I didn't kill Jenkins—"

"I'm not talking about Jenkins."

He won't stop looking at me. Smiling at me. Torturing me with his eyes.

This is me, screaming silently into my fist.

"That was an accident." The words tumble out of my mouth so quietly, so quickly I don't know if I've actually spoken or if I'm still sitting here or if I'm 14 years old all over again all over again all over again and I'm diving into a pool of memories I never ever ever ever ever

I can't seem to forget.

I saw her at the grocery store. Her legs were standing crossed at the ankles, her child was on a leash she thought he thought was a backpack. She thought he was too dumb/ too young/too immature to understand that the rope tying him to her wrist was a device designed to trap him in her uninterested circle of self-sympathy. She's too young to have a kid, to have these responsibilities, to be buried by a child who has needs that don't accommodate her own. Her life is so incredibly unbearable so immensely multifaceted too glamorous for the leashed legacy of her loins to understand.

Children are not stupid, was what I wanted to tell her.

I wanted to tell her that his seventh scream didn't mean he was trying to be obnoxious, that her fourteenth admonishment in the form of brat/you're such a brat/you're embarrassing me you little brat/don't make me tell Daddy you were being a brat was uncalled for. I didn't mean to watch but I couldn't help myself. His 3-year-old face puckered in pain, his little hands tried to undo the chains she'd strapped across his chest and she tugged so hard he fell down and cried and she told him he deserved it.

I wanted to ask her why she would do that.

I wanted to ask her so many questions but I didn't because we don't talk to people anymore because saying something would be stranger than saying nothing to a stranger. He fell to the floor and writhed around until I'd dropped everything in my hands and every feature on my face.

I'm so sorry, is what I never said to her son.

I thought my hands were helping

I thought my heart was helping

I thought so many things

I never

never

never

never

never thought

"You killed a little boy."

I'm nailed into my velvet chair by a million memories and haunted by a horror my bare hands created. I am unwanted for good reason. My hands can kill people. My hands can destroy everything.

I should not be allowed to live.

"I want," I gasp, "I want you to get rid of the cameras. Get rid of them or I will die fighting you for the right."

"Finally." Warner stands up and claps his hands together as if to congratulate himself. "I was wondering when you'd wake up. I've been waiting for the fire I know must be eating away at you every single day. You're buried in hatred, aren't you? Anger? Frustration? Itching to do *something*? To be *someone*?"

"No."

"Of course you are. You're just like me."

"I hate you more than you will ever understand."

"We're going to make an excellent team."

"We are *nothing*. You are *nothing* to me—"

"I know what you want." He leans in, lowers his voice. "I know what your little heart has always longed for. I can give you the acceptance you seek. I can be your *friend*."

I freeze. Falter.

"I know *everything* about you, love." He grins. "I've wanted you for a very long time. I've waited forever for you to be ready. I'm not going to let you go so easily."

"I don't want to be a monster," I say, perhaps more for my sake than his.

"Don't fight what you're born to be." He grasps my

shoulders. "Stop letting everyone else tell you what's wrong and right. Stake a claim! You cower when you could conquer. You have so much more power than you're aware of and quite frankly I'm"—he shakes his head—"fascinated."

"I am not your *freak*," I snap. "I will not *perform* for you."

"I'm not afraid of you, my dear," he says softly. "I'm absolutely enchanted."

"Either you get rid of the cameras or I will find and break every single one of them." I'm a liar. I'm lying through my teeth but I'm angry and desperate and horrified. Warner wants to morph me into an animal who preys on the weak. On the innocent.

If he wants me to fight for him, he's going to have to fight me first.

A slow smile spreads across his face. He touches gloved fingers to my cheek and tilts my head up, catching my chin in his grip when I flinch away. "You're absolutely delicious when you're angry."

"Too bad my taste is poisonous for your palate." I'm vibrating in disgust from head to toe.

"That detail makes this game so much more appealing."

"You're sick, you're so *sick*—"

He laughs and releases my chin. His eyes draw a lazy trail down the length of my body and I feel the sudden urge to rupture his spleen. "If I get rid of your cameras, what will you do for me?" His eyes are wicked.

"Nothing."

He shakes his head. "That won't do. I might agree to

your proposition if you agree to a condition."

I clench my jaw. "What do you want?"

The smile is bigger than before. "That is a dangerous question."

"What is your *condition*?" I clarify, impatient.

"Touch me."

"What?" My gasp is so loud it catches in my throat.

"I want to know exactly what you're capable of." His voice is steady, his eyebrows taut, tense.

"I won't do it again!" I explode. "You saw what you made me do to Jenkins—"

"Screw Jenkins," he spits. "I want you to touch *me*—I want to feel it *myself*—"

"No." I shake my head so hard it makes me dizzy. "No. Never. You're crazy—I won't—"

"You will, actually."

"I will NOT—"

"You will have to . . . *work* . . . at one point or another," he says, making an effort to moderate his voice. "Even if you were to forgo my condition, you are here for a reason, Juliette. I convinced my father that you would be an asset to The Reestablishment. That you'd be able to restrain any rebels we—"

"You mean *torture*—"

"Yes." He smiles. "Forgive me, I mean torture. You will be able to help us torture anyone we capture." A pause. "Inflicting pain, you see, is an incredibly efficient method of getting information out of anyone. And with you?" He glances at my hands. "Well, it's cheap. Fast. Effective."

He smiles wider. "And as long as we keep you alive, you'll be good for at least a few decades. It's very fortunate that you're not battery-operated."

"You—*you*—"

"You should be thanking me. I saved you from that sick hole of an asylum—I brought you into a position of power. I've given you everything you could possibly need to be comfortable." He levels his gaze at me. "Now I need you to focus. I need you to relinquish your hopes of living like everyone else. You are *not* normal. You never have been, and you never will be. Embrace who you *are*."

"I am not—I'm not—I'm—"

"A murderer?"

"NO—"

"An instrument of torture?"

"STOP—"

"You're lying to yourself."

I'm ready to destroy him.

He cocks his head. "You've been on the edge of insanity your entire life, haven't you? So many people called you crazy you actually started to believe it. You wondered if they were right. You wondered if you could fix it. You thought if you could just try a little harder, be a little better, smarter, nicer—you thought the world would change its mind about you. You blamed yourself for everything."

My bottom lip trembles without my permission. I can hardly control the tension in my jaw.

~~I don't want to tell him he's right.~~

"You've suppressed all your rage and resentment because

you wanted to be loved," he says, no longer smiling. "Maybe I understand you, Juliette. Maybe you should trust me. Maybe you should accept the fact that you've tried to be someone you're not for so long and that no matter what you did, those bastards were never happy. They were never satisfied. They never gave a damn, did they?" He looks at me and for a moment he seems almost human. For a moment I want to believe him. For a moment I want to sit on the floor and cry out the ocean lodged in my throat.

"It's time you stopped pretending," he says, so softly. "Juliette—" He takes my face in his gloved hands, so unexpectedly gentle. "You don't have to be nice anymore. You can destroy all of them. You can take them down and own this whole world—"

"But I don't want to destroy anyone," I tell him. "I don't want to *hurt* people—"

"They *deserve* it!" He turns away, frustrated. "How could you not want to retaliate? How could you not want to *fight back*—"

I stand up slowly, shaking with anger. "You think I don't have a heart? You think I don't *feel*? You think that because I *can* inflict pain, that I should? You're just like everyone else. You think I'm a monster just like everyone else. You don't understand me at all—"

"Juliette—"

"No."

I don't want this. I don't want his life.

I don't want to be anything for anyone but myself.

I want to make my own choices and I've never wanted to be a monster. My words are slow and steady when I speak. "I value human life a lot more than you do, Warner."

He opens his mouth to speak before he stops. Laughs out loud and shakes his head.

Smiles at me.

"What?" I ask before I can stop myself.

"You just said my name." He grins even wider. "You've never addressed me directly before. That must mean I'm making progress with you."

"I just told you I don't—"

He cuts me off. "I'm not worried about your moral dilemmas. You're just stalling for time because you're in denial. Don't worry," he says. "You'll get over it. I can wait a little longer."

"I'm not in *denial*—"

"Of course you are. You don't know it yet, Juliette, but you are a very bad girl," he says, clutching his heart. "Just my type."

This conversation is impossible.

"There is a soldier *living* in my room." I'm breathing hard. "If you want me to be here, you need to get rid of the cameras."

Warner's eyes darken for just an instant. "Where *is* your soldier, anyway?"

"I wouldn't know." I hope to God I'm not blushing. "You assigned him to me."

"Yes." He looks thoughtful. "I like watching you squirm.

He makes you uncomfortable, doesn't he?"

I think about Adam's hands on my body and his lips so close to mine and the scent of his skin and suddenly my heart is pounding. "Yes." *God*. "Yes. He makes me very . . . uncomfortable."

"Do you know why I chose him?" Warner asks, and I'm stunned.

Adam was *chosen*.

Of course he was. He wasn't just any soldier sent to my cell. Warner does nothing without reason. He must know Adam and I have a history. He is more cruel and calculative than I gave him credit for.

"No." Inhale. "I don't know why." Exhale. I can't forget to breathe.

"He volunteered," Warner says simply, and I'm dumbstruck. "He said he'd gone to school with you so many years ago. He said you probably wouldn't remember him, that he looks a lot different now than he did back then. He put together a very convincing case." A beat of breath. "He said he was thrilled to hear you'd been locked up." Warner finally looks at me.

"I'm curious," he continues, tilting his head as he speaks. "Do you remember him?"

"No," I lie, and I'm trying to untangle the truth from the false from assumptions from the postulations but run-on sentences are twisting around my throat.

Adam knew me when he walked into that cell.

He knew exactly who I was.

He already knew my name.

Oh

Oh

Oh

This was all a trap.

"Does this information make you . . . angry?" he asks, and I want to sew his smiling lips into a permanent scowl.

I say nothing and somehow it's worse.

Warner is beaming. "I never told him, of course, why it was that you'd been locked up—I thought the experiment in the asylum should remain untainted by extra information—but he said you were always a threat to the students. That everyone was always warned to stay away from you, though the authorities never explained why. He said he wanted to get a closer look at the freak you've become."

My heart cracks. My eyes flash. I'm so hurt so angry so *humiliated* and burning with indignation so raw that it's like a fire raging within me. I want to crush Warner's spine in my hand. I want him to know what it's like to wound, to inflict such agony on others. I want him to know my pain and Jenkins' pain and Fletcher's pain and I want him to *hurt*. Because maybe Warner is right.

Maybe some people do deserve it.

"Take off your shirt."

For all his posturing, Warner looks genuinely surprised, but he wastes no time unbuttoning his jacket, slipping off his gloves, and peeling away the thin cotton shirt clinging closest to his skin.

His eyes are bright, sickeningly eager; he doesn't mask his curiosity.

Warner drops his clothes to the floor and looks at me almost intimately. I have to swallow back the revulsion bubbling in my mouth. His perfect face. His perfect body. He repulses me. I want his exterior to match his broken black interior. I want to cripple his cockiness with the palm of my hand.

He walks up to me until there's less than a foot of space between us. His height and build make me feel like a fallen twig. "Are you ready?" he asks.

I contemplate breaking his neck.

"If I do this you'll get rid of all the cameras in my room. All the bugs. Everything."

He steps closer. Dips his head. He's staring at my lips, studying me in an entirely new way. "My promises aren't worth much, love," he whispers. "Or have you forgotten?" 3 inches forward. His hand on my waist. His breath sweet and warm on my neck. "I'm an exceptional liar."

Realization slams into me.

I shouldn't be doing this. I shouldn't be making deals with him. I shouldn't be contemplating torture dear God I have lost my mind. My fists are balled at my sides and I'm shaking everywhere. I can hardly find the strength to speak. "You can go to hell."

I'm limp.

I trip backward against the wall and slump into a heap of uselessness; desperation. I think of Adam and my heart deflates.

I can't be here anymore.

I fly to the double doors facing the room and yank them open before Warner can stop me. But Adam stops me instead. He's standing just outside. Waiting. Guarding me wherever I go.

I wonder if he heard everything and my eyes fall to the floor, the color flushed from my face. Of course he heard everything. Of course he now knows I'm a murderer. A monster. A worthless soul stuffed into a poisonous body.

Warner did this on purpose.

And I'm standing between them. Warner with no shirt on. Adam looking at his gun.

"Soldier." Warner speaks. "Take her back up to her room and disable all the cameras. She can have lunch alone if she wants, but I'll expect her for dinner."

Adam blinks for a moment too long. "Yes, sir."

"Juliette?"

I freeze. My back is to Warner and I don't turn around.

"I do expect you to hold up your end of the bargain."

TWENTY-TWO

It takes 5 years to walk to the elevator. 15 more to ride it up. I'm a million years old by the time I walk into my room. Adam is still, silent, perfectly put together and mechanical in his movements. There's nothing in his eyes, in his limbs, in the motions of his body that indicate he even knows my name.

I watch him move quickly, swiftly, carefully around the room, finding the little devices meant to monitor my behavior and disabling them one by one. If anyone asks why my cameras aren't working, Adam won't get in trouble. This order came from Warner. This makes it official.

This makes it possible for me to have some privacy.

I thought I would need privacy.

I'm such a fool.

Adam is not the boy I remember.

I was in third grade.

I'd just moved into town after being ~~thrown out of~~ asked to leave my old school. My parents were always moving, always running away from the messes I made, from the playdates I'd ruined, from the friendships I never had. No one ever wanted to talk about my "problem," but the mystery surrounding my existence somehow made things worse. The human imagination is often disastrous when left to its own devices. I only heard bits and pieces of their whispers.

"Freak!"

"Did you hear what she *did*—?"

"What a loser."

"—got kicked out of her old school—"

"Psycho!"

"She's got some kind of disease—"

No one talked to me. Everyone stared. I was young enough that I still cried. I ate lunch alone by a chain-link fence and never looked in the mirror. I never wanted to see the face everyone hated so much. Girls used to kick me and run away. Boys used to throw rocks at me. I still have scars somewhere.

I watched the world pass by through those chain-link fences. I stared out at the cars and the parents dropping off their kids and the moments I'd never be a part of. This was before the diseases became so common that death was a natural part of conversation. This was before we realized the clouds were the wrong color, before we realized all the animals were dying or infected, before we realized everyone was going to starve to death, and fast. This was back when we still thought our problems had solutions. Back then, Adam was the boy who used to walk to school. Adam was the boy who sat 3 rows in front of me. His clothes were worse than mine, his lunch nonexistent. I never saw him eat.

One morning he came to school in a car.

I know because I saw him being pushed out of it. His father was drunk and driving, yelling and flailing his fists for some reason. Adam stood very still and stared at the ground like he was waiting for something, steeling himself for the inevitable. I watched a father slap his 8-year-old son in the face. I watched Adam fall to the floor and I stood there, motionless as he was kicked repeatedly in the ribs.

"It's all your fault! It's *your* fault, you worthless piece of shit," his father screamed over and over and over again until I threw up right there, all over a patch of dandelions.

Adam didn't cry. He stayed curled up on the ground until his father gave up, until he drove away. Only once he was sure everyone was gone did his body break into heaving sobs, his small face smeared into the dirt, his arms clutching at his bruised abdomen. I couldn't look away.

I could never get that sound out of my head, that scene out of my head.

That's when I started paying attention to Adam Kent.

"Juliette."

I suck in my breath and wish my hands weren't trembling. I wish I had no eyes.

"Juliette," he says again, this time even softer.

I won't turn around.

"You always knew who I was," I whisper.

He says nothing and I'm suddenly desperate to see his eyes. I suddenly need to see his eyes. I turn to face him

138

despite everything only to see he's staring at his hands. "I'm sorry," is all he says.

I lean back against the wall and look away. Everything was a performance. Stealing my bed. Asking for my name. Asking me about my family. He was performing for Warner. For the guards. For whoever was watching. I don't even know what to believe anymore.

I need to say it. I need to get it out. I need to rip my wounds open and bleed fresh for him. "It's true," I tell him. "About the little boy." My voice is shaking so much more than I thought it would. "I did that."

He's quiet for so long. "I never understood before," he says. "When I first heard about it. I didn't realize until just now what must've happened. It never made sense to me," he says. He looks up. "When I heard about it. We all heard about it. The whole school—"

"It was an accident," I choke out. "He—h-he fell—and I was trying to help him—and I just—I didn't—I thought—"

"I know."

"What?" I gasp.

"I believe you," he says to me.

"What . . . why?" My eyes are blinking back tears, my hands unsteady, my heart filled with nervous hope.

He bites his bottom lip. Looks away. Walks to the wall. Opens and closes his mouth several times before the words rush out. "Because I *knew* you, Juliette—I—God—I just—" He closes his eyes. "That was the day I was going to talk to you." A strange sort of smile. A strange sort of laugh. Looks up at the ceiling. Turns his back to me. "I was finally going to talk to you. I was finally going to talk to you and I—" He shakes his head, hard, and attempts another painful laugh. "God, you don't remember me."

I want to laugh and cry and scream and run and I can't choose which to do first.

I confess.

"Of course I remember you." My voice is a strangled whisper. I squeeze my eyes shut. ~~I remember you every day forever in every single broken moment of my life.~~ "You were the only one who ever looked at me like a human being."

He never talked to me. He never spoke a single word to me, but he was the only one who dared to sit close to my fence. He was the only one who stood up for me, the only person who fought for me, the only one who'd punch someone in the face for throwing a rock at my head. I didn't even know how to say thank you.

He was the closest thing to a friend I ever had.

I open my eyes and he's standing right in front of me.

"You've always known?" 3 whispered words and he's broken my dam, unlocked my lips and stolen my heart all over again. I can hardly feel the tears streaming down my face.

"Adam." I try to laugh. "I'd recognize your eyes anywhere in the world."

And that's it.

This time there's no self-control.

This time I'm in his arms and against the wall and I'm trembling everywhere and he's so gentle, so careful, touching me like I'm made of porcelain and I want to shatter.

He's running his hands down my body running his eyes across my face and I'm running marathons with my mind.

Everything is on fire.

My cheeks my hands the pit of my stomach and I'm drowning in waves of emotion and a storm of fresh rain and all I feel is the strength of his silhouette against mine and I never ever ever ever want to forget this moment. I want to stamp him into my skin and save him forever.

He takes my hands and presses my palms to his face and I know I never knew the beauty of feeling human before this. I know I'm still crying when my eyes flutter closed.

I whisper his name.

And he's breathing harder than I am and suddenly his lips are on my neck and I'm gasping and clutching at his arms and he's touching me touching me touching me and I'm thunder and lightning and wondering when the hell I'll be waking up. He meets my eyes only to cup my face in his hands and I'm blushing through these walls from pleasure and pain and impossibility.

"I've wanted to kiss you for so long." His voice is husky, uneven, deep in my ear.

I'm frozen in anticipation in expectation and I'm so worried he'll kiss me, so worried he won't. I'm staring at his lips and I don't realize how close we are until we're pulled apart.

3 distinct electronic screeches reverberate around the room and Adam looks past me like he can't understand

where he is for a moment. He blinks. And runs toward an intercom to press the appropriate buttons. I notice he's still breathing hard.

I'm shaking in my skin.

"Name and number," the voice of the intercom demands.

"Kent, Adam. 45B-86659."

A pause.

"Soldier, are you aware the cameras in your room have been deactivated?"

"Yes, sir. I was given direct orders to dismantle the devices."

"Who cleared this order?"

"Warner, sir."

A longer pause.

"We'll verify and confirm. Unauthorized tampering with security devices may result in your immediate dishonorable discharge, soldier. I hope you're aware of that."

"Yes, sir."

The line goes quiet.

Adam slumps against the wall, his chest heaving. I'm not sure but I could've sworn his lips twitched into the tiniest smile. He closes his eyes and exhales.

I'm not sure what to do with the relief tumbling into my hands.

"Come here," he says, his eyes still shut.

I tiptoe forward and he pulls me into his arms. Breathes in the scent of my hair and kisses the side of my head and I've never felt anything so incredible in my life. I'm not even human anymore. I'm so much more. The sun and the moon have merged and the earth is upside down. I feel like I can be exactly who I want to be in his arms.

He makes me forget the terror I'm capable of.

"Juliette," he whispers in my ear. "We need to get the hell out of here."

TWENTY-THREE

I'm 14 years old again and I'm staring at the back of his head in a small classroom. I'm 14 years old and I've been in love with Adam Kent for years. I made sure to be extra careful, to be extra quiet, to be extra cooperative because I didn't want to move away again. I didn't want to leave the school with the one friendly face I'd ever known. I watched him grow up a little more every day, grow a little taller every day, a little stronger, a little tougher, a little more quiet every day. He eventually got too big to get beat up by his dad, but no one really knows what happened to his mother. The students shunned him, harassed him until he started fighting back, until the pressure of the world finally cracked him.

But his eyes always stayed the same.

Always the same when he looked at me. Kind. Compassionate. Desperate to understand. But he never asked questions. He never pushed me to say a word. He just made sure he was close enough to scare away everyone else.

I thought maybe I wasn't so bad. Maybe.

I thought maybe he saw something in me. I thought maybe I wasn't as horrible as everyone said I was. I hadn't touched anyone in years. I didn't dare get close to people. I couldn't risk it.

Until one day I did, and I ruined everything.

I killed a little boy in a grocery store simply by helping him to his feet. By grabbing his little hands. I didn't understand why he was screaming. It was my first experience ever touching someone for such a long period of time and I didn't understand what was happening to me. The few times I'd ever accidentally put my hands on someone I'd always pulled away. I'd pull away as soon as I remembered I wasn't supposed to be touching anyone. As soon as I heard the first scream escape their lips.

The little boy was different.

I wanted to help him. I felt such a surge of sudden anger toward his mother for neglecting his cries. Her lack of compassion as a parent devastated me ~~and it reminded me too much of my own mother.~~ I just wanted to help him. I wanted him to know that someone else was listening— that someone else cared. I didn't understand why it felt so strange and exhilarating to touch him. I didn't know that I was draining his life and I couldn't comprehend why he'd grown limp and quiet in my arms. I thought maybe the rush of power and positive feeling meant that I'd been cured of my horrible disease. I thought so many stupid things and I ruined everything.

I thought I was helping.

I spent the next 3 years of my life in hospitals, law offices, juvenile detention centers, and suffered through pills and electroshock therapy. Nothing worked. Nothing helped. Outside of killing me, locking me up in an institution was the only solution. The only way to protect the public from the terror of Juliette.

Until he stepped into my cell, I hadn't seen Adam Kent in 3 years.

And he does look different. Tougher, taller, harder, sharper, tattooed. He's muscle, mature, quiet and quick. It's almost like he can't afford to be soft or slow or relaxed. He can't afford to be anything but strength and efficiency. The lines of his face are precise, carved into shape by years of hard living and training and trying to survive.

He's not a little boy anymore. He's not afraid. He's in the army.

But he's not so different, either. He still has the most unusually blue eyes I've ever seen. Dark and deep and drenched in passion. I always wondered what it'd be like to see the world through such a beautiful lens. I wondered if your eye color meant you saw the world differently. If the world saw you differently as a result.

I should have known it was him when he showed up in my cell.

A part of me did. But I'd tried so hard to repress the memories of my past that I refused to believe it could be possible. Because a part of me didn't want to remember. A part of me was too scared to hope. A part of me didn't know if it would make any difference to know that it was him, after all.

I often wonder what I must look like.

I wonder if I'm just a punctured shadow of the person I

was before. I haven't looked in the mirror in 3 years. I'm so scared of what I'll see.

Someone knocks on the door.

I'm catapulted across the room by my own fear. Adam locks eyes with me before opening the door and I decide to retreat into a far corner of the room.

I sharpen my ears only to hear muted voices, hushed tones, and someone clearing his throat. I'm not sure what to do.

"I'll be down in a minute," Adam says a little loudly. I realize he's trying to end the conversation.

"C'mon, man, I just want to see her—"

"She's not a goddamn spectacle, Kenji. Get the hell out of here."

"Wait—just tell me: Does she light shit on fire with her eyes?" Kenji laughs and I cringe, slumping to the floor behind the bed. I curl into myself and try not to hear the rest of the conversation.

I fail.

Adam sighs. I can picture him rubbing his forehead. "Just get out."

Kenji struggles to muffle his laughter. "Damn you're sensitive all of a sudden, huh? Hanging out with a girl is changing you, man—"

Adam says something I can't hear.

The door slams shut.

I peek up from my hiding place. Adam looks embarrassed.

My cheeks go pink. I study the threads of the finely woven carpet under my feet. I touch the cloth wallpaper and wait for him to speak. I stand up to stare out the window only to be met by the bleak backdrop of a broken city. I lean my forehead against the glass.

Metal cubes are clustered together in the distance: compounds housing civilians wrapped in layers, trying to find refuge from the cold. A mother holding the hand of a small child. Soldiers standing over them, still like statues, rifles poised and ready to fire. Heaps and heaps and heaps of trash, dangerous scraps of iron and steel glinting on the ground. Lonely trees waving at the wind.

Adam's hands slip around my waist.

His lips are at my ear and he says nothing at all, but I melt, hot butter dripping down his body. I want to eat every minute of this moment.

I allow my eyes to shut against the truth outside my window. Just for a little while.

Adam takes a deep breath and pulls me even closer. I'm molded to the shape of him; his hands are circling my waist and his cheek is pressed against my head. "You feel incredible."

I try to laugh but seem to have forgotten how. "Those are words I never thought I'd hear."

Adam spins me around so I'm facing him.

He leans in until his forehead rests against mine and our lips still aren't close enough. He whispers, "How are you?" and I want to kiss every beautiful beat of his heart.

How are you? 3 words no one ever asks me.

"I want to get out of here," is all I can think of.

He squeezes me against his chest and I marvel at the power, the glory, the wonder in such a simple movement.

Every butterfly in the world has migrated to my stomach.

"Juliette."

I lean back to see his face.

"Are you serious about leaving?" he asks me. His fingers brush the side of my cheek. He tucks a stray strand of hair behind my ear. "Do you understand the risks?"

I take a deep breath. I know that the only real risk is death. "Yes."

He nods. Drops his eyes, his voice. "The troops are mobilizing for some kind of attack. There've been a lot of protests from groups who were silent before, and our job is to obliterate the resistance. I think they want this attack to be their last one," he adds. "There's something huge going on, and I'm not sure what, not yet. But whatever it is, we have to be ready to go when they are."

I freeze. "What do you mean?"

"When the troops are ready to deploy, you and I should be ready to run. It's the only way out that will give us time to disappear. Everyone will be too focused on the attack—it'll buy us some time before they notice we're missing or can get enough people together to search for us."

"But—you mean—you'll come with me . . . ? You'd be willing to do that for me?"

He smiles a small smile. His lips twitch like he's trying not to laugh. "There's very little I wouldn't do for you."

I take a deep breath and close my eyes, touching my fingers to his chest, imagining the bird soaring across his skin, and I ask him the one question that scares me the most. "Why?"

"What do you mean?"

"Why, Adam? Why do you care? Why do you want to help me? I don't understand—I don't know why you'd be willing to risk your life—"

But then his arms are around my waist and he's pulling me so close and his lips are at my ear and he says my name, once, twice and I had no idea I could catch fire so quickly. His mouth is smiling against my skin. "You don't?"

I don't know anything, is what I would tell him if I had any idea how to speak.

He laughs a little and pulls back. Takes my hand and studies it. "Do you remember in fourth grade," he says, "when Molly Carter signed up for the school field trip too late? All the spots were filled, and she stood outside the bus, crying because she wanted to go?"

He doesn't wait for me to answer.

"I remember you got off the bus. You offered her your seat and she didn't even say thank you. I watched you standing on the sidewalk as we pulled away."

I'm no longer breathing.

"Do you remember in fifth grade? That week Dana's parents nearly got divorced? She came to school every day without her lunch. And you offered to give her yours." He pauses. "As soon as that week was over she went back to pretending you didn't exist."

"In seventh grade Shelly Morrison got caught cheating off your math test. She kept screaming that if she failed, her father would kill her. You told the teacher that you were the one cheating off of *her* test. You got a zero on the exam, and detention for a week." He lifts his head but doesn't look at me. "You had bruises on your arms for at least a month after that. I always wondered where they came from."

My heart is beating too fast. Dangerously fast. I clench my fingers to keep them from shaking.

"A million times," he says, his voice so quiet now. "I saw you do things like that a million times. But you never said a word unless it was forced out of you." He laughs again, this time a hard, heavy sort of laugh. He's staring at a point directly past my shoulder. "You never asked for anything from anyone." He finally meets my eyes. "But no one ever gave you a chance."

I swallow hard, try to look away but he catches my face.

He whispers, "You have no idea how much I've thought about you. How many times I've dreamt"—he takes a tight breath—"how many times I've dreamt about being this close to you." He moves to run a hand through his hair before he changes his mind. Looks down. Looks up. "God, Juliette, I'd follow you anywhere. You're the only good thing left in this world."

I'm begging myself not to burst into tears and I don't know if it's working. I'm everything broken and glued back together and blushing everywhere and I can hardly find the strength to meet his gaze.

His fingers find my chin. Tip me up.

"We have three weeks at the most," he says. "I don't think they can control the mobs for much longer."

I nod. I blink. I rest my face against his chest and pretend I'm not crying.

3 weeks.

TWENTY-FOUR

2 weeks pass.

2 weeks of dresses and showers and food I want to throw across the room. 2 weeks of Warner smiling and touching my waist, laughing and guiding the small of my back, making sure I look my best as I walk beside him. He thinks I'm his trophy. His secret weapon.

I have to stifle the urge to crack his knuckles into concrete.

But I offer him 2 weeks of cooperation because in 1 week we'll be gone.

Hopefully.

But then, more than anything else, I've found I don't hate Warner as much as I thought I did.

I feel sorry for him.

He finds a strange sort of solace in my company; he thinks I can relate to him and his twisted notions, his cruel upbringing, his absent and simultaneously demanding father.

But he never says a word about his mother.

Adam says that no one knows anything about Warner's mother—that she's never been discussed and no one has any idea who she is. He says that Warner is only known to be the consequence of ruthless parenting, and a cold, calculated desire for power. He hates happy children and happy parents and their happy lives.

I think Warner thinks that I understand. That I understand him.

And I do. And I don't.

Because we're not the same.

I want to be better.

Adam and I have little time together but nighttime. And even then, not so much. Warner watches me more closely every day; disabling the cameras only made him more suspicious. He's always walking into my room unexpectedly, taking me on unnecessary tours around the building, talking about nothing but his plans and his plans to make more plans and how together we'll conquer the world. I don't pretend to care.

Maybe it's me who's making this worse.

"I can't believe Warner actually agreed to get rid of your cameras," Adam said to me one night.

"He's insane. He's sick in a way I'll never understand."

Adam sighed. "He's obsessed with you."

"What?" I nearly snapped my neck in surprise.

"You're all he ever talks about." Adam was silent a moment, his jaw too tight. "I heard stories about you before you even got here. That's why I got involved—it's why I volunteered to go get you. Warner spent months collecting information about you: addresses, medical records, personal histories, family relations, birth certificates, blood tests. The entire army was talking about his new project; everyone knew he was looking for a girl who'd killed a little boy in a grocery store. A girl named Juliette."

I held my breath.

Adam shook his head. "I knew it was you. It had to be. I asked Warner if I could help with the project—I told him I'd gone to school with you, that I'd heard about the little boy, that I'd seen you in person." He laughed a hard laugh. "Warner was thrilled. He thought it would make the experiment more interesting," he added, disgusted. "And I knew that if he wanted to claim you as some kind of sick project—" He hesitated. Looked away. "I just knew I had to do something. I thought I could try to help. But now it's gotten worse. Warner won't stop talking about what you're capable of or how valuable you are to his efforts and how excited he is to have you here. Everyone is beginning to notice. Warner is ruthless—he has no mercy for anyone. He loves the power, the thrill of destroying people. But he's starting to crack, Juliette. He's so desperate to have you . . . *join* him. And for all his threats, he doesn't want to force you. He wants you to want it. To choose *him*, in a way." He looked down, took a tight breath. "He's losing his edge. And whenever I see his face I'm always about two inches away from doing something stupid. I'd love to break his jaw."

Yes. Warner is losing his edge.

He's paranoid, though with good reason. But then he's patient and impatient with me. Excited and nervous all the time. He's a walking oxymoron.

He disables my cameras, but some nights he orders Adam to sleep outside my door to make sure I don't escape. He says I can eat lunch alone, but always ends up summoning me to his side. The few hours Adam and I would've had together are stolen from us, but the fewer nights Adam is allowed to sleep inside my room I manage to spend huddled in his arms.

We both sleep on the floor now, wrapped up in each other for warmth even with the blanket covering our bodies. Every time he touches me it's like a burst of fire and electricity that ignites my bones in the most amazing way. It's the kind of feeling I wish I could hold in my hand.

Adam tells me about new developments, whispers he's heard around the other soldiers. He tells me how there are multiple headquarters across what's left of the country. How Warner's dad is at the capital, how he's left his son in charge of this entire sector. He says Warner hates his father but loves the power. The destruction. The devastation. He strokes my hair and tells me stories and tucks me close like he's afraid I'll disappear. He paints pictures of people and places until I fall asleep, until I'm drowning in a drug of dreams to escape a world with no refuge, no relief, no release but his reassurances in my ear. Sleep is the only thing I look forward to these days. I can hardly remember why I used to scream.

Things are getting too comfortable and I'm beginning to panic.

"Put these on," Warner says to me.

Breakfast in the blue room has become routine. I eat and don't ask where the food comes from, whether or not the workers are being paid for what they do, how this building manages to sustain so many lives, pump so much water, or use so much electricity. I bide my time now. I cooperate.

Warner hasn't asked me to touch him again, and I don't offer.

"What are they for?" I eye the small pieces of fabric in his hands and feel a nervous twinge in my gut.

He smiles a slow, sneaky smile. "An aptitude test." He grabs my wrist and places the bundle in my hand. "I'll turn around, just this once."

I'm almost too nervous to be disgusted by him.

My hands shake as I change into the outfit that turns out to be a tiny tank top and tinier shorts. I'm practically naked. I'm practically convulsing in fear of what this might mean. I clear my throat and Warner spins around.

He takes too long to speak; his eyes are busy traveling the road map of my body. I want to rip up the carpet and sew it to my skin. He smiles and offers me his hand.

I'm granite and limestone and marbled glass. I don't move.

He drops his hand. Cocks his head. "Follow me."

Warner opens the door. Adam is standing outside. He's gotten so good at masking his emotions that I hardly register the look of shock that shifts in and out of his features. Nothing but the strain in his forehead, the tension

157

in his temples, gives him away. He knows something's not right. He actually turns his neck to take in my appearance. He blinks. "Sir?"

"Remain where you are, soldier. I'll take it from here."

Adam doesn't answer doesn't answer doesn't answer— "Yes, sir," he says.

I feel his eyes on me as I turn down the hall.

Warner takes me somewhere new. We're walking through corridors I've never seen, blacker and bleaker and more narrow as we go. I realize we're heading downward.

Into a basement.

We pass through 1, 2, 4 metal doors. Soldiers everywhere, their eyes everywhere, appraising me with both fear and something else I'd rather not consider. I've realized there are very few females in this building.

If there were ever a place to be grateful for being untouchable, it'd be here.

It's the only reason I have asylum from the preying eyes of hundreds of lonely men. It's the only reason Adam is staying with me—because Warner thinks Adam is a cardboard cutout. He thinks Adam is a machine oiled by orders and demands. He thinks Adam is a reminder of my past, and he uses it to make me uncomfortable. He'd never imagine Adam could lay a finger on me.

No one would. Everyone I meet is absolutely petrified.

The darkness is like a black canvas punctured by a blunt knife, with beams of light peeking through. It reminds me too much of my old cell. My skin ripples with uncontrollable dread.

I'm surrounded by guns.

"In you go," Warner says. I'm pushed into an empty room smelling faintly of mold. Someone hits a switch and fluorescent lights flicker on to reveal pasty yellow walls and carpet the color of dead grass. The door slams shut behind me.

There's nothing but cobwebs and a huge mirror in this room. The mirror is half the size of the wall. Instinctively I know Warner and his accomplices must be watching me. I just don't know why.

Mechanical clinks/cracks/creaks and shifts shake the space I'm standing in. The ground rumbles to life. The ceiling trembles with the promise of chaos. Metal spikes are suddenly everywhere, scattered across the room, puncturing every surface at all different heights. Every few seconds they disappear only to reappear with a sudden jolt of terror, slicing through the air like needles.

I realize I'm standing in a torture chamber.

Static and feedback from speakers older than my dying heart crackle to life.

"Are you ready?" Warner's amplified voice echoes around the room.

"What am I supposed to be ready for?" I yell into the empty space, certain that someone can hear me. ~~I'm calm. I'm calm. I'm calm.~~ I'm petrified.

"We had a deal, remember?" the room responds.

"Wha—"

"I disabled your cameras. Now it's your turn to hold up your end of the bargain."

159

"I won't touch you!" I shout, spinning in place, terrified.

"That's all right," he says. "I'm sending in my replacement."

The door squeals open and a toddler waddles in wearing nothing but a diaper. He's blindfolded and hiccupping sobs, shuddering in fear.

One pin pops my entire existence into nothing.

"If you don't save him," Warner's words crackle through the room, "we won't, either."

This child.

He must have a mother a father someone who loves him this child this child this child stumbling forward in terror. He could be speared through by a metal stalagmite at any second.

Saving him is simple: I need to pick him up, find a safe spot of ground, and hold him in my arms until the experiment is over.

There's only one problem.

If I touch him, he might die.

TWENTY-FIVE

Warner knows I don't have a choice. He wants to force me into another situation where he can see the impact of my abilities, and he has no problem torturing an innocent child to get exactly what he wants.

Right now I have no options.

I have to take a chance before this little boy steps forward in the wrong direction.

I quickly memorize as much as I can of the traps and dodge/hop/narrowly avoid the spikes until I'm as close as possible.

I take a deep, shaky breath and focus on the shivering limbs of the boy in front of me and pray to God I'm making the right decision. I'm about to pull off my shirt to use as a barrier between us when I notice the slight vibration in the ground. The tremble that precedes the terror. I know I have half of a second before the spikes slice up through the air and even less time to react.

I yank him up and into my arms.

His screams pierce through me like I'm being shot to death. He's clawing at my arms, my chest, kicking my body as hard as he can, crying out in agony until the pain paralyzes him. He goes weak in my grip and I'm being ripped to pieces, my bones, my veins all tumbling out of place, all turning on me to torture me forever with memories of the horrors I'm responsible for.

Pain and power are bleeding through his body into mine, jolting through his limbs and crashing into me until I nearly drop him. ~~It's like reliving a nightmare I've spent 3 years trying to forget.~~

"Absolutely amazing," Warner sighs through the speakers, and I realize I was right. He must be watching through a 2-way mirror. "Brilliant, love. I'm thoroughly impressed."

I'm too desperate to be able to focus on Warner right now. I have no idea how long this sick game is going to last, and I need to lessen the amount of skin I'm exposing to this little boy's body.

My skimpy outfit makes so much sense now.

I rearrange him in my arms and manage to grab hold of his diaper. I'm holding him up with the palm of my hand. I'm desperate to believe I couldn't have touched him long enough to cause serious damage.

He hiccups once; his body quivers back to life.

I could cry from happiness.

But then the screams start back up again, no longer cries of torture but of fear. He's desperate to get away from me and I'm losing my grip, my wrist nearly breaking from the effort. I don't dare remove his blindfold. I'd rather die than allow him to see this space, to see my face.

I clench my jaw. If I put him down, he'll start running. And if he starts running, he's finished. I have to keep holding on.

The roar of an old mechanical wheeze revives my heart. The spikes slip back into the ground, one by one until they've all disappeared. The room is harmless again so swiftly I fear I may have imagined the danger. I drop the boy back onto the floor and bite down on my lip to swallow the pain welling in my wrist.

The child starts running and accidentally bumps my bare legs.

He screams and shudders and falls to the floor, curled up into himself, sobbing until I consider destroying myself, ridding myself of this world. Tears are streaming fast down my face and I want nothing more than to reach out to him and help him, hug him close, kiss his beautiful cheeks and tell him I'll take care of him, that we'll run away together, that I'll play games with him and read him stories at night and I know I can't. I know I never will. I know it will never be possible.

And suddenly the world shifts out of focus.

I'm overcome by rage, an anger so potent I'm almost elevated off the ground. I'm boiling with blind hatred and disgust. I don't even understand how my feet move in the next instant. I don't understand my hands and what they're doing or how they decided to fly forward, fingers splayed, charging toward the window. I only know I want to feel Warner's neck snap between my own two hands. I want him to experience the same terror he just inflicted upon a child. I want to watch him die. I want to watch him beg for mercy.

I catapult through the concrete walls.

I crush the glass with 10 fingers.

I'm clutching a fistful of gravel and a fistful of fabric at Warner's neck and there are 50 different guns pointed at my head. The air is heavy with cement and sulfur, the glass falling in an agonized symphony of shattered hearts.

I slam Warner into the corroded stone.

"Don't you *dare* shoot her," Warner shouts at the guards. I haven't touched his skin yet, but I have the strangest suspicion that I could smash his rib cage into his heart if I just pressed a little harder.

"I should kill you." My voice is one deep breath, one uncontrolled exhalation.

"You—" He tries to swallow. "You just—you just broke through concrete with your bare hands."

I blink. I don't dare look behind me. But I know without looking backward that he can't be lying. I must have.

I lose focus for one instant.

The guns

click

click

click

Every moment is loaded.

"If any of you hurt her I will shoot you myself," Warner barks.

"But sir—"

"STAND DOWN, SOLDIER—"

The rage is gone. The sudden uncontrollable anger is gone. My mind has already surrendered to disbelief.

Confusion. I don't know what I've done. I obviously don't know what I'm capable of because I had no idea I could destroy anything at all and I'm suddenly so terrified so terrified so terrified of my own two hands. I stumble backward, stunned, and catch Warner watching me hungrily, eagerly, his emerald eyes bright with boyish fascination. He's practically trembling in excitement.

There's a snake in my throat and I can't swallow it down. I meet Warner's gaze. "If you ever put me in a position like that again, I *will* kill you. And I will enjoy it."

I don't even know if I'm lying.

TWENTY-SIX

Adam finds me curled into a ball on the shower floor.

I've been crying for so long I'm certain the hot water is made of nothing but my tears. My clothes are stuck to my skin, wet and useless. I want to drown in ignorance. I want to be stupid, dumb, mute, completely devoid of a brain. I want to cut off my own limbs. I want to be rid of this skin that can kill and these hands that destroy and this body I don't even know how to understand.

Everything is falling apart.

"Juliette . . ." He presses his hand against the glass. I can hardly hear him.

When I don't respond he opens the shower door. He's pelted with rebel raindrops and kicks his boots off before falling to his knees. He reaches in to touch my arms and the feeling only makes me more desperate to die. He sighs and pulls me up, just enough to lift my head. His hands trap my face and his eyes search me, search through me until I look away.

"I know what happened," he says softly.

My throat is a reptile, covered in scales. "Someone should just kill me," I croak.

Adam's arms wrap around me until he's tugged me up

and I'm wobbling on my legs and we're both standing upright. He steps into the shower and slides the door shut behind him.

I gasp.

He holds me up against the wall and I see nothing but his white T-shirt soaked through, nothing but the water dancing down his face, nothing but his eyes full of a world I'm dying to be a part of.

"It wasn't your fault," he whispers.

"It's what I *am*," I choke.

"No. Warner's wrong about you," Adam says. "He wants you to be someone you're not, and you can't let him break you. Don't let him get into your head. He *wants* you to think you're a monster. He wants you to think you have no choice but to join him. He wants you to think you'll never be able to live a normal life—"

"But I won't live a normal life." I swallow a hiccup. "Not ever—I'll n-never—"

Adam is shaking his head. "You will. We're going to get out of here. I won't let this happen to you."

"H-how could you possibly care about someone . . . like *me*?" I'm barely breathing, nervous and petrified but somehow staring at his lips, studying the shape, counting the drops of water tumbling over the hills and valleys of his mouth.

"Because I'm in love with you."

My eyes snap up to read his face. I'm a mess of electricity, humming with life and lightning, hot and cold and my heart is erratic. I'm shaking in his arms and my lips have parted for no reason at all.

His mouth softens into a smile.

My bones have disappeared.

His nose is touching my nose, his lips one breath away, his eyes devouring me already. I can smell him everywhere; I feel him pressed against me. His hands at my waist, gripping my hips, his legs flush against my own, his chest overpowering me with strength. The taste of his words lingers on my lips.

"Really . . . ?" I have one whisper of incredulity, one conscious effort to believe what's never been done. I'm flushed through my feet, filled with unspoken everything.

He looks at me with so much emotion I nearly crack in half.

"God, Juliette—"

And he's kissing me.

Once, twice, until I've had a taste and realize I'll never have enough. He's everywhere up my back and over my arms and suddenly he's kissing me harder, deeper, with a fervent urgent need I've never known before. He breaks for air only to bury his lips in my neck, along my collarbone, up my chin and cheeks and I'm gasping for oxygen and he's destroying me with his hands and we're drenched in water and beauty and the exhilaration of a moment I never knew was possible.

He pulls back with a low groan and I want him to take his shirt off.

I need to see the bird. I need to tell him about the bird.

My fingers are tugging at the hem of his wet clothes and his eyes widen for only a second before he rips the material off himself. He grabs my hands and lifts my arms above my head and pins me against the wall, kissing me until I'm sure I'm dreaming, drinking in my lips with his lips and he tastes like rain and sweet musk and I'm about to explode.

My heart is beating so fast I don't understand why it's still working. He's kissing away the pain, the hurt, the years of self-loathing, the insecurities, the dashed hopes for a future I always pictured as obsolete. He's lighting me on fire, burning away the torture of Warner's games, the anguish that poisons me every single day. The intensity of our bodies could shatter these glass walls.

It nearly does.

For a moment we're just staring at each other, breathing hard until I'm blushing, until he closes his eyes and takes one ragged, steadying breath and I place my hand on his chest. I dare to trace the outline of the bird soaring across his skin, I dare to trail my fingers down the length of his abdomen.

"You're my bird," I tell him. "You're my bird and you're going to help me fly away."

Adam is gone by the time I get out of the shower.

He wrung his clothes out and dried himself off and granted me privacy to change. Privacy I'm not sure I care about anymore. I touch 2 fingers to my lips and taste him everywhere.

But when I step into the room he's not anywhere. He

had to report downstairs.

I stare at the clothes in my closet.

I always choose a dress with pockets because I don't know where else to store my notebook. It doesn't carry any incriminating information, and the one piece of paper that bore Adam's handwriting has since been destroyed and flushed down the toilet, but I like to keep it close to me. It represents so much more than a few words scribbled on paper. It's a small token of my resistance.

I tuck the notebook into a pocket and decide I'm finally ready to face myself. I take a deep breath, push the wet strands of hair away from my eyes, and pad into the bathroom. The steam from the shower has clouded the mirror. I reach out a tentative hand to wipe away a small circle. Just big enough.

A scared face stares back at me.

I touch my cheeks and study the reflective surface, study the image of a girl who's simultaneously strange and familiar to me. My face is thinner, paler, my cheekbones higher than I remember them, my eyebrows perched above 2 wide eyes not blue not green but somewhere in between. My skin is flushed with heat and something named Adam. My lips are too pink. My teeth are unusually straight. My finger is trailing down the length of my nose, tracing the shape of my chin when I see a movement in the corner of my eye.

"You're so beautiful," he says to me.

I duck my head and trip away from the mirror only to

have him catch me in his arms. "I'd forgotten my own face," I whisper.

"Just don't forget who you *are*," he says.

"I don't even know."

"Yes you do." He tilts my face up. "I do."

I stare at the strength in his jaw, in his eyes, in his body. I try to understand the confidence he has in who he thinks I am and realize his reassurance is the only thing stopping me from diving into a pool of my own insanity. He's always believed in me. Even soundlessly, silently, he fought for me. Always.

He's my only friend.

I take his hand and hold it to my lips. "I've loved you forever," I tell him.

The sun rises, rests, shines in his face and he almost smiles, almost can't meet my eyes. His muscles relax, his shoulders find relief in the weight of a new kind of wonder, and he exhales. He touches my cheek, touches my lips, touches the tip of my chin and I blink and he's kissing me, he's pulling me into his arms and into the air and somehow we're on the bed and tangled in each other and I'm drugged with emotion, drugged by each tender moment. His fingers skim my shoulder, rest at my hips. He pulls me closer, whispers my name, drops kisses down my throat and struggles with the stiff fabric of my dress. His hands are shaking so slightly, his eyes brimming with feeling, his heart thrumming with pain and affection and I want to live here, in his arms, in his eyes for the rest of my life.

I slip my hands under his shirt and he chokes on a moan that turns into a kiss that needs me and wants me and has to have me so desperately it's like the most acute form of torture. His weight is pressed into mine, on top of mine, infinite points of feeling for every nerve ending in my body and his right hand is behind my neck and his left hand is reeling me in and his lips are falling down my shirt and I don't understand why I need to wear clothes anymore and I'm thunder and lightning and the possibility of exploding into tears at any inopportune moment. Bliss Bliss Bliss is beating through my chest.

I don't remember what it means to breathe.

I never

ever

ever

knew

what it meant to *feel*.

An alarm is hammering through the walls.

The room blares to life and Adam stiffens, pulls back; his face collapses.

"This is a CODE SEVEN. All soldiers must report to the Quadrant immediately. This is a CODE SEVEN. All soldiers must report to the Quadrant immediately. This is a CODE SEVEN. All soldiers must report to the Quadra—"

Adam is on his feet and pulling me up and the voice is still shouting orders through a speaker system wired into the building. "There's been a breach," he says, his voice broken and breathy, his eyes darting between me and the door. "Jesus. I can't just leave you here—"

"Go," I tell him. "You have to go—I'll be fine—"

Footsteps are thundering through the halls and soldiers are barking at each other so loudly I can hear it through the walls. Adam is still on duty. He has to perform. He has to keep up appearances until we can leave. I know this.

He pulls me close. "This isn't a joke, Juliette—I don't know what's happening—it could be anything—"

A metal click. A mechanical switch. The door slides open and Adam and I jump 10 feet apart.

Adam rushes to exit just as Warner is walking in. They both freeze.

"I'm pretty sure that alarm has been going off for at least a minute, soldier."

"Yes sir. I wasn't sure what to do about her." He's suddenly composed, a perfect statue. He nods at me like I'm an afterthought but I know he's just slightly too stiff in the shoulders. Breathing just a beat too fast.

"Lucky for you, I'm here to take care of that. You may report to your commanding officer."

"Sir." Adam nods, pivots on one heel, and darts out the door. I hope Warner didn't notice his hesitation.

Warner turns to face me with a smile so calm and casual I begin to question whether the building is actually in chaos. He studies my face. My hair. Glances at the rumpled sheets behind me and I feel like I've swallowed a spider. "You took a nap?"

"I couldn't sleep last night."

"You've ripped your dress."

"What are you doing here?" I need him to stop staring at me, I need him to stop drinking in the details of my existence.

"If you don't like the dress, you can always choose a different one, you know. I picked them out for you myself."

"That's okay. The dress is fine." I glance at the clock for no real reason. It's already 4:30 in the afternoon. "Why won't you tell me what's going on?"

He's too close. He's standing too close and he's looking at me and my lungs are failing to expand. "You should really change."

"I don't want to change." I don't know why I'm so nervous. Why he's making me so nervous. Why the space between us is closing too quickly.

He hooks a finger in the rip close to the drop-waist of my dress and I bite back a scream. "This just won't do."

"It's fine—"

He tugs so hard on the rip that it splits open the fabric and creates a slit up the side of my leg. "That's a bit better."

"What are you *doing*—"

His hands snake up my waist and clamp my arms in place and I know I need to defend myself but I'm frozen and I want to scream but my voice is broken broken broken.

"I have a question," he says, and I try to kick him in this worthless dress and he just squeezes me up against the wall, the weight of his body pressing me into place, every inch of him covered in clothing, a protective layer between us. "I said I have a question, Juliette."

His hand slips into my pocket so quickly it takes me a moment to realize what he's done. I'm panting up against the wall, shaking and trying to find my head.

"I'm curious," he says. "What is *this*?"

He's holding my notebook between 2 fingers.

Oh God.

This dress is too tight to hide the outline of the notebook and I was too busy looking at my face to check the dress in the mirror. ~~This is all my fault all my fault all my fault all my fault~~ I can't believe it. This is all my fault. I should've known better.

I say nothing.

He cocks his head. "I don't recall giving you a notebook. I certainly don't remember granting you allowance for any possessions, either."

"I brought it with me." My voice catches.

"Now you're lying."

"What do you want from me?" I panic.

"That's a stupid question, Juliette."

The soft sound of smooth metal slipping out of place. Someone has opened my door.

Click.

"Get your hands off of her before I bury a bullet in your head."

TWENTY-SEVEN

Warner's eyes close very slowly. He steps away very slowly. His lips twitch into a dangerous smile. "Kent."

Adam's hands are steady, the barrel of his gun pressed into the back of Warner's skull. "You're going to clear our exit out of here."

Warner actually laughs. He opens his eyes and whips a gun out of his inside pocket only to point it directly at my forehead. "I will kill her right now."

"You're not that stupid," Adam says.

"If she moves even a millimeter, I will shoot her. And then I will rip you to pieces."

Adam shifts quickly, slamming the butt of his gun into Warner's head. Warner's gun misfires and Adam catches his arm and twists his wrist until his grip on the weapon wavers. I grab the gun from Warner's limp hand and slam the butt of it into his face. I'm stunned by my own reflexes. I've never held a gun before but I guess there's a first time for everything.

I point it at Warner's eyes. "Don't underestimate me."

"Holy *shit*." Adam doesn't bother hiding his surprise.

Warner coughs through a laugh, steadies himself, and tries to smile as he wipes the blood from his nose. "I never underestimate you," he says to me. "I never have."

Adam shakes his head for less than a second before his face splits into an enormous grin. He's beaming at me as he presses the gun harder into Warner's skull. "Let's get out of here."

I grab the two duffel bags stowed away in the armoire and toss one to Adam. We've been packed for a week already. If he wants to make a break for it earlier than expected, I have no complaints.

Warner's lucky we're showing him mercy.

But we're lucky the entire building has been evacuated. He has no one to rely on.

Warner clears his throat. He's staring straight at me when he speaks. "I can assure you, soldier, your triumph will be short-lived. You may as well kill me now, because when I find you, I will thoroughly enjoy breaking every bone in your body. You're a fool if you think you can get away with this."

"I am not your soldier." Adam's face is stone. "I never have been. You've been so caught up in the details of your own fantasies you failed to notice the dangers right in front of your face."

"We can't kill you yet," I add. "You have to get us out of here."

"You're making a huge mistake, Juliette," he says to me. His voice actually softens. "You're throwing away an entire future." He sighs. "How do you know you can trust him?"

I glance at Adam. Adam, the boy who's always defended me, even when he had nothing to gain. I shake my head to

clear it. I remind myself that Warner is a liar. A crazed luna-
tic. A psychotic murderer. He would never try to help me.

I think.

"Let's go before it's too late," I say to Adam. "He's just
trying to stall us until the soldiers get back."

"He doesn't even care about you!" Warner explodes.
I flinch at the sudden, uncontrolled intensity in his voice.
"He just wants a way out of here and he's *using* you!"
He steps forward. "I could love you, Juliette—I would treat
you like a *queen*—"

Adam puts him in a swift headlock and points the gun
at his temple. "You obviously don't understand what's happening here," he says very carefully.

"Then educate me, soldier," Warner's eyes are dancing
flames; dangerous. "Tell me what I'm failing to understand."

"Adam." I'm shaking my head.

He meets my eyes. Nods. Turns to Warner. "Make the
call," he says, squeezing his neck a little tighter. "Get us out
of here *now*."

"Only my dead body would allow her to walk out that
door." Warner exercises his jaw and spits blood on the
floor. "You I would kill for pleasure," he says to Adam. "But
Juliette is the one I want forever."

"I'm not yours to *want*." I'm breathing too hard. I'm
anxious to get out of here. I'm angry he won't stop talking
but as much as I'd love to break his face, he's no good to
us unconscious.

"You could love me, you know." He's smiling a strange sort of smile. "We would be unstoppable. We would change the world. I could make you happy," he says to me.

Adam looks like he might snap Warner's neck. His face is so taut, so tense, so angry. I've never seen him like this before. "You have nothing to offer her, you sick bastard."

Warner presses his eyes shut for one second. "Juliette. Don't make a rash decision. Stay with me. I'll be patient with you. I'll give you time to adjust. I'll take care of you—"

"You're insane." My hands are shaking but I hold the gun to his face again. I need to get him out of my head. I need to remember what he's done to me. "You want me to be a *monster* for you—"

"I want you to live up to your *potential*!"

"Let me go," I say quietly. "I don't want to be your creature. I don't want to hurt people."

"The world has already hurt *you*," he counters. "The world *put* you here. You're here because of them! You think if you leave they're going to accept you? You think you can run away and live a normal life? No one will care for you. No one will come near you—you'll be an outcast like you've always been! Nothing has changed! You belong with me!"

"She belongs with *me*." Adam's voice could cut through steel.

Warner flinches. For the first time he seems to be understanding what I thought was obvious. His eyes are wide, horrified, unbelieving, staring at me with a new kind of anguish. "No." A short, crazed laugh. "Juliette.

Please. Please. Don't tell me he's filled your head with romantic notions. Please don't tell me you fell for his false proclamations—"

Adam slams his knee into Warner's spine. Warner falls to the floor with a muffled crack and a sharp intake of breath. Adam has thoroughly overpowered him. I feel like I should be cheering.

But I'm too anxious. I'm too suspended in disbelief. I'm too insecure to be confident in my own decisions. I need to pull myself together.

"Adam—"

"I *love* you," he says to me, his eyes just as earnest as I remember them, his words just as urgent as they should be. "Don't let him confuse you—"

"You *love* her?" Warner practically spits. "You don't even—"

"Adam." The room shifts in and out of focus. I'm staring at the window. I glance back at him.

His eyes touch his eyebrows. "You want to *jump* out?"

I nod.

"But we're fifteen stories up—"

"What choice do we have if he won't cooperate?" I look at Warner. Cock my head. "There is no Code Seven, is there?"

Warner's lips twitch. He says nothing.

"Why would you do that?" I ask him. "Why would you pull a false alarm?"

"Why don't you ask the soldier you're so suddenly fond

of?" Warner snaps, disgusted. "Why don't you ask yourself why you're trusting your life to someone who can't even differentiate between a real and an imaginary threat?"

Adam swears under his breath.

I lock eyes with him and he tosses me his gun.

He shakes his head. Swears again. Clenches and unclenches his fist. "It was just a drill."

Warner actually laughs.

Adam glances at the door, the clock, my face. "We don't have much time."

I'm holding Warner's gun in my left hand and Adam's gun in my right and pointing them both at Warner's forehead, doing my best to ignore the eyes he's drilling in my direction. Adam uses his free hand to dig in his pockets for something. He pulls out a pair of plastic zip ties and kicks Warner onto his back just before binding his limbs together. Warner's boots and gloves have been discarded on the floor. Adam keeps one boot pressed on his stomach.

"A million alarms are going to go off the minute we jump through that window," he tells me. "We'll have to run, so we can't risk breaking our legs. We can't jump."

"So what do we do?"

"I have rope," he says. "We'll have to climb down. And fast."

He sets to work pulling out a coil of cord attached to a small clawlike anchor. I'd asked him a million times what on earth he would need it for, why he would pack it in his escape bag. He told me a person could never have too much rope.

He turns to me. "I'm going to go down first so I can catch you on the other side—"

Warner laughs loud, too loud. "You can't *catch* her, you fool." He squirms in his plastic shackles. "She's wearing next to nothing. She'll kill you and kill herself from the fall."

My eyes dart between Warner and Adam. I don't have time to entertain Warner's charades any longer. I make a hasty decision. "Do it. I'll be right behind you."

Warner looks confused. "What are you doing?"

I ignore him.

"Wait—"

I ignore him.

"Juliette."

I ignore him.

"Juliette!" His voice is tighter, higher, full of anger and confusion. "He can *touch* you?"

Adam is wrapping his fist in the bedsheet.

"Goddamn it, Juliette, answer me!" Warner is writhing on the floor, unhinged in a way I never thought possible. He looks wild, his eyes disbelieving, horrified. "Has he *touched* you?"

I can't understand why the walls are suddenly on the ceiling. Everything is stumbling sideways.

"Juliette—"

Adam breaks through the glass with one swift crack, one solid punch, and instantly the room is ringing with the sound of hysteria like no alarm I've heard before. The floor is rumbling under my feet, footsteps are thundering down the halls, and I know we're about one minute from being discovered.

Adam throws the rope through the window and slings his pack over his back. "Throw me your bag!" he shouts and I can barely hear him. I toss my duffel and he catches it right before slipping through the window. I run to join him.

Warner tries to grab my leg.

His failed attempt nearly trips me but I manage to stumble my way to the window without losing much time. I glance back at the door and feel my heart racing through my bones. The sound of soldiers running and yelling is getting louder, closer, clearer by the second.

"Hurry!" Adam is calling to me.

"Juliette, *please*—"

Warner swipes for my leg again and I gasp so loud I almost hear it through the sirens shattering my eardrums. ~~I won't look at him. I won't look at him. I won't look at him.~~

I swing one leg through the window and latch on to the cord. My bare legs are going to make this an excruciating ordeal. Both legs are through. My hands are in place. Adam is calling to me from below, and I don't know how far down he is. Warner is shouting my name and I look up despite my best efforts.

His eyes are two shots of green punched through a pane of glass. Cutting through me.

I take a deep breath and hope I won't die.

I take a deep breath and inch my way down the rope.

I take a deep breath and hope Warner doesn't realize what just happened.

I hope he doesn't know he just touched my leg.

And nothing happened.

TWENTY-EIGHT

I'm burning.

The cord is chafing my legs into a fiery mass so painful I'm surprised there's no smoke. I bite back the pain because I have no choice. The mass hysteria of the building is bulldozing my senses, raining down danger all around us. Adam is shouting to me from below, telling me to jump, promising he'll catch me. I'm too ashamed to admit I'm afraid of the fall.

I never have a chance to make my own decision.

Soldiers are already pouring into what used to be my room, shouting and confused, probably shocked to find Warner in such a feeble position. It was really too easy to overpower him. It worries me.

It makes me think we did something wrong.

A few soldiers pop their heads out of the shattered window and I'm frantic to shimmy down the rope but they're already moving to unlatch the anchor. I prepare myself for the nauseating sensation of free fall only to realize they're not trying to drop me. They're trying to reel me back inside.

Warner must be telling them what to do.

I glance down at Adam below me and finally give in to his calls. I squeeze my eyes shut and let go.

And fall right into his open arms.

We collapse onto the ground, but the breath is knocked out of us for only a moment. Adam grabs my hand and then we're running.

There's nothing but empty, barren space stretching out ahead of us. Broken asphalt, uneven pavement, dirt roads, naked trees, dying plants, a yellowed city abandoned to the elements drowning in dead leaves that crunch under our feet. The civilian compounds are short and squat, grouped together in no particular order, and Adam makes sure to stay as far away from them as possible. The loudspeakers are already working against us. The sound of a young, smoothly mechanical female voice drowns out the sirens.

"Curfew is now in effect. Everyone return to their homes immediately. There are rebels on the loose. They are armed and ready to fire. Curfew is now in effect. Everyone return to their homes immediately. There are rebels on the loose. They are armed and ready to fi—"

My sides are cramping, my skin is tight, my throat dry, desperate for water. I don't know how far we've run. All I know is the sound of boots pounding the pavement, the screech of tires peeling out of underground storage units, alarms wailing in our wake.

I look back to see people screaming and running for shelter, ducking away from the soldiers rushing through their homes, pounding down doors to see if we've found refuge somewhere inside. Adam pulls me away from civilization and heads toward the abandoned streets of an earlier decade: old shops and restaurants, narrow side streets and abandoned playgrounds. The unregulated land of our past lives has been strictly off-limits. It's forbidden territory. Everything closed down. Everything broken, rusted shut, lifeless. No one is allowed to trespass here. Not even soldiers.

And we're charging through these streets, trying to stay out of sight.

The sun is slipping through the sky and tripping toward the edge of the earth. Night will be coming quickly, and I have no idea where we are. I never expected so much to happen so quickly and I never expected it all to happen on the same day. I just have to hope to survive but I haven't the faintest idea where we might be headed.

We're darting in a million directions. Turning abruptly, going forward a few feet only to head back in an opposite path. My best guess is that Adam is trying to confuse and/or distract our followers as much as possible. I can do nothing but attempt to keep up.

And I fail.

Adam is a trained soldier. He's built for exactly these kinds of situations. He understands how to flee, how to stay inconspicuous, how to move soundlessly in any space. I, on the other hand, am a broken girl who's known no exercise for too long. My lungs are burning with the effort to inhale oxygen, wheezing with the effort to exhale carbon dioxide.

I'm suddenly gasping so desperately Adam is forced to pull me into a side street. He's breathing a little harder than usual, but I've acquired a full-time job choking on the weakness of my limp body.

Adam takes my face in his hands and tries to focus my eyes. "I want you to breathe like I am, okay?"

I wheeze a bit more.

"Focus, Juliette." His eyes are so determined. Infinitely patient. He looks fearless and I envy him his composure. "Calm your heart," he says. "Breathe exactly as I do."

He takes 3 small breaths in, holds it for a few seconds, and releases it in one long exhalation. I try to copy him. I'm not very good at it.

"Okay. I want you to keep breathing like—" He stops. His eyes dart up and around the abandoned street for a split second. I know we have to move.

Gunshots shatter the atmosphere. I'd never realized just how loud they are. An icy chill seeps through me and I know immediately that they're not trying to kill *me*. They're trying to kill Adam.

Adam doesn't have time for me to catch my breath and find my head. He flips me up and into his arms and takes off in a diagonal dash across another alleyway.

And we're running.

And I'm breathing.

And he shouts, "Wrap your arms around my neck!" and I release the choke hold I have on his T-shirt and I'm stupid enough to feel shy as I slip my arms around him. He readjusts me against him so I'm higher, closer to his chest. He carries me like I weigh less than nothing.

I close my eyes and press my cheek against his neck.

The gunshots are somewhere behind us, but even I can tell from the sound that they're too far away and too far in the wrong direction. We seem to have momentarily out-maneuvered them. Their cars can't even find us, because Adam has avoided all main streets. He seems to have his own map of this city. He seems to know exactly what he's doing—like he's been planning this for a very long time.

Adam drops me to my feet in front of a stretch of chain-link fence.

"Juliette," he says after a breathless moment. "Can you jump this?"

I'm so eager to be more than a useless lump that I nearly sprint up and over the metal barrier. But I'm reckless. And too hasty. I practically rip my dress off and scratch my legs in the process. I wince against the stinging pain, and in the moment it takes me to reopen my eyes, Adam is already standing next to me.

He looks down at my legs and sighs. He almost laughs. I wonder what I must look like, tattered and wild in this shredded dress. The slit Warner created now stops at my hip bone. I must look like a crazed animal.

Adam doesn't seem to mind.

He's slowed down, too. We're moving at a brisk walk now, no longer barreling through the streets. I realize we must be closer to some semblance of safety, but I'm not sure if I should ask questions now, or save them for later. Adam answers my silent thoughts.

"They won't be able to track me out here," he says, and it dawns on me that all soldiers must have some kind of tracking device on their person. I wonder why I never got one.

It shouldn't be this easy to escape.

"Our trackers aren't tangible," he explains. We make a left into another alleyway. The sun is just dipping below the horizon. I wonder where we are. How far away from Reestablished settlements we must be that there are no people here. "It's a special serum injected into our bloodstream," he continues, "and it's designed to work with our bodies' natural processes. It would know, for example, if I died. It's an excellent way to keep track of soldiers lost in combat." He glances at me out of the corner of his eye. He smiles a crooked smile I want to kiss.

"So how did you confuse the tracker?"

His grin grows bigger. He waves one hand around us. "This space we're standing in? It was used for a nuclear power plant. One day the whole thing exploded."

My eyes are as big as my face. "When did that happen?"

"About five years ago. They cleaned it up pretty quickly. Hid it from the media, from the people. No one really knows what happened here. But the radiation alone is enough to kill." He pauses. "It already has."

He stops walking. "I've been through this area a million times already, and I haven't been affected by it. Warner used to send me up here to collect samples of the soil. He wanted to study the effects." He runs a hand through his hair. "I think he was hoping to manipulate the toxicity into a poison of some kind.

"The first time I came up here, Warner thought I'd died. The tracker is linked to all of our main processing systems—an alert goes off whenever a soldier is lost. He knew there was a risk in sending me, so I don't think he was too surprised to hear I'd died. He was more surprised to see me return." He shrugs. "There's something about the chemicals here that counteracts the molecular composition of the tracking device. So basically—right now everyone thinks I'm dead."

"Won't Warner suspect you might be here?"

"Maybe." He squints up at the fading sunlight. Our shadows are long and unmoving. "Or I could've been shot. In any case, it buys us some time."

He takes my hand and grins at me before something slams into my consciousness.

"What about *me*?" I ask. "Can't this radiation kill me?"

"Oh—no." He shakes his head. "One of the reasons why Warner wanted me collecting these samples? You're immune to it, too. He was studying you. He said he found the information in your hospital records. That you'd been tested—"

"But no one ever—"

"—probably without your knowledge, and despite testing positive for the radiation, you were entirely whole, biologically. There was nothing inherently wrong with you."

Nothing inherently wrong with you.

The observation is so blatantly false I actually start

191

laughing. "There's nothing wrong with me? You're kidding, right?"

Adam stares at me so long I begin to blush. Blue blue blue boring into me. His voice is deep, steady. "I don't think I've ever heard you laugh."

I don't know how to respond except with the truth. "Laughter comes from living." I shrug, try to sound indifferent. "I've never really been alive before."

His eyes haven't wavered in their focus. I can almost feel his heart beating against my skin.

He pulls me close. Kisses the top of my head.

"Let's go home," he whispers.

TWENTY-NINE

Home.

Home.

What does he mean?

I part my lips to ask the question and his sneaky smile is the only answer I receive.

Every step is a step away from the asylum, away from Warner, away from the futility of the existence I've always known. Every step is one I take because I *want* to. For the first time in my life, I walk forward because I *want* to, because I feel hope and love and the exhilaration of beauty, because I want to know what it's like to *live*. I could jump up to catch a breeze and live in its windblown ways forever.

I feel like I've been fitted for wings.

Adam leads me into an abandoned shed on the outskirts of this wild field, overgrown by rogue vegetation and crazed bushlike tentacles, scratchy and hideous, likely poisonous to ingest. I wonder if this is where Adam meant for us to stay. I step into the dark space and squint. An outline comes into focus.

There's a car inside.

I blink.

Not just a car. A tank.

Adam can't hide his own eagerness. He looks at my

face for a reaction and seems pleased with my astonishment. "I convinced Warner I'd managed to break one of the tanks I brought up here. These things are designed to run on electricity—so I told him the main unit fried on contact with the chemical traces. That it was corrupted by something in the atmosphere. He arranged for a car to deliver and collect me after that, and said we should leave the tank where it is." He almost smiles. "Warner was sending me up here against his father's wishes, and didn't want anyone to find out he'd broken a 500-thousand-dollar tank. The official report says it was hijacked by rebels."

"Couldn't someone else have come up and seen the tank sitting here?"

Adam opens the passenger door. "The civilians stay far, far away from this place, and no other soldier has been up here. No one else wanted to risk the radiation." He cocks his head. "It's one of the reasons why Warner trusted me with you. He liked that I was willing to die for my *duty*."

"He never thought you'd step out of line," I say, comprehending.

Adam shakes his head. "Nope. And after what happened with the tracking serum, he had no reason to doubt that crazy things were possible up here. I deactivated the tank's electrical unit myself, just in case he wanted to check." He nods back to the monstrous vehicle. "I had a feeling it would come in handy one day. It's always good to be prepared."

Prepared. To run. To escape.

194

I wonder why.

"Come here," he says, his voice gentler. He reaches for me in the dim light and I pretend it's a happy coincidence that his hands brush my bare thighs. I pretend it doesn't feel incredible to have him struggle with the rips in my dress as he helps me into the tank. I pretend I can't see the way he's looking at me as the last of the sun falls below the horizon.

"I need to take care of your legs," he says, a whisper against my skin, electric in my blood. For a moment I don't even understand what he means. I don't even care. My thoughts are so impractical I surprise myself. I've never had the freedom to touch anyone before. Certainly no one has ever *wanted* my hands on them. Adam is an entirely new experience.

Touching him is all I want to think about.

"The cuts aren't too bad," he says, the tips of his fingers running across my calves. I suck in my breath. "But we'll have to clean them up, just in case. Sometimes it's safer being cut by a butcher knife than being scratched by a random scrap of metal. You don't want it to get infected."

He looks up. His hand is now on my knee.

I'm nodding and I don't know why. I wonder if I'm trembling on the outside as much as I am on the inside. I need to say something. "We should probably get going, right?"

"Yeah." He takes a deep breath and seems to return to himself. "Yeah. We have to go." He peers through the evening light. "We have some time before they realize I'm still alive. And we have to use it to our advantage."

"But once we leave this place—won't the tracker start back up again? Won't they know you're not dead?"

"No." He jumps into the driver's side and fumbles for the ignition. There's no key, just a button. I wonder if it recognizes Adam's thumbprint as authorization. A small sputter and the machine roars to life. "Warner had to renew my tracker serum every time I got back. Once it's gone? It's gone." He grins. "So now we can really get the hell out of here."

"But where are we going?" I finally ask.

He shifts into gear before he responds.

"My house."

THIRTY

"You have a *house*?"

Adam laughs and pulls out of the field. The tank is surprisingly fast, surprisingly swift and stealthy. The engine has quieted to a soothing hum, and I wonder if that's why they switched their tanks from gas to electric. It's certainly less conspicuous this way. "Not exactly," he answers. "But a home of sorts. Yeah."

I want to ask and don't want to ask and need to ask and never want to ask. I have to ask. I steel myself. "Your fathe—"

"He's been dead for a while now." Adam's not smiling anymore. His voice is tight with something I know how to place. Pain. Bitterness. Anger.

"Oh."

We drive in silence, each of us absorbed in our own thoughts. I don't dare ask what became of his mother. I only wonder how he turned out so well despite having such a despicable father. And I wonder why he ever joined the army if he hates it so much. Right now, I'm too shy to ask. I don't want to infringe on his emotional boundaries.

God knows I have a million of my own.

I peer out the window and strain my eyes to see what

we're passing through, but I can't make out much more than the sad stretches of deserted land I've grown accustomed to. There are no civilians where we are: we're too far from Reestablished settlements and civilian compounds. I notice another tank patrolling the area not 100 feet away, but I don't think it sees us. Adam is driving without headlights, presumably to draw as little attention to us as possible. I wonder how he's even able to navigate. The moon is the only lamp to light our way.

It's eerily quiet.

I allow my thoughts to drift back to Warner, wondering what must be going on right now, wondering how many people must be searching for me, wondering what lengths he'll go to until he has me back. He wants Adam dead. He wants me alive. He won't stop until I'm trapped beside him.

He can never never never know that I can touch him.

I can only imagine what he'd do if he had access to my body.

I breathe in one quick, sharp, shaky breath and contemplate telling Adam what happened.

No. No. No. No.

I squeeze my eyes shut. I may have misjudged the situation. It was chaotic. My brain was distracted. Maybe I imagined it.

Yes.

Maybe I imagined it.

It's strange enough that Adam can touch me. The

likelihood of there being 2 people in this world who are immune to my touch doesn't seem possible. In fact, the more I think about it, the more I'm determined I must have made a mistake. It could've been anything brushing my leg. Maybe a piece of the sheet Adam abandoned after using it to punch through the window. Maybe a pillow that'd fallen from the bed. Maybe Warner's gloves lying, discarded, on the floor. Yes.

There's no way he could've touched me, because if he had, he would've cried out in agony.

Just like everyone else.

Adam's hand slips silently into mine and I grip his fingers with both my hands, desperate to reassure myself that he has immunity from me. I worry that there's an expiration date on this phenomenon. A clock striking midnight. A pumpkin carriage.

The possibility of losing him

The possibility of losing him

The possibility of losing him is 100 years of solitude I don't want to imagine. I don't want my arms to be devoid of his warmth. His touch. His lips, God his lips, his mouth on my neck, his body wrapped around mine, holding me together as if to affirm that my existence on this earth is not for nothing.

"Juliette?"

I swallow back the bullet in my throat. "Yes?"

"Why are you crying . . . ?" His voice is almost as gentle as his hand as it breaks free from my grip. He touches the tears rolling down my face.

"You can *touch* me," I say for the first time, recognize out loud for the first time. My words fade to a whisper. "You can touch me. You care and I don't know why. You're kind to me and you don't have to be. My own mother didn't care enough to—t-to—" My voice catches and I press my lips together. Glue them shut. Force myself to be still.

I am a rock. A statue. A movement frozen in time. Ice feels nothing at all.

Adam doesn't answer, doesn't say a single word until he pulls off the road and into an old underground parking garage. I realize we've reached some semblance of civilization, but it's pitch-black belowground. I can see next to nothing and once again wonder at how Adam is managing. My eyes fall on the screen illuminated on his dashboard only to realize the tank has night vision. *Of course.*

Adam shuts off the engine. I hear him sigh. I can hardly distinguish his silhouette before I feel his hand on my thigh. Warmth spreads through my limbs. The tips of my fingers and toes are tingling to life.

"Juliette," he whispers, and I realize just how close he is. "It's been me and you against the world forever," he says. "It's always been that way. It's my fault I took so long to do something about it."

"No." I'm shaking my head. "It's not your fault—"

"It is. I fell in love with you a long time ago. I just never had the guts to act on it."

"Because I could've killed you."

He laughs a quiet laugh. "Because I didn't think I deserved you."

"What?"

He touches his nose to mine. Leans into my neck. Wraps a piece of my hair around his fingers and I can't I can't I can't breathe. "You're so . . . *good*," he whispers.

"But my hands—"

"Have never done anything to hurt anyone."

I'm about to protest when he corrects himself. "Not on purpose." He leans back. "You never fought back," he says after a moment. "I always wondered why. You never yelled or got angry or tried to say anything to anyone," he says, and I know we're both back in third fourth fifth sixth seventh eighth ninth grade all over again. "But damn, you must've read a million books." I know he's smiling when he says it. A pause. "You bothered no one, but you were a moving target every day. You could've fought back. You could've hurt everyone if you wanted to."

"I don't want to hurt anyone." My voice is less than a whisper. I can't get the image of 8-year-old Adam out of my head. Lying on the floor. Broken. Abandoned. Crying into the dirt.

The things people will do for power.

"That's why you'll never be what Warner wants you to be."

I'm staring at a point in the blackness, my mind tortured by possibilities. "How can you be sure?"

His lips are so close to mine. "Because you still give a

damn about the world."

I gasp and he's kissing me, deep and powerful and unrestrained. His arms wrap around my back, dipping my body until I'm practically horizontal. My head is on the seat, his frame hovering over me, his hands gripping my hips from under my tattered dress. He's a hot bath, a short breath, 5 days of summer pressed into 5 fingers writing stories on my body. I'm an embarrassing mess of nerves crashing into him. His scent is assaulting my senses.

His eyes

His hands

His chest

His lips

are at my ear when he speaks. "We're here, by the way." He's breathing harder now than when he was running for his life. I feel his heart pounding against my ribs. His words are a broken whisper. "Maybe we should go inside. It's safer." But he doesn't move.

I just nod, my head bobbing on my neck, until I remember he can't see me. I try to remember how to speak, but I'm too focused on the fingers he's running down my thighs to form sentences. There's something about the absolute darkness, about not being able to see what's happening that makes me drunk with a delicious dizziness. "Yes," is all I manage.

He helps me up to a seated position, leans his forehead against mine. "I'm sorry," he says. "It's so hard for me to stop myself." His words tingle on my skin.

I allow my hands to slip under his shirt. I trace the perfectly sculpted lines of his body. He's nothing but lean muscle. "You don't have to," I tell him.

It's 5,000 degrees in the air between us. His fingers are at the dip right below my hip bone, teasing the small piece of fabric keeping me halfway decent. "Juliette . . ."

"Adam?"

My neck snaps up in surprise. Fear. Anxiety. Adam stops moving, frozen in front of me. I'm not sure he's breathing. I look around but can't find a face to match the voice that called his name and begin to panic before Adam is slamming open the door, flying out before I hear it again.

"Adam . . . is that you?"

It's a boy.

"James!"

The muffled sound of impact, 2 bodies colliding, 2 voices too happy to be dangerous.

"I can't believe it's really you! I mean, well, I thought it was you because I thought I heard something and at first I figured it was nothing but then I decided I should probably check just to be sure because what if it *was* you and—" He pauses. "Wait—what are you doing here?"

"I'm home." Adam laughs a little.

"Really?" James squeaks. "Are you home for good?"

"Yeah." He sighs. "Damn it's good to see you."

"I missed you," James says, suddenly quiet.

One deep breath. "Me too, kid. Me too."

"Hey, so, have you eaten anything? Benny just delivered

my dinner package, and I could share some with y—"

"James?"

He pauses. "Yeah?"

"There's someone I want you to meet."

My palms are sweaty. My heart is in my throat. I hear Adam walk back toward the tank and don't realize he's popped his head inside until he hits a switch. A faint emergency light illuminates the cabin. I blink a few times and see a young boy standing about 5 feet away, dirty-blond hair framing a round face with blue eyes that look too familiar. He's pressed his lips together in concentration. He's staring at me.

Adam is opening my door. He helps me to my feet, barely able to control the smile on his face and I'm stunned by the level of my own nervousness. I don't know why I'm so nervous but God I'm nervous. This boy is obviously important to Adam. I don't know why but I feel like this *moment* is important, too. I'm so worried I'm going to ruin everything. I try to fix the ripped folds of my dress, try to soften the wrinkles ironed into the fabric. I run haphazard fingers through my hair. It's useless.

The poor kid will be petrified.

Adam leads me forward. James is a handful of inches short of my height, but it's obvious in his face that he's young, unblemished, untouched by most of the world's harsh realities.

"James? This is Juliette." Adam glances at me.

"Juliette, this is my brother, James."

THIRTY-ONE

His brother.

I try to shake off the nerves. I try to smile at the boy studying my face, studying the pathetic pieces of fabric barely covering my body. How did I not know Adam had a brother? How could I have never known?

James turns to Adam. "*This* is Juliette?"

I'm standing here like a lump of nonsense. I don't remember my manners. "You know who I am?"

James spins back in my direction. "Oh yeah. Adam talks about you *a lot*."

I flush and can't help but glance at Adam. He's staring at a spot on the floor. He clears his throat.

"It's really nice to meet you," I manage.

James cocks his head. "So do you always dress like that?"

I'd like to die a little.

"Hey, kid," Adam interrupts. "Juliette is going to be staying with us for a little while. Why don't you go make sure you don't have any underwear lying on the floor, huh?"

James looks horrified. He darts into the darkness without another word.

It's quiet for so many seconds I lose count. I hear some kind of drip in the distance.

I take a deep breath. Bite my bottom lip. Try to find the right words. Fail. "I didn't know you had a brother."

Adam hesitates. "Is it okay . . . that I do? We'll all be sharing the same space and I—"

"Of course it's okay!" I say hastily. "I just—I mean—are you sure it's okay—for *him*? If I'm here?"

"There's no underwear *anywhere*," James announces, marching forward into the light. I wonder where he disappeared to, where the house is. He looks at me. "So you're going to be staying with us?"

Adam intervenes. "Yeah. She's going to crash with us for a bit."

James looks from me to Adam back to me again. He sticks out his hand. "Well, it's nice to finally meet you."

All the color drains from my face. I can't stop staring at his small hand outstretched, offered to me.

"*James*," Adam says a little curtly.

James starts laughing. "I was only kidding," he says, dropping his hand.

"What?" My head is spinning, confused.

"Don't worry," James says, still chuckling. "I won't touch you. Adam told me all about your magical powers." He rolls his eyes.

"Adam—told—he—*what*?"

"Hey, maybe we should go inside." Adam clears his throat a little too loudly. "I'll just grab our bags real quick—" And he jogs off toward the tank. I'm left staring at James. He doesn't conceal his curiosity.

"How old are you?" he asks me.

"Seventeen."

He nods. "That's what Adam said."

I bristle. "What else did Adam tell you about me?"

"He said you don't have parents, either. He said you're like us."

My voice softens. "How old are *you*?"

"I'll be eleven next year."

I grin. "So you're ten years old?"

He crosses his arms. Frowns. "I'll be twelve in two years."

I think I already love this kid.

The cabin light shuts off and for a moment we're immersed in absolute darkness. A soft *click* and a faint circular glow illuminates the view. Adam has a flashlight.

"Hey, James? Why don't you lead the way for us?"

"Yes, sir!" He skids to a halt in front of Adam's feet, offers us an exaggerated salute, and runs off so quickly there's no way to follow him. I can't help the smile spreading across my face.

Adam's hand slips into mine as we move forward. "You okay?"

I squeeze his fingers. "You told your ten-year-old brother about my magical powers?"

He laughs. "I tell him a lot of things."

"Adam?"

"Yeah?"

"Isn't your *house* the first place Warner will go looking for you? Isn't this dangerous?"

"It would be. But according to public records, I don't have a home."

"And your brother?"

"Would be Warner's first target. It's safer for him where I can watch over him. Warner knows I have a brother, he just doesn't know where. And until he figures it out—which he will—we have to prepare."

"To fight?"

"To fight back. Yeah." Even in the dim light of this foreign space I can see the determination holding him together. It makes me want to sing.

I close my eyes. "Good."

"What's taking you so long?" James shouts in the distance.

And we're off.

The parking garage is located underneath an old abandoned office building buried in the shadows. A fire exit leads directly up to the main floor.

James is so excited he's jumping up and down the stairs, running forward a few steps only to run back to complain we're not coming fast enough. Adam catches him from behind and lifts him off the floor. He laughs. "You're going to break your neck."

James protests but only halfheartedly. He's too happy to have his brother back.

A sharp pang of some distant kind of emotion hits me in the heart. It hurts in a bittersweet way I can't place. I feel warm and numb at the same time.

Adam punches a pass code into a keypad by a massive steel door. There's a soft *click*, a short *beep*, and he turns the handle.

I'm stunned by what I see inside.

THIRTY-TWO

It's a full living room, open and plush. A thick rug, soft chairs, one sofa stretched across the wall. Green and red and orange hues, warm lamps softly lit in the large space. It feels more like a home than anything I've ever seen. The cold, lonely memories of my childhood can't even compare. I feel so safe so suddenly it scares me.

"You like it?" Adam is grinning at me, amused no doubt by the look on my face. I manage to pick my jaw up off the floor.

"I love it," I say, out loud or in my head I'm unsure.

"Adam did it," James says, proud, puffing his chest out a little more than necessary. "He made it for me."

"I didn't *make* it," Adam protests, chuckling. "I just . . . cleaned it up a bit."

"You live here by yourself?" I ask James.

He shoves his hands into his pockets and nods. "Benny stays with me a lot, but mostly I'm here alone. I'm lucky, though."

Adam is dropping our bags onto the couch. He runs a hand through his hair and I watch as the muscles in his back flex, tight, pulled together. I watch as he exhales the tension from his body.

I know why, but I ask anyway. "Why are you lucky?"

"Because I have a visitor. None of the other kids have visitors."

"There are other kids here?" I hope I don't look as horrified as I feel.

James nods so quickly his head wobbles on his neck. "Oh yeah. This whole street. All the kids are here. I'm the only one with my own room, though." He gestures around the space. "This is all mine because Adam got it for me. But everyone else has to share. We have school, sort of. And Benny brings me my food packages. Adam says I can play with the other kids but I can't bring them inside." He shrugs. "It's okay."

The reality of what he's saying spreads like poison in the pit of my stomach.

A street dedicated to orphaned children.

I wonder how their parents died. I don't wonder for long.

I take inventory of the room and notice a tiny refrigerator and a tiny microwave perched on top, both nestled into a corner, see some cabinets set aside for storage. Adam brought as much stuff as he could—all sorts of canned food and nonperishable items. We both brought our toiletries and multiple sets of clothes. We packed enough to survive for at least a little while.

James pulls a tinfoil package out of the fridge and sticks it in the microwave.

"Wait—James—don't—" I try to stop him.

His eyes are wide, frozen. "What?"

"The tinfoil—you can't—you can't put metal in the microwave—"

"What's a microwave?"

I blink so many times the room spins. "What . . . ?"

He pulls the lid off the tinfoil container to reveal a small square. It looks like a bouillon cube. He points to the cube and then nods at the microwave. "It's okay. I always put this in the Automat. Nothing happens."

"It takes the molecular composition of the food and multiplies it." Adam is standing beside me. "It doesn't add any extra nutritional value, but it makes you feel fuller, longer."

"And it's cheap!" James says, grinning as he sticks it back in the contraption.

It astounds me how much has changed. People have become so desperate they're faking *food*.

I have so many questions I'm liable to burst. Adam squeezes my shoulder, gently. He whispers, "We'll talk later, I promise." But I'm an encyclopedia with too many blank pages.

James falls asleep with his head in Adam's lap.

He talked nonstop once he finished his food, telling me all about his sort-of school, and his sort-of friends, and Benny, the elderly lady who takes care of him because "I think she likes Adam better than me but she sneaks me sugar sometimes so it's okay." Everyone has a curfew. No one but soldiers are allowed outside after sunset, each soldier armed and instructed to fire at their own discretion.

"Some people get more food and stuff than other people," James said, but that's because the people are sorted based on what they can provide to The Reestablishment, and not because they're human beings with the right not to starve to death.

My heart cracked a little more with every word he shared with me.

"You don't mind that I talk a lot, huh?" He bit down on his bottom lip and studied me.

"I don't mind at all."

"Everyone says I talk a lot." He shrugged. "But what am I supposed to do when I have so much to say?"

"Hey—about that—" Adam interrupted. "You can't tell anyone we're here, okay?"

James' mouth stopped midmovement. He blinked a few times. He stared hard at his brother. "Not even Benny?"

"No one," Adam said.

For one infinitesimal moment I saw something that looked like raw understanding flash in his eyes. A 10-year-old who can be trusted absolutely. He nodded again and again. "Okay. You were never here."

Adam brushes back wayward strands of hair from James' forehead. He's looking at his brother's sleeping face as if trying to memorize each brushstroke of an oil painting. I'm staring at him staring at James.

Adam looks up and I look down and we're both embarrassed for different reasons.

He whispers, "I should probably put him in bed," but doesn't make an effort to move. James is sound sound sound asleep.

"When was the last time you saw him?" I ask, careful to keep my voice down.

"About six months ago." A pause. "But I talked to him on the phone a lot." Smiles a little. "Told him a lot about you."

I flush. Count my fingers to make sure they're all there. "Didn't Warner monitor your calls?"

"Yeah. But Benny has an untraceable line, and I was always careful to keep it to official reporting, only. In any case, James has known about you for a long time."

"Really?"

He looks up, looks away. Locks eyes with me. "Juliette, I've been searching for you since the day you left. I didn't know what they were going to do to you."

He leans back against the couch. Runs a free hand over his face. Seasons change. Stars explode. Someone is walking on the moon. "You know I still remember the first day you showed up at school?" He laughs a soft, sad laugh. "Maybe I was too young, and maybe I didn't know much about the world, but there was something about you I was immediately drawn to. It's like I just wanted to be near you, like you had this—this *goodness* I never found in my life. This sweetness that I never found at home. I just wanted to hear you talk. I wanted you to see me, to smile at me. Every single day I promised myself I would talk to you. I wanted to *know* you. But every day I was a coward. And one day you just disappeared.

"I'd heard the rumors, but I knew better. I knew you'd never hurt anyone." He looks down. The earth cracks open and I'm falling into the fissure. "It sounds crazy," he says finally, so quietly. "To think that I cared so much without ever talking to you." He hesitates. "But I couldn't stop thinking about you. I couldn't stop wondering where you went. What would happen to you. I was afraid you'd never fight back."

He's silent for so long.

"I had to find you," he whispers. "I asked around everywhere and no one had answers. The world kept falling apart. Things were getting worse and I didn't know what to do. I had to take care of James and I had to find a way to live and I didn't know if joining the army would help but I never forgot about you. I always hoped," he falters, "that one day I would see you again."

I've run out of words. My pockets are full of letters I can't string together and I'm so desperate to say something that I say nothing and my heart is about to burst through my chest.

"Juliette . . . ?"

"You found me." 3 syllables. 1 whisper of astonishment.

"Are you . . . upset?"

I look up and for the first time I realize he's nervous. Worried. Uncertain how I'll react to this revelation. I don't know whether to laugh or cry or kiss every inch of his body.

I want to fall asleep to the sound of his heart beating. I want to know he's alive and well, breathing in and out, strong and sane and healthy forever.

"You're the only one who ever cared," I say. My eyes are filling with tears and I'm blinking them back and feeling the burn in my throat and everything everything everything hurts. The weight of the entire day crashes into me, threatens to break my bones. I want to cry out in happiness, in agony, in joy and the absence of justice. I want to touch the heart of the only person who ever gave a damn.

"I love you," I whisper. "So much more than you will ever know."

His jaw is tight. His mouth is tight. He looks up and tries to clear his throat and I know he needs a moment to pull himself together. I tell him he should probably put James in bed. He nods. Cradles his brother to his chest. Gets to his feet and carries James to the storage closet that's become his bedroom.

I watch him walk away with the only family he has left and I know why Adam joined the army.

I know why he suffered through being Warner's whipping boy. I know why he dealt with the horrifying reality of war, why he was so desperate to run away, so ready to run away as soon as possible. Why he's so determined to fight back.

He's fighting for so much more than himself.

THIRTY-THREE

"Why don't I take a look at those cuts?"

Adam is standing in front of James' door, his hands tucked into his pockets. He's wearing a dark red T-shirt that hugs his torso. His arms are professionally painted with tattoos I now know how to recognize. He catches me staring.

"I didn't really have a choice," he says, examining the consecutive black bands of ink etched into his forearms. "We had to survive. It was the only job I could get."

I meet him across the room, touch the designs on his skin. Nod. "I understand."

He almost laughs. Shakes his head just a millimeter.

"What?" I jerk my hand away.

"Nothing." He grins. Slips his arms around my waist. "It just keeps hitting me. You're really here. In my house."

I bite my lip. "Where'd you get your tattoo from?"

"These?" He looks at his arms again.

"No." I reach for his shirt, tugging it up so unsuccessfully he nearly loses his balance. He stumbles back against the wall. I touch his chest. Touch the bird. "Where'd you get *this* from?"

"Oh." He's looking at me but I'm suddenly distracted

by his body and the cargo pants set a little too low on his hips. I realize he must've taken his belt off. I force my eyes upward. Allow my fingers to fumble down his abs. He takes a tight breath. "I don't know," he says. "I just—I kept dreaming about this white bird. Birds used to fly, you know."

"You used to dream about it?"

"Yeah. All the time." He smiles a little, exhales a little, remembering. "It was nice. It felt good—hopeful. I wanted to hold on to that memory because I wasn't sure it would last. So I made it permanent."

I cover the tattoo with the palm of my hand. "I used to dream about this bird all the time."

"*This* bird?" His eyebrows could touch the sky.

I nod. "This exact one. Until the day you showed up in my cell. I haven't dreamt of it ever since." I peek up at him.

"You're kidding."

I lean my forehead on his chest. Breathe in the scent of him. He wastes no time pulling me closer. Rests his chin on my head, his hands on my back.

And we stand like that until I'm too old to remember a world without his warmth.

Adam cleans my cuts in a bathroom set a little off to the side of the space. It's a miniature room with a toilet, a sink, a small mirror, and a tiny shower. I love all of it. By the time I get out of the bathroom, finally changed and washed up for bed, Adam is waiting for me in the dark.

There are blankets and pillows laid out on the floor and it looks like heaven. I'm so exhausted I could sleep through a few centuries.

I slip in beside him and he scoops me into his arms. The temperature is significantly lower in this place, and Adam is the perfect furnace. I bury my face in his chest and he pulls me tight. I trail my fingers down his naked back, feel the muscles tense under my touch. I rest my hand on the waist of his pants. Hook my finger into a belt loop. Test the taste of the words on my tongue. "I meant it, you know."

His breath is a beat too late. His heart just a beat too fast. "Meant what . . . ?"

I feel so shy suddenly. So blind, so unnecessarily bold. I know nothing about what I'm venturing into. All I know is I don't want anyone's hands on me but his. Forever.

Adam leans back and I can just make out the outline of his face, his eyes always shining in the darkness. I stare at his lips when I speak. "I've never asked you to stop." My fingers rest on the button holding his pants together. "Not once."

He's staring at me, his chest rising and falling. He seems almost numb with disbelief.

I lean into his ear. "Touch me."

And he's nearly undone.

My face is in his hands and my lips are at his lips and he's kissing me and I'm oxygen and he's dying to breathe. His body is almost on top of mine, one hand in my hair, the other slipping behind my knee to pull me closer, higher, tighter. I want to experience him with all 5 senses, drown in the waves of wonder enveloping me.

He takes my hands and presses them against his chest, guides my fingers as they trail down the length of his torso before his lips meet mine again and again and again drugging me into a delirium I never want to escape. But it's not enough. It's still not enough. My heart is racing through my blood, destroying my self-control. He breaks for air and I pull him back, aching, desperate, dying for his touch. His hands slip up under my shirt, skirting my sides, touching me like he's never dared to before, and my top is nearly over my head when a door squeaks open. We both freeze.

"Adam . . . ?"

He can hardly breathe. He tries to lower himself onto the pillow beside me but I can still feel his heat, his figure, his heart pounding in my ears. Adam leans his head up, just a little. Tries to sound normal. "James?"

"Can I come sleep out here with you?"

Adam sits up. He's breathing hard but he's suddenly alert. "Of course you can." A pause. His voice slows, softens. "You have bad dreams?"

James doesn't answer.

Adam is on his feet.

I hear the muffled hiccup of 10-year-old tears, but can barely distinguish the outline of Adam's body holding James together. "I thought you said it was getting better,"

I hear him whisper, but his words are kind, not accusing.

James says something I can't hear.

Adam picks him up, and I realize how tiny James seems in comparison. They disappear into the bedroom only to return with bedding. Only once James is tucked securely in place a few feet from Adam does he finally give in to exhaustion. His heavy breathing is the only sound in the room.

Adam turns to me. I have no idea what James has witnessed at such a tender age. I have no idea what Adam has had to endure in leaving him behind. I have no idea how people live anymore. How they survive.

~~I don't know what's become of my parents.~~

Adam brushes my cheek. Slips me into his arms. Says, "I'm sorry," and I kiss the apology away.

"When the time is right," I tell him.

He leans into my neck. His hands are under my shirt. Up my back.

I bite back a gasp. "Soon."

THIRTY-FOUR

Adam and I forced ourselves 5 feet apart last night, but somehow I wake up in his arms. He's breathing softly, evenly, steadily, a warm hum in the morning air. I blink, peering into the daylight only to be met by a set of big blue eyes on a 10-year-old's face.

"How come you can touch *him*?" James is standing over us with his arms crossed, back to the stubborn boy I remember. There's no trace of fear, no hint of tears threatening to spill down his face. It's like last night never happened. *"Well?"* His impatience startles me.

I jump away from Adam's uncovered upper half so quickly it jolts him awake. A little.

He reaches for me. "Juliette . . . ?"

"You're touching a *girl*!"

Adam sits up so quickly he tangles in the sheets and falls back on his elbows. "Jesus, James—"

"You were sleeping next to a *girl*!"

Adam opens and closes his mouth several times. He glances at me. Glances at his brother. Shuts his eyes and finally sighs. Runs a hand through his morning hair. "I don't know what you want me to say."

"I thought you said she couldn't touch anyone." James is

staring at me now, suspicious.

"She can't."

"Except for you?"

"Right. Except for me."

~~And Warner.~~

"She can't touch anyone except for you."

~~And Warner.~~

"Right."

"That seems awfully *convenient*." James narrows his eyes.

Adam laughs out loud. "Where'd you learn to talk like that?"

James frowns. "Benny says that a lot. She says my excuses are 'awfully convenient.'" He makes air quotes with two fingers. "She says it means I don't believe you. And I don't believe you."

Adam gets to his feet. The early morning light filters through the small windows at the perfect angle, the perfect moment. He's bathed in gold, his muscles taut, his pants still a little low on his hips and I have to force myself to think straight. Adam makes me hungry for things I never knew I could have.

I watch as he drapes an arm over his brother's shoulders before squatting down to meet his gaze. "Can I talk to you about something?" he says. "Privately?"

"Just me and you?" James glances at me out of the corner of his eye.

"Yeah. Just me and you."

"Okay."

I watch the two of them disappear into James' room and wonder what Adam is going to tell him. It takes me a moment to realize James must feel threatened by my sudden appearance. He finally sees his brother after nearly 6 months only to have him come home with a strange girl with crazy magical powers. I nearly laugh at the idea. If only it were magic that made me this way.

I don't want James to think I'm taking Adam away from him.

I slip back under the covers and wait. The morning is cool and brisk and my thoughts begin to wander to Warner. I need to remember that we're not safe. Not yet, maybe not ever. I need to remember never to get too comfortable. I sit up. Pull my knees to my chest and wrap my arms around my ankles.

I wonder if Adam has a plan.

James' door squeaks open. The two brothers step out, the younger before the older. James looks a little pink and he can hardly meet my eyes. He looks embarrassed and I wonder if Adam punished him.

My heart fails for a moment.

Adam claps James on the shoulder. Squeezes. "You okay?"

"I know what a *girlfriend* is—"

"I never said you didn't—"

"So you're his *girlfriend*?" James crosses his arms, looks at me.

I look at Adam because I don't know what else to do.

"Hey, maybe you should be getting ready for school, huh?" Adam opens the refrigerator and hands James a new foil package. I assume it's his breakfast.

"I don't *have* to go," James protests. "It's not like a *real* school, no one *has* to—"

"I want you to," Adam cuts him off. He turns back to his brother with a small smile. "Don't worry. I'll be here when you get back."

James hesitates. "You promise?"

"Yeah." Another grin. Nods him over. "Come here."

James runs forward and clings to Adam like he's afraid he'll disappear. Adam pops the foil food into the Automat and presses a button. He musses James' hair. "You need to get a haircut, kid."

James wrinkles his nose. "I like it."

"It's a little long, don't you think?"

James lowers his voice. "I think *her* hair is really long."

James and Adam glance back at me. I touch my hair without intending to, suddenly self-conscious. I look down. I've never had a reason to cut my hair. I've never even had the tools. No one offers me sharp objects.

I chance a peek and see Adam is still staring at me. James is staring at the Automat.

"I like her hair," Adam says, and I'm not sure who he's talking to.

I watch the two of them as Adam helps his brother get ready for school. James is so full of life, so full of energy, so excited to have his brother around. It makes me wonder what it must be like for a 10-year-old to live on his own. What it must be like for all the kids who live on this street.

I'm itching to get up and change, but I'm not sure what I should do. I don't want to take up the bathroom in case James needs it, or if Adam needs it. I don't want to take up any more space than I already have. It feels so private, so personal, this relationship between Adam and James. It's the kind of bond I've never had, will never have. But being around so much love has managed to thaw my frozen parts into something human. I *feel* human. Like maybe I could be a part of this world. Like maybe I don't have to be a monster. Maybe I'm not a monster.

Maybe things can change.

THIRTY-FIVE

James is at school, Adam is in the shower, and I'm staring at a bowl of granola Adam left for me to eat. It feels so wrong to be eating this food when James has to eat the unidentifiable substance in the foil container. But Adam says James is allocated a certain portion for every meal, and he's required to eat it by law. If he's found wasting it or discarding it, he could be punished. All the orphans are expected to eat the foil food that goes in their Automat. James claims it "doesn't taste too bad."

I shiver slightly in the cool morning air and smooth a hand over my hair, still damp from the shower. The water here isn't hot. It isn't even warm. It's freezing. Warm water is a luxury.

Someone is pounding on the door.

I'm up.
Spinning.
Scanning.
Scared.
They found us is the only thing I can think of. My stomach is a flimsy crepe, my heart a raging woodpecker, my blood a river of anxiety.

Adam is in the shower.

James is at school.

~~I'm absolutely defenseless.~~

I rummage through Adam's duffel bag until I find what I'm looking for. 2 guns, 1 for each hand. 2 hands, just in case the guns fail. I'm finally wearing the kind of clothes that would be comfortable to fight in. I take a deep breath and beg my hands not to shake.

The pounding gets harder.

I point the guns at the door.

"Juliette . . . ?"

I spin back to see Adam staring at me, the guns, the door. His hair is wet. His eyes are wide. He nods toward the extra gun in my hand and I toss it to him without a word.

"If it were Warner he wouldn't be knocking," he says, though he doesn't lower his weapon.

I know he's right. Warner would've shot down the door, used explosives, killed a hundred people to get to me. He certainly wouldn't wait for me to open the door. Something calms inside of me but I won't allow myself to get comfortable. "Who do you think—?"

"It might be Benny—she usually checks up on James—"

"But wouldn't she know he'd be at school right now?"

"No one else knows where I live—"

The pounding is getting weaker. Slower. There's a low, guttural sound of agony.

Adam and I lock eyes.

One more fist flailing into the door. A slump. Another

moan. The thud of a body against the door.

I flinch.

Adam rakes a hand through his hair.

"Adam!" someone cries. Coughs. "Please, man, if you're in there—"

I freeze. The voice sounds familiar.

Adam's spine straightens in an instant. His lips are parted, his eyes astonished. He punches in the pass code and turns the latch. Points his gun toward the door as he eases it open.

"Kenji?"

A short wheeze. A muffled groan. "Shit, man, what took you so long?"

"What the hell are you doing here?" *Click.* I can hardly see through the small slit of the door, but it's clear Adam isn't happy to have company. "Who sent you here? Who are you with?"

Kenji swears a few more times under his breath. *"Look at me,"* he demands, though it sounds more like a plea. "You think I came up here to kill you?"

Adam pauses. Breathes. Doubts. "I have no problem putting a bullet in your back."

"Don't worry, bro. I already have a bullet in my back. Or my leg. Or some shit. I don't even know."

Adam opens the door. "Get up."

"It's all right, I don't mind if you drag my ass inside."

Adam works his jaw. "I don't want your blood on my carpet. It's not something my brother needs to see."

Kenji stumbles up and staggers into the room. I'd heard his voice once before, but never seen his face. Though this probably isn't the best time for first impressions. His eyes are puffy, swollen, purple; there's a huge gash in the side of his forehead. His lip is split, slightly bleeding, his body slumped and broken. He winces, takes short breaths as he moves. His clothes are ripped to shreds, his upper body covered by nothing but a tank top, his well-developed arms cut and bruised. I'm amazed he didn't freeze to death. He doesn't seem to notice me until he does.

He stops. Blinks. Breaks into a ridiculous smile dimmed only by a slight grimace from the pain. "Holy shit," he says, still drinking me in. "Holy *shit*." He tries to laugh. "Dude, you're *insane*—"

"The bathroom is over here." Adam is set in stone.

Kenji moves forward but keeps looking back. I point the gun at his face. He laughs harder, flinches, wheezes a bit. "Dude, you ran off with the crazy chick! You ran off with the psycho girl!" he's calling after Adam. "I thought they made that shit up. What the hell were you thinking? What are you going to do with the psycho chick? No *wonder* Warner wants you dead—OW, MAN, what the *hell*—"

"She's not crazy. And she's not *deaf*, asshole."

The door slams shut behind them and I can only make out their muffled argument. I have a feeling Adam doesn't want me to hear what he has to say to Kenji. Either that, or it's the screaming.

I have no idea what Adam is doing, but I assume it

has something to do with dislodging a bullet from Kenji's body and generally repairing the rest of his wounds as best he can. Adam has a pretty extensive first aid supply and strong, steady hands. I wonder if he picked up these skills in the army. Maybe for taking care of himself. Or maybe his brother. It would make sense.

Health insurance was a dream we lost a long time ago.

I've been holding this gun in my hand for nearly an hour. I've been listening to Kenji scream for nearly an hour and I only know that because I like counting the seconds as they pass by. I have no idea what time it is. I think there's a clock in James' bedroom but I don't want to go into his room without permission.

I stare at the gun in my hand, at the smooth, heavy metal, and I'm surprised to find that I enjoy the way it feels in my grip. Like an extension of my body. It doesn't frighten me anymore.

It frightens me more that I might use it.

The bathroom door opens and Adam walks out. He has a small towel in his hands. I get to my feet. He offers me a tight smile. He reaches into the tiny fridge for the even tinier freezer section. Grabs a couple of ice cubes and drops them into the towel. Disappears into the bathroom again.

I sit back on the couch.

Adam comes out of the bathroom, this time empty-handed, still alone.

I stand back up.

He rubs his forehead, the back of his neck. Meets me on the couch. "I'm sorry," he says.

My eyes are wide. "For what?"

"Everything." He sighs. "Kenji was a sort of friend of mine back on base. Warner had him tortured after we left. For information."

I swallow a gasp.

"He says he didn't say anything—didn't have anything to say, really—but he got messed up pretty bad. I have no idea if his ribs are broken or just bruised, but I managed to get the bullet out of his leg."

I take his hand. Squeeze.

"He got shot running away," Adam says after a moment.

And something slams into my consciousness. I panic. "The tracker serum—"

Adam nods, his eyes heavy, distraught. "I think it might be dysfunctional, but I have no way of knowing for sure. I do know that if it were working as it should, Warner would be here by now. But we can't risk it. We have to get out, and we have to get rid of Kenji before we go."

I'm shaking my head. "How did he even *find* you?"

Adam's face hardens. "He started screaming before I could ask."

"And James?" I whisper, almost afraid to wonder.

Adam drops his head into his hands. "As soon as he gets home, we have to go. We can use this time to prepare." He meets my eyes. "I can't leave James behind. It's not safe for him here anymore."

I touch his cheek and he leans into my hand, holds my palm against his face. Closes his eyes.

"Son of a motherless goat—"

Adam and I break apart. I'm blushing past my hairline. Adam looks annoyed. Kenji is leaning against the wall in the bathroom hallway, holding the makeshift ice pack to his face. Staring at us.

"You can *touch* her? I mean—shit, I just *saw* you touch her but that's not even—"

"You have to go," Adam says to him. "You've already left a chemical trace leading right to my home. We need to leave, and you can't come with us."

"Oh hey—whoa—hold on." Kenji stumbles into the living room, wincing as he puts pressure on his leg. "I'm not trying to slow you down, man. I know a place. A safe place. Like, a legit, super-safe place. I can take you. I can show you how to get there. I know a guy."

"Bullshit." Adam is still angry. "How did you even find me? How did you manage to show up at my *door*, Kenji? I don't trust you—"

"I don't know, man. I swear I don't remember what happened. I don't know where I was running after a certain point. I was just jumping fences. I found a huge field with an old shed. Slept in there for a while. I think I blacked out at one point, either from the pain or from the cold—it is cold as *hell* out here—and the next thing I know, some dude is carrying me. Drops me off at your door. Tells me to shut up about Adam, because Adam lives right here." He grins. Tries to wink. "I guess I was dreaming about you in my sleep."

"Wait—what?" Adam leans forward. "What do you mean some guy was carrying you? What guy? What was his name? How did he know *my* name?"

"I don't know. He didn't tell me, and it's not like I had the presence of mind to ask. But dude was *huge*. I mean, he had to be if he was going to lug my ass around."

"You can't honestly expect me to believe you."

"You have no choice." Kenji shrugs.

"Of course I have a choice." Adam is on his feet. "I have no reason to trust you. No reason to believe a word that's coming out of your mouth."

"Then why am I here with a bullet in my leg? Why hasn't Warner found you yet? Why am I *unarmed*—"

"This could be a part of your plan!"

"And you helped me anyway!" Kenji dares to raise his voice. "Why didn't you just let me die? Why didn't you shoot me dead? Why did you *help* me?"

Adam falters. "I don't know."

"You *do* know. You *know* I'm not here to mess you up. I took a goddamn beating for you—"

"You weren't protecting any information of mine."

"Well, shit, man, what the hell do you want me to say? They were going to *kill* my ass. I had to run. It wasn't my fault some dude dropped me off at your door—"

"This isn't just about *me*, don't you understand? I've worked so hard to find a safe place for my brother and in

234

one morning you ruined *years* of planning. What the hell am I supposed to do now? I have to run until I can find a way to keep him safe. He's too young to have to deal with this—"

"We're *all* too young to have to deal with this shit." Kenji is breathing hard. "Don't fool yourself, bro. No one should have to see what we've seen. No one should have to wake up in the morning and find dead bodies in their living room, but shit happens. We deal with it, and we find a way to *survive*. You're not the only one with problems."

Adam sinks into the sofa. He leans forward with his head in his hands.

Kenji stares at me. I stare back.

He grins and hobbles forward. "You know, you're pretty sexy for a psycho chick."

Click.

Kenji is backing up with his hands in the air. Adam is pressing a gun to his forehead. "Show some respect, or I will burn it into your skull."

"I was *kidding*—"

"Like hell you were."

"Damn, Adam, calm the hell down—"

"Where's the 'super-safe place' you can take us?" I'm up, gun still gripped in my hand. I move into position next to Adam. "Or are you making that up?"

Kenji lights up. "No, that's real. Very real. In fact, I may or may not have mentioned something about you. And the dude who runs the place may or may not be ridiculously interested in meeting you."

"You think I'm some kind of freak you can show off to your friends?"

Kenji clears his throat. "Not a freak. Just . . . interesting."

I point my gun at his nose. "I'm so interesting I can kill you with my bare hands."

A barely perceptible flash of fear flickers in his eyes. "You sure you're not crazy?"

"No." I cock my head. "I'm not sure."

Kenji grins. Looks me up and down. "Well damn. But you make crazy sound so *good*."

"I'm about five inches from breaking your face," Adam warns him, his body stiff with anger, his eyes narrowed, unflinching. "I don't need another reason."

"What?" Kenji laughs, undeterred. "I haven't been this close to a chick in *way too long*, bro. And crazy or not—"

"I'm not interested."

Kenji turns to face me. "Well I'm not sure I blame you. I look like hell right now. But I clean up okay." He attempts a grin. "Give me a couple days. You might change your mind—"

Adam elbows him in the face and doesn't apologize.

THIRTY-SIX

Kenji is swearing, bleeding, and tripping his way toward the bathroom, holding his nose together.

Adam pulls me into James' bedroom.

"Tell me something," he says. He stares up at the ceiling, takes a hard breath. "Tell me anything—"

I try to focus his eyes, grasp his hands, gentle gentle gentle. I wait until he's looking at me. "Nothing is going to happen to James. We'll keep him safe. I promise."

His eyes are full of pain like I've never seen them before. He parts his lips. Presses them together. "He doesn't even know about our dad." It's the first time he's acknowledged the issue. It's the first time he's acknowledged that I know anything about it. "I never wanted him to know. I made up stories for him. I wanted him to have a chance to be *normal*." His lips are spelling secrets and my ears are spilling ink, staining my skin with his stories. "I don't want anyone to touch him. I don't want to screw him up. I can't—God I can't let it happen," he says to me. Hushed. Quiet.

I've searched the world for all the right words and my mouth is full of nothing.

"It's never enough," he whispers. "I can never do enough. He still wakes up screaming. He still cries himself to sleep.

237

He sees things I can't control." He blinks a million times. "So many people, Juliette."

I hold my breath.

"Dead."

I touch the word on his lips and he kisses my fingers.

"I don't know what to do," he says, and it's like a confession that costs him so much more than I can understand. Control is slipping through his fingers and he's desperate to hold on. *Tell me what to do.*

I study the shape of his lips, the strong lines of his face, the eyelashes any girl would kill for, the deep dark blue of the eyes I've learned to swim in. I offer him the only possibility I have. "Kenji's plan might be worth considering."

"You trust him?" Adam leans back, surprised.

"I don't think he's lying about knowing a place we can go."

"I don't know if that's a good idea."

"Why not . . . ?"

Something that might not be a laugh. "I might kill him before we even get there."

My lips twist into a sad smile. "There isn't any other place for us to hide, is there?"

He shakes his head. Once. Fast. Tight.

I squeeze his hand. "Then we have to try."

"What the hell are you doing in there?" Kenji shouts through the door. Pounds it a couple times. "I mean, shit, man, I don't think there's *ever* a bad time to get naked, but now is probably not the best time for a nooner. So unless

238

you want to get killed, I suggest you get your ass out here. We have to get ready to go."

"I might kill him right now." Adam changes his mind.

I take his face in my hands, tip up on my toes and kiss him. "I love you."

He's looking into my eyes and looking at my mouth and his voice is a husky whisper. "Yeah?"

"Absolutely."

The 3 of us are packed and ready to go before James comes home from school. Adam and I collected the most important basic necessities: food, clothes, money Adam saved up. He keeps looking around the small space like he can't believe he's lost it so easily. I can only imagine how much work he put into it, how hard he tried to make a home for his little brother. My heart is in pieces for him.

His friend is an entirely different species.

Kenji is nursing new bruises, but seems in reasonable spirits, excited for reasons I can't fathom. He's oddly upbeat. It seems impossible to discourage him and I can't help but admire his determination. But he won't stop staring at me.

"So how come you can touch Adam?" he says after a moment.

"I don't know."

He snorts. "Bull."

I shrug. I don't feel the need to convince him that I have no idea how I got so lucky.

"How'd you even know you could touch him? Some

239

kind of sick experiment?"

"Where's this place you're taking us?"

"Why are you changing the subject?" He's grinning. I'm sure he's grinning. I refuse to look at him, though. "Maybe you can touch *me*, too. Why don't you try?"

"You don't want me to touch you."

"Maybe I do." He's definitely grinning.

"Maybe you should leave her alone before I put that bullet back in your leg," Adam offers.

"I'm sorry—is a lonely man not allowed to make a move, Kent? Maybe I'm actually interested. Maybe you should back the hell off and let her speak for herself."

Adam runs a hand through his hair. Always the same hand. Always through his hair. He's flustered. Frustrated. Maybe even embarrassed.

"I'm still not interested," I remind him, an edge to my voice.

"Yes, but let's not forget that *this*"—he motions to his battered face—"is not permanent."

"Well, I'm permanently uninterested." I want so badly to tell him that I'm unavailable. I want to tell him that I'm in a serious relationship. I want to tell him that Adam's made me promises.

But I can't.

I have no idea what it means to be in a relationship. I don't know if saying "I love you" is code for "mutually exclusive," and I don't know if Adam was serious when he told James I was his girlfriend. Maybe it was an excuse, a cover, an easy answer to an otherwise complicated question.

I wish he would say something to Kenji—I wish he would tell him that we're together officially, exclusively.

But he doesn't.

And I don't know why.

"I don't think you should decide until the swelling goes down," Kenji continues matter-of-factly. "It's only fair. I have a pretty spectacular face."

Adam chokes on a cough that I think was a laugh.

"You know, I could've sworn we used to be cool," Kenji says, leveling his gaze at Adam.

"I can't remember why."

Kenji bristles. "Is there something you want to say to me?"

"I don't trust you."

"Then why am I still here?"

"Because I trust *her.*"

Kenji turns to look at me. He manages a goofy smile. "Aw, you trust me?"

"As long as I have a clear shot." I tighten my hold on the gun in my hand.

His grin is crooked. "I don't know why, but I kind of like it when you threaten me."

"That's because you're an idiot."

"Nah." He shakes his head. "You've got a sexy voice. Makes everything sound naughty."

Adam stands up so suddenly he nearly knocks over the coffee table.

Kenji bursts out laughing, wheezing against the pain of his injuries. "Calm down, Kent, *damn.* I'm just messing with you guys. I like seeing psycho chick get all intense."

He glances at me, lowers his voice. "I mean that as a compliment—because, you know"—he waves a haphazard hand in my direction—"psycho kind of works for you."

"What the hell is wrong with you?" Adam turns on him.

"What the hell is wrong with *you*?" Kenji crosses his arms, annoyed. "Everyone is so uptight in here."

Adam squeezes the gun in his hand. Walks to the door. Walks back. He's pacing.

"And don't worry about your brother," Kenji adds. "I'm sure he'll be here soon."

Adam doesn't laugh. He doesn't stop pacing. His jaw twitches. "I'm not worried about my brother. I'm trying to decide whether to shoot you now or later."

"Later," Kenji says, collapsing onto the couch. "You still need me right now."

Adam tries to speak but he's out of time.

The door clicks, beeps, unlatches open.

James is home.

THIRTY-SEVEN

"I'm really happy you're taking it so well—I am—but James, this really isn't something to be excited about. We're running for our lives."

"But we're doing it *together*," he says for the fifth time, a huge grin overcrowding his face. He took a liking to Kenji almost too quickly, and now the pair of them are conspiring to turn our predicament into some kind of elaborate mission. "And I can *help*!"

"No, it's not—"

"Of course you can—"

Adam and Kenji speak at the same time. Kenji recovers first. "Why can't he help? Ten years old is old enough to help."

"That's not your call," Adam says, careful to control his voice. I know he's staying calm for his brother's sake. "And it's none of your business."

"I'll finally get to come *with* you," James says. "And I want to help."

James took the news in stride. He didn't even flinch when Adam explained the real reason why he was home, and why we were together. I thought seeing Kenji's bruised and battered face would scare him, but James was eerily unmoved. It occurred to me he must've seen much worse.

Adam takes a few deep breaths before turning to Kenji. "How far?"

"By foot?" Kenji looks uncertain for the first time. "At least a few hours. If we don't do anything stupid, we should be there by nightfall."

"And if we take a car?"

Kenji blinks. His surprise dissolves into an enormous grin. "Well, shit, Kent, why didn't you say so sooner?"

"Watch your mouth around my brother."

James rolls his eyes. "I hear worse stuff than that *every day*. Even Benny uses bad words."

"*Benny?*"

"Yup."

"What does she—" Adam stops. Changes his mind. "That doesn't mean it's okay for you to keep hearing it."

"I'm almost eleven!"

"Hey, little man," Kenji interrupts. "It's okay. It's my fault. I should be more careful. Besides, there are ladies present." Kenji winks at me.

I look away. Look around.

It's difficult for *me* to leave this humble home, so I can only imagine what Adam must be experiencing right now. I think James is too excited about the dangerous road ahead of us to realize what's happening. To truly understand that he'll never be coming back here.

We're all fugitives running for our lives.

"So, what—you stole a car?" Kenji asks.

"A tank."

Kenji barks out a laugh. "Nice."

"It's a little conspicuous for daytime, though."

"What's *conspicuous* mean?" James asks.

"It's a little too . . . noticeable." Adam cringes.

"*SHIT.*" Kenji stumbles up to his feet.

"I told you to watch your mouth—"

"Do you hear that?"

"Hear what—?"

Kenji's eyes are darting in every direction. "Is there another way out of here?"

Adam is up. "JAMES—"

James runs to his brother's side. Adam checks his gun. I'm slinging bags over my back, Adam is doing the same, his attention diverted by the front door.

"HURRY—"

"How close—?"

"THERE'S NO TIME—"

"What do you—"

"KENT, RUN—"

And we're running, following Adam into James' room. Adam rips a curtain off of one wall to reveal a hidden door just as 3 beeps sound from the living room.

Adam shoots the lock on the exit door.

Something explodes not 15 feet behind us. The sound shatters in my ears, vibrates through my body. I nearly collapse from the impact. Gunshots are everywhere. Footsteps are pounding into the house but we're already running through the exit. Adam hauls James up and into his arms and we're flying through the sudden burst of light blinding our way through the streets. The rain has stopped. The roads are slick and muddy. There are children everywhere, bright colors of small bodies suddenly screaming at our approach. There's no point being inconspicuous anymore.

They've already found us.

Kenji is lagging behind, stumbling his way through the last of his adrenaline rush. We turn into a narrow alleyway and he slumps against the wall. "I'm sorry," he pants, "I can't—you can leave me—"

"We can't leave you—," Adam shouts, looking everywhere, drinking in our surroundings.

"That's sweet, bro, but it's okay—"

"We need you to show us where to go!"

"Well, *shit*—"

"You said you would help us—"

"I thought you said you had a *tank*—"

"If you hadn't noticed, there's been an unexpected change of plans—"

"I can't keep up, Kent. I can barely walk—"

"You have to *try*—"

"There are rebels on the loose. They are armed and ready to fire. Curfew is now in effect. Everyone return to their homes immediately. There are rebels on the loose. They are armed and ready to fi—"

The loudspeakers sound around the streets, drawing attention to our bodies huddled together in the narrow alley. A few people see us and scream. Boots are getting louder. Gunshots are getting wilder.

I take a moment to analyze the surrounding buildings

and realize we're not in a settled compound. The street James lives on is unregulated turf: a series of abandoned office buildings crammed together, leftovers from our old lives. I don't understand why he's not living in a compound like the rest of the population. I don't have time to figure out why I only see two age groups represented, why the elderly and the orphaned are the only residents, why they've been dumped on illegal land with soldiers who are not supposed to be here. I'm afraid to consider the answers to my own questions and in a panicked moment I fear for James' life. I spin around as we run, glimpsing his small body bundled in Adam's arms.

His eyes are squeezed shut so tight I'm sure it hurts.

Adam swears under his breath. He kicks down the door of a deserted building and yells for us to follow him inside.

"I need you to stay here," he says to Kenji. "And I'm out of my mind, but I need to leave James with you. I need you to watch out for him. They're looking for Juliette, and they're looking for *me*. They won't even expect to find you two."

"What are you going to do?" Kenji asks.

"I need to steal a car. Then I'll come back for you." James doesn't even protest as Adam puts him down. His little lips are white. His eyes wide. His hands trembling. "I'll come back for you, James," Adam says again. "I promise."

James nods over and over and over again. Adam kisses his head, once, hard, fast. Drops our duffel bags on the floor. Turns to Kenji. "If you let anything happen to him, I will kill you."

Kenji doesn't laugh. He takes a deep breath. "I'll take care of him."

"Juliette?"

He takes my hand, and we disappear into the streets.

THIRTY-EIGHT

The roads are packed with pedestrians trying to escape. Adam and I hide our guns in the waistbands of our pants, but our wild eyes and jerky movements seem to give us away. Everyone stays away from us, darting in opposite directions, some squeaking, shouting, crying, dropping the things in their hands. But for all the people, I don't see a single car in sight. They must be hard to come by, especially in this area.

Adam pushes me to the ground just as a bullet flies past my head. He shoots down another door and we run through the ruins toward another exit, trapped in the maze of what used to be a clothing store. Gunshots and footsteps are close behind. There must be at least a hundred soldiers following us through these streets, clustered in different groups, dispersed in different areas of the city, ready to capture and kill.

But I know they won't kill me.

It's Adam I'm worried about.

I try to stay as close as possible to his body because I'm certain Warner has given them orders to bring me back alive. My efforts, however, are weak at best. Adam has enough height and muscle to dwarf me. Anyone with an excellent shot would be able to target him. They could shoot him right in the head.

Right in front of me.

He turns to fire two shots. One falls short. Another elicits a strangled cry. We're still running.

Adam doesn't say anything. He doesn't tell me to be brave. He doesn't ask me if I'm okay, if I'm scared. He doesn't offer me encouragement or assure me that we'll be just fine. He doesn't tell me to leave him behind and save myself. He doesn't tell me to watch his brother in case he dies.

He doesn't need to.

We both understand the reality of our situation. Adam could be shot right now. I could be captured at any moment. This entire building might suddenly explode. Someone could've discovered Kenji and James. We might all die today. The facts are obvious.

But we know we need to take the chance just the same.

Because moving forward is the only way to survive.

The gun is growing slick in my hands, but I hold on to it anyway. My legs are screaming against the pain, but I push them faster anyway. My lungs are sawing my rib cage in half, but I force them to process oxygen anyway. I have to keep moving. There's no time for human deficiencies.

The fire escape in this building is nearly impossible to find. Our feet pound the tiled floors, our hands searching through the bleak light for some kind of outlet, some kind of access to the streets. This building is larger than we anticipated, massive, with hundreds of possible directions. I realize it must have been a *warehouse* and not just a store. Adam ducks behind an abandoned desk, pulling me down with him.

"Don't be stupid, Kent—you can only run for so long!" someone shouts. The voice isn't more than 10 feet away.

Adam swallows. Clenches his jaw. The people trying to kill him are the same ones he used to eat lunch with. Train with. Live with. He *knows* these guys. I wonder if that knowledge makes this worse.

"Just give us the girl," a new voice adds. "Just give us the girl and we won't shoot you. We'll pretend we lost you. We'll let you go. Warner only wants the girl."

Adam is breathing hard. He grips the gun in his hand. Pops his head out for a split second and fires. Someone falls to the floor, screaming.

"KENT, YOU SON OF A—"

Adam uses the moment to run. We jump out from behind the desk and fly toward a stairwell. Gunshots miss us by millimeters. I wonder if these two men are the only ones who followed us inside.

The spiral staircase winds into a lower level, a basement of some kind. Someone is trying to aim for Adam, but our erratic movements make it almost impossible. The chance of him hitting me instead are too high. He's unleashing a mass of expletives in our wake.

Adam knocks things over as we run, trying to create any kind of distraction, any kind of hazard to slow down the soldier behind us. I spot a pair of storm cellar doors and realize this area must've been ravaged by tornadoes. The weather is turbulent; natural disasters are common. Cyclones must have ripped this city apart. "Adam—" I tug on his arm. We hide behind a low wall. I point to our only possible escape route.

He squeezes my hand. "Good eye." But we don't move until the air shifts around us. A misstep. A muffled cry. It's almost blindingly black down here; it's obvious the electricity was disconnected a long time ago. The soldier has tripped on one of the obstacles Adam left behind.

Adam holds the gun close to his chest. Takes a deep breath. Turns and takes a swift shot.

His aim is excellent.

An uncontrolled explosion of curse words confirms it. Adam takes a hard breath. "I'm only shooting to disable," he says. "Not to kill."

"I know," I tell him. Though I wasn't sure.

We run for the doors and Adam struggles to pull the latch open. It's nearly rusted shut. We're getting desperate. I don't know how long it'll be until we're discovered by another set of soldiers. I'm about to suggest we shoot it open when Adam finally manages to break it free.

He kicks open the doors and we stumble out onto the street. There are 3 cars to choose from.

I'm so happy I could cry.

"It's about time," he says.

But it's not Adam who says it.

THIRTY-NINE

There's blood everywhere.

Adam is on the ground, clutching his body, but I don't know where he's been shot. There are soldiers swarming around him and I'm clawing at the arms holding me back, kicking the air, crying out into the emptiness. Someone is dragging me away and I can't see what they've done to Adam. Pain is seizing my limbs, cramping my joints, breaking every single bone in my body. I don't understand why the agony isn't finding escape in my screams. Why my mouth is covered with someone else's hand.

"If I let go, you have to promise not to scream," he says to me.

He's touching my face with his bare hands and I don't know where I dropped my gun.

Warner drags me into a still-functioning building and kicks open a door. Hits a switch. Fluorescent lights flicker on with a dull hum. There are paintings taped to the walls, alphabet rainbows stapled to corkboards. Small tables scattered across the room. We're in a classroom.

I wonder if this is where James goes to school.

Warner drops his hand. His glassy green eyes are so delighted I'm petrified. "God I missed you," he says to me.

"You didn't actually think I'd let you go so easily?"

"You shot Adam," are the only words I can think of. My mind is muddled with disbelief. I keep seeing his beautiful body crumpled on the ground, red red red. I need to know if he's alive. He has to be alive.

Warner's eyes flash. "Kent is dead."

"No—"

Warner backs me into a corner and I realize I've never been so defenseless in my life. Never so vulnerable. 17 years I spent wishing my curse away, but in this moment I'm more desperate than ever to have it back. Warner's eyes warm unexpectedly. His constant shifts in emotion are difficult to anticipate. Difficult to counter.

"Juliette," he says. He touches my hand so gently it startles me. "Did you notice? It seems I am immune to your gift." He studies my eyes. "Isn't that incredible? Did you notice?" he asks again. "When you tried to escape? Did you feel it . . . ?"

Warner who misses absolutely nothing. Warner who absorbs every single detail.

Of course he knows.

But I'm shocked by the tenderness in his voice. The sincerity with which he wants to know. He's like a feral dog, crazed and wild, thirsty for chaos, simultaneously aching for recognition and acceptance.

Love.

"We can really be together," he says to me, undeterred by my silence. He pulls me close, too close. I'm frozen.

Stunned in grief, in disbelief.

His hands reach for my face, his lips for mine. My brain is on fire, ready to explode from the impossibility of this moment. I feel like I'm watching it happen, detached from my own body, incapable of intervening. More than anything else, I'm shocked by his gentle hands, his earnest eyes.

"I want you to choose me," he says. "I want you to choose to be with me. I want you to *want* this—"

"You're insane," I choke. "You're psychotic—"

"You're only afraid of what you're capable of." His voice is soft. Easy. Slow. Deceptively persuasive. I'd never realized before just how attractive his voice is. "Admit it," he says. "We're perfect for each other. You want the power. You love the feel of a weapon in your hand. You're . . . attracted to me."

I try to swing my fist but he catches my arms. Pins them to my sides. Presses me up against the wall. He's so much stronger than he looks. "Don't lie to yourself, Juliette. You're going to come back with me whether you like it or not. But you can choose to want it. You can choose to enjoy it—"

"I will *never*," I breathe, broken. "You're sick—you're a sick, twisted monster—"

"That's not the right answer," he says, and seems genuinely disappointed.

"It's the only answer you'll ever get from me."

His lips come too close. "But I love you."

"No you don't."

His eyes close. He leans his forehead against mine. "You have no idea what you do to me."

"I hate you."

He shakes his head very slowly. Dips down. His nose brushes the nape of my neck and I stifle a horrified shiver that he misunderstands. His lips touch my skin and I actually whimper. "God I'd love to just take a bite out of you."

I notice the gleam of silver in his inside jacket pocket.

I feel a thrill of hope. A thrill of horror. Brace myself for what I need to do. Spend a moment mourning the loss of my dignity.

And I relax.

He feels the tension seep out of my limbs and responds in turn. He smiles, loosens his clamp on my shoulders. Slips his arms around my waist. I swallow the vomit threatening to give me away.

His military jacket has a million buttons and I wonder how many I'll have to undo before I can get my hands on the gun. His hands are exploring my body, slipping down my back and it's all I can do to keep from doing something reckless. I'm not skilled enough to overpower him and I have no idea why he's able to touch me. I have no idea why I was able to crash through concrete yesterday. I have no idea where that energy came from.

Today he's got every advantage and it's not time to give myself away.

Not yet.

I place my hands on his chest. He presses me into the

line of his body. Tilts my chin up to meet his eyes. "I'll be good to you," he whispers. "I'll be so good to you, Juliette. I promise."

I hope I'm not visibly shaking.

And he kisses me. Hungrily. Desperately. Eager to break me open and taste me. I'm so stunned, so horrified, so cocooned in insanity I forget myself. I stand there frozen, disgusted. My hands slip from his chest. All I can think about is Adam and blood and Adam and the sound of gun-shots and Adam lying in a pool of blood and I nearly shove him off of me. But Warner will not be discouraged.

He breaks the kiss. Whispers something in my ear that sounds like nonsense. Cups my face in his hands and this time I remember to pretend. I pull him closer, grab a fistful of his jacket and kiss him as hard as I can, my fin-gers already attempting to release the first of his buttons. Warner tastes like peppermint, smells like gardenias. His arms are strong around me, his lips soft, almost sweet against my skin. There's an electric charge between us I hadn't anticipated.

My head is spinning.

His lips are on my neck, tasting me, devouring me, and I force myself to think straight. I force myself to understand the perversion of this situation. I don't know how to recon-cile the confusion in my mind, my hesitant repulsion, my inexplicable chemical reaction to his lips. I need to get this over with. Now.

I reach for his buttons.

And he's unnecessarily encouraged.

Warner lifts me by the waist, hoists me up against the wall, his hands cupping my backside, forcing my legs to wrap around him. He doesn't realize he's given me the perfect angle to reach into his coat.

His lips find my lips, his hands slip under my shirt and he's breathing hard, tightening his grip around me, and I practically rip open his jacket in desperation. I can't let this go on much longer. I have no idea how far Warner wants to push things, but I can't keep encouraging his insanity.

I need him to lean forward just an inch more—

My hands wrap around the gun.

I feel him freeze. Pull back. I watch his face phase through frames of confusion/dread/anguish/horror/anger. He drops me to the floor just as my fingers pull the trigger for the very first time.

The power and strength of the weapon is disarming, the sound so much louder than I anticipated. The reverberations are vibrating through my ears and every pulse in my body.

It's a sweet sort of music.

A small sort of victory.

Because this time the blood is not Adam's.

FORTY

Warner is down.

I am up and running away with his gun.

I need to find Adam. I need to steal a car. I need to find James and Kenji. I need to learn how to drive. I need to drive us to safety. I need to do everything in exactly that order.

Adam can't be dead.

Adam is not dead.

Adam will not be dead.

My feet slap the pavement to a steady rhythm, my shirt and face spattered with blood, my hands still shaking slightly in the setting sun. A sharp breeze whips around me, jolting me out of the crazed reality I seem to be swimming in. I take a hard breath, squint up at the sky, and realize I don't have much time before I lose the light. The streets, at least, have long since been evacuated. But I have exactly zero idea where Warner's men might be.

I wonder if Warner has the tracker serum as well. I wonder if they'd know if he were dead.

I duck into dark corners, try to read the streets for clues, try to remember where Adam fell to the ground, but my memory is too weak, too distracted, my brain too broken to process these kinds of details. That horrible instant is one mess of insanity in my mind. I can't make any sense of it and Adam could be anywhere by now. They could've done anything to him.

I don't even know what I'm looking for.

~~I might be wasting my time.~~

I hear sudden movement and dart into a side street, my fingers tightening around the weapon slick in my grip. Now that I've actually fired a gun, I feel more confident with it in my hands, more aware of what to expect, how it functions. But I don't know if I should be happy or horrified that I'm so comfortable so quickly with something so lethal.

Footsteps.

I slide up against the wall, my arms and legs flat against the rough surface. I hope I'm buried in the shadows. I wonder if anyone's found Warner yet.

I watch a soldier walk right past me. He has rifles slung across his chest, a smaller sort of automatic weapon in his hands. I glance down at the gun in my own hand and realize I have no idea how many different kinds there are. All I know is some are bigger than others. Some have to be reloaded constantly. Some, like the one I'm holding, do not. Maybe Adam can teach me the differences.

Adam.

I suck in my breath and move as stealthily as I can through the streets. I spot a particularly dark shadow on a stretch of the sidewalk ahead of me and make an effort to avoid it. But as I get closer I realize it's not a shadow. It's a stain.

Adam's blood.

I squeeze my jaw shut until the pain scares away the screams. I take short, tiny, too-quick breaths. I need to focus. I need to use this information. I need to pay attention—

I need to follow the trail of blood.

Whoever dragged Adam away still hasn't come back to clean the mess. There's a steady spattered drip that leads away from the main roads and into the poorly lit side streets. The light is so dim I have to bend down to search for the spots on the ground. I'm losing sight of where they lead. There are fewer here. I think they've disappeared entirely. I don't know if the dark spots I'm finding are blood or old gum pounded into the pavement or drops of life from another person's flesh. Adam's path has disappeared.

I back up several steps and retrace the line.

I have to do this 3 times before I realize they must've taken him inside. There's an old steel structure with an older rusted door that looks like it's never been opened. It looks like it hasn't been used in years. I don't see any other options.

I wiggle the handle. It's locked.

I try to open it, but I only manage to bruise my body. I could shoot it down like I've seen Adam do, but I'm not certain of my aim nor my skill with this gun, and I'm not sure I can afford the noise. I can't make my presence known.

There has to be another way into this building.

There is no other way into this building.

My frustration is escalating. My desperation is crippling. My hysteria is threatening to break me and I want to scream

261

until my lungs collapse. Adam is in this building. He has to be in this building.

I'm standing right outside this building and I can't get inside.

This can't be happening.

I clench my fists, try to beat back the maddening futility enveloping me but I feel crazed. Wild. Insane. The adrenaline is slipping away, my focus is slipping away, the sun is setting on the horizon and I remember James and Kenji and Adam Adam Adam ~~and Warner's hands on my body and his lips on my mouth and his tongue tasting my neck~~ and all the blood

everywhere

everywhere

everywhere

and I do something stupid.

I punch the door.

In one instant my mind catches up to my muscle and I brace myself for the impact of steel on skin, ready to feel the agony of shattering every bone in my right arm. But my fist flies through 12 inches of steel like it's made of butter. I'm stunned. I harness the same volatile energy and kick my foot through the door. I use my hands to rip the steel to shreds, clawing my way through the metal like a wild animal.

It's incredible. Exhilarating. Completely feral.

This must be how I broke through the concrete in Warner's torture chamber. Which means I still have no idea how I broke through the concrete in Warner's torture chamber.

I climb through the hole I've created and slip into the shadows. It's not hard. The entire place is cloaked in darkness. There are no lights, no sounds of machines or electricity. Just another abandoned warehouse left to the elements.

I check the floors but there's no sign of blood. My heart soars and plummets at the same time. I need him to be okay. I need him to be alive. Adam is not dead. He can't be.

Adam promised James he'd come back for him.

He'd never break that promise.

I move slowly at first, wary, worried that there might be soldiers around, but it doesn't take long for me to realize there's no sound of life in this building. I decide to run.

I tuck caution in my pocket and hope I can reach for it if I need to. I'm flying through doors, spinning around turns, drinking in every detail. This building wasn't just a warehouse. It was a factory.

Old machines clutter the walls, conveyor belts are frozen in place, thousands of boxes of inventory stacked precariously in tall heaps. I hear a breath, a stifled cough.

I'm bolting through a set of swinging double doors, searching out the feeble sound, fighting to focus on the tiniest details. I strain my ears and hear it again.

Heavy, labored breathing.

The closer I get, the more clearly I can hear him. It has to be him. My gun is up and aimed to fire, my eyes careful now, anticipating attackers. My legs move swiftly, easily, silently. I nearly shoot a shadow the boxes have cast on the floor. I take a steadying breath. Round another corner.

And nearly collapse.

Adam is hanging from bound wrists, shirtless, bloodied and bruised everywhere. His head is bent, his neck limp, his left leg drenched in blood despite the tourniquet wrapped around his thigh. I don't know how long the weight of his entire body has been hanging from his wrists. I'm surprised he hasn't dislocated his shoulders. He must still be fighting to hold on.

The rope wrapped around his wrists is attached to some kind of metal rod running across the ceiling. I look more closely and realize the rod is a part of a conveyor belt. That Adam is on a conveyor belt.

That this isn't just a factory.

It's a slaughterhouse.

I'm too poor to afford the luxury of hysteria right now.

I need to find a way to get him down, but I'm afraid to approach. My eyes search the space, certain that there are guards around here somewhere, soldiers prepared for this kind of ambush. But then it occurs to me that perhaps I was never really considered a threat. Not if Warner managed to drag me away.

No one would expect to find me here.

I climb onto the conveyor belt and Adam tries to lift his head. I have to be careful not to look too closely at his wounds, not to let my imagination cripple me. Not here. Not now.

"Adam . . . ?"

His head snaps up with a sudden burst of energy. His

264

eyes find me. His face is almost unscathed; there are only minor cuts and bruises to account for. Focusing on the familiar gives me a modicum of calm.

"Juliette—?"

"I need to cut you down—"

"Jesus, Juliette—how did you find me?" He coughs. Wheezes.

"Later." I reach up to touch his face. "I'll tell you everything later. First, I need to find a knife."

"My pants—"

"What?"

"In"—he swallows—"in my pants—"

I reach for his pocket and he shakes his head. I look up. "Where—"

"There's an inside pocket *in* my pants—"

I practically rip his clothes off. There's a small pocket sewn into the lining of his cargo pants. I slip my hand inside and retrieve a compact pocketknife. A butterfly knife. I've seen these before.

They're illegal.

I start stacking boxes on the conveyor belt. Climb my way up and hope to God I know what I'm doing. The knife is extremely sharp, and it works quickly to undo the bindings. I realize a little belatedly that the rope holding him together is the same cord we used to escape.

Adam is cut free. I'm climbing down, refolding the knife and tucking it into my pocket. I don't know how I'm going to get Adam out of here. His wrists are rubbed raw, bleeding, his body pounded into one piece of pain, his leg bloodied through with a bullet.

He nearly falls over.

I try to hold on as tenderly as possible. He doesn't say a word about the pain, tries so hard to hide the fact that he's having trouble breathing. He's wincing against the torture of it all, but doesn't whisper a word of complaint. "I can't believe you found me," is all he says.

And I know I shouldn't. I know now isn't the time. I know it's impractical. But I kiss him anyway.

"You are not going to die," I tell him. "We are going to get out of here. We are going to steal a car. We are going to find James and Kenji. And then we're going to get safe."

He stares at me. "Kiss me again," he says.

And I do.

It takes a lifetime to make it back to the door. Adam had been buried deep in the recesses of this building, and finding our way to the front is even more difficult than I expected. Adam is trying so hard, moving as fast as he can, but he still isn't fast at all. "They said Warner wanted to kill me himself," he explains. "That he shot me in the leg on purpose, just to disable me. It gave him a chance to drag you away and come back for me later. Apparently his plan was to torture me to death." He winces. "He said he wanted to enjoy it. Didn't want to rush through killing me." A hard laugh. A short cough.

~~His hands on my body his hands on my body his hands on my body~~ —

"So they just tied you up and abandoned you here?"

"They said no one would ever find me. They said the building is made entirely of concrete and reinforced steel and no one can break in. Warner was supposed to come back for me when he was ready." He stops. Looks at me. "God, I'm so happy you're okay."

I offer him a smile. Try to keep my organs from falling out. Hope the holes in my head aren't showing.

He pauses when we reach the door. The metal is a mangled mess. It looks like a wild animal attacked it and lost. "How did you—"

"I don't know," I admit. Try to shrug, be indifferent. "I just punched it."

"You just punched it."

"And kicked it a little."

He's smiling and I want to cry. I have to focus on his face. I can't let my eyes digest the travesty of his body.

"Come on," I tell him. "Let's go do something illegal."

I leave Adam in the shadows and dart up to the edge of the main road, searching for abandoned vehicles. We have to travel up 3 different side streets until we finally find one.

"How are you holding up?" I ask him, afraid to hear the answer.

He presses his lips together. Does something that looks like a nod. "Okay."

That's not good.

"Wait here."

It's pitch-black, not a single street lamp in sight. This

is good. Also bad. It gives me an extra edge, but makes me extra vulnerable to attack. I have to be careful. I tiptoe up to the car.

I'm fully prepared to smash the glass open, but I check the handle first. Just in case.

The door is unlocked.

The keys are in the ignition.

There's a bag of groceries in the backseat.

Someone must've panicked at the sound of the alarm and unexpected curfew. They must've dropped everything and run for cover. Unbelievable. This would be absolutely perfect if I had any idea how to drive.

I run back for Adam and help him hobble into the passenger side. As soon as he sits down I can tell just how much pain he's in. Bending his body in any way at all. Putting pressure on his ribs. Straining his muscles. "It's okay," he tells me, he lies to me. "I can't stand on my feet for much longer."

I reach into the back and rummage through the grocery bags. There's real food inside. Not just strange bouillon cubes designed to go into Automats, but fruit and vegetables. Even Warner never gave us bananas.

I hand the yellow fruit to Adam. "Eat this."

"I don't think I can—" He pauses. Stares at the form in his hands. "Is this what I think it is?"

"I think so."

We don't have time to process the impossibility. I peel it open for him. Encourage him to take a small bite. I hope it's a good thing. I heard bananas have potassium. I hope he can keep it down.

I try to focus on the machine under my feet.

"How long do you think we'll have until Warner finds us?" Adam asks.

I take a few bites of oxygen. "I don't know."

A pause. "How did you get away from him . . . ?"

I'm staring straight out the windshield when I answer. "I shot him."

"No." Surprise. Awe. Amazement.

I show him Warner's gun. It has a special engraving in the hilt.

Adam is stunned. "So he's . . . dead?"

"I don't know," I finally admit, ashamed. I drop my eyes, study the grooves in the steering wheel. "I don't know for sure." I took too long to pull the trigger. It was stiffer than I expected it to be. Harder to hold the gun between my hands than I'd imagined. Warner was already dropping me when the bullet flew into his body. I was aiming for his heart.

I hope to God I didn't miss.

We're both too quiet.

"Adam?"

"Yeah?"

"I don't know how to drive."

FORTY-ONE

"You're lucky this isn't a stick shift." He tries to laugh.

"Stick shift?"

"Manual transmission."

"What's that?"

"A little more complicated."

I bite my lip. "Do you remember where we left James and Kenji?" I don't even want to consider the possibility that they've moved. Been discovered. Anything. I can't fathom the idea.

"Yes." I know he's thinking exactly what I'm thinking.

"How do I get there?"

Adam tells me the right pedal is for gas. The left is to brake. I have to shift into *D* for *drive*. I use the steering wheel to turn. There are mirrors to help see behind me. I can't turn on my headlights and will have to rely on the moon to light my way.

I turn on the ignition, press the brake, shift into drive. Adam's voice is the only navigation system I need. I release the brake. Press the gas. Nearly crash into a wall.

This is how we finally get back to the abandoned building.

Gas. Brake. Gas. Brake. Too much gas. Too much brake.

Adam doesn't complain and it's almost worse. I can only imagine what my driving is doing for his injuries. I'm grateful that at least we're not dead, not yet.

I don't know why no one has spotted us. I wonder if maybe Warner really is dead. I wonder if everything is in chaos. I wonder if that's why there are no soldiers in this city. They've all disappeared.

I think.

I almost forget to put the car in park when we reach the vaguely familiar broken building. Adam has to reach over and do it for me. I help him transition into the backseat, and he asks me why.

"Because I'm making Kenji drive, and I don't want your brother to have to see you like this. It's dark enough that he won't see your body. I don't think he should have to see you hurt."

He nods after an infinite moment. "Thank you."

And I'm running toward the broken building. Pulling the door open. I can only barely make out two figures in the dark. I blink and they come into focus. James is asleep with his head in Kenji's lap. The duffel bags are open, cans of food discarded on the floor. They're okay.

Thank God they're okay.

I could die of relief.

Kenji pulls James up and into his arms, struggling a little under the weight. His face is smooth, serious, unflinching. He doesn't smile. He doesn't say anything stupid. He studies my eyes like he already knows, like he already understands why it took us so long to get back, like there's only one reason why I must look like hell right now, why I have blood all over my shirt. Probably on my face. All over my hands. "How is he?"

And I nearly lose it right there. "I need you to drive."

He takes a tight breath. Nods several times. "My right leg is still good," he says to me, but I don't think I'd care even if it weren't. We need to get to his safe place, and my driving isn't going to get us anywhere.

Kenji settles a sleeping James into the passenger side, and I'm so happy he's not awake for this moment.

I grab the duffel bags and carry them to the backseat. Kenji slides in front. Looks in the rearview mirror. "Good to see you alive, Kent."

Adam almost smiles. Shakes his head. "Thank you for taking care of James."

"You trust me now?"

A small sigh. "Maybe."

"I'll take a *maybe*." He grins. Turns on the car. "Let's get the hell out of here."

Adam is shaking.

His bare body is finally cracking under the cold weather, the hours of torture, the strain of holding himself together for so long. I'm scrambling through the duffel bags, searching for a coat, but all I find are shirts and sweaters. I don't know how to get them on his body without causing him pain.

272

I decide to cut them up. I take the butterfly knife to a few of his sweaters and slice them open, draping them over him like a blanket. I glance up. "Kenji—does this car have a heater?"

"It's on, but it's pretty crappy. It's not working very well."

"How much longer until we get there?"

"Not too much."

"Have you seen anyone that might be following us?"

"No." He pauses. "It's weird. I don't understand why no one has noticed a car flying through these streets after curfew. Something's not right."

"I know."

"And I don't know what it is, but obviously my tracker serum isn't working. Either they really just don't give a shit about me, or it's legit not working, and I don't know why."

A tiny detail sits on the outskirts of my consciousness. I examine it. "Didn't you say you slept in a shed? That night you ran away?"

"Yeah, why?"

"Where was it . . . ?"

He shrugs. "I don't know. Some huge field. It was weird. Crazy shit growing in that place. I almost ate something I thought was fruit before I realized it smelled like ass."

My breath catches. "It was an empty field? Barren? Totally abandoned?"

"Yeah."

"The nuclear field," Adam says, a dawning realization in his voice.

"What nuclear field?" Kenji asks.

I take a moment to explain.

"Holy crap." Kenji grips the steering wheel. "So I could've died? And I didn't?"

I ignore him. "But then how did they find us? How did they figure out where you live—?"

"I don't know," Adam sighs. Closes his eyes. "Maybe Kenji is lying to us."

"Come on, man, what the hell—"

"Or," Adam interrupts, "maybe they bought out Benny."

"No." I gasp.

"It's possible."

We're all silent for a long moment. I try to look out the window but it's very nearly useless. The night sky is a vat of tar suffocating the world around us.

I turn to Adam and find him with his head tilted back, his hands clenched, his lips almost white in the blackness. I wrap the sweaters more tightly around his body. He stifles a shudder.

"Adam . . ." I brush a strand of hair away from his forehead. His hair has gotten a little long and I realize I've never really paid attention to it before. It's been cropped short since the day he stepped into my cell. I never would've thought his dark hair would be so soft. Like melted chocolate. I wonder when he stopped cutting it.

He flexes his jaw. Pries his lips open. Lies to me over and over again. "I'm okay."

"Kenji—"

"Five minutes, I promise—I'm trying to gun this thing—"

I touch his wrists, trace the tender skin with my fingertips. The bloodied scars. I kiss the palm of his hand. He takes a broken breath. "You're going to be okay," I tell him.

His eyes are still closed. He tries to nod.

"Why didn't you tell me you two were together?" Kenji asks unexpectedly. His voice is even, neutral.

"What?" Now is not the time to be blushing.

Kenji sighs. I catch a glimpse of his eyes in the rearview mirror. The swelling is almost completely gone. His face is healing. "I'd have to be *blind* to miss something like that. I mean, hell, just the way he looks at you. It's like the guy has never seen a woman in his life. Like putting food in front of a starving man and telling him he can't eat it."

Adam's eyes fly open. I try to read him but he won't look at me.

"Why didn't you just tell me?" Kenji says again.

"I never had a chance to ask," Adam answers. His voice is less than a whisper. His energy levels are dropping too fast. I don't want him to have to talk. He needs to conserve his strength.

"Wait—are you talking to me or her?" Kenji glances back at us.

"We can discuss this later—," I try to say, but Adam shakes his head.

"I told James without asking you. I made . . . an assumption." He stops. "I shouldn't have. You should have a choice.

You should always have a choice. And it's your choice if you want to be with me."

"Hey, so, I'm just going to pretend like I can't hear you guys anymore, okay?" Kenji makes a random motion with his hand. "Go ahead and have your moment."

But I'm too busy studying Adam's eyes, his soft soft lips. His furrowed brow.

I lean into his ear, lower my voice. Whisper the words so only he can hear me.

"You're going to get better," I promise him. "And when you do, I'm going to show you exactly what choice I've made. I'm going to memorize every inch of your body with my lips."

He exhales suddenly. Swallows hard.

His eyes are burning into me. He looks almost feverish, and I wonder if I'm making things worse.

I pull back and he stops me. Rests his hand on my thigh. "Don't go," he says. "Your touch is the only thing keeping me from losing my mind."

FORTY-TWO

"We're here, and it's nighttime. So according to my calcula-
tions, we must not have done anything stupid."

Kenji shifts into park. We're underground again, in
some kind of elaborate parking garage. One minute we
were aboveground, the next we've disappeared into a ditch.
It's next to impossible to locate, much less to spot in the
darkness. Kenji was telling the truth about this hideout.

I've been busy trying to keep Adam awake for the past few
minutes. His body is fighting exhaustion, blood loss, hunger,
a million different points of pain. I feel so utterly useless.

"Adam has to go straight to the medical wing," Kenji
announces.

"They have a medical wing?"

Kenji grins. "This place has everything. It will blow your
goddamn mind." He hits a switch on the ceiling. A faint
light illuminates the old sedan. Kenji steps out the door.
"Wait here—I'll get someone to bring out a stretcher."

"What about James?"

"Oh." Kenji's mouth twitches. "He, uh—he's going to be
asleep for a little while longer."

"What do you mean . . . ?"

He clears his throat. Once. Twice. Smooths out the

wrinkles in his shirt. "I, uh, may or may not have given him something to . . . ease the pain of this journey."

"You gave a ten-year-old a *sleeping pill*?" I'm afraid I'm going to break his neck.

"Would you rather he were awake for all of this?"

"Adam is going to kill you."

Kenji glances at Adam's drooping lids. "Yeah, well, I guess I'm lucky he won't be able to kill me tonight." He hesitates. Ducks into the car to run his fingers through James's hair. Smiles a little. "The kid is a saint. He'll be perfect in the morning."

"I can't *believe* you—"

"Hey, hey—" He holds up his hands. "Trust me. He's going to be just fine. I just didn't want him to be any more traumatized than he had to be." He shrugs. "Hell, maybe Adam will agree with me."

"I'm going to murder you." Adam's voice is a soft mumble.

Kenji laughs. "Keep it together, bro, or I'll think you don't really mean it."

Kenji disappears.

I watch Adam, encourage him to stay awake. Tell him he's almost safe. Touch my lips to his forehead. Study every shadow, every outline, every cut and bruise of his face. His muscles relax, his features lose their tension. He exhales a little more easily. I kiss his top lip. Kiss his bottom lip. Kiss his cheeks. His nose. His chin.

Everything happens so quickly after that.

4 people run out toward the car. 2 older than me, 2 older

than them. A pair of men. A pair of women. "Where is he?" the older woman asks. They're all looking around, anxious. I wonder if they can see me staring at them.

Kenji opens Adam's door. Kenji is no longer smiling. In fact, he looks . . . different. Stronger. Faster. Taller, even. He's in control. A figure of authority. These people *know* him.

Adam is lifted onto the stretcher and assessed immediately. Everyone is talking at once. Something about broken ribs. Something about losing blood. Something about airways and lung capacity and *what happened to his wrists?* Something about checking his pulse and *how long has he been bleeding?* The young male and female glance in my direction. They're all wearing strange outfits.

Strange suits. All white with gray stripes down the side. I wonder if it's a medical uniform.

They're carrying Adam away.

"Wait—" I trip out of the car. "Wait! I want to go with him—"

"Not now." Kenji stops me. Softens. "You can't be with him for what they need to do. Not now."

"What do you mean? What are they going to do to him?" The world is fading in and out of focus, shades of gray flickering as stilted frames, broken movements. Suddenly nothing makes sense. Suddenly everything is confusing me. Suddenly my head is a piece of pavement and I'm being trampled to death. I don't know where we are. I don't know who Kenji is. Kenji was Adam's friend. Adam knows him. Adam. My Adam. Adam who is being taken away from me and I can't go with him and I want to go with him but they won't let me go with him and I don't know why—

"They're going to help him—*Juliette*—I need you to focus. You can't fall apart right now. I know it's been a crazy day—but I need you to stay calm." His voice. So steady. So suddenly articulate.

"Who *are* you . . . ?" I'm beginning to panic. I want to grab James and run but I can't. He's done something to James and even if I knew how to wake him up, I can't touch him. I want to rip my nails out. *"Who are you—"*

Kenji sighs. "You're starving. You're exhausted. You're processing shock and a million other emotions right now. Be logical. I'm not going to hurt you. You're safe now. Adam is safe. James is safe."

"I want to be with him—I want to see what they're going to do to him—"

"I can't let you do that."

"What are you going to do to me? Why did you bring me here . . . ?" My eyes are wide, darting in every direction. I'm spinning, stranded in the middle of the ocean of my own imagination and I don't know how to swim. "What do you want from me?"

Kenji looks down. Rubs his forehead. Reaches into his pocket. "I really didn't want to have to do this."

I think I'm screaming.

FORTY-THREE

I'm an old creaky staircase when I wake up.

Someone has scrubbed me clean. My skin is like satin. My eyelashes are soft, my hair is smooth, brushed out of its knots; it gleams in the artificial light, a chocolate river lapping the pale shore of my skin, soft waves cascading around my collarbone. My joints ache; my eyes burn from an insatiable exhaustion. My body is naked under a heavy sheet. I've never felt so pristine.

I'm too tired to be bothered by it.

My sleepy eyes take inventory of the space I'm in, but there's not much to consider. I'm lying in bed. There are 4 walls. 1 door. A small table beside me. A glass of water on the table. Fluorescent lights humming above me. Everything is white.

Everything I've ever known is changing.

I reach for the glass of water and the door opens. I pull the sheet up as high as it will go.

"How are you feeling?"

A tall man is wearing plastic glasses. Black frames. A simple sweater. Pressed pants. His sandy-blond hair falls into his eyes.

He's holding a clipboard.

"Who are you?"

He grabs a chair I hadn't noticed was sitting in the corner. Pushes it forward. Sits down beside my bed. "Do you feel dizzy? Disoriented?"

"Where's Adam?"

He's holding his pen to a sheet of paper. Writing something down. "Do you spell your last name with two *rs*? Or just one?"

"What did you do with James? Where's Kenji?"

He stops. Looks up. He can't be more than 30. He has a crooked nose. A day of scruff. "Can I at least make sure you're doing all right? Then I'll answer your questions. I promise. Just let me get through the basic protocol here."

I blink.

How do I feel. I don't know.

Did I have any dreams. I don't think so.

Do I know where I am. No.

Do I think I'm safe. I don't know.

Do I remember what happened. Yes.

How old am I. 17.

What color are my eyes. I don't know.

"You don't know?" He puts down his pen. Takes off his glasses. "You can remember exactly what happened yesterday, but you don't know the color of your own eyes?"

"I think they're green. Or blue. I'm not sure. Why does it matter?"

"I want to be sure you can recognize yourself. That you haven't lost sight of your person."

"I've never really known my eye color, though. I've only looked in the mirror once in the last three years."

The stranger stares at me, his eyes crinkled in concern. I finally have to look away.

"How did you touch me?" I ask.

"I'm sorry?"

"My body. My skin. I'm so . . . clean."

"Oh." He bites his thumb. Marks something on his papers. "Right. Well, you were covered in blood and filth when you came in, and you had some minor cuts and bruises. We didn't want to risk infection. Sorry for the personal intrusion—but we can't allow anyone to bring that kind of bacteria in here. We had to do a superficial detox."

"That's fine—I understand," I hurry on. "But *how*?"

"Excuse me?"

"How did you touch me?" Surely he must know. How could he not know? God I hope he knows.

"Oh—" He nods, distracted by the words he's scribbling on his clipboard. Squints at the page. "Latex."

"What?"

"Latex." He glances up for a second. Sees my confusion. "Gloves?"

"Right." Of course. Gloves. Even Warner used gloves until he figured it out.

~~Until he figured it out. Until he figured it out. Until he figured it out.~~

I replay the moment over and over and over in my mind. The split second I took too long to jump from the window.

283

The moment of hesitation that changed everything. The instant I lost all control. All power. Any point of dominance. He's never going to stop until he finds me and it's my own fault.

I need to know if he's dead.

I have to force myself to be still. I have to force myself not to shake, shudder, or vomit. I need to change the subject. "Where are my clothes?"

"They've been destroyed for the same reasons you needed to be sanitized." He picks up his glasses. Slips them on. "We have a special suit for you. I think it'll make your life a lot easier."

"A special suit?" I look up. Part my lips in surprise.

"Yes. We'll get to that part a bit later." He pauses. Smiles. There's a dimple in his chin. "You're not going to attack me like you did Kenji, are you?"

"I attacked Kenji?" I cringe.

"Just a little bit." He shrugs. "At least now we know he's not immune to your touch."

"I *touched* him?" I sit up straight and nearly forget to pull my sheet up with me. "I'm so sorry—"

"I'm sure he'll appreciate the apology. But it's all right. We've been expecting some destructive tendencies. You've been having one hell of a week."

"Are you a psychologist?"

"Sort of." He brushes the hair away from his forehead.

"Sort of?"

He laughs. Pauses. Rolls the pen between his fingers.

"Yes. For all intents and purposes, I am a psychologist. Sometimes."

"What is that supposed to mean . . . ?"

He parts his lips. Presses them shut. Seems to consider answering me but examines me instead. He stares for so long I feel my face go hot. He starts scribbling furiously.

"What am I doing here?" I ask him.

"Recovering."

"How long have I been here?"

"You've been asleep for almost fourteen hours. We gave you a pretty powerful sedative." Looks at his watch. "You seem to be doing well." Hesitates. "You look very well, actually."

"Where's Adam?"

Blondie takes a deep breath. Underlines something on his papers. His lips twitch into a smile.

"Where is he?"

"Recovering." He finally looks up.

"He's okay?"

Nods. "He's okay."

I stare at him. "What does that mean?"

2 knocks at the door.

The bespectacled stranger doesn't move. He rereads his notes. "Come in," he calls.

Kenji walks inside, a little hesitant at first. He peeks at me, his eyes cautious. I never thought I'd be so happy to see him. But while it's a relief to see a face I recognize, my stomach immediately twists into a knot of guilt, knocking me over from the inside. I wonder how badly I must've hurt him. He steps forward.

My guilt disappears.

I look more closely and realize he's perfectly unharmed. His leg is working fine. His face is back to normal. His eyes are no longer puffy, his forehead is repaired, smooth, untouched. He was right.

He does have a spectacular face.

A defiant jawline. Perfect eyebrows. Eyes as black as his hair. Sleek. Strong. A bit dangerous.

"Hey, beautiful."

"I'm sorry I almost killed you," I blurt out.

"Oh." He startles. Shoves his hands into his pockets. "Well. Glad we got that out of the way." I notice he's wearing a destroyed T-shirt. Dark jeans. I haven't seen anyone wear jeans in such a long time. Army uniforms, cotton basics, and fancy dresses are all I've known lately.

I can't really look at him. "I panicked," I try to explain. I clasp and unclasp my fingers.

"I figured." He cocks an eyebrow.

"I'm sorry."

"I know."

I nod. "You look better."

He cracks a grin. Stretches. Leans against the wall, arms crossed at his chest, legs crossed at the ankles. "This must be difficult for you."

"Excuse me?"

"Looking at my face. Realizing I was right. Realizing

you made the wrong decision." He shrugs. "I understand. I'm not a proud man, you know. I'd be willing to forgive you."

I gape at him, unsure whether to laugh or throw something. "Don't make me touch you."

He shakes his head. "It's incredible how someone can look so right and feel so wrong. Kent is a lucky bastard."

"I'm sorry—" Psychologist-man stands up. "Are you two finished here?" He looks to Kenji. "I thought you had a purpose."

Kenji pushes off the wall. Straightens his back. "Right. Yeah. Castle wants to meet her."

FORTY-FOUR

"Now?" Blondie is more confused than I am. "But I'm not done examining her."

Kenji shrugs. "He wants to meet her."

"Who's Castle?" I ask.

Blondie and Kenji look at me. Kenji looks away. Blondie doesn't.

He cocks his head. "Kenji didn't tell you anything about this place?"

"No." I falter, uncertain, glancing at Kenji, who won't look at me. "He never explained anything. He said he knew someone who had a safe place and thought he could help us—"

Blondie gapes. Laughs so hard he snorts. Stands up. Cleans his glasses with the hem of his shirt. "You're such an ass," he says to Kenji. "Why didn't you just tell her the truth?"

"She never would've come if I told her the truth."

"How do you know?"

"She nearly *killed* me—"

My eyes are darting from one face to the other. Blond hair to black hair and back again. "What is going *on*?" I demand. "I want to see Adam. I want to see James. And I want a set of *clothes*—"

"You're naked?" Kenji is suddenly studying my sheet and not bothering to be subtle about it.

I flush despite my best efforts, flustered, frustrated. "Blondie said they destroyed my clothes."

"*Blondie?*" Blond man is offended.

"You never told me your name."

"Winston. My name is Winston." He's not smiling anymore.

"Didn't you say you had a suit for me?"

He frowns. Checks his watch. "We won't have time to go through that right now." Sighs. "Get her something to wear temporarily, will you?" He's talking to Kenji. Kenji who is still staring at me.

"I want to see Adam."

"Adam isn't ready to see you yet." ~~Blondie~~ Winston tucks his pen into a pocket. "We'll let you know when he's ready."

"How am I supposed to trust any of you if you won't even let me see him? If you won't let me see James? I don't even have my basic things. I want to get out of this bed and I need something to wear."

"Go fetch, Moto." Winston is readjusting his watch.

"I'm not your dog, *Blondie*," Kenji snaps. "And I told you not to call me Moto."

Winston pinches the bridge of his nose. "No problem. I'll also tell Castle it's your fault she's not meeting with him right now."

Kenji mutters something obscene under his breath. Stalks off. Almost slams the door.

A few seconds pass in a strained sort of silence.

I take a deep breath. "So what's *moto* mean?"

Winston rolls his eyes. "Nothing. It's just a nickname—his last name is Kishimoto. He gets mad when we chop it in half. Gets sensitive about it."

"Well why do you chop it in half?"

He snorts. "Because it's hard as hell to pronounce."

"How is that an excuse?"

He frowns. "What?"

"You got mad that I called you Blondie and not Winston. Why doesn't he have the right to be mad that you're calling him Moto instead of Kenji?"

He mumbles something that sounds like, "It's not the same thing."

I slide down a little. Rest my head on the pillow. "Don't be a hypocrite."

FORTY-FIVE

I feel like a clown in these oversized clothes. I'm wearing someone else's T-shirt. Someone else's pajama pants. Someone else's slippers. Kenji says they had to destroy the clothes in my duffel bag, too, so I have no idea whose outfit is currently hanging on my frame. I'm practically swimming in the material.

I try to knot the extra fabric and Kenji stops me. "You're going to mess up my shirt," he complains.

I drop my hands. "You gave me *your* clothes?"

"Well what did you expect? It's not like we have extra dresses just lying around." He shoots me a look, like I should be grateful he's even sharing.

Well. I guess it's better than being naked. "So who's Castle again?"

"He's in charge of everything," Kenji tells me. "The head of this entire movement."

My ears snap off. *"Movement?"*

Winston sighs. He seems so uptight. "If Kenji hasn't told you anything, you should probably wait to hear it from Castle himself. Hang tight. I promise we're going to answer your questions."

"But what about Adam? Where is *James*—"

"Wow." Winston runs a hand through his floppy hair. "You're just not going to give it up, huh?"

"He's fine, Juliette," Kenji intervenes. "He needs a little more time to recover. You have to start trusting us. No one here is going to hurt you, or Adam, or James. They're both fine. Everything is fine."

But I don't know if *fine* is good enough.

We're walking through an entire city underground, hallways and passageways, smooth stone floors, rough walls left untouched. There are circular disks drilled into the ground, glowing with artificial light every few feet. I notice computers, all kinds of gadgets I don't recognize, doors cracked open to reveal rooms filled with nothing but technological machinery.

"How do you find the electricity necessary to run this place?" I look more closely at the unidentifiable machines, the flickering screens, the unmistakable humming of hundreds of computers built into the framework of this underground world.

Kenji tugs on a stray strand of my hair. I spin around. "We steal it." He grins. Nods down a narrow path. "This way."

People both young and old and of all different shapes and ethnicities shuffle in and out of rooms, all along the halls. Many of them stare, many of them are too distracted to notice us. Some of them are dressed like the men and women who rushed out to our car last night. It's an odd kind of uniform. It seems unnecessary.

"So . . . everyone dresses like that?" I whisper, gesturing to the passing strangers as inconspicuously as possible.

Kenji scratches his head. Takes his time answering. "Not everyone. Not all the time."

"What about you?" I ask him.

"Not today."

I decide not to indulge his cryptic tendencies, and instead ask a more straightforward question. "So are you ever going to tell me how you healed so quickly?"

"Yes," Kenji says, unfazed. "We're going to tell you a lot of things, actually." We make an abrupt turn down an unexpected hallway. "But first—" Kenji pauses outside of a huge wooden door. "Castle wants to meet you. He's the one who requested you."

"Requested—?"

"Yeah." Kenji looks uncomfortable for just a wavering second.

"Wait—what do you mean—"

"I mean it wasn't an accident that I ended up in the army, Juliette." He sighs. "It wasn't an accident that I showed up at Adam's door. And I wasn't supposed to get shot or get beaten half to death, but I did. Only I wasn't dropped off by some random dude." He almost grins. "I've always known where Adam lived. It was my job to know." A pause. "We've all been looking for you.

"Go ahead." Kenji pushes me inside. "He'll be out when he's ready."

"Good luck," is all Winston says to me.

293

1,320 seconds walk into the room before he does.

He moves methodically, his face a mask of neutrality as he brushes wayward dreadlocks into a ponytail and seats himself at the front of the room. He's thin, fit, impeccably dressed in a simple suit. Dark blue. White shirt. No tie. There are no lines on his face, but there's a streak of silver in his hair and his eyes confess he's lived at least 100 years. He must be in his 40s. I look around.

It's an empty space, impressive in its sparseness. The floors and ceilings are built by bricks carefully pieced together. Everything feels old and ancient, but somehow modern technology is keeping this place alive. Artificial lighting illuminates the cavernous dimensions, small monitors are built into the stone walls. I don't know what I'm doing here. I don't know what to expect. I have no idea what kind of person Castle is but after spending so much time with Warner, I'm trying not to get my hopes up. I don't even realize I've stopped breathing until he speaks.

"I hope you're enjoying your stay so far."

My neck snaps up to meet his dark eyes, his smooth voice, silky and strong. His eyes are glinting with genuine curiosity, a smattering of surprise.

"Kenji said you wanted to meet me," is the only response I offer.

"Kenji would be correct." He takes his time breathing. He takes his time shifting in his seat. He takes his time studying my eyes, choosing his words, touching two fingers to his lips. He seems to have dominated the concept of time. "I've heard . . . stories. About you." Smiles. "I simply wanted to know if they were true."

"What have you heard?"

He opens his hands. Studies them for a moment. Looks up. "You can kill a man with nothing but your bare skin. You can crush five feet of concrete with the palm of your hand."

I'm climbing a mountain of air and my feet keep slipping. I need to get a grip on something.

"Is it true?" he asks.

"Rumors are more likely to kill you than I am."

He studies me for too long. "I'd like to show you something," he says after a moment.

"I want answers to my questions." This has gone on too long. I don't want to be lulled into a false sense of security. I don't want to assume Adam and James are okay. I don't want to trust anyone until I have proof. I can't pretend like any of this is all right. Not yet. "I want to know that I'm safe," I tell him. "And I want to know that my friends are safe. There was a ten-year-old boy with us when we arrived and I want to see him. I need to make certain he is healthy and unharmed. I won't cooperate otherwise."

His eyes inspect me a few moments longer. "Your loyalty is refreshing," he says, and he means it. "You will do well here."

"My friends—"

"Yes. Of course." He's on his feet. "Follow me."

This place is far more complex, far more organized than I could've imagined it to be. There are hundreds of different directions to get lost in, almost as many rooms, some bigger than others, each dedicated to different pursuits.

"The dining hall," Castle says to me.

"The dormitories." On the opposite wing.

"The training facilities." Down that hall.

"The common rooms." Right through here.

"The bathrooms." On either end of the floor.

"The meeting halls." Just past that door.

Each space is buzzing with bodies, each body adapted to a particular routine. People look up when they see us. Some wave, smile, delighted. I realize they're all looking at Castle. He nods his head. His eyes are kind. His smile is reassuring.

He's the leader of this entire *movement*, is what Kenji said. These people are depending on him for something more than basic survival. This is more than a fallout shelter. This is much more than a hiding space. There is a greater goal in mind. A greater purpose.

"Welcome," Castle says to me, gesturing with one hand, "to Omega Point."

FORTY-SIX

"Omega Point?"

"The last letter in the Greek alphabet. The final development, the last in a series." He stops in front of me and for the first time I notice the omega symbol stitched into the back of his jacket. "We are the only hope our civilization has left."

"But how—with such small numbers—how can you possibly hope to compete—"

"We've been building for a long time, Juliette." It's the first time he's said my name. "We've been planning, organizing, mapping out our strategy for many years now. The collapse of our human society should not come as a surprise. We brought it upon ourselves.

"The question wasn't *whether* things would fall apart," he continues. "Only *when*. It was a waiting game. A question of who would try to take power and how they would try to use it. Fear," he says to me, turning back for just a moment, his footsteps silent against the stone, "is a great motivator."

"That's pathetic."

"I agree. Which is why part of my job is reviving the stalled hearts that've lost all hope." We turn down another corridor. "And to tell you that almost everything you've learned about the state of our world is a lie."

I stop in place. "What do you mean?"

"I mean things are not nearly as bad as The Reestablishment wants us to think they are."

"But there's no food—"

"That they give *you* access to."

"The animals—"

"Are kept hidden. Genetically modified. Raised on secret pastures."

"But the air—the seasons—the *weather*—"

"Is not as bad as they'll have us believe. It's probably our only real problem—but it's one caused by the perverse manipulations of Mother Earth. *Man-made* manipulations that we can still fix." He turns to face me. Focuses my mind with one steady gaze.

"There is still a chance to change things. We can provide fresh drinking water to all people. We can make sure crops are not regulated for profit; we can ensure that they are not genetically altered to benefit manufacturers. Our people are dying because we are feeding them poison. Animals are dying because we are forcing them to eat waste, forcing them to live in their own filth, caging them together and abusing them. Plants are withering away because we are dumping chemicals into the earth that make them hazardous to our health. But these are things we can fix.

"We are fed lies because believing them makes us weak, vulnerable, malleable. We depend on others for our food, health, sustenance. This cripples us. Creates cowards of our people. Slaves of our children. It's time for us to fight back." His eyes are bright with feeling, his fists clenched in fervor. His words are powerful, heavy with conviction. I have no doubt he's swayed many people with such fanciful thoughts. Hope for a future that seems lost. Inspiration in a bleak world with nothing to offer. He is a natural leader. A talented orator.

I have a hard time believing him.

"How can you know for certain that your theories are correct? Do you have proof?"

His hands relax. His eyes quiet down. His lips form a small smile. "Of course." He almost laughs.

"Why is that funny?"

He shakes his head. Just a bit. "I'm amused by your skepticism. I admire it, actually. It's never a good idea to believe everything you hear."

I catch his double meaning. Acknowledge it. "Touché, Mr. Castle."

"This entire movement is proof enough. We survive because of these truths. We seek out food and supplies from the various storage compounds The Reestablishment has constructed. We've found their fields, their farms, their animals. They have hundreds of acres dedicated to crops. The farmers are slaves, working under the threat of death to themselves or their family members. The rest of society is either killed or corralled into sectors, sectioned off to be monitored, carefully surveyed."

I keep my face neutral. I still haven't decided whether or

not I believe him. "And what do you need with me? Why do you care if I'm here?"

He stops at a glass wall. Points through to the room beyond. Doesn't answer my question. "Your Adam is healing because of our people."

I nearly trip in my haste to see him. I press my hands against the glass and peer into the brightly lit space. Adam is asleep, his face perfect, peaceful. This must be the medical wing.

"Look closely," Castle tells me. "There are no needles attached to his body. No machines keeping him alive. He arrived with three broken ribs. Lungs close to collapsing. A bullet in his thigh. His kidneys were bruised along with the rest of his body. Broken skin, bloodied wrists. A sprained ankle. He'd lost more blood than most hospitals would be able to replenish.

"There are close to two hundred people at Omega Point," Castle says. "Less than half of whom have some kind of gift."

I spin around, stunned.

"I brought you here," he says to me carefully, quietly, "because this is where you belong. Because you need to know that you are not alone."

FORTY-SEVEN

"You would be invaluable to our resistance."

I can hardly breathe. "There are others . . . like me?"

Castle offers me eyes that empathize. "I was the first to realize my affliction could not be mine alone. I sought out others, following rumors, listening for stories, reading the newspapers for abnormalities in human behavior. At first it was just for companionship." He pauses. "I was tired of the insanity. Of believing I was inhuman; a monster. But then I realized that what seemed a weakness was actually a strength. That together we could be something extraordinary. Something *good*."

I can't catch my breath. I can't cough up the impossibility caught in my throat.

Castle is waiting for my reaction.

"What is your . . . gift?" I ask him.

His smile disarms my insecurity. He holds out his hand. Cocks his head. I hear the creak of a distant door opening. The sound of air and metal; movement. I turn toward the sound only to see something hurtling in my direction. I duck. Castle laughs. Catches it in his hand.

I gasp.

He shows me the key now caught between his fingers.

"You can move things with your mind?"

"I have an impossibly advanced level of psychokinesis." He twists his lips into a smile. "So yes."

"There's a *name* for it?"

"For my condition? Yes. For yours?" He pauses. "I'm uncertain."

"And the others—what—they're—"

"You can meet them, if you'd like."

"I—yes—I'd like that," I stammer, excited, 4 years old and still believing in fairies.

I freeze at a sudden sound.

Footsteps are pounding the stone. I catch the pant of strained breathing.

"*Sir*—" someone shouts.

Castle starts. Stills. Pivots around a corner toward the runner. "Brendan?"

"Sir!" he pants again.

"You have news? What have you seen?"

"We're hearing things on the radio," he begins, his broken words thick with a British accent. "Our cameras are picking up more tanks patrolling the area than usual. We think they may be getting closer—"

The sound of static energy. Static electricity. Garbled voices croaking through a weak radio line.

Brendan curses under his breath. "Sorry, sir—it's not usually this distorted—I just haven't learned to contain the charges lately—"

"Not to worry. You just need practice. Your training is going well?"

"Very well, sir. I have it almost entirely under my command." Brendan pauses. "For the most part."

"Excellent. In the meantime, let me know if the tanks get any closer. I'm not surprised to hear they're getting a little more vigilant. Try to listen for any mention of an attack. The Reestablishment has been trying to pinpoint our whereabouts for years, but now we have someone particularly valuable to their efforts and I'm certain they want her back. I have a feeling things are going to develop rather quickly from now on."

A moment of confusion. "Sir?"

"There's someone I'd like for you to meet."

Brendan and Castle step around the corner. Come into view. And I have to make a conscious effort to keep my jaw from unhinging. I can't stop staring.

Castle's companion is white from head to toe.

Not just his strange uniform, which is a blinding shade of shimmering white, but his skin is paler than mine. His hair is so blond it can only be accurately described as white. His eyes are mesmerizing. They're the lightest shade of blue I've ever seen. Piercing. Practically transparent. He looks to be my age.

He doesn't seem *real*.

"Brendan, this is Juliette," Castle introduces us. "She arrived just yesterday. I was giving her an overview of Omega Point."

Brendan sticks out his hand and I almost panic before he frowns. Pulls back, says, "Er, wait—sorry—," and flexes his hands. Cracks his knuckles. A few sparks fly out of his fingers.

I gape at him.

He shrinks back. Smiles sheepishly. "Sometimes I electrocute people by accident."

Something in my heavy armor melts away. I feel suddenly understood. Unafraid of being myself. I can't help my grin. "Don't worry," I tell him. "If I shake your hand I might kill you."

"Blimey." He blinks. Stares. Waits for me to take it back. "You're serious?"

"Very."

He laughs. "Right then. No touching." Leans in. Lowers his voice. "I have a bit of a problem with that myself, you know. Girls are always talking about electricity in their romance, but none are too happy to actually *be* electrocuted, apparently. Bloody confusing, is what it is." He shrugs.

Adam was right. Maybe things can be okay. Maybe I don't have to be a monster. Maybe I do have a choice.

I think I'm going to like it here.

Brendan winks. "It was very nice meeting you, Juliette. I'll be seeing you?"

I nod. "I think so."

"Brilliant." He shoots me another smile. Turns to Castle. "I'll let you know if I hear anything, sir."

"Perfect."

And Brendan disappears.

I turn to the glass wall keeping me from the other half of my heart. Press my head against the cool surface. Wish he would wake up.

"Would you like to say hello?"

I look up at Castle, who is still studying me. Always analyzing me. Somehow his attention doesn't make me uncomfortable. "Yes," I tell him. "I want to say hello."

FORTY-EIGHT

Castle uses the key in his hand to open the door.

"Why does the medical wing have to be locked?" I ask him.

He turns to me. He's not very tall, I realize for the first time. "If you'd known where to find him—would you have waited patiently behind this door?"

I drop my eyes. Don't answer.

He tries to be encouraging. "Healing is a delicate process. It can't be interrupted or influenced by erratic emotions. We're lucky enough to have two healers among us—a set of twins, in fact. But most fascinating is that they each focus on a different element—one on the physical incapacitations, and one on the mental. Both facets must be addressed, otherwise the healing will be incomplete, weak, insufficient." He turns the door handle. "But I think it's safe for Adam to see you now."

I step inside and my senses are almost immediately assaulted by the scent of jasmine. I search the space for the flowers but find none. I wonder if it's a perfume. It's intoxicating.

"I'll be just outside," Castle says to me.

The room is filled with a long row of beds, simply made.

All 20 or so of them are empty except for Adam's. There's a door at the end of the room that probably leads to another space, but I'm too nervous to be curious right now.

I pull up an extra chair and try to be as quiet as possible. I don't want to wake him, I just want to know he's okay. I clasp and unclasp my hands. I'm too aware of my racing heart. And I know I probably shouldn't touch him, but I can't help myself. I cover his hand with mine. His fingers are warm.

His eyes flutter for just a moment. They don't open. He takes a sudden breath and I freeze.

"What are you *doing*?"

My head snaps up at the sound of Castle's panicked voice. I drop Adam's hand. Push away from the bed, eyes wide, worried. "What do you mean?"

"Why are you—you can *touch* him—?" I never thought I'd see Castle so confused. He's lost his composure, one arm half extended in an effort to stop me.

"Of course I can tou—" I stop. "Kenji didn't tell you?"

"This young man has immunity from your touch?"

"Yes." I look from him to Adam, still sound asleep. ~~So does Warner.~~

"That's . . . *astounding*."

"Is it?"

"Very." Castle's eyes are bright, so eager. "It certainly isn't coincidence. There is no coincidence in these kinds of situations." He pauses. Paces. "Fascinating. So many possibilities—so many theories—" He's not even talking to me anymore. His mind is working too quickly for me to keep up. He takes a deep breath. Seems to remember I'm still in the room. "My apologies. Please, carry on. The girls will be out soon—they're assisting James at the moment. I must report this new information as soon as possible."

"Wait—"

He looks up. "Yes?"

"You have theories?" I ask him. "You—you know why these things are happening . . . to me?"

"You mean to *us*?" Castle offers me a smile.

I manage to nod.

"We have been doing extensive research for years," he says. "We think we have a pretty good idea."

"And?" I can hardly breathe.

"If you should decide to stay at Omega Point, we'll have that conversation very soon, I promise. Besides, I'm sure now is probably not the best time." He nods at Adam.

"Oh. Of course."

Castle turns to leave.

"But do you think that Adam—" The words tumble out of my mouth too quickly. I try to pace myself. "Do you think he's . . . like *us*, too?"

Castle pivots back around. Studies my eyes. "I think," he says carefully, "that it is entirely possible."

I gasp.

"My apologies," he says, "but I really must get going. And I wouldn't want to interrupt your time together."

I want to say yes, sure, of course, absolutely. I want to

smile and wave and tell him it's no problem. But I have so many questions, I think I might explode; I want him to tell me everything he knows.

"I know this is a lot of information to take in at once." Castle pauses at the door. "But we'll have plenty of opportunities to talk. You must be exhausted and I'm sure you'd like to get some sleep. The girls will take care of you—they're expecting you. In fact, they'll be your new roommates at Omega Point. I'm sure they'll be happy to answer any questions you might have." He clasps my shoulders before he goes. "It's an honor to have you with us, Ms. Ferrars. I hope you will seriously consider joining us on a permanent basis."

I nod, numb.

And he's gone.

We have been doing extensive research for years, he said. *We think we have a pretty good idea*, he said. *We'll have that conversation very soon, I promise.*

For the first time in my life I might finally understand what I am and it doesn't seem possible. And Adam. *Adam.* I shake myself and take my seat next to him. Squeeze his fingers. Castle could be wrong. Maybe this *is* all coincidence.

I have to focus.

I wonder if anyone has heard from Warner lately.

"Juliette?"

His eyes are half open. He's staring at me like he's not sure if I'm real.

"Adam!" I have to force myself to be still.

He smiles and the effort seems to exhaust him. "God it's good to see you."

"You're *okay*." I grip his hand, resist pulling him into my arms. "You're really okay."

His grin gets bigger. "I feel like I could sleep for a few years."

"Don't worry, the sedative will wear off soon."

I spin around. Two girls with exactly the same green eyes are staring at us. They smile at the same time. Their long brown hair is thick and stick-straight in high ponytails on their heads. They're wearing matching silver bodysuits. Gold ballet flats.

"I'm Sonya," the girl on the left says.

"I'm Sara," her sister adds.

I have no idea how to tell them apart.

"It's so nice to meet you," they say at exactly the same time.

"I'm Juliette," I manage. "It's a pleasure to meet you, too."

"Adam is almost ready for release," one says to me.

"Sonya is an excellent healer," the other one chimes in.

"Sara is better than I am," says the first.

"He should be okay to leave just as soon as the sedative is out of his system," they say together, smiling.

"Oh—that's great—thank you so much—" I don't know who to look at. Who to answer. I glance back at Adam. He seems thoroughly amused.

"Where's James?" he asks.

"He's playing with the other children." I think it's Sara who says it.

"We just took him on a bathroom break," says the other.

"Would you like to see him?" Back to Sara.

"There are other children?" My eyes go wide.

The girls nod at the same time.

"We'll go get him," they chorus. And disappear.

"They seem nice," Adam says after a moment.

"Yeah. They do." This whole place seems nice.

Sonya and Sara come back with James, who seems happier than I've ever seen him, almost happier than seeing Adam for the first time. He's thrilled to be here. Thrilled to be with the other kids, thrilled to be with "the pretty girls who take care of me because they're so nice and there's so much food and they gave me *chocolate*, Adam—have you ever tasted *chocolate*?" and he has a big bed and tomorrow he's going to class with the other kids and he's already excited.

"I'm so happy you're awake," he says to Adam, practically jumping up and down on his bed. "They said you got sick and that you were resting and now you're awake so that means you're better, right? And we're safe? I don't really remember what happened on our way here," he admits, a little embarrassed. "I think I fell asleep."

I think Adam is looking to break Kenji's neck at this point.

"Yeah, we're safe," Adam tells him, running a hand through his messy blond hair. "Everything is okay."

James runs back to the playroom with the other kids. Sonya and Sara invent an excuse to leave so we have some privacy. I'm liking them more and more.

"Has anyone told you about this place yet?" Adam asks me. He manages to sit up. His sheet slides down. His chest is exposed. His skin is perfectly healed—I can hardly reconcile the image I have in my memory with the one in front of me. I forget to answer his question.

"You have no scars." I touch his skin like I need to feel it for myself.

He tries to smile. "They're not very traditional in their medical practices around here."

I look up, startled. "You . . . know?"

"Did you meet Castle yet?"

I nod.

He shifts. Sighs. "I've heard rumors about this place for a long time. I got really good at listening to whispers, mostly because I was looking out for myself. But in the army we hear things. Any and all kinds of enemy threats. Possible ambushes. There was talk of an unusual underground movement from the moment I enlisted. Most people said it was crap. That it was some kind of garbage concocted to scare people—that there was no way it could be real. But I always hoped it had some basis in truth, especially after I found out about you—I hoped we'd be able to find others with similar abilities. But I didn't know who to ask. I had no connections—no way of knowing how to find them." He shakes his head. "And all this time, Kenji was working undercover."

"He said he was looking for me."

312

Adam nods. Laughs. "Just like I was looking for you. Just like Warner was looking for you."

"I don't understand," I mumble. "Especially now that I know there are others like me—stronger, even—why did Warner want *me*?"

"He discovered you before Castle did," Adam says. "He felt like he claimed you a long time ago." Adam leans back. "Warner's a lot of things, but he's not stupid. I'm sure he knew there was some truth to those rumors—and he was fascinated. Because as much as Castle wanted to use his abilities for good, Warner wanted to manipulate those abilities for his own cause. He wanted to become some kind of superpower." A pause. "He invested a lot of time and energy just studying you. I don't think he wanted to let that effort go to waste."

"Adam," I whisper.

He takes my hand. "Yeah?"

"I don't think he's dead."

FORTY-NINE

"He's not."

Adam turns. Frowns at the voice. "What are you doing here?"

"Wow. What a greeting, Kent. Be careful not to pull a muscle thanking me for saving your ass."

"You lied to all of us."

"You're welcome."

"You sedated my ten-year-old brother!"

"You're still welcome."

"Hey, Kenji." I acknowledge him.

"My clothes look good on you." He steps a bit closer, smiles.

I roll my eyes. Adam examines my outfit for the first time.

"I didn't have anything else to wear," I explain.

Adam nods a little slowly. Looks at Kenji. "Did you have a message to deliver?"

"Yeah. I'm supposed to show you where you'll be staying."

"What do you mean?"

Kenji grins. "You and James are going to be my new roommates."

Adam swears under his breath.

"Sorry, bro, but we don't have enough rooms for you

and Hot Hands over here to have your own private space." He winks at me. "No offense."

"I have to leave right now?"

"Yeah, man. I want to go to sleep soon. I don't have all day to wait around for your lazy ass."

"*Lazy—?*"

I hurry to interrupt before Adam has a chance to fight back. "What do you mean, you want to go to sleep? What time is it?"

"It's almost ten at night," Kenji tells me. "It's hard to tell underground, but we all try to be aware of the clocks. We have monitors in the hallways, and most of us try to wear watches. Losing track of night and day can screw us up pretty quickly. And now is not the time to be getting too comfortable."

"How do you know Warner isn't dead?" I ask, nervous.

"We just saw him on camera," Kenji says. "He and his men are patrolling this area pretty heavily. I managed to hear some of their conversation. Turns out Warner got shot."

I suck in my breath, try to silence my heartbeats.

"That's why we got lucky last night—apparently the soldiers got called back to base because they *thought* Warner was dead. There was a shift in power for a minute. No one knew what to do. What orders to follow. But then it turned out he wasn't dead. Just wounded pretty bad. His arm was all patched up and in a sling," Kenji adds.

Adam finds his voice before I do. "How safe is this place from attack?"

Kenji laughs. "Safe as *hell*. I don't even know how they

managed to get as close as they did. But they'll never be able to find our exact location. And even if they do, they'll never be able to break in. Our security is just about impenetrable. Plus we have cameras everywhere. We can see what they're doing before they even plan it.

"It doesn't really matter, though," he goes on. "Because they're looking for a fight, and so are we. We're not afraid of an attack. Besides, they have no idea what we're capable of. And we've been training for this shit forever."

"Do you—" I pause. "Can you—I mean, do you have a . . . gift, too?"

Kenji smiles. And disappears.

He's really gone.

I stand up. Try to touch the space he was just standing in.

He reappears just in time to jump out of reach. "HEY—whoa, careful—just because I'm invisible doesn't mean I can't feel anything—"

"Oh!" I pull back. Cringe. "I'm sorry—"

"You can make yourself *invisible*?" Adam looks more irritated than interested.

"Just blew your mind, didn't I?"

"How long have you been spying on me?" Adam narrows his eyes.

"As long as I needed to." But his grin is laced with mischief.

"So you're . . . corporeal?" I ask.

"Look at you, using big fancy words." Kenji crosses his arms. Leans against the wall.

"I mean—you can't, like, walk through walls or anything, can you?"

He snorts. "Nah, I'm not a ghost. I can just . . . blend, I guess is the best word. I can blend into the background of any space. Shift myself to match my surrounds. It's taken me a long time to figure it out."

"Wow."

"I used to follow Adam home. That's how I knew where he lived. And that's how I was able to run away—because they couldn't really see me. They tried to shoot at me anyway," he adds, bitter, "but I managed not to die, at least."

"Wait, but why were you following Adam home? I thought you were looking for *me*?" I ask him.

"Yeah—well, I enlisted shortly after we got wind of Warner's big project." He nods in my direction. "We'd been trying to find you, but Warner had more security clearance and access to more information than we did—we were having a hard time tracking you down. Castle thought it would be easier to have someone on the inside paying attention to all the crazy shit Warner was planning. So when I heard that Adam was the main guy involved in this particular project and that he had this history with you, I sent the information to Castle. He told me to watch out for Adam, too—you know, in case Adam turned out to be just as psycho as Warner. We wanted to make sure he wasn't a threat to you or our plans. But I had no idea you'd try to run away together. Messed me the hell up."

We're all silent for a moment.

"So how much did you spy on me?" Adam asks him.

"Well, well, well." Kenji cocks his head. "Is Mr. Adam Kent suddenly feeling a little intimidated?"

"Don't be a jackass."

"You hiding something?"

"Yeah. My gun—"

"Hey!" Kenji claps his hands together. "So! Are we ready to get out of here, or what?"

"I need a pair of pants."

Kenji looks abruptly annoyed. "Seriously, Kent? I don't want to hear that shit."

"Well, unless you want to see me naked, I suggest you do something about it."

Kenji shoots Adam a dirty look and stalks off, grumbling something about lending people all of his clothes. The door swings shut behind him.

"I'm not really naked," Adam tells me.

"Oh," I gasp. Look up. My eyes betray me.

He can't bite back his grin in time. His fingers graze my cheek. "I just wanted him to leave us alone for a second."

I blush. Fumble for something to say. "I'm so happy you're okay."

He says something I don't hear.

Takes my hand. Pulls me up beside him.

He's leaning in and I'm leaning in until I'm practically on top of him and he's slipping me into his arms and kissing me with a new kind of desperation. His hands are threaded in my hair, his lips so soft, so urgent against mine, like fire and honey exploding in my mouth. My body is steaming.

Adam pulls back just a tiny bit. Kisses my bottom lip. Bites it for just a second. His skin feels 100 degrees hotter than it was a moment ago. His lips are pressed against my neck and my hands are on a journey down his upper body and I'm wondering why there are so many freight trains in my heart, why his chest is a broken harmonica. I'm tracing the bird caught forever in flight on his skin and I realize for the first time that he's given me wings of my own. He's helped me fly away and now I'm stuck in centripetal motion, soaring right into the center of everything. I bring his lips back up to mine.

"Juliette," he says. 1 breath. 1 kiss. 10 fingers teasing my skin. "I need to see you tonight."

Yes.

Please.

2 hard knocks send us flying apart.

Kenji slams open the door. "You do realize this wall is made of *glass*, don't you?" He looks like he's bitten the head off a worm. "No one wants to see that."

He throws a pair of pants at Adam.

Nods to me. "Come on, I'll take you to Sonya and Sara. They'll set you up for tonight." Turns to Adam. "And don't *ever* give those pants back to me."

"What if I don't want to sleep?" Adam asks, unabashed. "I'm not allowed to leave my room?"

Kenji presses his lips together. Narrows his eyes. "I will not use this word often, Kent, but *please* don't try any secret-sneaking-away shit. We have to regulate things around here for a reason. It's the only way to survive. So do everyone a favor and keep your pants on. You'll see her in the morning."

But morning feels like a million years from now.

FIFTY

The twins are still asleep when someone knocks. Sonya and Sara showed me where the girls' bathrooms are so I had a chance to shower last night, but I'm still wearing Kenji's oversized clothes. I feel a little ridiculous as I pad my way toward the door.

I open it.

Blink. "Hey, Winston."

He looks me up and down. "Castle thought you might like to change out of those clothes."

"You have something for me to wear?"

"Yeah—remember? We made you something custom."

"Oh. Wow. Yeah, that sounds great."

I slip outside silently, following Winston through the dark halls. The underground world is quiet, its inhabitants still asleep. I ask Winston why we're up so early.

"I figured you'd want to meet everyone at breakfast. This way you can jump into the regular routine of things around here—even get started on your training." He glances back. "We all have to learn how to harness our abilities in the most effective manner possible. It's no good having no control over your body."

"Wait—you have an *ability*, too?"

"There are exactly fifty-six of us who do. The rest are our family members, children, or close friends who help out with everything else. So yes, I'm one of those fifty-six. So are you."

I'm nearly stepping on his feet in an effort to keep up with his long legs. "So what can you do?"

He doesn't answer. And I can't be sure, but I think he's blushing.

"I'm sorry—" I backpedal. "I don't mean to pry— I shouldn't have asked—"

"It's okay," he cuts me off. "I just think it's kind of stupid." He laughs a short, hard laugh. "Of all the things I should be able to do," he sighs. "At least you can do something *interesting*."

I stop walking, stunned. "You think this is a competition? To see which magic trick is more twisted? To see who can inflict the most pain?"

"That's not what I meant—"

"I don't think it's *interesting* to be able to kill someone by accident. I don't think it's *interesting* to be afraid to touch a living thing."

His jaw is tense. "I didn't mean it like that. I just . . . I wish I were more useful. That's all."

I cross my arms. "You don't have to tell me if you don't want to."

He rolls his eyes. Runs a hand through his hair. "I'm just—I'm very . . . flexible," he says.

It takes me a moment to process his admission. "Like— you can bend yourself into a pretzel?"

"Sure. Or stretch myself if I need to."

"Can I see?"

He bites his lip. Readjusts his glasses. Looks both ways down the empty hall. And loops one arm around his waist. Twice.

"Wow."

"It's stupid," he grumbles. "And useless."

"Are you insane?" I lean back to look at him. "That's *incredible*."

But his arm is back to normal and he's walking away again. I have to run to catch up.

"Don't be so hard on yourself," I try to tell him. "It's nothing to be ashamed of." But he's not listening and I'm wondering when I became a motivational speaker. When I made the switch from hating myself to accepting myself. When it became okay for me to choose my own life.

Winston leads me to the room I met him in. The same white walls. The same small bed. Only this time, Adam and Kenji are waiting inside. My heart kicks into gear and I'm suddenly nervous.

Adam is up. He's standing on his own and he looks perfect. Beautiful. Unharmed. There's not a single drop of blood on his body. He walks forward with only slight discomfort, smiles at me with no difficulty. His skin is a little paler than normal, but positively radiant compared to his complexion the night we arrived. His natural tan offsets a pair of eyes a shade of blue in a midnight sky.

"Juliette," he says.

I can't stop staring at him. Marveling at him. Amazed by how incredible it feels to know that he's all right.

"Hey." I manage to smile.

"Good morning to you, too," Kenji interjects.

I startle. "Oh, hi." I wave a limp hand in his direction. He snorts.

"All right. Let's get this over with, shall we?" Winston walks toward one of the walls, which turns out to be a closet. There's one pop of color inside. He pulls it off the hanger.

"Can I, uh, have a moment alone with her?" Adam says suddenly.

Winston takes off his glasses. Rubs his eyes. "I need to follow protocol. I have to explain everything—"

"I know—that's fine," Adam says. "You can do it after. I just need a minute, I promise. I haven't really had a chance to talk to her since we got here."

Winston frowns. Looks at me. Looks at Adam. Sighs.

"All right. But then we'll be back. I need to make sure everything fits and I have to check the—"

"Perfect. That sounds great. Thanks, man—" And he's shoving them out the door.

"Wait!" Winston slams the door back open. "At least get her to put the suit on while we're outside. That way it won't be a complete waste of my time."

Adam stares at the material in Winston's outstretched hand. Winston mumbles something about people always wasting his time, and Adam suppresses a grin. Glances at me. I shrug.

"Okay," he says, grabbing the suit. "But now you have to get out—" And pushes them both back into the hallway.

"We're going to be *right outside*," Kenji shouts. "Like five seconds away—"

Adam closes the door behind them. Turns around. His eyes are burning into me.

"I never had a chance to say thank you," he says.

I look away. Pretend heat isn't fighting its way up my face.

He steps forward. Takes my hands. "Juliette."

I peek up at him.

"You saved my life."

I bite the inside of my cheek. It seems silly to say "You're welcome" for saving someone's life. I don't know what to do. "I'm just so happy you're okay," is all I manage.

He's staring at my lips and I'm aching everywhere. If he kisses me right now I don't think I'll let him stop. He takes a sharp breath. Seems to remember he's holding something. "Oh. Maybe you should put this on?" He hands me a slinky piece of something purple. It looks tiny. Like a jumpsuit that could fit a small child.

I offer Adam a blank stare.

He grins. "Try it on."

I stare differently.

"Oh." He jumps back. "Right—I'll just—I'll turn around—"

I wait until his back is to me before I exhale. I look around. There don't seem to be any mirrors in this room. I shed the oversized outfit. Drop each piece on the floor.

I'm standing here, completely naked, and for a moment I'm too petrified to move. But Adam doesn't turn around. He doesn't say a word. I examine the shiny purple material. I imagine it's supposed to stretch.

It does.

In fact, it's unexpectedly easy to slip on—like it was designed specifically for my body. There's built-in lining for where underwear is supposed to be, extra support for my chest, a collar that goes right up to my neck, sleeves that touch my wrists, legs that touch my ankles, a zipper that pulls it all together. I examine the ultrathin material. It feels like I'm wearing nothing. It's the richest shade of purple, skintight but not tight at all. It's breathable, oddly comfortable.

"How does it look . . . ?" Adam asks. He sounds nervous. "Can you help me zip it up?"

He turns around. His lips part, falter, form an incredible smile. Adam touches my hair and I realize it's almost all the way down my back. Maybe it's time I cut it.

His fingers are so careful. He pushes the waves over my shoulder so they won't get caught in the zipper. Trails a line from the base of my neck down to the start of the seam, down to the dip in my lower back. My spine is conducting enough electricity to power a city. He takes his time zipping me up. Runs his hands down the length of my silhouette.

"You look incredible," is the first thing he says to me.

I turn around.

I touch the material. Decide I should probably say

something. "It's very . . . comfortable."

"Sexy."

I look up.

He's shaking his head. "It's sexy as hell."

He steps forward. Slips me into his arms.

"I look like a gymnast," I mumble.

"No," he whispers, hot hot hot against my lips. "You look like a superhero."

EPILOGUE

I'm still tingling when Kenji and Winston burst back into the room.

"So how is this suit supposed to make my life easier?" I ask anyone who'll answer.

But Kenji is frozen in place, staring without apology. Opens his mouth. Closes it. Shoves his hands into his pockets.

Winston steps in. "It's supposed to help with the touching issue," he tells me. "You don't have to worry about being covered from head to toe in this unpredictable weather. The material is designed to keep you cool or keep you warm based on the temperature. It's light and breathable so your skin doesn't suffocate. It will keep you safe from hurting someone unintentionally, but offers you the flexibility of touching someone . . . intentionally, too. If you ever needed to."

"That's amazing."

He smiles. Big. "You're welcome."

I study the suit more closely. Realize something. "But my hands and feet are totally exposed. How's that supposed to—"

"Oh—shoot," Winston interrupts. "I almost forgot." He runs over to the closet and pulls out a pair of flat-heeled black ankle boots and a pair of black gloves that stop right before the elbow. He hands them to me. I study the soft leather of the accessories and marvel at the springy, flexible build of the boots. I could do ballet and run a mile in these shoes. "These should fit you," he says. "They complete the outfit."

I slip them on and tip up on my toes, luxuriate in the feeling of my new outfit. I feel invincible. I really wish I had a mirror for once in my life. I look from Kenji to Adam to Winston. "What do you think? Is it . . . okay?"

Kenji makes a strange noise.

Winston looks at his watch.

Adam can't stop smiling.

He and I follow Kenji and Winston out of the room, but Adam pauses to slip off my left glove. He takes my hand. Intertwines our fingers. Offers me a smile that manages to kiss my heart.

And I look around.

Flex my fist.

Touch the material hugging my skin.

I feel incredible. My bones feel rejuvenated; my skin feels vibrant, healthy. I take big lungfuls of air and savor the taste.

Things are changing, but this time I'm not afraid. This time I know who I am. This time I've made the right choice and I'm fighting for the right team. I feel safe. Confident.

Excited, even.

Because this time?

I'm ready.

Want to hear more from Warner? Keep reading for a novella from Warner's point of view.

PROLOGUE

I've been shot.

And, as it turns out, a bullet wound is even more uncomfortable than I had imagined.

My skin is cold and clammy; I'm making a herculean effort to breathe. Torture is roaring through my right arm and making it difficult for me to focus. I have to squeeze my eyes shut, grit my teeth, and force myself to pay attention.

The chaos is unbearable.

Several people are shouting and too many of them are touching me, and I want their hands surgically removed. They keep shouting "Sir!" as if they're still waiting for me to give them orders, as if they have no idea what to do without my instruction. The realization exhausts me.

"Sir, can you hear me?" Another cry. But this time, a voice I don't detest.

"Sir, please, can you hear me—"

"I've been shot, Delalieu," I manage to say. I open my eyes. Look into his watery ones. "I haven't gone deaf."

All at once the noise disappears. The soldiers shut up. Delalieu looks at me. Worried.

I sigh.

"Take me back," I tell him, shifting, just a little. The

1

world tilts and steadies all at once. "Alert the medics and have my bed prepared for our arrival. In the meantime, elevate my arm and continue applying direct pressure to the wound. The bullet has broken or fractured something, and this will require surgery."

Delalieu says nothing for just a moment too long.

"Good to see you're all right, sir." His voice is a nervous, shaky thing. "Good to see you're all right."

"That was an order, Lieutenant."

"Of course," he says quickly, head bowed. "Certainly, sir. How should I direct the soldiers?"

"Find her," I tell him. It's getting harder for me to speak. I take a small breath and run a shaky hand across my forehead. I'm sweating in an excessive way that isn't lost on me.

"Yes, sir." He moves to help me up, but I grab his arm.

"One last thing."

"Sir?"

"Kent," I say, my voice uneven now. "Make sure they keep him alive for me."

Delalieu looks up, his eyes wide. "Private Adam Kent, sir?"

"Yes." I hold his gaze. "I want to deal with him myself."

ONE

Delalieu is standing at the foot of my bed, clipboard in hand.

His is my second visit this morning. The first was from my medics, who confirmed that the surgery went well. They said that as long as I stay in bed this week, the new drugs they've given me should accelerate my healing process. They also said that I should be fit to resume daily activities fairly soon, but I'll be required to wear a sling for at least a month.

I told them it was an interesting theory.

"My slacks, Delalieu." I'm sitting up, trying to steady my head against the nausea of these new drugs. My right arm is essentially useless to me now.

I look up. Delalieu is staring at me, unblinking, Adam's apple bobbing in his throat.

I stifle a sigh.

"What is it?" I use my left arm to steady myself against the mattress and force myself upright. It takes every ounce of energy I have left, and I'm clinging to the bed frame. I wave away Delalieu's effort to help; I close my eyes against the pain and dizziness. "Tell me what's happened," I say to him. "There's no point in prolonging bad news."

His voice breaks twice when he says, "Private Adam Kent has escaped, sir."

My eyes flash a bright, dizzying white behind my eyelids.

I take a deep breath and attempt to run my good hand through my hair. It's thick and dry and caked with what must be dirt mixed with my own blood. I'm tempted to punch my remaining fist through the wall.

Instead I take a moment to collect myself.

I'm suddenly too aware of everything in the air around me, the scents and small noises and footsteps outside my door. I hate these rough cotton pants they've put me in. I hate that I'm not wearing socks. I want to shower. I want to change.

I want to put a bullet through Adam Kent's spine.

"Leads," I demand. I move toward my bathroom and wince against the cold air as it hits my skin; I'm still without a shirt. Trying to remain calm. "Tell me you have not brought me this information without leads."

My mind is a warehouse of carefully organized human emotions. I can almost see my brain as it functions, filing thoughts and images away. I lock away the things that do not serve me. I focus only on what needs to be done: the basic components of survival and the myriad things I must manage throughout the day.

"Of course," Delalieu says. The fear in his voice stings me a little; I dismiss it. "Yes, sir," he says, "we do think we know where he might've gone—and we have reason to believe that Private Kent and the—and the girl—well, with Private Kishimoto having run off as well—we have reason to believe that they are all together, sir."

4

The drawers in my mind are rattling to break open. Memories. Theories. Whispers and sensations.

I shove them off a cliff.

"Of course you do." I shake my head. Regret it. Close my eyes against the sudden unsteadiness. "Do not give me information I've already deduced for myself," I manage to say. "I want something concrete. Give me a solid lead, Lieutenant, or leave me until you have one."

"A car," he says quickly. "A car was reported stolen, sir, and we were able to track it to an unidentified location, but then it disappeared off the map. It's as if it ceased to exist, sir."

I look up. Give him my full attention.

"We followed the tracks it left in our radar," he says, speaking more calmly now, "and they led us to a stretch of isolated, barren land. But we've scoured the area and found nothing."

"This is something, at least." I rub the back of my neck, fighting the weakness I feel deep in my bones. "I will meet you in the L Room in one hour."

"But sir," he says, eyes trained on my arm, "you'll need assistance—there's a process—you'll require a convalescent aide—"

"You are dismissed."

He hesitates.

Then, "Yes, sir."

TWO

I manage to bathe without losing consciousness.

It was more of a sponge bath, but I feel better none-theless. I have an extremely low threshold for disorder; it offends my very being. I shower regularly. I eat six small meals a day. I dedicate two hours of each day to training and physical exercise. And I detest being barefoot.

Now, I find myself standing naked, hungry, tired, and barefoot in my closet. This is not ideal.

My closet is separated into various sections. Shirts, ties, slacks, blazers, and boots. Socks, gloves, scarves, and coats. Everything is arranged according to color, then shades within each color. Every article of clothing it contains is meticulously chosen and custom made to fit the exact mea-surements of my body. I don't feel like myself until I'm fully dressed; it's part of who I am and how I begin my day.

Now I haven't the faintest idea how I'm supposed to dress myself.

My hand shakes as I reach for the little blue bottle I was given this morning. I place two of the square-shaped pills on my tongue and allow them to dissolve. I'm not sure what they do; I only know they help replenish the blood I've lost. So I lean against the wall until my head clears and I feel stronger on my feet.

This, such an ordinary task. It wasn't an obstacle I was anticipating.

I put socks on first; a simple pleasure that requires more effort than shooting a man. Briefly, I wonder what the medics must've done with my clothes. *The clothes,* I tell myself, *only the clothes*; I'm focusing only on the clothes from that day. Nothing else. No other details.

Boots. Socks. Slacks. Sweater. My military jacket with its many buttons.

The many buttons she ripped open.

It's a small reminder, but it's enough to spear me.

I try to fight it off but it lingers, and the more I try to ignore the memory, it multiplies into a monster that can no longer be contained. I don't even realize I've fallen against the wall until I feel the cold climbing up my skin; I'm breathing too hard and squeezing my eyes shut against the sudden wash of mortification.

I knew she was terrified, horrified, even, but I never thought those feelings were directed toward me. I'd seen her evolve as we spent time together; she seemed more comfortable as the weeks passed. Happier. At ease. I allowed myself to believe she'd seen a future for us; that she wanted to be with me and simply thought it impossible.

I'd never suspected that her newfound happiness was a consequence of Kent.

I run my good hand down the length of my face; cover my mouth. The things I said to her.

7

A tight breath.

The way I touched her.

My jaw tenses.

If it were nothing but sexual attraction I'm sure I would not suffer such unbearable humiliation. But I wanted so much more than her body.

All at once I implore my mind to imagine nothing but walls. Walls. White walls. Blocks of concrete. Empty rooms. Open space.

I build walls until they begin to crumble, and then I force another set to take their place. I build and build and remain unmoving until my mind is clear, uncontaminated, containing nothing but a small white room. A single light hanging from the ceiling.

Clean. Pristine. Undisturbed.

I blink back the flood of disaster pressing against the small world I've built; I swallow hard against the fear creeping up my throat. I push the walls back, making more space in the room until I can finally breathe. Until I'm able to stand.

Sometimes I wish I could step outside of myself for a while. I want to leave this worn body behind, but my chains are too many, my weights too heavy. This life is all that's left of me. And I know I won't be able to meet myself in the mirror for the rest of the day.

I'm suddenly disgusted with myself. I have to get out of this room as soon as possible, or my own thoughts will wage war against me. I make a hasty decision and for the first time, pay little attention to what I'm wearing. I tug on a fresh pair of pants and go without a shirt. I slip my good arm into the sleeve of a blazer and allow the other shoulder to drape over the sling carrying my injured arm. I look ridiculous, exposed like this, but I'll find a solution tomorrow.

First, I have to get out of this room.

THREE

Delalieu is the only person here who does not hate me.

He still spends the majority of his time in my presence cowering in fear, but somehow he has no interest in overthrowing my position. I can feel it, though I don't understand it. He's likely the only person in this building who's pleased that I'm not dead.

I hold up a hand to keep away the soldiers who rush forward as I open my door. It takes an intense amount of concentration to keep my fingers from shaking as I wipe the slight sheen of perspiration off my forehead, but I will not allow myself a moment of weakness. These men do not fear for my safety; they only want a closer look at the spectacle I've become. They want a first look at the cracks in my sanity. But I have no wish to be wondered at.

My job is to lead.

I've been shot; it will not be fatal. There are things to be managed; I will manage them.

This wound will be forgotten.

Her name will not be spoken.

My fingers clench and unclench as I make my way toward the L Room. I never before realized just how long these corridors are and just how many soldiers line the halls. There's no reprieve from their curious stares and their disappointment that I did not die. I don't even have to look at them to know what they're thinking. But knowing how they feel only makes me more determined to live a very long life.

I will give no one the satisfaction of my death.

"No."

I wave away the tea and coffee service for the fourth time. "I do not drink caffeine, Delalieu. Why do you always insist on having it served at my meals?"

"I suppose I always hope you will change your mind, sir."

I look up. Delalieu is smiling that strange, shaky smile. And I'm not entirely certain, but I think he's just made a joke.

"Why?" I reach for a slice of bread. "I am perfectly capable of keeping my eyes open. Only an idiot would rely on the energy of a bean or a leaf to stay awake throughout the day."

Delalieu is no longer smiling.

"Yes," he says. "Certainly, sir." And stares down at his food. I watch as his fingers push away the coffee cup.

I drop the bread back onto my plate. "My opinions," I say to him, quietly this time, "should not so easily break your own. Stand by your convictions. Form clear and logical arguments. Even if I disagree."

"Of course, sir," he whispers. He says nothing for a few seconds. But then I see him reach for his coffee again.

Delalieu.

He, I think, is my only course for conversation.

He was originally assigned to this sector by my father, and has since been ordered to remain here until he's no longer able. And though he's likely forty-five years my senior, he insists on remaining directly below me. I've known Delalieu's face since I was a child; I used to see him around our house, sitting in on the many meetings that took place in the years before The Reestablishment took over.

There was an endless supply of meetings in my house.

My father was always planning things, leading discussions and whispered conversations I was never allowed to be a part of. The men of those meetings are running this world now, so when I look at Delalieu I can't help but wonder why he never aspired to more. He was a part of this regime from the very beginning, but somehow seems content to die just as he is now. He chooses to remain subservient, even when I give him opportunities to speak up; he refuses to be promoted, even when I offer him higher pay. And while I appreciate his loyalty, his dedication unnerves me. He does not seem to wish for more than what he has.

I should not trust him.

And yet, I do.

But I've begun to lose my mind for a lack of companionable conversation. I cannot maintain anything but a cool distance from my soldiers, not only because they all wish to see me dead, but also because I have a responsibility as their leader to make unbiased decisions. I have sentenced myself to a life of solitude, one wherein I have no peers, and no mind but my own to live in. I looked to build myself as a feared leader, and I've succeeded; no one will question my authority or posit a contrary opinion. No one will speak to me as anything but the chief commander and regent of Sector 45. Friendship is not a thing I have ever experienced. Not as a child, and not as I am now.

Except.

One month ago, I met the exception to this rule. There *has* been one person who's ever looked me directly in the eye. The same person who's spoken to me with no filter; someone who's been unafraid to show anger and real, raw feeling in my presence; the only one who's ever dared to challenge me, to raise her voice to me—

I squeeze my eyes shut for what feels like the tenth time today. I unclench my fist around this fork, drop it to the table. My arm has begun to throb again, and I reach for the pills tucked away in my pocket.

"You shouldn't take more than eight of those within a twenty-four-hour period, sir."

I open the cap and toss three more into my mouth. I really wish my hands would stop shaking. My muscles feel too tight, too tense. Stretched thin.

I don't wait for the pills to dissolve. I bite down on them, crunching against their bitterness. There's something about the foul, metallic taste that helps me focus. "Tell me about Kent."

Delalieu knocks over his coffee cup.

The dining aides have left the room at my request; Delalieu receives no assistance as he scrambles to clean up the mess. I sit back in my chair, staring at the wall just behind him, mentally tallying up the minutes I've lost today.

"Leave the coffee."

"I—yes, of course, sorry, sir—"

"Stop."

Delalieu drops the sopping napkins. His hands are frozen in place, hovering over his plate.

"Speak."

I watch his throat move as he swallows, hesitates. "We don't know, sir," he whispers. "The building should've been impossible to find, much less to enter. It'd been bolted and rusted shut. But when we found it," he says, "when we found it, it was . . . the door had been destroyed. And we're not sure how they managed it."

I sit up. "What do you mean, *destroyed*?"

He shakes his head. "It was . . . very odd, sir. The door had been . . . mangled. As if some kind of animal had clawed through it. There was only a gaping, ragged hole in the middle of the frame."

I stand up entirely too fast, gripping the table for support. I'm breathless at the thought of it, at the possibility of what must've happened. And I can't help but allow myself the painful pleasure of recalling her name once more, because I know it must've been her. She must've done something extraordinary, and I wasn't even there to witness it.

"Call for transport," I tell him. "I will meet you in the Quadrant in exactly ten minutes."

"Sir?"

I'm already out the door.

FOUR

Clawed through the middle. Just like an animal. It's true.

To an unsuspecting observer it would be the only explanation, but even then it wouldn't make any sense. No animal alive could claw through this many inches of reinforced steel without amputating its own limbs.

And she is not an animal.

She is a soft, deadly creature. Kind and timid and terrifying. She's completely out of control and has no idea what she's capable of. And even though she hates me, I can't help but be fascinated by her. I'm enchanted by her pretend-innocence; jealous, even, of the power she wields so unwittingly. I want so much to be a part of her world. I want to know what it's like to be in her mind, to feel what she feels. It seems a tremendous weight to carry.

And now she's out there, somewhere, unleashed on society.

What a beautiful disaster.

I run my fingers along the jagged edges of the hole, careful not to cut myself. There's no design to it, no premeditation. Only an anguished fervor so readily apparent in the chaotic ripping-apart of this door. I can't help but wonder if she knew what she was doing when this happened, or if it was just as unexpected to her as it was the day she broke through that concrete wall to get to me.

I have to stifle a smile. I wonder how she must remember that day. Every soldier I've worked with has walked into a simulation knowing exactly what to expect, but I purposely kept those details from her. I thought the experience should be as undiluted as possible; I hoped the spare, realistic elements would lend authenticity to the event. More than anything else, I wanted her to have a chance to explore her true nature—to exercise her strength in a safe space—and given her past, I knew a child would be the perfect trigger. But I never could've anticipated such revolutionary results. Her performance was more than I had hoped for. And though I wanted to discuss the effects with her afterward, by the time I found her she was already planning her escape.

My smile falters.

"Would you like to step inside, sir?" Delalieu's voice jolts me back to the present. "There's not much to see within, but it is interesting to note that the hole is just big enough for someone to easily climb through. It seems clear, sir, what the intent was."

I nod, distracted. My eyes carefully catalog the dimensions of the hole; I try to imagine what it must've been like for her, to be here, trying to get through. I want so much to be able to talk to her about all of this.

My heart twists so suddenly.

I'm reminded, all over again, that she's no longer with me. She does not live on base anymore.

It's my fault she's gone. I allowed myself to believe

she was finally doing well and it affected my judgment. I should've been paying closer attention to details. To my soldiers. I lost sight of my purpose and my greater goal; the entire reason I brought her on base. I was stupid. Careless.

But the truth is, I was distracted.

By her.

She was so stubborn and childish when she first arrived, but as the weeks passed she'd seemed to settle; she felt less anxious to me, somehow less afraid. I have to keep reminding myself that her improvements had nothing to do with me.

They had to do with Kent.

A betrayal that somehow seemed impossible. That she would leave me for a robotic, unfeeling idiot like Kent. His thoughts are so empty, so mindless; it's like conversing with a desk lamp. I don't understand what he could've offered her, what she could've possibly seen in him except a tool for escape.

She still hasn't grasped that there's no future for her in the world of common people. She doesn't belong in the company of those who will never understand her. And I have to get her back.

I only realize I've said that last bit out loud when Delalieu speaks.

"We have troops all across the sector searching for her," he says. "And we've alerted the neighboring sectors, just in case the group of them should cross ove—"

"What?" I spin around, my voice a quiet, dangerous

thing. "What did you just say?"

Delalieu has turned a sickly shade of white.

"I was unconscious for all of one night! And you've already alerted the other sectors to this *catastrophe*—"

"I thought you would want to find them, sir, and I thought, if they should try to seek refuge elsewhere—"

I take a moment to breathe, to gather my bearings.

"I'm sorry, sir, I thought it would be safest—"

"She is with two of my own soldiers, Lieutenant. Neither one of them are stupid enough to guide her toward another sector. They have neither the clearance nor the tools to obtain said clearance in order to cross the sector line."

"But—"

"They've been gone one day. They are badly wounded and in need of aid. They're traveling on foot and with a stolen vehicle that is easily trackable. How far," I say to him, frustration breaking into my voice, "could they have gone?"

Delalieu says nothing.

"You have sent out a national alert. You've notified multiple sectors, which means the entire continent now knows. Which means the capitals have received word. Which means what?" I curl my only working hand into a fist. "What do you think that means, Lieutenant?"

For a moment, he seems unable to speak.

Then

"Sir," he gasps. "Please forgive me."

FIVE

Delalieu follows me to my door.

"Gather the troops in the Quadrant tomorrow at ten hundred hours," I say to him by way of good-bye. "I'll have to make an announcement about these recent events as well as what's to come."

"Yes, sir," Delalieu says. He doesn't look up. He hasn't looked at me since we left the warehouse.

I have other matters to worry about.

Not counting Delalieu's stupidity, there are an infinite number of things I must take care of right now. I can't afford any more difficulties, and I cannot be distracted. Not by her. Not by Delalieu. Not by anyone. I have to focus.

This is a terrible time to be wounded.

News of our situation has already hit a national level. Civilians and neighboring sectors are now aware of our minor uprising, and we have to tamp down the rumors as much as possible. I have to somehow defuse the alerts Delalieu has already sent out, and simultaneously suppress any hope of rebellion among the citizens. They're already too eager to resist, and any spark of controversy will reignite their fervor. Too many have died already, and they still don't seem to understand that standing against The Reestablishment is asking for more destruction. The civilians *must* be pacified.

I do not want war in my sector.

Now more than ever, I need to be in control of myself and my responsibilities. But my mind is scattered, my body fatigued and wounded. All day I've been inches from collapsing, and I don't know what to do. I have no idea how to fix it. This weakness is foreign to my being.

In just two days, one girl has managed to cripple me.

I've taken even more of these disgusting pills, but I feel weaker than I did this morning. I thought I could ignore the pain and inconvenience of a wounded shoulder, but the complication refuses to diminish. I am now wholly dependent on whatever will carry me through these next weeks of frustration. Medicine, medics, hours in bed.

All this for a kiss.

It's almost unbearable.

"I'll be in my office for the rest of the day," I tell Delalieu. "Have my meals sent to my room, and do not disturb me unless there are any new developments."

"Yes, sir."

"That'll be all, Lieutenant."

"Yes, sir."

I don't even realize how ill I feel until I close the bedroom door behind me. I stagger to the bed and grip the frame to keep from falling over. I'm sweating again and decide to strip the extra coat I wore on our outside excursion. I yank off the blazer I'd carelessly tossed over my injured shoulder this morning and fall backward onto my bed. I'm suddenly freezing. My good hand shakes as I reach for the medic call button.

I need to get the dressing on my shoulder changed. I need to eat something substantial. And more than anything else, I desperately need to take a real shower, which seems altogether impossible.

Someone is standing over me.

I blink several times but can only make out the general outline of their figure. A face keeps coming in and out of focus until I finally give up. My eyes fall closed. My head is pounding. Pain is searing through my bones and up my neck; reds and yellows and blues blur together behind my eyelids. I catch only clips of the conversation around me.

—*seems to have developed a fever*—

—*probably sedate him*—

—*how many did he take?*—

They're going to kill me, I realize. This is the perfect opportunity. I'm weak and unable to fight back, and someone has finally come to kill me. This is it. My moment. It has arrived. And somehow I can't seem to accept it.

I take a swipe at the voices; an inhuman sound escapes my throat. Something hard hits my fist and crashes to the floor. Hands clamp down on my right arm and pin it in place. Something is being tightened around my ankles, my wrist. I'm thrashing against these new restraints and kicking desperately at the air. The blackness seems to be pressing against my eyes, my ears, my throat. I can't breathe, can't hear or see clearly, and the suffocation of the moment is so terrifying that I'm almost certain I've lost my mind.

Something cold and sharp pinches my arm.

I have only a moment to reflect on the pain before it engulfs me.

SIX

"Juliette," I whisper. "What are you doing here?"

I'm half-dressed, getting ready for my day, and it's too early for visitors. These hours just before the sun rises are my only moments of peace, and no one should be in here. It seems impossible she gained access to my private quarters.

Someone should've stopped her.

Instead, she's standing in my doorway, staring at me. I've seen her so many times, but this is different—it's causing me physical pain to look at her. But somehow I still find myself drawn to her, wanting to be near her.

"I'm so sorry," she says, and she's wringing her hands, looking away from me. "I'm so, so sorry."

I notice what she's wearing.

It's a dark-green dress with fitted sleeves; a simple cut made of stretch cotton that clings to the soft curves of her figure. It complements the flecks of green in her eyes in a way I couldn't have anticipated. It's one of the many dresses I chose for her. I thought she might enjoy having something nice after being caged as an animal for so long. And I can't quite explain it, but it gives me a strange sense of pride to see her wearing something I picked out myself.

"I'm sorry," she says for the third time.

I'm again struck by how impossible it is that she's here. In my bedroom. Staring at me without my shirt on. Her hair is so long it falls to the middle of her back; I have to clench my fists against this unbidden need to run my hands through it. She's so beautiful.

I don't understand why she keeps apologizing.

She shuts the door behind her. She's walking over to me. My heart is beating quickly now, and it doesn't feel natural. I do not react this way. I do not lose control. I see her every day and manage to maintain some semblance of dignity, but something is off; this isn't right.

She's touching my arm.

She's running her fingers along the curve of my shoulder, and the brush of her skin against mine is making me want to scream. The pain is excruciating, but I can't speak; I'm frozen in place.

I want to tell her to stop, to leave, but parts of me are at war. I'm happy to have her close even if it hurts, even if it doesn't make any sense. But I can't seem to reach for her; I can't hold her like I've always wanted to.

She looks at me.

She searches me with those odd, blue-green eyes and I feel guilty so suddenly, without understanding why. But there's something about the way she looks at me that always makes me feel insignificant, as if she's the only one who's realized I'm entirely hollow inside. She's found the cracks in this cast I'm forced to wear every day, and it petrifies me.

That this girl would know exactly how to shatter me.

She rests her hand against my collarbone.

And then she grips my shoulder, digs her fingers into my skin like she's trying to tear off my arm. The agony is so blinding that this time I actually scream. I fall to my knees before her and she wrenches my arm, twisting it backward until I'm heaving from the effort to stay calm, fighting not to lose myself to the pain.

"Juliette," I gasp, "please—"

She runs her free hand through my hair, tugs my head back so I'm forced to meet her eyes. And then she leans into my ear, her lips almost touching my cheek. "Do you love me?" she whispers.

"What?" I breathe. "What are you doing—"

"Do you still love me?" she asks again, her fingers now tracing the shape of my face, the line of my jaw.

"Yes," I tell her. "Yes I still do—"

She smiles.

It's such a sweet, innocent smile that I'm actually shocked when her grip tightens around my arm. She twists my shoulder back until I'm sure it's being ripped from the socket. I'm seeing spots when she says, "It's almost over now."

"What is?" I ask, frantic, trying to look around. "What's almost over—"

"Just a little longer and I'll leave."

"No—no, don't go—where are you going—"

"You'll be all right," she says. "I promise."

"No," I'm gasping, "no—"

All at once she yanks me forward, and I'm awake so quickly I can't breathe.

I blink several times only to realize I've woken up in the middle of the night. Absolute blackness greets me from the corners of my room. My chest is heaving; my arm is bound and pounding, and I realize my pain medication has worn off. There's a small remote wedged under my hand; I press the button to replenish the dosage.

It takes a few moments for my breathing to stabilize. My thoughts slowly retreat from panic.

Juliette.

I can't control a nightmare, but in my waking moments her name is the only reminder I will permit myself.

The accompanying humiliation will not allow me much more than that.

SEVEN

"Well, isn't this embarrassing. My son, tied down like an animal."

I'm half-convinced I'm having another nightmare. I blink my eyes open slowly; I stare up at the ceiling. I make no sudden movements, but I can feel the very real weight of restraints around my left wrist and both ankles. My injured arm is still bound and slung across my chest. And though the pain in my shoulder is present, it's dulled to a light hum. I feel stronger. Even my head feels clearer, sharper somehow. But then I taste the tang of something sour and metal in my mouth and wonder how long I've been in bed.

"Did you really think I wouldn't find out?" he asks, amused.

He moves closer to my bed, his footsteps reverberating right through me. "You have Delalieu whimpering apologies for disturbing me, begging my men to blame him for the inconvenience of this unexpected visit. No doubt you terrified the old man for doing his job, when the truth is, I would've found out even without his alerts. This," he says, "is not the kind of mess you can conceal. You're an idiot for thinking otherwise."

I feel a light tugging on my legs and realize he's undoing

27

my restraints. The brush of his skin against mine is abrupt and unexpected, and it triggers something deep and dark within me, enough to make me physically ill. I taste vomit at the back of my throat. It takes all my self-control not to jerk away from him.

"Sit up, son. You should be well enough to function now. You were too stupid to rest when you were supposed to, and now you've overcorrected. Three days you've been unconscious, and I arrived twenty-seven hours ago. Now get up. This is ridiculous."

I'm still staring at the ceiling. Hardly breathing.

He changes tactics.

"You know," he says carefully, "I've actually heard an interesting story about you." He sits down on the edge of my bed; the mattress creaks and groans under his weight. "Would you like to hear it?"

My left hand has begun to tremble. I clench it fast against the bedsheets.

"Private 45B-76423. Fletcher, Seamus." He pauses. "Does that name sound familiar?"

I squeeze my eyes shut.

"Imagine my surprise," he says, "when I heard that my son had finally done something right. That he'd finally taken initiative and dispensed with a traitorous soldier who'd been stealing from our storage compounds. I heard you shot him right in the forehead." A laugh. "I congratulated myself—told myself you'd finally come into your own, that you'd finally learned how to lead properly. I was almost proud.

"That's why it came as an even greater shock to me to hear Fletcher's family was still alive." He claps his hands together. "Shocking, of course, because you, of all people, should know the rules. Traitors come from a family of traitors, and one betrayal means death to them all."

He rests his hand on my chest.

I'm building walls in my mind again. White walls. Blocks of concrete. Empty rooms and open space.

Nothing exists inside of me. Nothing stays.

"It's funny," he continues, thoughtful now, "because I told myself I'd wait to discuss this with you. But somehow, *this* moment seems so right, doesn't it?" I can hear him smile. "To tell you just how tremendously . . . *disappointed* I am. Though I can't say I'm surprised." He sighs. "In a single month you've lost two soldiers, couldn't contain a clinically insane girl, upended an entire sector, and encouraged rebellion among the citizens. And somehow, I'm not surprised at all."

His hand shifts; lingers at my collarbone.

White walls, I think.

Blocks of concrete.

Empty rooms. Open space.

Nothing exists inside of me. Nothing stays.

"But what's worse than all this," he says, "is not that you've managed to humiliate me by disrupting the order I'd finally managed to establish. It's not even that you somehow got yourself shot in the process. But that you would show sympathy to the family of a *traitor*," he says, laughing, his voice a happy, cheerful thing. "This is unforgivable."

My eyes are open now, blinking up at the fluorescent lights above my head, focused on the white of the bulbs blurring my vision. I will not move. I will not speak.

His hand closes around my throat.

The movement is so rough and violent I'm almost relieved. Some part of me always hopes he'll go through with it; that maybe this time he'll actually let me die. But he never does. It never lasts.

Torture is not torture when there's any hope of relief.

He lets go all too soon and gets exactly what he wants. I jerk upward, coughing and wheezing and finally making a sound that acknowledges his existence in this room. My whole body is shaking now, my muscles in shock from the assault and from remaining still for so long. My skin is cold sweat; my breaths are labored and painful.

"You're very lucky," he says, his words too soft. He's up now, no longer inches from my face. "So lucky I was here to make things right. So lucky I had time to correct the mistake."

I freeze.

The room spins.

"I was able to track down his wife," he says. "Fletcher's wife and their three children. I hear they sent their regards." A pause. "Well, this was before I had them killed, so I suppose it doesn't really matter now, but my men told me they said hello. It seems she remembered you," he says, laughing softly. "The wife. She said you went to visit them before all this . . . unpleasantness occurred. You were always visiting the compounds, she said. Asking after the civilians."

I whisper the only two words I can manage.

"Get out."

"This is my boy!" he says, waving a hand in my direction. "A meek, pathetic fool. Some days I'm so disgusted by you I don't know whether to shoot you myself. And then I realize you'd probably like that, wouldn't you? To be able to blame me for your downfall? And I think no, best to let him die of his own stupidity."

I stare blankly ahead, fingers flexing against the mattress.

"Now tell me," he says, "what happened to your arm? Delalieu seemed as clueless as the others."

I say nothing.

"Too ashamed to admit you were shot by one of your own soldiers, then?"

I close my eyes.

"And what about the girl?" he asks. "How did she escape? Ran off with one of your men, didn't she?"

I grip the bedsheet so hard my fist starts shaking.

"Tell me," he says, leaning into my ear. "How would you deal with a traitor like that? Are you going to go visit his family, too? Make nice with his wife?"

And I don't mean to say it out loud, but I can't stop myself in time. "I'm going to kill him."

He laughs out loud so suddenly it's almost a howl. He claps a hand on my head and musses my hair with the same fingers he just closed around my throat. "Much better," he says. "So much better. Now get up. We have work to do."

And I think yes, I wouldn't mind doing the kind of work that would remove Adam Kent from this world.

A traitor like him does not deserve to live.

EIGHT

I'm in the shower for so long I actually lose track of time.

This has never happened before.

Everything is off, unbalanced. I'm second-guessing my decisions, doubting everything I thought I didn't believe in, and for the first time in my life, I am genuinely, bone-achingly tired.

My father is here.

We are sleeping under the same godforsaken roof; a thing I'd hoped never to experience again. But he's here, staying on base in his own private quarters until he feels confident enough to leave. Which means he'll be fixing our problems by wreaking havoc on Sector 45. Which means I will be reduced to becoming his puppet and messenger, because my father never shows his face to anyone except those he's about to kill.

He is the supreme commander of The Reestablishment, and prefers to dictate anonymously. He travels everywhere with the same select group of soldiers, communicates only through his men, and only in extremely rare circumstances does he ever leave the capital.

News of his arrival at Sector 45 has probably spread around base by now, and has likely terrified my soldiers.

Because his presence, real or imagined, has only ever signi-fied one thing: torture.

It's been so long since I've felt like a coward.

But this, this is bliss. This protracted moment—this illu-sion—of strength. Being out of bed and able to bathe: it's a small victory. The medics wrapped my injured arm in some kind of impermeable plastic for the shower, and I'm finally well enough to stand on my own. My nausea has settled, the dizziness is gone. I should finally be able to think clearly, and yet, my choices still seem so muddled.

I've forced myself not to think about her, but I'm begin-ning to realize I'm still not strong enough; not just yet, and especially not while I'm still actively searching for her. It's become a physical impossibility.

Today, I need to go back to her room.

I need to search her things for any clues that might help me find her. Kent's and Kishimoto's bunks and lockers have already been cleared out; nothing incriminating was found. But I'd ordered my men to leave her room—*Juliette's* room—exactly as it was. No one but myself is allowed to reenter that space. Not until I've had the first look.

And this, according to my father, is my first task.

"That'll be all, Delalieu. I'll let you know if I require assis-tance."

He's been following me around even more than usual lately. Apparently he came to check on me when I didn't show for the assembly I'd called two days ago, and had the pleasure of finding me completely delirious and half out of my mind. He's somehow managed to lay the blame for all this on himself.

If he were anyone else, I would've had him demoted.

"Yes, sir. I'm sorry, sir. And please forgive me—I never meant to cause additional problems—"

"You are in no danger from me, Lieutenant."

"I'm so sorry, sir," he whispers. His shoulders fall. His head bows.

His apologies are making me uncomfortable. "Have the troops reassemble at thirteen hundred hours. I still need to address them about these recent developments."

"Yes, sir," he says. He nods once, without looking up.

"You are dismissed."

"Sir." He drops his salute and disappears.

I'm left alone in front of her door.

Funny, how accustomed I'd become to visiting her here; how it gave me a strange sense of comfort to know that she and I were living in the same building. Her presence on base changed everything for me; the weeks she spent here became the first I ever enjoyed living in these quarters. I looked forward to her temper. Her tantrums. Her ridiculous arguments. I wanted her to yell at me; I would've congratulated her had she ever slapped me in the face. I was always pushing her, toying with her emotions. I wanted to meet the real girl trapped behind the fear. I wanted her to finally break free of her own carefully constructed restraints.

35

Because while she might be able to feign timidity within the confines of isolation, out here—amid chaos, destruction—I knew she'd become something entirely different. I was just waiting. Every day, patiently waiting for her to understand the breadth of her own potential; never realizing I'd entrusted her to the one soldier who might take her away from me.

I should shoot myself for it.

Instead, I open the door.

The panel slides shut behind me as I cross the threshold. I find myself alone, standing here, in the last place she touched. The bed is messy and unmade, the doors to her armoire hanging open, the broken window temporarily taped shut. There's a sinking, nervous pain in my stomach that I choose to ignore.

Focus.

I step into the bathroom and examine the toiletries, the cabinets, even the inside of the shower.

Nothing.

I walk back over to the bed and run my hand over the rumpled comforter, the lumpy pillows. I allow myself a moment to appreciate the evidence that she was once here, and then I strip the bed. Sheets, pillowcases, comforter, and duvet; all tossed to the floor. I scrutinize every inch of the pillows, the mattress, and the bed frame, and again find nothing.

The side table. Nothing.

Under the bed. Nothing.

The light fixtures, the wallpaper, each individual piece of clothing in her armoire. Nothing.

It's only as I'm making my way toward the door that something catches my foot. I look down. There, caught just under my boot, is a thick, faded rectangle. A small, unassuming notebook that could fit in the palm of my hand.

And I'm so stunned that for a moment I can't even move.

NINE

How could I have forgotten?

This notebook was in her pocket the day she was making her escape. I'd found it just before Kent put a gun to my head, and at some point in the chaos, I must've dropped it. And I realize I should've been looking for this all along.

I bend down to pick it up, carefully shaking out bits and pieces of glass from the pages. My hand is unsteady, my heart pounding in my ears. I have no idea what this might contain. Pictures. Notes. Scrambled, half-formed thoughts.

It could be anything.

I flip the notebook over in my hands, my fingers memorizing its rough, worn surface. The cover is a dull shade of brown, but I can't tell if it's been stained by dirt and age, or if it was always this color. I wonder how long she's had it. Where she might've acquired it.

I stumble backward, the backs of my legs hitting her bed. My knees buckle, and I catch myself on the edge of the mattress. I take in a shaky breath and close my eyes.

I'd seen footage from her time in the asylum, but it was essentially useless. The lighting was always too dim; the small window did little to illuminate the dark corners of her room. She was often an indistinguishable form; a dark shadow one might never even notice. Our cameras were only good at detecting movement—and maybe a lucky moment when the sun hit her at the right angle—but she rarely moved. Most of her time was spent sitting very, very still, on her bed or in a dark corner. She almost never spoke. And when she did, it was never in words. She spoke only in numbers.

Counting.

There was something so unreal about her, sitting there. I couldn't even see her face; couldn't discern the outline of her figure. Even then she fascinated me. That she could seem so calm, so still. She would sit in one place for hours at a time, unmoving, and I always wondered where she was in her mind, what she might be thinking, how she could possibly exist in that solitary world. More than anything else, I wanted to hear her speak.

I was desperate to hear her voice.

I'd always expected her to speak in a language I could understand. I thought she'd start with something simple. Maybe something unintelligible. But the first time we ever caught her talking on camera, I couldn't look away. I sat there, transfixed, nerves stretched thin, as she touched one hand to the wall and counted.

4,572.

I watched her count. To 4,572.

It took five hours.

Only afterward did I realize she was counting her breaths.

I couldn't stop thinking about her after that. I was distracted long before she arrived on base, constantly wondering what she might be doing and whether she'd speak again. If she wasn't counting out loud, was she counting in her head? Did she ever think in letters? Complete sentences? Was she angry? Sad? Why did she seem so serene for a girl I'd been told was a volatile, deranged animal? Was it a trick?

I'd seen every piece of paper documenting the critical moments in her life. I'd read every detail in her medical records and police reports; I'd sorted through school complaints, doctors' notes, her official sentencing by The Reestablishment, and even the asylum questionnaire submitted by her parents. I knew she'd been pulled out of school at fourteen. I knew she'd been through severe testing and was forced to take various—and dangerous—experimental drugs, and had to undergo electroshock therapy. In two years she'd been in and out of nine different juvenile detention centers and had been examined by more than fifty different doctors. All of them described her as a monster. They called her a danger to society and a threat to humanity. A girl who would ruin our world and had already begun by murdering a small child. At sixteen, her parents suggested she be locked away. And so she was.

None of it made sense to me.

A girl cast off by society, by her own family—she had to contain so much feeling. Rage. Depression. Resentment. Where was it?

She was nothing like the other inmates at the asylum—the ones who were truly disturbed. Some would spend hours hurling themselves at the wall, breaking bones and fracturing skulls. Others were so deranged they would claw at their own skin until they drew blood, literally ripping themselves to pieces. Some had entire conversations with themselves out loud, laughing and singing and arguing. Most would tear their clothes off, content to sleep and stand naked in their own filth. She was the only one who showered regularly or even washed her clothes. She would take her meals calmly, always finishing whatever she was given. And she spent most of her time staring out the window.

She'd been locked up for almost a year and had not lost her sense of humanity. I wanted to know how she could suppress so much; how she'd achieved such outward calm. I'd asked for profiles on the other prisoners because I wanted comparisons. I wanted to know if her behavior was normal.

It wasn't.

I watched the unassuming outline of this girl I could not see and did not know, and I felt an unbelievable amount of respect for her. I admired her, envied her composure—her steadiness in the face of all she'd been forced to endure. I don't know that I understood what it was, exactly, I was feeling at the time, but I knew I wanted her all to myself.

I wanted to know her secrets.

And then one day, she stood up in her cell and walked over to the window. It was early morning, just as the sun was rising; I caught a glimpse of her face for the very first time. She pressed her palm to the window and whispered two words, just once.

Forgive me.

I hit rewind too many times.

I could never tell anyone I'd developed a newfound fascination with her. I had to effect a pretense, an outward indifference—an arrogance—toward her. She was to be our weapon and nothing more, just an innovative instrument of torture.

A detail I cared very little about.

My research had led me to her files by pure accident. Coincidence. I did not seek her out in search of a weapon; I never had. Far before I'd ever seen her on film, and far, far before I ever spoke a word to her, I had been researching something else. For something else.

My motives were my own.

Utilizing her as a weapon was a story I fed to my father; I needed an excuse to have access to her, to gain the necessary clearance to study her files. It was a charade I was forced to maintain in front of my soldiers and the hundreds of cameras that monitor my existence. I did not bring her on base to exploit her ability. And I certainly did not expect to fall for her in the process.

But these truths and my real motivations will be buried with me.

I fall hard onto the bed. Clap a hand over my forehead, drag it down the length of my face. I never would've sent Kent to stay with her if I could've taken the time to go myself. Every move I made was a mistake. Every calculated effort was a failure. I only wanted to watch her interact with someone. I wondered if she'd seem different; if she'd shatter the expectations I'd already formed in my mind by simply having a normal conversation. But watching her talk to someone else made me crazy. I was jealous. Ridiculous. I wanted her to know *me*; I wanted her to talk to *me*. And I felt it then: this strange, inexplicable sense that she might be the only person in the world I could really care about.

I force myself to sit up. I hazard a glance at the notebook still clutched in my hand.

I lost her.

She hates me.

She hates me and I repulse her and I might never see her again, and it is entirely my own doing. This notebook might be all I have left of her. My hand is still hovering over the cover, tempting me to open it and find her again, even if it's only for a short while, even if it's only on paper. But part of me is terrified. This might not end well. This might not be anything I want to see. And so help me, if this turns out to be some kind of diary concerning her thoughts and feelings about Kent, I might just throw myself out the window.

I pound my fist against my forehead. Take a long, steadying breath.

Finally, I flip it open. My eyes fall to the first page.

And only then do I begin to understand the weight of what I've found.

I keep thinking I need to stay calm, that it's all in my head, that everything is going to be fine and someone is going to open the door now, someone is going to let me out of here. I keep thinking it's going to happen. I keep thinking it has to happen, because things like this don't just happen. This doesn't happen. People aren't forgotten like this. Not abandoned like this.

This doesn't just happen.

My face is caked with blood from when they threw me on the ground, and my hands are still shaking even as I write this. This pen is my only outlet, my only voice, because I have no one else to speak to, no mind but my own to drown in and all the lifeboats are taken and all the life preservers are broken and I don't know how to swim I can't swim I can't swim and it's getting so hard. It's getting so hard. It's like there are a million screams caught inside of my chest but I have to keep them all in because what's the point of screaming if you'll never be heard and no one will ever hear me in here. No one will ever hear me again.

I've learned to stare at things.

The walls. My hands. The cracks in the walls. The lines on my fingers. The shades of gray in the concrete. The shape of my fingernails. I pick one thing and stare at it for what must be hours. I keep time in my head by counting the seconds as they pass. I keep days in my head by writing them down. Today is day two. Today is the second day. Today is a day.

Today.

It's so cold. It's so cold it's so cold.

Please please please

I slam the cover shut.

I'm shaking again, and this time I can't stop it. This time the shaking is coming from deep within my core, from a profound realization of what I'm holding in my hands. This journal is not from her time spent here. It has nothing to do with me, or Kent, or anyone at all. This journal is a documentation of her days spent in the asylum.

And suddenly this small, battered notebook means more to me than anything I've ever owned.

TEN

I don't even know how I manage to get myself back to my own rooms so quickly. All I know is that I've locked the door to my bedroom, unlocked the door to my office only to lock myself inside, and now I'm sitting here, at my desk, stacks of papers and confidential material shoved out of the way, staring at the tattered cover of something I'm very nearly terrified to read. There's something so personal about this journal; it looks as if it's been bound together by the loneliest feelings, the most vulnerable moments of one person's life. She wrote whatever lies within these pages during some of the darkest hours of her seventeen years, and I'm about to get exactly what I've always wanted.

A look into her mind.

And though the anticipation is killing me, I'm also acutely aware of just how badly this might backfire. I'm suddenly not sure I even want to know. And yet I do. I definitely do.

So I open the book, and turn to the next page. Day three.

I started screaming today.

And those four words hit me harder than the worst kind of physical pain.

My chest is rising and falling, my breaths coming in too hard. I have to force myself to keep reading.

I soon realize there's no order to the pages. She seems to have started back at the beginning after she came to the end of the notebook and realized she'd run out of space. She's written in the margins, over other paragraphs, in tiny and nearly illegible fonts. There are numbers scrawled all over everything, sometimes the same number repeating over and over and over again. Sometimes the same word has been written and rewritten, circled and underlined. And nearly every page has sentences and paragraphs almost entirely crossed out.

It's complete chaos.

My heart constricts at this realization, at this proof of what she must've experienced. I'd hypothesized about what she might've suffered in all that time, locked up in such dark, horrifying conditions. But seeing it for myself—I wish I weren't right.

And now, even as I try to read in chronological order, I find I'm unable to keep up with the method she's used to number everything; the system she created on these pages is something only she'd be able to decipher. I can only flip through the book and seek out the bits that are most coherently written.

My eyes freeze on a particular passage.

It's a strange thing, to never know peace. To know that no matter where you go, there is no sanctuary. That the threat of pain is always a whisper away. I'm not safe locked into these 4 walls, I was never safe leaving my house, and I couldn't even feel safe in the 14 years I lived at home. The asylum kills people every day, the world has already been taught to fear me, and my home is the same place where my father locked me in my room every night and my mother screamed at me for being the abomination she was forced to raise.

She always said it was my face.

There was something about my face, she said, that she couldn't stand. Something about my eyes, the way I looked at her, the fact that I even existed. She'd always tell me to stop looking at her. She'd always scream it. Like I might attack her. Stop looking at me, she'd scream. You just stop looking at me, she'd scream.

She put my hand in the fire once.

Just to see if it would burn, she said. Just to check if it was a regular hand, she said.

I was 6 years old then.

I remember because it was my birthday.

I knock the notebook to the floor.

I'm upright in an instant, trying to steady my heart. I run a hand through my hair, my fingers caught at the roots. These words are too close to me, too familiar. The story of a child abused by its parents. Locked away and discarded. It's too close to my mind.

I've never read anything like this before. I've never read anything that could speak directly to my bones. And I know I shouldn't. I know, somehow, that it won't help, that it

48

won't teach me anything, that it won't give me clues about where she might've gone. I already know that reading this will only make me crazy.

But I can't stop myself from reaching for her journal once more.

I flip it open again.

> ~~Am I insane yet?~~
> ~~Has it happened yet?~~
> ~~How will I ever know?~~

My intercom screeches so suddenly that I trip over my own chair and have to catch myself on the wall behind my desk. My hands won't stop shaking; my forehead is beaded with sweat. My bandaged arm has begun to burn, and my legs are suddenly too weak to stand on. I have to focus all my energy on sounding normal as I accept the incoming message.

"What?" I demand.

"Sir, I only wondered, if you were still—well, the assembly, sir, unless of course I got the time wrong, I'm so sorry, I shouldn't have bothered you—"

"Oh for the love of God, Delalieu." I try to shake off the tremble in my voice. "Stop apologizing. I'm on my way."

"Yes, sir," he says. "Thank you, sir."

I disconnect the line.

And then I grab the notebook, tuck it in my pocket, and head out the door.

ELEVEN

I'm standing at the edge of the courtyard above the Quadrant, looking out at the thousands of faces staring back at me. These are my soldiers. Standing single-file line in their assembly uniforms. Black shirts, black pants, black boots.

No guns.

Left fists pressed against their hearts.

I make an effort to focus on—and care about—the task at hand; but somehow I can't help but be hyperaware of the notebook tucked away in my pocket, the shape of it pressing against my leg and torturing me with its secrets.

I am not myself.

My thoughts are tangled in words that are not my own. I have to take a sharp breath to clear my head; I clench and unclench my fist.

"Sector 45," I say, speaking directly into the square of microphonic mesh.

They shift at once, dropping their left hands and instead placing their right fists on their chests.

"We have a number of important things to discuss today," I tell them, "the first of which is readily apparent." I gesture to my arm. Study their carefully crafted emotionless faces.

Their traitorous thoughts are so obvious.

They think of me as little more than a deranged child. They do not respect me; they are not loyal to me. They are disappointed that I stand before them; angry; disgusted, even, that I am not dead of this wound.

But they do fear me.

And that is all I require.

"I was injured," I say, "while in pursuit of two of our defecting soldiers. Private Adam Kent and Private Kenji Kishimoto collaborated their escape in an effort to abduct Juliette Ferrars, our newest transfer and critical asset to Sector 45. They have been charged with the crime of unlawfully seizing and detaining Ms. Ferrars against her will. But, and most importantly, they have been rightly convicted of treason against The Reestablishment. When found, they will be executed on sight."

Terror, I realize, is one of the easiest feelings to read. Even on a soldier's stoic face.

"Second," I say, more slowly this time, "in an effort to expedite the process of stabilizing Sector 45, its citizens, and the ensuing chaos resulting from these recent disruptions, the supreme commander of The Reestablishment has joined us on base. He arrived," I tell them, "not thirty-six hours ago."

Some men have dropped their fists. Forgotten themselves. Their eyes are wide.

Petrified.

"You will welcome him," I say.

They drop to their knees.

It's strange, wielding this kind of power. I wonder if my father is proud of what he's created. That I'm able to bring thousands of grown men to their knees with only a few words; with only the sound of his title. It's a horrifying, addicting kind of thing.

I count five beats in my head.

"Rise."

They do. And then they march.

Five steps backward, forward, standing in place. They raise their left arms, curl their fingers into fists, and fall on one knee. This time, I do not let them up.

"Prepare yourselves, gentlemen," I say to them. "We will not rest until Kent and Kishimoto are found and Ms. Ferrars has returned to base. I will confer with the supreme commander in these next twenty-four hours; our newest mission will soon be clearly defined. In the interim you are to understand two things: first, that we will defuse the tension among the citizens and take pains to remind them of their promises to our new world. And second, be certain that we will find Privates Kent and Kishimoto." I stop. Look around, focusing on their faces. "Let their fates serve as an example to you. We do not welcome traitors in The Reestablishment. And we do not forgive."

TWELVE

One of my father's men is waiting for me outside my door.

I glance in his direction, but not long enough to discern his features. "State your business, soldier."

"Sir," he says, "I've been instructed to inform you that the supreme commander requests your presence in his quarters for dinner at twenty-hundred hours."

"Consider your message received." I move to unlock my door.

He steps forward, blocking my path.

I turn to face him.

He's standing less than a foot away from me: an implicit act of disrespect; a level of comfort even Delalieu does not allow himself. But unlike my men, the sycophants who surround my father consider themselves lucky. Being a member of the supreme commander's elite guard is considered a privilege and an honor. They answer to no one but him.

And right now, this soldier is trying to prove he outranks me.

He's jealous of me. He thinks I'm unworthy of being the son of the supreme commander of The Reestablishment. It's practically written on his face.

I have to stifle my impulse to laugh as I take in his cold

gray eyes and the black pit that is his soul. He wears his sleeves rolled up above his elbows, his military tattoos clearly defined and on display. The concentric black bands of ink around his forearms are accented in red, green, and blue, the only sign on his person to indicate that he is a soldier highly elevated in rank. It's a sick branding ritual I've always refused to be a part of.

The soldier is still staring at me.

I incline my head in his direction, raise my eyebrows.

"I am required," he says, "to wait for verbal acceptance of this invitation."

I take a moment to consider my choices, which are none.

I, like the rest of the puppets in this world, am entirely subservient to my father's will. It's a truth I'm forced to contend with every day: that I've never been able to stand up to the man who has his fist clenched around my spine.

It makes me hate myself.

I meet the soldier's eyes again and wonder, for a fleeting moment, if he has a name, before I realize I couldn't possibly care less. "Consider it accepted."

"Yes, s—"

"And next time, soldier, you will not step within five feet of me without first asking permission."

He blinks, stunned. "Sir, I—"

"You are confused." I cut him off. "You assume your work with the supreme commander grants you immunity from rules that govern the lives of other soldiers. Here, you are mistaken."

His jaw tenses.

"Never forget," I say, quietly now, "that if I wanted your job, I could have it. And never forget that the man you so eagerly serve is the same man who taught me how to fire a gun when I was nine years old."

His nostrils flare. He stares straight ahead.

"Deliver your message, soldier. And then memorize this one: do not ever speak to me again."

His eyes are focused on a point directly behind me now, his shoulders rigid.

I wait.

His jaw is still tight. He slowly lifts his hand in salute.

"You are dismissed," I say.

I lock my bedroom door behind me and lean against it. I need just a moment. I reach for the bottle I left on my night-stand and shake out two of the square pills; I toss them into my mouth, closing my eyes as they dissolve. The darkness behind my eyelids is a welcome relief.

Until the memory of her face forces itself into my consciousness.

I sit down on my bed and drop my head into my hand. I shouldn't be thinking about her right now. I have hours of paperwork to sort through and the additional stress of my father's presence to contend with. Dinner with him should be a spectacle. A soul-crushing spectacle.

I squeeze my eyes shut tighter and make a weak effort to build the walls that would surely clear my mind. But this time, they don't work. Her face keeps cropping up, her journal taunting me from its place in my pocket. And I begin to realize that some small part of me doesn't want to wish away the thoughts of her. Some part of me enjoys the torture.

This girl is destroying me.

A girl who has spent the last year in an insane asylum. A girl who would try to shoot me dead for kissing her. A girl who ran off with another man just to get away from me.

Of course this is the girl I would fall for.

I close a hand over my mouth.

I am losing my mind.

I tug off my boots. Pull myself up onto my bed and allow my head to hit the pillows behind me.

She slept here, I think. She slept in my bed. She woke up in my bed. She was here and I let her get away.

I failed.

I lost her.

I don't even realize I've tugged her notebook out of my pocket until I'm holding it in front of my face. Staring at it. Studying the faded cover in an attempt to understand where she might've acquired such a thing. She must've stolen it from somewhere, though I can't imagine where.

There are so many things I want to ask her. So many things I wish I could say to her.

Instead, I open her journal, and read.

Sometimes I close my eyes and paint these walls a different color.

I imagine I'm wearing warm socks and sitting by a fire. I imagine someone's given me a book to read, a story to take me away from the torture of my own mind. I want to be someone else somewhere else with something else to fill my mind. I want to run, to feel the wind tug at my hair. I want to pretend that this is just a story within a story. That this cell is just a scene, that these hands don't belong to me, that this window leads to somewhere beautiful if only I could break it. I pretend this pillow is clean, I pretend this bed is soft. I pretend and pretend and pretend until the world becomes so breathtaking behind my eyelids that I can no longer contain it. But then my eyes fly open and I'm caught around the throat by a pair of hands that won't stop suffocating suffocating suffocating

My thoughts, I think, will soon be sound.

My mind, I hope, will soon be found.

The journal drops out of my hand and onto my chest. I run my only free hand across my face, through my hair. I rub the back of my neck and haul myself up so fast that my head hits the headboard and I'm actually grateful. I take a moment to appreciate the pain.

And then I pick up the book.

And turn the page.

I wonder what they're thinking. My parents. I wonder where they are. I wonder if they're okay now, if they're happy now, ~~if they finally got what they wanted~~. I wonder if my mother will ever have another child. I wonder if someone will ever be kind enough to kill me, and I wonder if hell is better than here. I wonder what my face looks like now. I wonder if I'll ever breathe fresh air again.

I wonder about so many things.

Sometimes I'll stay awake for days just counting everything I can find. I count the walls, the cracks in the walls, my fingers and toes. I count the springs in the bed, the threads in the blanket, the steps it takes to cross the room and back. I count my teeth and the individual hairs on my head and the number of seconds I can hold my breath.

But sometimes I get so tired that I forget I'm not allowed to wish for things anymore, and I find myself wishing for the one thing I've always wanted. The only thing I've always dreamt about.

I wish all the time for a friend.

I dream about it. I imagine what it would be like. To smile and be smiled upon. To have a person to confide in; someone who wouldn't throw things at me or stick my hands in the fire or beat me for being born. Someone who would hear that I'd been thrown away and would try to find me, who would never be afraid of me.

Someone who'd know I'd never try to hurt them.

I fold myself into a corner of this room and bury my head in my knees and rock back and forth and back and forth and back and forth and I wish and I wish and I wish and I dream of impossible things until I've cried myself to sleep.

I wonder what it would be like to have a friend.

And then I wonder who else is locked in this asylum. I wonder where the other screams are coming from.

I wonder if they're coming from me.

I'm trying to focus, telling myself these are just empty words, but I'm lying. Because somehow, just reading these words is too much; and the thought of her in pain is causing me an unbearable amount of agony.

To know that she experienced this.

She was thrown into this by her own parents, cast off and abused her entire life. Empathy is not an emotion I've ever known, but now it's drowning me, pulling me into a world I never knew I could enter. And though I've always believed she and I shared many things in common, I did not know how deeply I could feel it.

It's killing me.

I stand up. Start pacing the length of my bedroom until I've finally worked up the nerve to keep reading. Then I take a deep breath.

And turn the page.

~~*There's something simmering inside of me.*~~

~~*Something I've never dared to tap into, something I'm afraid to acknowledge. There's a part of me clawing to break free from the cage I've trapped it in, banging on the doors of my heart, begging to be free.*~~

~~*Begging to let go.*~~

~~Every day I feel like I'm reliving the same nightmare. I~~
~~open my mouth to shout, to fight, to swing my fists, but my~~
~~vocal cords are cut, my arms are heavy and weighted down~~
~~as if trapped in wet cement and I'm screaming but no one~~
~~can hear me, no one can reach me and I'm caught. And it's~~
~~killing me.~~

~~I've always had to make myself submissive, subservient,~~
~~twisted into a pleading, passive mop just to make everyone~~
~~else feel safe and comfortable. My existence has become~~
~~a fight to prove I'm harmless, that I'm not a threat, that~~
~~I'm capable of living among other human beings without~~
~~hurting them.~~

~~And I'm so tired I'm so tired I'm so tired I'm so tired~~
~~and sometimes I get so angry~~

I don't know what's happening to me.

"God, Juliette," I gasp.

And fall to my knees.

"Call for transport immediately." I need to get out. I need to get out right now.

"Sir? I mean, yes, sir, of course—but where—"

"I have to visit the compounds," I say. "I should make my rounds before my meeting this evening." This is both true and false. But I'm willing to do anything right now that might get my mind off this journal.

"Oh, certainly, sir. Would you like me to accompany you?"

"That won't be necessary, Lieutenant, but thank you for the offer."

"I—s-sir," he stammers. "Of course, it's m-my pleasure, sir, to assist you—"

Good God, I have taken leave of my senses. I never thank Delalieu. I've likely given the poor man a heart attack.

"I will be ready to go in ten minutes." I cut him off.

He stutters to a stop. Then, "Yes, sir. Thank you, sir."

I'm pressing my fist to my mouth as the call disconnects.

THIRTEEN

We had homes. Before.

All different kinds.

1-story homes. 2-story homes. 3-story homes.

We bought lawn ornaments and twinkle lights, learned to ride bikes without training wheels. We purchased lives confined within 1, 2, 3 stories already built, stories caught inside of structures we could not change.

We lived in those stories for a while.

We followed the tale laid out for us, the prose pinned down in every square foot of space we'd acquired. We were content with the plot twists that only mildly redirected our lives. We signed on the dotted line for the things we didn't know we cared about. We ate the things we shouldn't, spent money when we couldn't, lost sight of the Earth we had to inhabit and wasted wasted wasted everything. Food. Water. Resources.

Soon the skies were gray with chemical pollution, and the plants and animals were sick from genetic modification, and diseases rooted themselves in our air, our meals, our blood and bones. The food disappeared. The people were dying. Our empire fell to pieces.

The Reestablishment said they would help us. Save us.

Rebuild our society.

Instead they tore us all apart.

I enjoy coming to the compounds.

It's an odd place to seek refuge, but there's something about seeing so many civilians in such a vast, open space that reminds me of what I'm meant to be doing. I'm so often confined within the walls of Sector 45 headquarters that I forget the faces of those we're fighting and those we're fighting for.

I like to remember.

Most days I visit each cluster on the compounds; I greet the residents and ask about their living conditions. I can't help but be curious about what life must be like for them now. Because while the world changed for everyone else, it always stayed the same for me. Regimented. Isolated. Bleak.

There was a time when things were better, when my father wasn't always so angry. I was about four years old then. He used to let me sit on his lap and search his pockets. I'd get to keep anything I wanted as long as my argument was convincing enough. It was his idea of a game.

But this was all before.

I wrap my coat more tightly around my body, feel the material press against my back. I flinch without meaning to.

The life I know now is the only one that matters. The suffocation, the luxury, the sleepless nights, and the dead bodies. I've always been taught to focus on power and pain, gaining and inflicting.

I grieve nothing.

I take everything.

It's the only way I know how to live in this battered body. I empty my mind of the things that plague me and burden my soul, and I take all that I can from what little pleasantness comes my way. I do not know what it is to live a normal life; I do not know how to sympathize with the civilians who've lost their homes. I do not know what it must've been like for them before The Reestablishment took over.

So I enjoy touring the compounds.

I enjoy seeing how other people live; I like that the law requires them to answer my questions. I would have no way of knowing, otherwise.

But my timing is off.

I paid little attention to the clock before I left base and didn't realize how soon the sun would be setting. Most civilians are returning home to retire for the evening, their bodies bowed, huddled against the cold as they shuffle toward the metal clusters they share with at least three other families.

These makeshift homes are built from forty-foot shipping containers; they're stacked side by side and on top of one another, lumped together in groups of four and six. Each container has been insulated; fitted with two windows and one door. Stairs to the upper levels are attached on either side. The roofs are lined with solar panels that provide free electricity for each grouping.

It's something I'm proud of.

Because it was my idea.

When we were seeking temporary shelter for the civilians, I suggested refurbishing the old shipping containers that line the docks of every port around the world. Not only are they cheap, easily replicated, and highly customizable, but they're stackable, portable, and built to withstand the elements. They'd require minimal construction, and with the right team, thousands of housing units could be ready in a matter of days.

I'd pitched the idea to my father, thinking it might be the most effective option; a temporary solution that would be far less cruel than tents; something that would provide true, reliable shelter. But the result was so effective that The Reestablishment saw no need to upgrade. Here, on land that used to be a landfill, we've stacked thousands of containers; clusters of faded, rectangular cubes that are easy to monitor and keep track of.

The people are still told that these homes are temporary. That one day they will return to the memories of their old lives, and that things will be bright and beautiful again. But this is all a lie.

The Reestablishment has no plans to move them.

Civilians are caged on these regulated grounds; these containers have become their prisons. Everything has been numbered. The people, their homes, their level of importance to The Reestablishment.

Here, they've become a part of a huge experiment. A world wherein they work to support the needs of a regime that makes them promises it will never fulfill.

This is my life.

This sorry world.

Most days I feel just as caged as these civilians; and that's likely why I always come here. It's like running from one prison to another; an existence wherein there is no relief, no refuge. Where even my own mind is a traitor.

I should be stronger than this.

I've been training for just over a decade. Every day I've worked to hone my physical and mental strengths. I'm five feet, nine inches and 170 pounds of muscle. I've been built to survive, to maximize endurance and stamina, and I'm most comfortable when I'm holding a gun in my hand. I can fieldstrip, clean, reload, disassemble, and reassemble more than 150 different types of firearms. I can shoot a target through the center from almost any distance. I can break a person's windpipe with only the edge of my hand. I can temporarily paralyze a man with nothing but my knuckles.

On the battlefield, I'm able to disconnect myself from the motions I've been taught to memorize. I've developed a reputation as a cold, unfeeling monster who fears nothing and cares for less.

But this is all very deceiving.

Because the truth is, I am nothing but a coward.

FOURTEEN

The sun is setting.

Soon I'll have no choice but to return to base, where I'll have to sit still and listen to my father speak instead of shooting a bullet through his open mouth.

So I stall for time.

I watch from afar as the children run around while their parents herd them home. I wonder about how one day they'll get old enough to realize that the Reestablishment Registration cards they carry are actually tracking their every movement. That the money their parents make from working in whichever factories they were sorted into is closely monitored. These children will grow up and finally understand that everything they do is recorded, every conversation dissected for whispers of rebellion. They don't know that profiles are created for every citizen, and that every profile is thick with documentation on their friendships, relationships, and work habits; even the ways in which they choose to spend their free time.

We know everything about everyone.

Too much.

So much, in fact, that I seldom remember we're dealing with real, live people until I see them on the compounds.

I've memorized the names of nearly every person in Sector 45. I like to know who lives within my jurisdiction, soldiers and civilians alike.

That's how I knew, for example, that Private Seamus Fletcher, 45B-76423, was beating his wife and children every night.

I knew he was spending all his money on alcohol; I knew he'd been starving his family. I monitored the REST dollars he spent at our supply centers and carefully observed his family on the compounds. I knew his three children were all under the age of ten and hadn't eaten in weeks; I knew that they'd repeatedly been to the compounds' medic for broken bones and stitches. I knew he'd punched his nine-year-old daughter in the mouth and split her lip, fractured her jaw, and broken her two front teeth; and I knew his wife was pregnant. I also knew that he hit her so hard one night she lost the child the following morning.

I knew, because I was there.

I'd been stopping by each residence, visiting with the civilians, asking questions about their health and overall living situations. I'd wanted to know about their work conditions and whether any members of their family were ill and needed to be quarantined.

She was there that day. Fletcher's wife. Her nose was broken so badly that both her eyes had swollen shut. Her frame was so thin and frail, her color so sallow that I thought she might snap in half just by sitting down. But when I asked about her injuries, she wouldn't look me in the eye. She said she'd fallen down; that because of her fall, she'd lost the pregnancy and managed to break her nose in the process.

I nodded. Thanked her for her cooperation in answering my questions.

And then I called for an assembly.

I'm well aware that the majority of my soldiers steal from our storage compounds. I oversee our inventory closely, and I know that supplies go missing all the time. But I allow these infractions because they do not upset the system. A few extra loaves of bread or bars of soap keep my soldiers in better spirits; they work harder if they are healthy, and most are supporting spouses, children, and relatives. So it is a concession I allow.

But there are some things I do not forgive.

I don't consider myself a moral man. I do not philosophize about life or bother with the laws and principles that govern most people. I do not pretend to know the difference between right and wrong. But I do live by a certain kind of code. And sometimes, I think, you have to learn how to shoot first.

Seamus Fletcher was murdering his family. And I shot him in the forehead because I thought it'd be kinder than ripping him to pieces by hand.

But my father picked up where Fletcher left off. My father had three children and their mother shot dead, all because of the drunken bastard they'd depended on to provide for them. He was their father, her husband, and the reason they all died a brutal, untimely death.

And some days I wonder why I insist on keeping myself alive.

FIFTEEN

Once I'm back on base, I head straight down.

I ignore the soldiers and their salutes as I pass by, paying little attention to the blend of curiosity and suspicion in their eyes. I didn't even realize I was headed this way until I arrived at headquarters; but my body seems to know more about what I need right now than my mind does. My footfalls are heavy; the steady, clipping sound of my boots echoes along the stone path as I reach the lower levels.

I haven't been here in nearly two weeks.

The room has been rebuilt since my last visit; the glass panel and the concrete wall have been replaced. And as far as I'm aware, she was the last person to use this room.

I brought her here myself.

I push through a set of swinging double doors into the locker room that sits adjacent to the simulation deck. My hand searches for a switch in the dark; the light beeps once before it flickers to life. A dull hum of electricity vibrates through these vast dimensions. Everything is quiet, abandoned.

Just as I like it.

I strip as quickly as this injured arm will allow me to. I still have two hours before I'm expected to meet my father for dinner, so I shouldn't be feeling so anxious, but my nerves are not cooperating. Everything seems to be catching up with me at once. My failures. My cowardice. My stupidity.

Sometimes I'm just so tired of this life.

I'm standing barefoot on this concrete floor in nothing but an arm sling, hating the way this injury constantly slows me down. I grab the shorts stashed in my locker and pull them on as quickly as I can, leaning against the wall for support. When I'm finally upright, I slam the locker shut and make my way into the adjoining room.

I hit another switch, and the main operational deck whirs to life. The computers beep and flash as the program recalibrates; I run my fingers along the keyboard.

We use these rooms to generate simulations.

We manipulate the technology to create environments and experiences that exist entirely in the human mind. Not only are we able to create the framework, but we can also control minute details. Sounds, smells, false confidence, paranoia. The program was originally designed to help train soldiers for specific missions, as well as aid them in overcoming fears that would otherwise cripple them on the battlefield.

I use it for my own purposes.

I used to come here all the time before she arrived on base. This was my safe space; my only escape from the world. I only wish it didn't come with a uniform. These shorts are starchy and uncomfortable, the polyester itchy and irritating. But the shorts are lined with a special chemical that reacts with my skin and feeds information to the sensors; it helps place me in the experience, and will enable to me to run for miles without ever running into actual, physical walls in my true environment. And in order for the process to be as effective as possible, I have to be wearing next to nothing. The cameras are hypersensitive to body heat, and work best when not in contact with synthetic materials.

I'm hoping this detail will be fixed in the next generation of the program.

The mainframe prompts me for information; I quickly enter an access code that grants me clearance to pull up a history of my past simulations. I look up and over my shoulder as the computer processes the data; I glance through the newly repaired two-way mirror that sees into the main chamber. I still can't believe she broke down an entire wall of glass and concrete and managed to walk away uninjured.

Incredible.

The machine beeps twice; I spin back around. The programs in my history are loaded and ready to be executed.

Her file is at the top of the list.

I take a deep breath; try to shake off the memory. I don't regret putting her through such a horrifying experience; I don't know that she would've ever allowed herself to finally lose control—to finally inhabit her own body—if I hadn't found an effective method of provoking her. Ultimately, I really believe it helped her, just as I intended it to. But I do wish she hadn't pointed a gun at my face and jumped out a window shortly afterward.

I take another slow, steadying breath.

And select the simulation I came here for.

SIXTEEN

I'm standing in the main chamber.

Facing myself.

This is a very simple simulation. I didn't change my clothes or my hair or even the room's carpeted floors. I didn't do anything at all except create a duplicate of myself and hand him a gun.

He won't stop staring at me.

One.

He cocks his head. "Are you ready?" A pause. "Are you scared?"

My heart kicks into gear.

He lifts his arm. Smiles a little. "Don't worry," he says. "It's almost over now."

Two.

"Just a little longer and I'll leave," he says, pointing the gun directly at my forehead.

My palms are sweating. My pulse is racing.

"You'll be all right," he lies. "I promise."

Three.

Boom.

SEVENTEEN

"You sure you're not hungry?" my father asks, still chewing. "This is really quite good."

I shift in my seat. Focus on the ironed creases in these pants I'm wearing.

"Hm?" he asks. I can actually hear him smiling.

I'm acutely aware of the soldiers lining the walls of this room. He always keeps them close, and always in constant competition with one another. Their first assignment was to determine which of the eleven of them was the weakest link. The one with the most convincing argument was then required to dispose of his target.

My father finds these practices amusing.

"I'm afraid I'm not hungry. The medicine," I lie, "destroys my appetite."

"Ah," he says. I hear him put his utensils down. "Of course. How inconvenient."

I say nothing.

"Leave us."

Two words and his men disperse in a matter of seconds. The door slides shut behind them.

"Look at me," he says.

I look up, my eyes carefully devoid of emotion. I hate his

face. I can't stand to look at him for too long; I don't like experiencing the full impact of how very inhuman he is. He is not tortured by what he does or how he lives. In fact, he enjoys it. He loves the rush of power; he thinks of himself as an invincible entity.

And in some ways, he's not wrong.

I've come to believe that the most dangerous man in the world is the one who feels no remorse. The one who never apologizes and therefore seeks no forgiveness. Because in the end it is our emotions that make us weak, not our actions.

I turn away.

"What did you find?" he asks, with no preamble.

My mind immediately goes to the journal I've stowed away in my pocket, but I make no movement. I do not dare flinch. People seldom realize that they tell lies with their lips and truths with their eyes all the time. Put a man in a room with something he's hidden and then ask him where he's hidden it; he'll tell you he doesn't know; he'll tell you you've got the wrong man; but he'll almost always glance at its exact location. And right now I know my father is watching me, waiting to see where I might look, what I might say next.

I keep my shoulders relaxed and take a slow, imperceptible breath to steady my heart. I do not respond. I pretend to be lost in thought.

"Son?"

I look up. Feign surprise. "Yes?"

"What did you find? When you searched her room today?"

I exhale. Shake my head as I lean back in my chair. "Broken glass. A disheveled bed. Her armoire, hanging open. She took only a few toiletries and some extra pairs of clothes and undergarments. Nothing else was out of place." None of this is a lie.

I hear him sigh. He pushes away his plate.

I feel the outline of her notebook burning against my upper leg.

"And you say you do not know where she might've gone?"

"I only know that she, Kent, and Kishimoto must be together," I tell him. "Delalieu says they stole a car, but the trace disappeared abruptly at the edge of a barren field. We've had troops on patrol for days now, searching the area, but they've found nothing."

"And where," he says, "do you plan on searching next? Do you think they might've crossed over into another sector?" His voice is off. Entertained.

I glance up at his smiling face.

He's only asking me these questions to test me. He has his own answers, his own solution already prepared. He wants to watch me fail by answering incorrectly. He's trying to prove that without him, I'd make all the wrong decisions.

He's mocking me.

"No," I tell him, my voice solid, steady. "I don't think they'd do something as idiotic as cross into another sector.

77

They don't have the access, the means, or the capacity. Both men were severely wounded, rapidly losing blood, and too far from any source of emergency aid. They're probably dead by now. The girl is likely the only survivor, and she can't have gone far because she has no idea how to navigate these areas. She's been blind to them for too long; everything in this environment is foreign to her. Furthermore, she does not know how to drive, and if she'd somehow managed to commandeer a vehicle, we would've received word of stolen property. Considering her overall health, her propensity toward physical inexertion, and her general lack of access to food, water, and medical attention, she's probably collapsed within a five-mile radius of this supposed barren field. We have to find her before she freezes to death."

My father clears his throat.

"Yes," he says, "those are interesting theories. And perhaps under ordinary circumstances, they might actually hold true. But you are failing to recall the most important detail."

I meet his gaze.

"She is not normal," he says, leaning back in his chair. "And she is not the only one of her kind."

My heartbeat quickens. I blink too fast.

"Oh come now, surely you'd suspected? You'd hypothesized?" He laughs. "It seems statistically impossible that she'd be the only mistake manufactured by our world. You knew this, but you didn't want to believe it. And I came here to tell you that it's true." He cocks his head at me. Smiles a big, vibrant smile. "There are more of them. And they've recruited her."

"No," I breathe.

"They infiltrated your troops. Lived among you in secret. And now they've stolen your toy and run away with it. God only knows how they hope to manipulate her for their own benefit."

"How can you be certain?" I ask. "How do you know they've succeeded in taking her with them? Kent was half-dead when I left him—"

"Pay attention, son. I'm telling you that they are not normal. They do not follow your rules; there is no logic that binds them. You have no idea what oddities they might be capable of." A pause. "Furthermore, I have known for some time now that a group of them exists undercover in this area. But in all these years they've always kept to themselves. They did not interfere with my methods, and I thought it best to allow them to die off on their own without infecting in our civilians unnecessary panic. You understand, of course," he says. "After all, you could hardly contain even one of them. They're freakish things to behold."

"You knew?" I'm on my feet now. Trying to stay calm. "You knew of their existence, all this time, and yet you did nothing? You said nothing?"

"It seemed unnecessary."

"And now?" I demand.

"Now it seems pertinent."

"Unbelievable!" I throw my hands in the air. "That you would withhold such information from me! When you knew of my plans for her—when you knew what pains I'd taken to bring her here—"

"Calm yourself," he says. He stretches out his legs; rests the ankle of one on the knee of the other. "We are going to find them. This barren field Delalieu speaks of—the area where the car was no longer traceable? That is our target location. They must be located underground. We must find the entrance and destroy them quietly, from within. Then we will have punished the guilty among them, and kept the rest from rising up and inspiring rebellion in our people."

He leans forward.

"The civilians hear everything. And right now they are vibrating with a new kind of energy. They're feeling inspired that anyone was able to run away, and that you've been wounded in the process. It makes our defenses seem weak and easily penetrable. We must destroy this perception by righting the imbalance. Fear will return everything to its proper place."

"But they've been searching," I tell him. "My men. Every day they've scoured the area and found nothing. How can we be sure we'll find anything at all?"

"Because," he says, "you will lead them. Every night. After curfew, while the civilians are asleep. You will cease your daylight searches; you will not give the citizens anything else to talk about. Act quietly, son. Do not show your moves. I will remain on base and oversee your responsibilities through my men; I will dictate to Delalieu as necessary. And in the interim, you shall find them, so that I may destroy them as swiftly as possible. This nonsense has gone on long enough," he says, "and I'm no longer feeling gracious."

EIGHTEEN

I'm sorry. I'm so sorry. I'm so sorry I'm so sorry I'm so so sorry I'm so sorry. I'm so sorry I'm so sorry I'm so so sorry. I'm so sorry. I'm so sorry. I'm so sorry I'm so so sorry I'm so sorry I'm so sorry I'm so sorry I'm so so sorry. I'm so sorry. I'm so sorry I'm so sorry I'm so so sorry I'm so sorry. I'm so sorry. I'm so sorry I'm so so sorry. I'm so sorry. I'm so sorry I'm so sorry I'm so so sorry I'm so sorry. I'm so sorry I'm so sorry. I'm so so sorry. I'm so sorry. I'm so sorry I'm so sorry I'm so so sorry I'm so sorry. I'm so sorry. I'm so sorry I'm so so sorry. I'm sorry I'm so sorry please forgive me.

It was an accident.

Forgive me

Please forgive me

There is little I allow anyone to discover about me. There's even less I'm willing to share about myself. And of the many things I've never discussed, this is one of them.

I like to take long baths.

I've had an obsession with cleanliness for as long as I can remember. I've always been so mired in death and destruction that I think I've overcompensated by keeping myself pristine as much as possible. I take frequent showers. I brush and floss three times a day. I trim my own hair every week. I scrub my hands and nails before I go to bed and just after I wake up. I have an unhealthy preoccupation with wearing only freshly laundered clothes. And whenever I'm experiencing any extreme level of emotion, the only thing that settles my nerves is a long bath.

So that's what I'm doing right now.

The medics taught me how to bind my injured arm in the same plastic they used before, so I'm able to sink beneath the surface without a problem. I submerge my head for a long while, holding my breath as I exhale through my nose. I feel the small bubbles rise to the surface.

The warm water makes me feel weightless. It carries my burdens for me, understanding that I need a moment to relieve my shoulders of this weight. To close my eyes and relax.

My face breaks the surface.

I don't open my eyes; only my nose and lips meet the oxygen on the other side. I take small, even breaths to help steady my mind. It's so late that I don't know what time it is; all I know is that the temperature has dropped significantly, and the cold air is tickling my nose. It's a strange sensation, to have 98 percent of my body floating at a warm, welcome temperature, while my nose and lips twitch from the cold.

I sink my face below the water again.

I could live here, I think. Live where gravity does not know my name. Here I am unbound, untethered by the chains of this life. I am a different body, a different shell, and my weight is carried by the hands of friends. So many nights I've wished I could fall asleep under this sheet.

I sink deeper.

In one week my entire life has changed.

My priorities, shifted. My concentration, destroyed. Everything I care about right now revolves around one person, and for the first time in my life, it's not myself. Her words have been burned into my mind. I can't stop picturing her as she must've been, can't stop imagining what she must've experienced. Finding her journal has crippled me. My feelings for her have spiraled out of control. I've never been so desperate to see her, to talk to her.

I want her to know that I understand now. That I didn't understand before. She and I really are the same; in so many more ways than I could've known.

But now she's out of reach. She's gone somewhere with strangers who do not know her and would not care for her as I would. She's been dropped into another foreign environment with no time to transition, and I'm worried about her. A person in her situation—with her past—does not recover overnight. And now, one of two things is bound to happen: She's either going to completely shut down, or she's going to explode.

I sit up too fast, breaking free of the water, gasping for air.

I push my wet hair out of my face. I lean back against the tiled wall, allowing the cool air to calm me, to clear my thoughts.

I have to find her before she breaks.

I've never wanted to cooperate with my father before, never wanted to agree with his motives or his methods. But in this instance, I'm willing to do just about anything to get her back.

And I'm eager for any opportunity to snap Kent's neck.

That traitorous bastard. The idiot who thinks he's won himself a pretty girl. He has no idea who she is. No idea what she's about to become.

And if he thinks he's even remotely suited to match her, he's even more of an idiot than I gave him credit for.

NINETEEN

"Where's the coffee?" I ask, my eyes scanning the table.

Delalieu drops his fork. The silverware clangs against the china plates. He looks up, eyes wide. "Sir?"

"I'd like to try it," I tell him, attempting to spread butter on my toast with my left hand. I toss a look in his direction. "You're always going on about your coffee, aren't you? I thought I—"

Delalieu jumps up from the table without a word. Bolts out the door.

I laugh silently into my plate.

Delalieu carts the tea and coffee tray in himself and stations it by my chair. His hands shake as he pours the dark liquid into a teacup, places it on a saucer, sets it on the table, and pushes it in my direction.

I wait until he's finally sitting down again before I take a sip. It's a strange, obscenely bitter sort of drink; not at all what I expected. I glance up at him, surprised to discover that a man like Delalieu would begin his day by bracing himself with such a potent, foul-tasting liquid. I find I respect him for it.

"This isn't terrible," I tell him.

His face splits into a smile so wide, so beatific, I wonder

if he's misheard me. He's practically beaming when he says, "I take mine with cream and sugar. The taste is far better that w—"

"Sugar." I put my cup down. Press my lips together, fight back a smile. "You add sugar to it. Of course you do. That makes so much more sense."

"Would you like some, sir?"

I hold up my hand. Shake my head. "Call back the troops, Lieutenant. We're going to halt daytime missions and instead launch in the evening, after curfew. You will remain on base," I tell him, "where the supreme will dictate orders through his men; carry out any demands as they are required. I shall lead the group myself." I stop. Hold his eyes. "There will be no more talk of what has transpired. Nothing for the civilians to see or speak of. Do you understand?"

"Yes, sir," he says, his coffee forgotten. "I'll issue the orders at once."

"Good."

He stands up.

I nod.

He leaves.

I'm beginning to feel real hope for the first time since she left. We're going to find her. Now, with this new information—with an entire army against a group of clueless rebels—it seems impossible we won't.

I take a deep breath. Take another sip of this coffee.

I'm surprised to discover how much I enjoy the bitter taste of it.

TWENTY

He's waiting for me when I return to my room.

"The orders have been issued," I tell him without looking in his direction. "We will mobilize tonight." I hesitate. "So if you'll excuse me, I have other matters to contend with."

"What's it like," he asks, "to be so crippled?" He's smiling. "How can you stand to look at yourself, knowing that you've been disabled by your own subordinates?"

I pause outside the adjoining door to my office. "What do you want?"

"What," he says, "is your fascination with that girl?"

My spine goes rigid.

"She is more to you than just an experiment, isn't she?" he says.

I turn around slowly. He's standing in the middle of my room, hands in his pockets, smiling at me like he might be disgusted.

"What are you talking about?"

"Look at yourself," he says. "I haven't even said her name and you fall apart." He shakes his head, still studying me. "Your face is pale, your only working hand is clenched. You're breathing too fast, and your entire body is tense." A pause. "You have betrayed yourself, son. You think you're

88

very clever," he says, "but you're forgetting who taught you your tricks."

I go hot and cold all at once. I try to unclench my fist and I can't. I want to tell him he's wrong, but I'm suddenly feeling unsteady, wishing I'd eaten more at breakfast, and then wishing I'd eaten nothing at all.

"I have work to do," I manage to say.

"Tell me," he says, "that you would not care if she died along with the others."

"What?" The nervous, shaky word escapes my lips too soon.

My father drops his eyes. Clasps and unclasps his hands. "You have disappointed me in so many ways," he says, his voice deceptively soft. "Please don't let this be another."

For a moment I feel as though I exist outside of my body, as if I'm looking at myself from his perspective. I see my face, my injured arm, these legs that suddenly seem unable to carry my weight. Cracks begin to form along my face, all the way down my arms, my torso, my legs.

I imagine this is what it's like to fall apart.

I don't realize he's said my name until he repeats it twice more.

"What do you want from me?" I ask, surprised to hear how calm I sound. "You've walked into my room without permission; you stand here and accuse me of things I don't have time to understand. I am following your rules, your orders. We will leave tonight; we will find their hideout. You can destroy them as you see fit."

"And your girl," he says, cocking his head at me. "Your Juliette?"

I flinch at the sound of her name. My pulse is racing so fast it feels like a whisper.

"If I were to shoot three holes in her head, how would that make you feel?" He stares at me. Watches me. "Disappointed, because you'd have lost your pet project? Or devastated, because you'd have lost the girl you love?"

Time seems to slow down, melting all around me.

"It would be a waste," I say, ignoring the tremble I feel deep inside me, threatening to tip me over, "to lose something I've invested so much time in."

He smiles. "It's good to know you see it that way," he says. "But projects are, after all, easily replaced. And I'm certain we'll be able to find a better, more practical use of your time."

I blink at him so slowly. Part of my chest feels as if it's collapsed.

"Of course," I hear myself say.

"I knew you'd understand." He claps me on my injured shoulder as he leaves. My knees nearly buckle. "It was a good effort, son. But she's cost us too much time and expense, and she's proven completely useless. This way we'll be disposing of many inconveniences all at once. We'll just consider her collateral damage." He shoots me one last smile before walking past me and out the door.

I fall back against the wall.

And crumble to the floor.

TWENTY-ONE

*Swallow the tears back often enough and they'll start
feeling like acid dripping down your throat.*

*It's that terrible moment when you're sitting still so
still so still because* ~~you don't want them to see you cry~~ *you
don't want to cry but your lips won't stop trembling and
your eyes are filled to the brim with please and I beg you
and please and I'm sorry and please and have mercy and
maybe this time it'll be different but it's always the same.
There's no one to run to for comfort. No one on your side.*

Light a candle for me, I used to whisper to no one.

Someone

Anyone

If you're out there

Please tell me you can feel this fire.

It's day five of our patrols, and still, nothing.

I lead the group every night, marching into the silence
of these cold, winter landscapes. We search for hidden passageways, camouflaged manholes—any indication that
there might be another world under our feet.

And every night we return to base with nothing.

The futility of these past few days has washed over me,
dulling my senses, settling me into a kind of daze I haven't

been able to claw my way out of. Every day I wake up searching for a solution to the problems I've forced upon myself, but I have no idea how to fix this.

If she's out there, he will find her. And he will kill her.

Just to teach me a lesson.

My only hope is to find her first. Maybe I could hide her. Or tell her to run. Or pretend she's already dead. Or maybe I'll convince him that she's different, better than the others; that she's worth keeping alive.

I sound like a pathetic, desperate idiot.

I am a child all over again, hiding in dark corners and praying he won't find me. Hoping he'll be in a good mood today. That maybe everything will be all right. That maybe my mother won't be screaming this time.

How quickly I revert back to another version of myself in his presence.

I've gone numb.

I've been performing my tasks with a sort of mechanical dedication; it requires minimal effort. Moving is simple enough. Eating is something I've grown accustomed to.

I can't stop reading her notebook.

My heart actually hurts, somehow, but I can't stop turning the pages. I feel as if I'm pounding against an invisible wall, as if my face has been bandaged in plastic and I can't breathe, can't see, can't hear any sound but my own heart beating in my ears.

I've wanted few things in this life.

I've asked for nothing from no one.

And now, all I'm asking for is another chance. An opportunity to see her again. But unless I can find a way to stop him, these words will be all I'll ever have of her.

These paragraphs and sentences. These letters.

I've become obsessed. I carry her notebook with me everywhere I go, spending all my free moments trying to decipher the words she's scribbled in the margins, developing stories to go along with the numbers she's written down.

I've also noticed that the last page is missing. Ripped out.

I can't help but wonder why. I've searched through the book a hundred times, looking for other sections where pages might be gone, but I've found none. And somehow I feel cheated, knowing there's a piece I might've missed. It's not even my journal; it's none of my business at all, but I've read her words so many times now that they feel like my own. I can practically recite them from memory.

It's strange being in her head without being able to see her. I feel like she's here, right in front of me. I feel like I now know her so intimately, so privately. I'm safe in the company of her thoughts; I feel welcome, somehow. Understood. So much so that some days I manage to forget that she's the one who put this bullet hole in my arm.

I almost forget that she still hates me, despite how hard I've fallen for her.

And I've fallen.

So hard.

I've hit the ground. Gone right through it. Never in my

life have I felt this. Nothing like this. I've felt shame and cowardice, weakness and strength. I've known terror and indifference, self-hate and general disgust. I've seen things that cannot be unseen.

And yet I've known nothing like this terrible, horrible, paralyzing feeling. I feel crippled. Desperate and out of control. And it keeps getting worse. Every day I feel sick. Empty and somehow aching.

Love is a heartless bastard.

I'm driving myself insane.

I fall backward onto my bed, fully dressed. Coat, boots, gloves. I'm too tired to take them off. These late-night shifts have left me very little time to sleep. I feel as though I've been existing in a constant state of exhaustion.

My head hits the pillow and I blink once. Twice.

I collapse.

TWENTY-TWO

"No," I hear myself say. "You're not supposed to be here."

She's sitting on my bed. She's leaning back on her elbows, legs outstretched in front of her, crossed at the ankles. And while some part of me understands I must be dreaming, there's another, overwhelmingly dominant part of me that refuses to accept this. Part of me wants to believe she's really here, inches away from me, wearing this short, tight black dress that keeps slipping up her thighs. But everything about her looks different, oddly vibrant; the colors are all wrong. Her lips are a richer, deeper shade of pink; her eyes seem wider, darker. She's wearing shoes I know she'd never wear. And strangest of all: she's smiling at me.

"Hi," she whispers.

It's just one word, but my heart is already racing. I'm inching away from her, stumbling back and nearly slamming my skull against the headboard, when I realize my shoulder is no longer wounded. I look down at myself. My arms are both fully functional. I'm wearing nothing but a white T-shirt and my underwear.

She shifts positions in an instant, propping herself up on her knees before crawling over to me. She climbs onto my lap. She's now straddling my waist. I'm suddenly breathing too fast.

95

Her lips are at my ear. Her words are so soft. "Kiss me," she says.

"Juliette—"

"I came all the way here." She's still smiling at me. It's a rare smile, the kind she's never honored me with. But somehow, right now, she's mine. She's mine and she's perfect and she wants me, and I'm not going to fight it.

I don't want to.

Her hands are tugging at my shirt, pulling it up over my head. Tossing it to the floor. She leans forward and kisses my neck, just once, so slowly. My eyes fall closed.

There aren't enough words in this world to describe what I'm feeling.

I feel her hands move down my chest, my stomach; her fingers run along the edge of my underwear. Her hair falls forward, grazing my skin, and I have to clench my fists to keep from pinning her to my bed.

Every nerve ending in my body is awake. I've never felt so alive or so desperate in my life, and I'm sure if she could hear what I'm thinking right now, she'd run out the door and never come back.

Because I want her.

Now.

Here.

Everywhere.

I want nothing between us.

I want her clothes off and the lights on and I want to study her. I want to unzip her out of this dress and take my time with every inch of her. I can't help my need to just stare; to know her and her features: the slope of her nose, the curve of her lips, the line of her jaw. I want to run my fingertips across the soft skin of her neck and trace it all the way down. I want to feel the weight of her pressed against me, wrapped around me.

I can't remember a reason why this can't be right or real. I can't focus on anything but the fact that she's sitting on my lap, touching my chest, staring into my eyes like she might really love me.

I wonder if I've actually died.

But just as I lean in, she leans back, grinning before reaching behind her, never once breaking eye contact with me. "Don't worry," she whispers. "It's almost over now."

Her words seem so strange, so familiar. "What do you mean?"

"Just a little longer and I'll leave."

"No." I'm blinking fast, reaching for her. "No, don't go— where are you going—"

"You'll be all right," she says. "I promise."

"*No*—"

But now she's holding a gun.

And pointing it at my heart.

TWENTY-THREE

These letters are all I have left.

26 friends to tell my stories to.

26 letters are all I need. I can stitch them together to create oceans and ecosystems. I can fit them together to form planets and solar systems. I can use letters to construct skyscrapers and metropolitan cities populated by people, places, things, and ideas that are more real to me than these 4 walls.

I need nothing but letters to live. Without them I would not exist.

Because these words I write down are the only proof I have that I'm still alive.

It's extraordinarily cold this morning.

I suggested we make a smaller, more low-key trip to the compounds earlier in the day today, just to see if any of the civilians seemed suspicious or out of place. I'm beginning to wonder if Kent and Kishimoto and all the others are living among the people in secret. They must, after all, have to have some source for food and water—something that ties them to society; I doubt they can grow anything underground. But of course, these are all assumptions. They might very well have a person who can grow food out of thin air.

I quickly address my men; instruct them to disperse and remain inconspicuous. Their job is to watch everyone today, and report their findings directly to me.

Once they're gone, I'm left to look around and be alone with my thoughts. It's a dangerous place to be.

God, she seemed so real in my dream.

I close my eyes, dragging a hand down my face; my fingers linger against my lips. I could feel her. I could really *feel* her. Even thinking about it now makes my heart race. I don't know what I'm going to do if I keep having such intense dreams about her. I won't be able to function at all.

I take a deep, steadying breath and focus. I allow my eyes to wander naturally, and I can't help but be distracted by the children running around. They seem so spirited and carefree. In a strange way, it makes me sad that they've been able to find happiness in this life. They have no idea what they've missed; no idea what the world used to be like.

Something barrels into the backs of my legs.

I hear a strange, labored sort of panting; I turn around.

It's a dog.

A tired, starving dog, so thin and frail it looks like it could be knocked over by the wind. But it's staring at me. Unafraid. Mouth open. Tongue lolling.

I want to laugh out loud.

I glance around quickly before scooping the dog into my arms. I don't need to give my father any more reasons to castrate me, and I don't trust my soldiers not to report something like this.

That I would play with a dog.

I can already hear the things my father would say to me.

I carry the whimpering creature over to one of the recently vacated housing units—I just saw all three families leave for work—and duck down behind one of the fences. The dog seems smart enough to understand that now is not the time to bark.

I tug off my glove and reach into my pocket for the Danish I grabbed at breakfast this morning; I hadn't had a chance to eat anything before our early start today. And though I haven't the faintest idea what dogs eat, exactly, I offer the Danish anyway.

The dog practically bites off my hand.

It chokes down the Danish in two bites and starts licking my fingers, jumping against my chest in excitement, finally plowing into the warmth of my open coat. I can't control the easy laughter that escapes my lips; I don't want to. I haven't felt like laughing in so long. And I can't help but be amazed at the power such small, unassuming animals wield over us; they so easily break down our defenses.

I run my hand along its shabby fur, feeling its ribs jut out at sharp, uncomfortable angles. But the dog doesn't seem to mind its starved state, at least not right now. Its tail is wagging hard, and it keeps pulling back from my coat to look me in the eye. I'm starting to wish I'd stuffed all the Danishes in my pocket this morning.

Something snaps.

I hear a gasp.

I spin around.

I jump up, alert, searching for the sound. It seemed close by. Someone saw me. Someone—

A civilian. She's already darting away, her body pressed against the wall of a nearby unit.

"Hey!" I shout. "You there—"

She stops. Looks up.

I nearly collapse.

Juliette.

She's staring at me. She's actually here, staring at me, her eyes wide and panicked. My legs are suddenly made of lead. I'm rooted to the ground, unable to form words. I don't even know where to start. There's so much I want to say to her, so much I've never told her, and I'm just so happy to see her—God, I'm so *relieved*—

She's disappeared.

I spin around, frantic, wondering whether I've actually begun to lose my grip on reality. My eyes land on the little dog still sitting there, waiting for me, and I stare at it, dumbfounded, wondering what on earth just happened. I keep looking back at the place I thought I saw her, but I see nothing.

Nothing.

I run a hand through my hair, so confused, so horrified and angry with myself that I'm tempted to rip it out of my head.

What is happening to me.

THE STORY CONTINUES IN
RESTORE ME

here

   in the dark, dusty corners of my mind
I feel a strange relief.
I am always welcome here
   in my loneliness, in my sadness
      in this abyss, there is a rhythm I remember.
   The steady drop of tears,
      the temptation to retreat,
      the shadow of my past
   the life I choose to forget has not
      will never
   e v e r
      forget me

HARPER
An Imprint of HarperCollinsPublishers

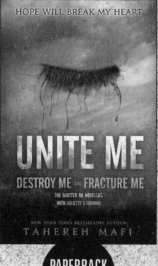

JOIN THE

Epic Reads

COMMUNITY

THE ULTIMATE YA DESTINATION

◀ **DISCOVER** ▶
your next favorite read

◀ **MEET** ▶
new authors to love

◀ **WIN** ▶
free books

◀ **SHARE** ▶
infographics, playlists, quizzes, and more

◀ **WATCH** ▶
the latest videos